ALAN WARNER

Alan Warner is the author of nine novels: *Morvern Callar*, which was filmed in 2002, *These Demented Lands*, *The Sopranos/Our Ladies*, which was adapted for the cinema as *Our Ladies*, *The Man Who Walks*, *The Worms Can Carry Me To Heaven*, *The Stars in the Bright Sky*, which was long listed for the Man Booker Prize 2010, The Deadman's Pedal won the 2012 James Tait Black Prize. *Their Lips Talk of Mischief* and *Kitchenly 434*.

ALSO BY ALAN WARNER

Fiction

Morvern Callar
These Demented Lands
The Man Who Walks
The Worms Can Carry Me To Heaven
The Stars in the Bright Sky
The Deadman's Pedal
Their Lips Talk of Mischief
Kitchenly 434

Non-fiction

Tago Mago: Permission to Dream

ALAN WARNER

Our Ladies

Previously published as *The Sopranos*

VINTAGE

Vintage is part of the Penguin Random House group
of companies whose addresses can be found
at global.penguinrandomhouse.com

Penguin
Random House
UK

First published by Jonathan Cape in 1998 with the title *The Sopranos*
First published in Vintage in 1999 with the title *The Sopranos*
This edition published in 2020 with the title *Our Ladies*

penguin.co.uk/vintage

A CIP catalogue record for this book is available
from the British Library

ISBN 9781529113631

Printed and bound in Great Britain by Clays Ltd, Elcograf S.p.A.

Penguin Random House is committed to a sustainable future for
our business, our readers and our planet. This book is made
from Forest Stewardship Council® certified paper.

MIX
Paper from
responsible sources
FSC® C018179

To Hollie

Lie Down.
Cold Hand.
Slow Heart.
Breathe Deep.
Close Eyes Now
Please. Close Eyes Now

'Every Second Hurts', Superstar

'They *do* live more in earnest, more in themselves and less in surface change, and frivolous external things. I could fancy a love for life here almost possible . . .'

Wuthering Heights

Our Lady of Perpetual Succour
School for Girls

No sweat, we'll never win; other choirs sing about Love, all our songs are about cattle or death!

Fionnula (the Cooler) spoke that way, last words pitched a little bit lower with a sexyish sideways look at none of the others. The fifth-year choir all laughed.

Orla, still so thin she had her legs crossed to cover up her skinniness, keeked along the line and says, When they from the Fort, Hoors of the Sacred Heart, won the competition last year, they got kept down the whole night and put up in a big posh hotel and ... everything, no that I want that! Sooner be snogged in the Mantrap.

Know what the Hoor's school motto is? Fionnula spoke again, from the longest-legs-position on the wall. She spoke louder this time, in that blurred, smoked voice, It's 'Noses up ... knickers DOWN'!

The Sopranos all chorted and hootsied; the Seconds and Thirds mostly smiled in per-usual admiration. Quietly, so's only the Sopranos-half of the wall could hear, Fionnula goes, Look girls, the Hoors're no even IN it this year. Shows how chronic the standard is; we stick thegether on this and there's no ways we'll win, won't even get in the second round! We'll be plonked on the bus an back here in plenty time for the Mantrap slow dances and all manner of sailors' jigs.

That's IF submarin-ers are in the Mantrap. And that's IF we get past that new bouncer, he hasn't got off wi a single one of us! (Ra)Chell was calling out, just from along, where some taller Seconds and Thirds separated her.

(A)Manda Tassy recrossed her legs, looking a little uncomfortable, cleared her throat and announced, I've got in the Mantrap three Saturdays running! Manda who could never afford cigarettes an was aye bumming them, placed one of her big sister's duty free Camels into her lips without even offering round, an from a pack of twenty!

Kylah squinted severely, though Manda was next her, Kylah went, That's cause you're the dying image of your big sister.

Are you JOKING Kylah? Manda blew smoke, Have you SEEN Catriona's suntan!

I'll no see a thing the day, Kylah muttered.

Orla giggled and smiled, her braces showed, Yon medallion man, the bouncer, he's only there cause he couldn't get a chef's job anywhere. He's from the Island. He'd get on well with Chell cause he has a love of animals; he can only tell the ages of sheep!

Aye, goes Chell, From behind.

Those within earshot laughed. Manda coughed.

Kylah chortled, frowning up and down the line as if watching a fast tennis rally and says, The Island, where no horse is safe as long as there's a table or chair left!

Fionnula shrugged shoulders laughing, lit another cigarette an goes, As long as we ALL stick thegether. It was spoken as what it was: a warning to any Seconds or Thirds who might be taking the competition too seriously and who didn't have the priority of a night on the town later; it was a threat to anyone with delusions of grandeur.

The Sopranos leaned forward an looked at Kay Clarke from Seconds who, virtue of her limb-length, sat trapped, sombre and silent amongst them, then they glared down the length-of-legs school wall towards the short-arse end and Ana-Bessie.

Snobby Kay Clarke and Ana-Bessie Baberton fee-paying (their Old Men, one Port Solicitor, one Consultant up the Chest Infirmary) stared stubborn cross-square to the statue of JL McAdam, surveyor, advocate of tarmacadam and national hero. Kay and Ana-Bessie were aye willing to admit bursary girls like Fionnula had 'colourful character'. Inwardly, the two middle-class girls consoled themselves: Fionnula's legs were 'actually' too thin and there was always the fact Fionnula's parents only had a bought council house up the Complex.

The school wall afront the square, with its iron railings, curved round to the slope by the side entrance (the polishy-smooth stubs were the old iron bars, sawed off for the war effort in the forties); the upward slope of pavement delineated the precise order the choir aye sat in, 'ccording to the length of each girl's legs from arse on the old polished stubs down to the chewing-gum-blotched macadam.

CHOIR ORDER ON LENGTH-OF-LEGS SCHOOL WALL

GIRL	VOICE	INSIDE LEG
Fionnula (the Cooler)	Sopranos	35"
Kylah	Sopranos	35"

(n.b. Fionnula (the Cooler) and Kylah an agreed First Equal but Fionnula always sits on outside.)

(A)Manda Tassy	Sopranos	$34\frac{3}{4}$"

Kay Clarke	Seconds	$34\frac{1}{2}''$
Yolanda McCormack	Thirds	$34\frac{1}{4}''$
Assumpta	Thirds	$33\frac{1}{2}''$
(Ra)Chell	Sopranos	$32\frac{3}{4}''$
Orla	Sopranos	$32\frac{1}{2}''$
Aisling	Seconds	$32''$
Iona	Seconds	$31\frac{1}{2}''$
Shuna	Thirds	$30''$
Fionnula (ordinary)	Seconds	$30\frac{1}{4}''$
English Katie	Seconds	$29\frac{1}{2}''$
Ana-Bessie	Seconds	$29\frac{1}{4}''$
Fat Clodagh	Thirds	$28\frac{1}{4}''$
Wee Maria	Thirds	$27\frac{3}{4}''$

On the flat, leaden school roof above the fifth-year choir and close to the speeding dawn clouds, Our Lady stood. Her sculpted shawl surmounted by an alert, perched seagull with a hooked, yellow beak – the cheeriest colour around. A scrawk from Lord Bolivia down in the New Chapel below, made the gull lean and fly forward off the BVM.

Our Lady of Perpetual Succour's dead, stone eyes were cast way over the teenagers below. The gaze looked above the slates of McAdam Square and the railway station clock, to the bay, beyond. She stared constant at some theoretical point, dependent on the angle of the reinforced concrete block Kirkham & Sons Construction had power-bolted her onto, year she descended down from heaven, under a Westland helicopter.

Her left arm was held out with a daft and neverending finality, offertory fingers appealing, though only ever receiving a tiny curlicue of sparrow's dropping; only ever delivering a slow sequence of rain drips to the sheered height way down onto the concrete playground below, where, every September, girls on their first day would bawl up to her: Don't jump, things can't be that bad! Don't do it! Suicide's a sin.

That morning, the statue's rampant gaze drove across the surface of the port's baywaters as perusual but, it seemingly settled for once on the long black vessel now anchored there, even the communications aerials on the nuclear submarine's conning tower, no reaching above the cloud-looped summits of the distant island mountains.

Orla yawned, moved her hand over her still-short hair, looked at her palm as if still surprised. She yawned, poked a finger in to the back of her mouth, took it out again and proclaimed, Chell's right enough, wi these navies from all countries, yous never can be sure if they've shore leave. Those greeny uniform ones did, but yon last destroyer didn't and you never know if you can count on them going to the Mantrap; who's to no say they'll go get taxis out the Barn or somewhere we can't get to?

They always go to the Mantrap for a drink even if they do go on, some aye stay. And funny though if those last didnie come ashore how come Michelle McLaughlin still managed to get pregnant offof it!

A few cassandras of laugh tremelled along the wall.

From top the wall Fionnula burred, Aye, it's a disgrace if they don't come ashore and them signed to NATO an everything! She sighed.

Everyone laughed. Even the girls who wernie doing Higher History.

Spotty Fat Clodagh from right along yelled out, cross square, By the way Manda, Michelle did not get pregnant by yon destroyer, it was one the Pakistani lads come up for Saturday market in their van.

There was dubious silence. Cross square, two gulls crawed an tugged at a fat binliner on the pavement by the amusement arcade, boarded for offseason.

Rural depopulation? NO chance with Our Ladys about, Kay Clarke sighed.

Manda leaned forward and met eyes with Fionnula across Kylah's thighs, the look meaning: No that you'll ever contribute, you lightweight, university-bound virgin.

There is an old county-council Ceud Mille Failte road sign just outside port, before you swing steering wheels round the high hairpin above the roofs below. When Fionnula and Manda were Second Years they nicked a little pot Airfix paint offof Kylah's big brother Calum

It was the time that First Year herself, a thirteen-year-old from Our Lady's got pregnant in the van, her bare back below the lifted blouse, sticking to the uncomfy cellophane-wrapped cartons. He was twenty-nine, refiller of cigarette machines, responsible for the entire West Coast!

Fionnula can still mind wearing their tight jeans and very white and pink trainers, being crouched up, faces close, gigglestifling in the dry ditch next the main road, then leaping out the gain when each last vehicle headlights passed and carrying on the handiwork with a make-up brush.

Population 6700
+ ONE

Then leaping back into the ditch as a great shift of headlight oozed round in the dark and them both cooried up, part of the tremulous, excited-feeling cause the vandalism, but also reaching for their own little, convexy belly-buttons snipped into shape by the National Health, knowing one day they would give in to some lad.

I read somewhere that submarine-ers . . .

Submariners, Fionnula grunted.

Submar-in-ers; that if they get a cut or something, cause they've been away under the waters for so long, it's done something to their . . . (Wee Maria McGill, who'd once used Vanish soap stain-remover to try get a bad henna out, had kinda stumbled into this, but she just looked along to Orla and bravely soldiered on) . . . Done something to their, blood.

Aye. Haemophilia. It's in Biology. Orla, who'd had chemotherapy, let Wee Maria go on.

Aye. Well if they get cut or that it won't stop bleeding for ages cause the air stuff they've been breathing down there.

There was contemplative silence then Orla spoke out their collective image, Aye! And when they submariners spunk with all their wanks down there, it just keeps coming out and coming out . . .

Everybody laughed cause it was Orla's crack.

. . . Inside their submarine – it would all just fill up with spunk and they'd all drown in it!

Yeauch!

Ah, dinnae scum us out! goes Chell.

Here in their spunky grave lie the hundred brave sailors, Fionnula's voice came from top the wall.

We'll test it out the night girls! Manda's filthy laugh came.
AYE!

7

Yolanda dropped her cigarette and yawned, Condom. Fuck!

Nine or ten limbs of the smokers, all in flesh-coloured tights, with socks pulled up above the knee to make the legs appear longer, pulverised half-smoked cigarettes into the tarmac pavement. Each black, flat-bottom shoe that did the grinding, sported completely different, luminous, day-glo, interwoven, painted or rainbowy laces: the only means of self-expression remaining.

Various novelty lighters that played tunes (ironic wedding marches and Lambadas) B&H, Regal, Embassy, Marlboro reds and Light, Silk Cut and Yolanda's Lambert & Butler! All packs of ten, part from Manda, were returned to suspiciously full backpacks. Some cigarettes were rapidly nibbed then slipped into the secret, folded hems of the specially shortened tartan skirts.

Orla grit her teeth, bared her retainer braces in a fake smile, says, Look at her walk, its like she's got the most gi-normous sanitary towel jammed between her legs.

Carrying her famous blue bucket, today full of parental consent forms and her own choral arrangements, held wind-safe under a hefty nineteenth-century bible, Sister Condron approached cross McAdam Square, beneath the collapsing and hanging dramatics of dawn clouds.

Aisling was mumbling, I'd a dream like that.

What? Shuna goes, but smiling straight ahead.

You know? A guy got handjobbed offof me and it not stopping, it just gushing an gushing out, goggles, whole goggles of it just gushing an gushing out filling ma bedroom an just knowing mum would find out!

Kay Clarke goes, I'll look that up in my Freud Dream Dictionary. Don't know what I'll look under.

Try Wanker, Manda coughed.

Fionnula spat out a laugh.

Shush.

Good morning girls.

MORNING SISTER CONDOM. Perfectly synchronised, each of the sixteen girls slithered off the wall to lengthen the look of their specially-shortened skirts.

Sister Condron breached the kerb, canted, swayed, straightened, spoke: All together, *Forth Let The Cattle Roam*! She dropped the bucket, lifted one arm pointing at heaven.

Sister, it's half eight in the morn, Fionnula snapped.

So Fionnula McConnel. Is your voice still in your bed?

Ana-Bessie and Kay Clarke alone giggled.

In a bland, soft whisper, Manda says, *Good King Wenceslas*.

Fionnula let out a spirtle of crack-up, waggled her tongue, looked left and right, eyes away wi it then says, One, two, three. The Sopranos sung in the tight dawn air, an immediate beauty, like flags cracking in the wind. The sound moved cross square:

> Good King Wenceslas
> Last looked out
> On the Feast of Stephen
> The snow lay round about
> Deep and crisp and even

NO. GIRLS! FORTH LET THE CATTLE ROAM.

But recalling December humiliations on Port streets with stupid hats on, the Seconds joined the Sopranos in a two-parter, cuddled in the neath, the Thirds waited and bassed the thing, even splitting the carol, messing about with a four-parter, looking each other in the eye to keep silent times.

A window canted out cross square, a night shifter fro the Alginate just a-bed leaned out roaring, Christmas so soon? Fuckin shut it ya wicked wee Catholic heathens.

Lord Bolivia

As each girl moved through, touching holy water to forehead, the ones with chewing gum ceased then began chewing again after they passed Sister Fagan the Pagan in the vestibule and entered New Chapel. An odd whistle of the Christmas carol brought a seething back glance from Sister Condron down the front.

Girls passed on inwards to the glooms, genuflected in coloured shapes of light then scattered among the pine benches.

The Sopranos took their usual back row. Kylah closed one eye to begin her counting of the mosaic tiles beyond the altar.

Orla nudged, What's wrong with your eye?

Kylah's mouth trembled to the soundless, hermetic rosary of her tile-counting.

There was a doldrum wait for Father Ardlui who must've been polishing off 7 a.m. Mass at the cathedral.

Kylah was whispering, alternatively to Orla's side and to Fionnula's, Here's a cracker, she was smiling, Saturday there, ma brother invites this sixth year from the high school out for a date. Never guess where?

Where?

I know.

Where then?

Plough Queen Contest.

Got it in one.

The Sopranos began to wheeze thegether.

Kylah kept on, She's a townie, no long moved up here, Laura Graham, her old man works on the newspaper.

Aye, ah seen her in the Mantrap, she's really pretty . . . says Fionnula.

In a kind of Aerobics Barbie sort of way . . . Manda went.

Aye, well, Calum vites her to the Plough Queen, right? Laura Graham says she'll meet him at Silvermines hotel by the fields. Calum turns up, jeans, gum boots y'know? Laura Graham is early: fucking stilettos, stockings, wonderbra, G-string, skimpy little red mini-dress and full make-up . . .

The Sopranos did their famous snigger, 'cept Kylah who just smiled with a hand over one eye.

Ah've *seen* that dress, Fionnula murmured.

Och that's a shame, Manda whispered, She must really fancy him.

Shush right, I'm telling a story. Calum *tries* to be polite. They have a drink and he doesn't mention her clothes but he realises he's totally fucked it up and he's no ways even getting a snog out of this. They walk over the fields and she's giving him queer-enough looks then she sees what it's all about; know what she says?

What?

'Plough Queen. I thought it was a beauty contest for farmers' daughters'!

The Sopranos' giggles started running away.

'A ploughing contest for big muscley women! I thought we were on a *date*!' goes Kylah, still staring over at the tiles. 'We *are* on a date,' ma brother goes, but she stomps off, side-stepping the cow pats an the spike on one of her stiletto heels sinks into the field and she has to get out them and walk in stocking soles back to the hotel to phone Tommy's taxi, Billy Farlane was on loudspeakers an he made some snide comment, like '... Amazed the JCB formation didn't ask that young lady to join the diggers in a waltz...!'

Manda let out one of her donkey honks.

Hsss, Sister Condron shushed backwards.

Then Father Ardlui rumbled in from the left and all rose without looking at him, seeking anything to improvise interest on: rafters with the peeling silver stars painted between, or imperfections in the stained glass sheets, or beyond the wall of coloured glass to the slight, reptilian movements and hops: Lord Bolivia, perched above yuccas and flourishing poinsettias in the little courtyard.

Fionnula peered that way, jaloused Sister Fagan the Pagan's method of hysterically increased growth for her poinsettia tubs – the Sister's own hormone-replacement-therapy patches wrapped tight around the stalks of the plants.

Father Ardlui suddenly produced his pipe from beneath his emblazoned togs, You *may* smoke but stub them out before you come up please.

The girls of the choir looked round, mouths forming perfect Os. Pink chewing gum (that was all they normally removed for communion) visible.

Father, Father! Sister Condron waved the hanky she kept tucked up her sleeve from where she sat on front row. Father, you're in the *girls'* school, the girls' school, you're not in the Seamen's Mission! No smoking *what* so *ever*.

A unison of tuts came from the rear, two enthusiasts even fumbled lighter and cigs back in bags.

Umm. Mmm. Oh-Umph. Father Ardlui repocketed his pipe, within the swelling Minoa of his inner garmenting.

Yolanda McCormack let out a rich, rounded smoker's cough,

tinted with goggles of potential phlegm. The Father reached a wide sleeve within his wrappings, removed half a deposited tube of Tunes cough lozenges, thumbed one out with his shovel-like nail and threw it, expertly at Yolanda. It missed her eye, slapped on her shiny forehead then cracked instantly to the floor by the kneeling cushion. She immediately stooped, peeled and popped it in her mouth. (It amused Father Ardlui to see the bent-over fur on the little tongues, their greyness stained artificially raspberry; the warm little menthol breath of acceptance, quivering on his thick fingers before he placed the host there.)

The Father got busy initiating a whole lot of wheels, cogs and judgings up in heaven: twisting a spiritual valve here and pressing in a redemptive switch there; a little bit fine tuning of forgiveness when needed.

The girls' minds wandered over immense dimensions of diversion.

Regardless, the Father pressed on with his planned opening words, You are all men of the sea. Toilers of the deep. Perhaps, like me, when you saw the vessel anchored in our bay this, morning, your memory was cast back to the excitements of seeing submarines tied up when you were young. I know *my* mind was cast back to the first time I ever saw a sub. I was young, and left our house to walk to the sweetie shop. As I came down from the Folly Heights, using Jacob's Ladder, I looked out Westly.

Imagine my Mother's shock when I arrived breathless, in tears back at our house, crying out that I did not want to be swallowed whole! For my Mother would read, not the gospels, but the *Old* Testament to me at night. My favourite was, of course, the story of Jonah and I was in such a state, for I believed the submarine was actually a whale, come into the bay to swallow me whole! You will recall from the story of Jonah . . .

The two nuns laughed at something the Father had says. Some stuff he was dithering on about, he'd mentioned the submarine but now he was on about whales!

Orla turned to her right, whispered, I've got a wisdom tooth coming through. Look. After a few seconds, Orla removed a flat, grey blob of chewed gum from out her mouth that, using her tongue, she'd jammed up the back and squeezed. Fionnula took the shiny, slavery block of chuddy, squinted at it and using two erect fingers, passed it on to Manda. The imprint of the emergent tooth had been embossed on the gum. Manda nodded sagely at the little indication of continued life, spoke out a response to one Father Ardlui's calls and passed back directly to Chell who'd missed it on the way up cos her thumbs were hooked, in boredom, into her skirt. Chell had it placed centre palm and peered at it, curious. She passed it by Orla and touched Kylah who had resumed a recount of the tiles; not wanting to lose her count, Kylah took the gum and glancing at it, popped it into her own mouth, never dropping her one uncovered eye from the tiles behind Father Ardlui; she chewed.

Father Ardlui was going full-tilt now.

I remember once I was in the Capital on a tram, way back in the days when they had trams which shows you how long ago *this* was! I was sitting right at the front and behind the driver there was a little sign which read, 'Standing Room only for Twelve persons'. Now some cheeky little child had taken out its pencil and written under the sign, 'and a wee boy!'

The two nuns giggled delightedly.

Now this of course is interesting for when you think about it, the twelve disciples had their lives changed . . . a little boy. For the Lord Jesus Christ was just an ordinary little boy . . .

Father Ardlui was still gesticulating and active up at the altar. The two Sisters had just laughed at something he says. Kylah's uncovered eye looked above him. She dropped the hand and muttered, Different. Different *every* fucking time. One hundred and seventy tiles or one hundred and sixty nine or one hundred and seventy one. I'm going to come in here one Saturday and sort this out once and for all, she whispered.

Then you'll have nothing to do. What is it with your eye?

Ah . . . don't have my contact lens.

You're just wearing one contact lens?

I swallowed the other.

Swallowed it?

It was a bet with ma *wee* brother. He won.

You're gonna go round all day with just one lens in?

Aye. Fucked if I'm going on the telly with glasses on.

The girls all beamed at each other as Father Ardlui got his bearings and before he invited everyone up to scoff body and blood, he was asking all to join in thanks and claiming celestial credit, for Orla Johnstone's healing.

All the girls mumbled together.

> Hail Mary Full of Grace
> The Lord is with thee
> THEEEEE!

All the girls' heads swung towards Lord Bolivia.

> Blessed art though amongst women
> WIMMANG . . . AGH . . . CUCK CUK PUTAS!
> Blessed is the fruit of Thy womb

BLESSED FRUIT WOMB ... PUTAS!

Sister Fagan frowned.

Lord Bolivia had been brought back from Sister Fagan's South American sabbatical, sealed tight in a beautiful, hand-carved wooden cage.

Somewhere near Ciudad Bolivar (formerly Angostura) the big bird had flown into an Iglesia de Santa Barbara and stunned itself near death on the ruby glass image of our Saviour's Ascension. The parrot had helicoptered down between the pews.

Lord Bolivia returned to consciousness caged in the Venezuelan convent surrounded by muttering nuns, the old women suspicious of a glaring beast – uneasy at its red and green slow-turning head, following the nuns scheming movements across the tiles; at night, prayers became troubled, doubting no soul was within the beast, seeing Satan in its black eyes.

Three technicians brought from the capital to refit the air conditioning (the convent was the only fitted building in the town) taught Lord Bolivia a succession of such profound obscenities, the old nuns could only listen to the parrot's catechism of unknowable, unimaginable sexual practices, like some language from far into the interior.

> Jesus
> JEEEZZZUSSS
> Holy Mary Mother of God
> CHUPATE LOS COJONES
> Pray for us sinners,
> COÑO
> Now

Naaa-How
And
Duh
At the hour of our death
HOUR UFF DEATH OUR DEATH
LOS COÑOS
DANDOME POR DETRAS!

No Snogging Through Tennis Fence

AWW Sister!

The girls of the fifth-year choir were assembled in room 37. The Mud Bucket was due: twenty minutes at the gates.

Sister Condron stood top of the room, before a chalk abstract of first-year blackboard graffiti, Now you ALL *know* make-up is not allowed in Our Lady's but since you are going to be on the television set we shall allow you it, *modestly* used. However it will *not* be applied until we are at the concert hall.

AWW Sister!

What about shopping, Sister Condron?

Amanda. Be quiet.

Manda tutted. She received a hard stare.

Shoelaces. These rid*iculous* shoelaces. It has gone far enough and from tomorrow coloured shoelaces will *not* be allowed . . .

AWW Sister!

This rule will be properly introduced next year when *some* of you (she smiled at Kay and Ana-Bessie though they'd followed fashion by sporting colourful shoelaces) will remain with us as sixth-year students. And here . . .

AWW Sister!

. . . I have sixteen pairs of regulation black shoelaces. I want them put on now, before we board the bus.

The girls threw their bags down in a right cheesed-off

manner. They tore laces out and shoved them into blazer pockets. They knelt and bent and perched on edges of desks so their hair, long and loose, plaited or gathered with regulation black scrunchies, slipped over one or other shoulder. Sister Condron spoke, cross their bended spines, BE QUIET! I paid for these laces.

Manda Tassy looked up, face flushed from efforts of bending and tugging tight the new laces, Are Sopranos or Seconds practising last, Sister Condron?

Be. Quiet. I have other announcements with regard school rules and general attitude today.

There was anticipatory hushedness.

It has come to Sister Fagan and I's attention, and this has been passed on to Mother Superior, that some girls are *still* wearing more than one earring in each ear. School rules are quite clear about this. Only *one* earring *per* ear and (in a hushed tone the little sister added) in no other part of the body.

There was a mush of shrugging smiles and rustle as many turned towards Chell of the Sopranos; they were smiling broadly at her eyebrow socket. Chell and Manda turned their heads busily towards each other.

Sister Condron went on, There are no excuses for two earrings. Although the school cannot prevent you, we will not accept the excuse you are wearing these stud things because your ear has recently been pierced. If you *must* get your ears pierced and wear these horrible studs for so long, then you must do it at the start of the summer holidays. Personally I think any more than one per ear is an ugly mutilation and I should say we have sent a letter to the hairdresser we hold responsible for this hysterical fad which has broken out among you. Sister Condron looked down at her notes and sullenly announced, The Best Little Hairhouse in Town.

The girls roared. Manda was turning back and forth in excitement, Ma sister's practise manageress . . . Catriona . . . Her that does all the piercings, Sister . . . it used to be called Kurl Up and Dye. Do you get that one?

A shriek of appreciation then anticipation went up.

Amanda Tassy. I know you must be excited at the thought of visiting the Capital . . .

Manda straightened to full height to absorb Sister Condron's attack.

. . . But you really shouldn't display your excitement like a giggly little *eight-year-old*.

When it was clear Manda wasn't going to blush beetroot all heads turned to the nun, smiling, mocking.

Even one earring per ear, the use of your gold Gaelic League lapel buttons as earrings is *not* to continue.

A gasp of laughter went up in full commotion, several girls flicked at their neighbour's lobes.

BE QUIET! The first crack up of the day and room 37 was silent. Though it was May, the fluorescents lined the strands of the dark-haired ones. A lorry from the Superstore crossed McAdam Square going away to the outlying villages.

GROW UP! You have an important day ahead, for each of you and for Our Lady's. You each have a responsibility to fulfil, not selfish little indulgences to perpetuate. We *have* a chance of winning tonight if you would all just believe it and I *won't* have a single individual or minority spoiling that chance for others. Yes, school doesn't start for you till eleven tomorrow but if we can win tonight there will be no school tomorrow. If only you could learn to see the long term. We will all stay in a fine Hotel tonight, *if* you sing as I taught you on the Judged Songs.

All day today you are representatives of the school. The entire Port is counting on you tonight, as well as your parents.

Think of them all day today. And God is watching too. God, d'you hear?

The girls looked at their hands and stared off, except Ana-Bessie; even Kay stared down glumly at her new laces.

The nun repeated deadly slow, The wearing of Gaelic League lapel buttons as earrings will not be tolerated today or any day from now on. Understood? Also. Also, she lifted her notes as if reading from them, The shaving of eyebrows is a perversion which shall not go on in this school.

Unable to laugh, fair flabbergasted, some scrutiny of eyebrows went on. For the nun's intelligence to be ahead gossip was virtually unknown.

And a last point. *Practices* have been occurring along the tennis court fence. A pre-Wimbledon passion for the game has clutched our school like multiple ear piercings. These gatherings have been happening at breaks and luncheon hour since, for reasons you well know, all years were banned from going down town.

It is *forbidden* to gather at the tennis court fence on the edge of the school grounds. We have already warned that loitering on this fence where a large pack of . . . Boys from the *Protestant* High School are also seen from Mother Superior's window to be gathering, is not permitted. The tennis courts are out of bounds unless you are playing on them. This does NOT permit, as happened yesterday, over fifty girls bringing tennis rackets down to the fence with them. Rackets which, from where we were watching, were being put to *very* little use.

The girls smiled, turning to look over their shoulders.

Now to today.

Who's practising first, Sister Condron?

The bus shall take us directly to the Concert Hall in the Capital.

Are we not stopping at Rest & Be Thankful?

Yes, yes; if we need toilets, then directly to the Concert Hall. There is no doubt, despite how hard you've worked, that you need more work, especially on *All Round the House* . . .

The nun smiled, touched, as the Thirds set up a hushed little whisper:

> All round the house
> Is the jet black night
> It stares through the window panes
> Crawls in the corners

Manda smirked.

I'm being realistic when I say the Seconds and Thirds need more work than the Sopranos . . .

Fionnula (the Cooler), Orla, Chell, Manda and squinting Kylah punched air, tamely hopped and turned beaming at each other.

Girls . . . you *all* need work, don't get blasé or you'll be here at 11 a.m. before you know it. I'll be practising the Thirds then the Seconds . . .

A babble had frothed up.

Quie-*et*. Then the Sopranos.

Sister? Fionnula's almost American-like, creamy voice rose, Are we permitted up the city till group rehearsals start. Aye?

Yes Fionnula, you can all go shopping and make your pilgrimage to McDonald's hamburgers . . .

A hubbub began . . .

But you will *all* be back from those streets on the price of your scalps for your rehearsal time at the Concert Hall. You will *not* get lost, you wear your uniforms at *all* times, you keep your blazers and ties *on*, your new shoelaces remain *in* your shoes and you conduct yourselves in a manner befitting Our Lady of Perpetual Succour School for Girls. Is that understood by each and every person in this room?

YES SISTER CONDOM.

Yes, Orla?

Sister. Have you seen any sailors from the submarine down town this morning?

Hymn to Orla Johnstone

Kylah, Fionnula (the Cooler), Chell, Manda Tassy and Orla! The Sopranos swinging or shouldering their bags from Room 37 towards the understairs toilets for final cigarettes.

They've youth; they'll walk it out like a favourite pair trainers. It's a poem this youth and why should they know it, as the five of them move up the empty corridors? We *should* get shoved aside cause they *have* it now, in glow of skin and liquid clarity of deep eye on coming June nights and cause it *will* go . . . After all what do *we* amount to but a load of old worn-out shoes?

Issues forth . . . the simple soul in . . . uh, God's eyes, Old Ardlui ground his teeth, tapped his tongue on the chewed end of his unlit pipe inside his mouth. *What is it that allows the soul, alma or anima, its delicate structure, to emerge into the things the girls have become, a sinful illusion? An Anatomy of the Soul that is what the world needs*. He growled. He really growled and squinted. At least he'd remembered the Johnstone lassie, the one they helped to Lourdes, at least he'd remembered her name.

Father Ardlui opened the scraping, wobbling wall of red and yellow glass before him; he stooped, bended inwards to the humid well of courtyard among the yuccas, the florid poinsettia petals like distressed fingers – the hormone patches peeled or fallen, curled aside on the dry humus of the tubs. *Sister Fagan, women!* He shivered, lifting one shoulder straight and he began the massive fumigations of lighting his pipe – the Falcon he would hold upside down in his mouth to stop it filling with rain, whipping it in beneath his vestments just as he approached the gravesides and earliest arrivals of the family clusters . . . He pulled the door closed behind him.

Characterisation, the Catholic priest mouthed the word. He was writing a novel, was the Father, up in his house at St Orans, on the dining-room table below the hole in the ceiling where the scandalous chandelier had fallen down as the school bus passed. Many of his villagers took it as act of God on Father Ardlui for having such a sinful extravagance fitted; especially the old women who believed two black cats together were messengers from the devil. The Father had it fitted cause the light was good for the writing.

He wasn't the only one writing a novel within two hundred miles; times were changing, and there *was* the possibility Niall Dubh, the poet, was sneakily making the biggest typing effort of his life over at Little Australia.

Father Ardlui felt he had almost perfected the grievous, seated stance worthy of a writer, the small Spanish cigar, emerging from the extreme edge of his mouth (left or right – he would roll it between), his seat pulled as close to the dining-room table as stomach would allow – transferring rough draftings of sentences from the left tablet of white paper sheets to the right one using the infinite supply of Sensor Technology pens; the grievous novelistic stance interrupted by the filling of the coffee mug from the large thermos Mrs Mac had left for him. After each five pages in clean handwriting, he would allow himself a pipe and grimace up at the hole. A good novel too, with a reductive style and dangerous vision.

*

26

The priest had an unknowing stir as he lifted his face and laughed, the word, Vision, and thick-scented tobacco smoke to the perspex circle two storeys up. The Sister had supervised the hoisting of the transparent ceiling, now besmattered with black and green seagull shit; the sky beyond momentarily blue between lumbering clouds (further through a mess of chicken wire to prevent nestings). It was badly needing cleaned by the janitor that, for surely it prevented light falling to the plants? The janitor here; *just a boy. Once in the world all janitors were old. Now young.*

Suddenly Father Ardlui says, In a village of La Mancha, whose name I prefer not to recall, there lived not long ago one of those ... the priest spoke out, his voice like a stomach rumble, laced with sand, in English, The Sons of Something ... Then continued, Those 'hidalgos' with lance in rack, ancient buckler, lean nag and fleet hound.

All this from old Father Ardlui in the well of the tiny courtyard, spoken in perfect Castilian Spanish as warily, Lord Bolivia eyed the staring priest and shuffled further along his perch.

Four them were locked inside one cubicle with window above. Orla stood on the pan in the next cubicle, her arms leaned on the top, holding a Benson & Hedges in her fingies that she was pretending to smoke, saying, ... So the chandelier fell down when we were going past in the Mud Bucket ...

The other Sopranos laughed and a canopy of cigarette smoke arose. Orla assisted it out the window with an arm wave, ... All the old dearies says it was act of God.

Fionnula's black eyes in her white face looked up at Orla, two pure little globes of bulb-reflection in the blackness, Long ago that happen?

Och ages ago, says Orla, showing her braces.

It was a month back, goes Kylah.

Aye. Orla turned, Ages ago.

You'd think it's the loco weed he smokes in his pipe.

The girls laughed.

What an old fucking . . . *cunt* the Condom was, eh?

Ya can see she's gonna be right on our fucking tits all day. And that cheeky little besom Kay Clarke and Ana, did ya hear them, fucking laughing . . .

Talking of tits did *you* . . . , Fionnula podged a finger gently into Manda's left, Bring yur wonderbra?

Course.

Intercourse!

Ooo, Eva Hercegovina, goes Chell.

Fionnula drawled, raised her eyebrows, Eva Herzigova. Hercegovina is where that killing went on . . .

It was in History . . .

Eva Herz-athingmy is married to Jon Bon Jovi's drummer, goes Kylah.

Whats the point in that? Less you're married to Jon Bon Jovi, what's the big deal in being married to his drummer, eh? Fuck that.

Fionnula laughed and smiled up at Orla, who grinned back.

Ever thought? Chell goes, That Emilio Estevez and Charlie Sheen, really look like Martin Sheen, their dad, but Emilio Estevez and Charlie Sheen don't look anything like each other!? I really ponder that some nights, Chell nodded.

Once, Orla started excessively farting; all of one day then at night in the toilet closet of their summer caravan at Tralee Bay.

She was making more noise in that cubicle, the Old Man and

Old Dear just outside ... More trying to stifle her laughs than anything.

Back home she couldn't get out of bed, just filling the big top of her duvet with the gas, then it stopped and she was scared.

She remembers nothing of the ambulance took her away from her bedroom, neighbours gathered watching and the night passage down through long concatenation of villages, south towards the Capital.

Now you know when you are really hungry, Orla?

Orla nodded. She was wearing daft pyjamas. Aye.

Specialist had big glasses and hairs grew out of his nose ... not out of snotholes but nose itself.

Now you know when you are *really* hungry, Orla? Well, these cells in your blood are terribly hungry and they are such greedy guts they gobble up your healthy blood cells and that's why you are feeling so poorly, feeling like bed all the time so, what Mr Sharma is going to do, every morning, is take you up here to radiotherapy. All right?

Uhhuh.

Now *I*'ll come with you tomorrow, but then Mr Sharma will have you taken up on your own, by one of the nurses, and what we'll be doing, is buzzing you with our machine here so it cleans the bad blood that's eating up your good stuff. He leaned forwarders and touched his pen (he never touched *her* once apart from on that day when they all knew nothing was working and she was jiggered), Now this will make you feel even poorlier than you do just now and you are going to think we are daft doing this but you remember how terrible those bad cells will feel because we are bashing them. He shook his clipboard. You be brave and see.

Uhhuh.

Orla had smiled, not even thinking, turned and smiled – not even afraid at that point, just thoughtless for a blessed moment of relief. She smiled at her Old Dear who, like having a sneezy fit, burst out, just bubbling and bubbling and no ways would've Orla too less bloody Old Dear hadn't and gone to.

Your pubes fall out too! Leaned forward in Barrels Bar with a red baseball cap on, Orla had hushed even quieter to the leaned-forward Sopranos, All ma pubes in the gusset of ma panties; under oxters, *legs*, ah tell you girls it's fucking brilliant, out the window with the Ladyshave and the fucking Immac Bikini Line when you're getting bombarded by the radioactive waves! Orla roared, loud as she could an the Sopranos followed with screams that made the barman, Angie Badhainn, look cross the empty bar from his Free Press (Angie was fortyish and two of the Sopranos had mashed the face offof him in the Mantrap, on summer Saturdays). Each the girls now lifted their Hooch (all diff flavours, Fionnula on her usual Shott's Vanilla seltzer, Orla: Appeltize). Chell kept going to the toilet and each time she came back her eye make-up was totally fucked. Fionnula swung an arm round her.

They tried to insist Orla didn't pay for a round but she needed to so she felt alive, still one of *them*, na a dying virgin who'd lost two stone and still had to wear retainer braces cause no to wear them would mean there was no future.

It wasn't cause politeness they didn't want Orla to pay. It was cause they all knew the twenty she was paying with was the money she was saving for the maybe-Greece-or-Spain holiday all five them were going on.

Chell went off to the toilet fore Orla came back from the bar, slowly with a tray, that red baseball cap and the long earrings only highlighting there was no hair hung at the back there.

If Orla Johnstone hud had a wee brother he'd have looked like her that afternoon.

The holiday had been their chimera, already talked about in hushed tones on account the alcohol that was going to be guzzled, the suntans obtained, the boys ravished. Much of it was fed by mythic tales of Manda's big sister Catriona on Lloret de Mar package holidays. The drinking so excessive she'd got seasick on the pedalos and vomited over the side, got car sick on the dodgems and vomited down on her high heels and the accelerator, the food so pungent she'd diarrhoea-ed back in the apartment and only had sanitary towels to wipe her ass with, so hot she'd take her bikini from the fridge in the self-catering and put bra and knickers in for the night.

Course Orla didn't have a wee brother cause Orla's Old Dear'd only Orla an lost a child when they still lived out the village.

Out the village. Above, moonhusk, hung like an abandoned wasp-comb.

Orla's mother had woke in the railway cottages, bleeding from out between her legs. No one had telephone in the cottages in the sixties but it was going to be just as quick.

Mrs Johnstone dressed and put Alec's mac over her, holding it onto her tumtum and walking funny to stop the little blood drips from touching the inside the coat as they sometimes fell, rather than running down her leg. She didn't want to wear the coat and ruin it but Alec shouted at her.

She did slip into her best shoes since blood would wash off the leather and she insisted Alec clip the gold chain round her neck. That couldn't get harmed in any way, I'm no going, turning up looking like a tinker, Alec!

They shuffled down the brae, neighbour's curtains still closed.

Past the phone box. Alec held her arm and pointed the Ever Ready bicycle torch – jittering yellowed beam making him all the more nervous of the time, though they hardly needed it with yon moon; it could dazzle you.

They waved down the nightshift bus collecting through the villages. On board, Mrs Johnstone insisted on them both struggling all the way to the back seat. Then she just had to have that cigarette to steady her nerves.

When she stood up at the Chest stop, there was a puddle blood on the old leather seat, Just as well I wore the dark skirt, Mrs Johnstone said, before apologising at length, to the driver.

In the Chest, once they got the skirt off and her up on the chair with her legs apart, the young nurse turned pale at what was down there. There were these little gutters sloped away from the chair so's the blood trick-trickled away.

Hurried her to the theatre. When they removed what was down there, she was under local anaesthetic. Her short fingers felt up her big belly, she could only feel nothingness where all her awareness had been centred before – as if she ended there. It felt terrible queer. Then they removed, what was down there. They put it in a white plastic basin, the youngest nurse, used to general anaesthetic, no thinking, passed the basin across Orla's mother's recumbent body, the basin moved over her face and that circle of big powerful overhead lights revealed everything in the basin, so the mother saw the floating expression on her dead, infant daughter's face.

She had been back, rested in her bed, crying for two days, when Orla's mother began the bleeding again from between her legs – the doctor had not removed everything of the unborn child – pieces were still in her, going rotten. Again the ride on the night shift bus, the Chest stop . . . the chair.

What Orla hated most about therapy was that they wouldn't let you walk. They put Orla flat on her back on a trolley from the first day and straight aways she sussed why. It was only going to get rougher here on in. Didn't let her walk up to start with cause soon she'd be so fucking poisoned she wouldn't be able to get to the lift up to radiotherapy.

When they moved her into the room on her own she knew what that meant too. Orla thought it should be the other way. Comfortable room when you had a chance. Into the ward when you were doomed.

Each time her parents came, the word hospice was mentioned by the specialist. Orla didn't know what that meant then. That 'spyce' sound made her think it was just an only-child hospital, still with the idea of making you better.

When Sharma stopped the radiation, she started to feel stronger . . . and she knew how dangerous and what a cruel lie that was. She was strong enough to want to go back home from the Capital, back through the long orphanage of railway stations to the port, to the Sopranos.

Good thing about the six days in the private ward was, you could play walkman loud as you wanted; other good thing: the corridor was mixed, not like the women's ward but there weren't any bonks.

She saw a guy lift his pyjama top off, four rooms up, but he was ancient, at least thirty and dying too of course, difference being he'd had a life – all skinny.

Then they wheeled the guy in next door. You could hear his splurbles and rants all the time. He was Norway or Sweden or Finland or something – nobody seemed to know.

Orla wouldn't use her toilet; she'd walk up the corridor to the big one with the hydraulic bath. She'd pass the room, see him lying there. Stop at his door on the way back. See his flat chest with its black hairs (his man-ness-that-wasn't-Dadness), his chest lifting and falling, his mouth mumbling those words at the ceiling – talking quick, away right up, the morphine drips hung like wires between telegraph poles, into his arms.

He speaks in two voices that one. It's frightening.

You mean two languages?

No. No, two *voices*. You listen. First he's speaking in one voice then it changes, another – another *person*. I don't know what languages he's speaking or what he's saying. No family ever visit, he's alone, alone at the end, it's terrible.

Orla says, He was a sailor. You can see the tattoos.

A sailor? Yes that would be his type. No possessions.

Do you understand what he's dying of?

The cleaner looked, nervous at Orla who was on the bed with knees cuddled to her chin.

He's dying of pancreas cancer. The cancer's ate it all up so's those dead strong digestive juices are running right into his stomach and they're digesting it. He's eating up his own stomach. Sometimes, way in the night when I'm lying here ah can hear it pop-popping; sure as fate, those digesting sounds all in the inside of him. Missus, you don't need to know what words he's speaking; ah know the things that are raving through his mind all through the night. He's girning up at God saying, 'Take me now, take me now out of this sheer, fucking agony.'

All that, Orla told them in Barrels, day before she went to Lourdes.

Manda was up getting crisps and shouting, Hello, Mountain Rescue, I'm in Barrels stuck at the bar and I'm needing a helicopter ta winch me back ta mah seat.

She'd also hit the wrong number on the juke box and grimly, *Elizabeth My Dear* on the first album was sounding in every nook and crannie.

In the bathroom, Fionnula had got Orla alone at last. Fionnula had noticed how dying folk are never left alone for a minute. For Saturday nights there was a speaker in there too, the song had almost finished and Fionnula never listened to any music anyway, she didn't even own a tape recorder, she'd play Condom's practice tapes on their living-room music centre.

I wouldn't mind but, Orla giggled, I want everything to be as it was . . .

Don't . . . shush.

Orla stepped towards her, stepped towards that voice she thought she could collapse into.

Fionnula took two full steps backwards till the top of her thighs at the rear came against the sink edge.

Orla had stopped coming forwards and was just forming an odd look when Fionnula stepped towards, wrapped her arms all round Orla's shoulders and laid her cheek against the canvas of the red baseball cap. They separated. Orla wanted to tell what had happened, she rubbed tears away with her palms, her hands turned outwards as if her nail varnish was wet.

I'm going to pee, goes Fionnula.

See you then.

Aye. Orla?

What?

Orla, you know we're coming to see you when you get back?

I'll come and see *yous*.

Good. Good, Fionnula tried to add that they loved her, but

Orla was already out of the door, using all the weight down her arm to shove the spring-lock outwards.

Fionnula slammed the cubicle shut, let the door swing back and touch her knee as she hovered, not sat on the pan. . . . She'd screwed one fist so's her brilliant nails dug into the palm – half in response to the way Orla'd rubbed her eyes. Fionnula hissed, Fuck. Fuck, fuck, fuck, fuck, fuck, fuck, fuck.

The toilet door was the raised type, so there was space between the bottom of the door and the floor. In magic marker someone had drawn:

WATCH OUT FOR
LIMBO DANCERS!!!

↓

When the night sister was up with the Ancient One, Orla had stepped into the mumbling sailor's room. She pushed the door back shut that the night sister kept like that to stop the sailor's two voices from bothering her too much; distracting her from those pink-covered books, swooning chicks with huge tresses of auburn hair on. Orla'd lent her *My Darling My Hamburger* but'd heard nothing back.

Orla stood to the side of the door, listening to the gurgle of Number Two voice. His bedside reading lamp was at a queer, never-used angle, anyone compos mentis would never've had it at.

Orla'd stepped forwarders, looked down on his tattoos; they were the floor of a seen-from-above forest. His wrists were held back – kind of poofy like-style – but that wasn't his fault. The silvery eyes looked straight up, the lips sort of chopped, he seemed to speak those foreigny things through teeth, the chalky dribbles dried down the sides of his mouth and round his neck, that cause he was dying, the nurses hadn't shaved for three mornings.

Orla walked round the bed glancing back over her shoulder. When she cornered the bottom she kneeled, looked at the piss bag and saw the little clear bit coming from the water feed they gave him. She touched the bag, followed with fingers up the clear tube, stopping before it went under the blanket.

Orla whispered, You're no all alone in the world, *I'm* with you. She took the cold hand, it'd the tacky damp of aliveness. She squeezed, I'm *with* you. She bent to the ear, I'll be like you soon. She kissed his forehead and she smiled.

Thing about Lourdes was the spooky silence: so many under open skies or close to the Grotto of Our Lady but everyone whispered. Then the occasional sound of planes taking off and landing, beyond the Ravine of Light, at the airport, flying in the sick and flying them out.

Orla stood in the cloisters of the underground basilica. She was under an enormous black and white photograph, smiling. It said the fucking pillars of the basilica were earthquake-proof, that's what Orla was smiling about. They were expecting the worst in the home of miracles.

She knew what the photo reminded her of. It was a photo of some place in the Pyrenees, a marathon of mountain penitents – maybe fifty or sixty of the loonies, hulking crosses, tied to their backs. It was making her feel horny, those rampant-looking bits where the ropes joined the wrists, tight, tight at the back.

Orla shifted the way she was standing. She looked at the bent backs, bare feet among the jaggy rocks and cactus. Climbing up the top the mountain where they were gonna stand those crosses up in their holes.

What all that row of bodies winding up the height reminded her of was the Rapids water chute at the Time Capsule. You had to carry your rubber tyre up the top, the queue of naked torsos, up the ascent, each waited for the moment of release where the ride started at the top, down thro' pools and rapids.

Orla! Old Dear called and she walked quickly after her. Quickly!

Next night, nurse had vanished away beyond the Ancient One. Orla stepped inside, amongst that breathing, amongst that murmuring. When the nurse had come to clean him she'd left the door blind down. Orla could feel her heart bumping. He wasn't shaved.

Suddenly she moved forward and dropped onto her pyjama knees. She lifted up the blanket and peeked under.

First thing was to check he hadn't shat himself. When you're dying and away with it they slip this sort of rice papery tissue beneath arse to prevent bedsores and catch shite.

She rolled him, the skin of his arse hadn't even puckered and pruned in bedsoreness. Orla rolled him but didn't have the strength to lift him enough, she found, biting her tongue and looking down behind his balls you could judge there was nothing there, like when Kylah babysat for English Katie's sister and Kylah'd check the nappies.

Orla took the tube out the end of his cock the way she'd ease a skelf from her Old Man's thumb when he came in from the garden. A single piss-drop rose up out of the little eye-hole and raced down the wrinkled skin and across the awful smoothness of his tummy-side.

In the little toilet she got the bowl and cloth, identical to in hers. She clothed the cock. She kept looking up at his face but the mutters continued. What word came to mind about the cock was its awful 'unusedness' neither anymore for pissing or even a wank.

She tried everything. Lying thinking about it for so long she'd realised she couldn't put what weight was left of her on *him* so she'd go like in Fionnula's porno mags.

She put her hands on the bottom of the bed and began shaking with turned-on-ness as she lowered herself, her legs spread over his, while reaching back with another hand to force it up, into the saturatedness that was between her there. The cock just flipped from side to side and he continued burbling behind her. She tried to force the limpness in her, sliding herself up and down; she realised *she* could get *off*, but that wasn't the point. She had to get him hard.

She took it in her mouth, eyes shut. She'd crawled backward so her fanny was over the burbling lips; when those rambles came round to the every-so-often-excited-bit, the breath touched her hairlessness there and she kept shivering all over. Despite the images of Night Sister with the Ancient One peering over her shoulder, suddenly opening the door, she sucked and sucked, using her hand too, like it said in *More*, but it

39

was the same. She sighed, legs stiff as she swung round off and pyjama bottoms back up and the sailor sat straight and stared at her.

. Orla took two steps back before the huge leap of adrenalin hit her face. She thumped almightily into the wall, as she shot to the side, she saw he was staring at the same spot. He lunged forward but as his left leg came free of the bed, it buckled, canted onto the bathroom wall; the morphine drip on his right arm caught up with him, violently tautened and the stand the clearbag hung on, flew onto the bed and dragged across.

The sailor was shouting, both arms out sudden. The other glucose drip, tightened up, but instead of following his Frankenstein walk, they tore free at his arm. Orla turned to the door but he was going to reach her and she didn't want that to happen with her back to him. She turned, saw the long spread of blood on both arms where he'd lost his drip. She ran forward, hands out and she hit him with both palms on his chest. She stopped and the sailor fell backward, crashed down against the curtains. There was a sound and Orla watched as a huge puddle of skitter spread under his skinny buttock and then pee was squirting up helplessly out of him and the blood was all down his arms and it was the look, that awful look, helplessness, bewildered pain that Orla saw, a look like that would be in her eye soon.

Orla burst out crying as the man swung his arms round in any old way, pleading, she stepped forward and kneeled down in the piss and the shit and pulled her arms tight round the nude man, his cock like a shrivelled fossil, his face suddenly ancient but infantile in pain. Orla cried and the man shuffled weakly, little pained sounds from his mouth.

Sorry, Sorry, Sorry, Orla whispered until the door flung in

and Night Sister called out. In the morning the nurses had tied him to the bed with belts.

In Lourdes, shops sold only souvenirs. Worse than the Port in high season. Every form of Virgin you'd ever require, every permutation: egg-timers to alarm clocks. Each shop was a cave of trash.

It was when she was in, maybe, the tenth cave of trinkets she realised *why* she was going from shop to shop with Old Dear in Lourdes. It was cause Old Dear kept saying, Are you sure you're okay? And she *was*.

After Orla and her folks returned from the Lourdes trip, funded by gatherings through the cathedral, it was a bit obvious Orla wasn't dying quite that quick, so they drove south again.

For one hundred miles and more, down long, slow swerves between the blackest Mounts, the clouds then above, moving faster over behind them than the wide land seemed to go below the tyres. The drooping then leaping wire, rubber-wrapped against snow-cling, hung between the telegraph poles of the railway line that comes close to the car then retreats away, over the glens, the neat symmetry of track, insinuating it knows a better route south, to cities.

At each village of the hundred miles, Orla, her Old Dear and Old Man stop yapping cause there're sudden human beings to look at rather than the uninhabited lands with the deeply rich commission plantations, runway-wide boulevards of desolate fire-breaks, suddenly blocked in their ascent by solid walls of mist-choke. Cultivated front gardens in the villages with chrysanths amongst the inhuman mountains that have always been around Orla and her parents – they even know the gaelic names of some – but on those wide flanks, stotted with rolled boulders and the dots of sheep two thousand feet up, they have never, nor will they ever set a foot.

Though Alec Johnstone can't afford it on top petrol and won't be able to have a few pints in the Gluepot for two weekends, he swings off the road for pub lunch at Rest & Be Thankful. In, its embarrassingly quiet. They hear the big lorries swish by from where they sit in the empty lounge by the real log fire. The targe and crossed claymores above, Orla dousing her fat scampi (really took from a blue bay round the cliffs) in lemon, vinegaring her chips with inundations till the ones at the bottom are disintegrating and fairly swimming in it – leaving her wee cluster of cress, lettuce and greenish tomato slice, untouched as always. Her parents watching her, just watching and watching her.

Back in the car a frizzle of post-food chatter as they descend corners (several of them claiming to be The Devil's Elbow) to where the valleys meet and . . . out of the Westlands, the mountain ranges are receding, like the advance clouds on an overtaken weather front. Then the three in the car fall silent with the huge arrival of constant streetlights, the massed flow of the first dual carriageway, and like an inaudible hum all round them, the theme of great cities, an oppressiveness; helpless ugliness; a people cowered in numbers for reasons they can't remember.

The Specialist smiles a lot and says, With Hodgkinson's Disease at this age there is always a good chance. The malignancy has completely vanished as you can see.

Can it ever come back? Mr Johnstone asks.

Mrs Johnstone almost turns and tells her husband not to ask such a thing. For Mrs Johnstone her daughter has been saved by Our Lady and all this is not needed.

At this age, the Specialist tells them, Every six months that passes makes a relapse less likely. In our experience, after three or four years any recurrence would be, unusual, highly unusual. In our experience. We shall ask for regular blood samples from her for the immediate future.

Can I ask, why the radiotherapy seemed to no work, then she, recovered?

Sometimes trauma therapy like that can take a time, as you know I was extremely pessimistic. It's unusual for such an eleventh hour reversal. But wonderful, of course, he laughed. Shall we bring her in?

Her Old Man brought Orla in. She knew she was going to live cause the way the Specialist came round from the back his desk and kissed her on the cheek. He wouldn't have wasted otherwise.

This means I'll be back to school next week, eh? she asked. The three adults chuckled.

Hymn to Single Parents

Reluctant to refrain, knowing a long journey was ahead them, Sopranos were last down the pavement to the bus stop, though there was no sign of the nuns.

It's prove that smoking adds to the ageing process, Kylah says.

Good, we'll get into over 21's nights sooner, snapped Fionnula.

Chell and Kylah barked out laughs and Manda honked.

There was a whoop from among the girls assembled there. Cross square, tummy seeming as per-usual, laughing and pointing at them, showing teeth – Michelle McLaughlin.

Ooo . . . goes Manda.

She might know if there's any sailors come ashore, Chell was smiling.

Cmon. That's no fair, Fionnula warned.

Who is it? Kylah was squinting.

Michelle McLaughlin, says Orla. She's no belly at all.

A few of the Seconds and Thirds were calling out and Michelle was crossing the square towards. Fat Clodagh swung round and glanced back at the Sopranos. Manda stuck out her tongue and Clodagh looked away.

The choir formed three deep round Michelle, apart from Kay Clarke who stood a-way-away, as if she was disapproving of Michelle. Manda now scowled at Kay.

The inner circle round Michelle – Shuna, Iona, Aisling, Asumpta and Maria: gleering between their shoulders were Manda Tassy and Chell, Fat Clodagh and Yolanda. Fionnula (Ordinary) and Fionnula (the Cooler), English Katie, Ana-Bessie and Orla circled the cluster.

Clodagh was *just* talking about you, Manda announced.

Aye? Michelle peeped.

Clodagh tutted and went beetroot, Where are you going, at this time?

Yous are all off to the Finals, eh? Whah-ow. I'm off up pre-natal at the Chest.

At this time in the morn?

Oh aye, it's to get ya used to the idea of sleepless nights when the baby comes ah guess . . .

A rubble of chuckles rose up.

. . . Ah tell yous, think pre-natal at nine in the morn is bad yous should see the fucking *post*-natal up there; all the lassies from the villages and that . . . mental . . . all fourteen and that, ah swear on the bible to yous, there's three lassies in post-natal there, and they come in a horse box pulled by boyfriend's tractor, three of them in the shitey horse box wi their wee babies and this ugly, bogger guy, driving the tractor, ah mean, fair enough, they used to arrive the Mantrap in that horse box . . . that's quite a laugh no think? But it's no exactly a 'family' vehicle now, is it. Fucksake! Eh? She laughed.

Chell went, That's right enough, it's yon Dempster boy, Fuckin 'Dumpster' they call him. Aye, his house is built three quarter out of old railway wagons, ah swear! They used the box as a bar once at a plough contest.

Michelle went on, Theyve got these signs on *every* table on the cafeteria up at the Chest, right:

45

It's cause they post-natal lassies are aye taking the ends of their wee wet tits and dipping them into the sugar bowls so's their babies'll sook away at them quiet-like and they can get on having a smoke and a good ceilidh.

A huge, Awww, had taken place.

Ah, dinnae *scum* us out! goes Chell.

How many pregnant this year? Michelle nodded up towards Our Lady of Perpetual Succour.

Twenty-seven, beamed Manda, she turned to Fionnula (the Cooler) and says, Y'know Moira Grierson got hers off of Iain Dickinson?

The dick! He's a fucking bonk, a right spunker.

A couple girls looked back at Fionnula (the Cooler) who'd famously handjobbed Dickinson infront Moira at New Year Dance.

How are ya Orla – you look great, I'd heard you'd got better, honey.

Aye, it's great to see ya Michelle. Girls moved specially aside to let Orla through and the two girls hug-huggd.

Ah hear you went to Lourdes and all?

Aye, didn't get off with a single guy.

Everyone laughed.

That a ring on your engaged finger, Michelle? Clodagh pointed.

Nah, nah, it's just a crappy-nothing-ring. You slip it on just for the post-natals ... some of the fathers to the village girls come along just to chat up the pre-natals so ah says I'm engaged to a big guy that'll burst their faces if they fucking *touch* me!

The girls all laughed. Here was a silence. On Michelle's side, it signified how Out-Of-School she was now; she lived in an adult world wi mysterious quantities of time on her hands and she'd moved into the exclusive world of teenage pregnancy, an infinite distance from the few virgins present. In some ways this silence confirmed Michelle's young life was over; pure and intense, she'd devoured the few opportunities for the wee bit sparkle that was ever going to come her way. Part of the remaining tension came from the obscurity of her child's fatherhood; the choir were just too embarrassed to mention top news of the submarine.

Can you feel your baby kick at all? Wee Maria piped up.
Aye.
Can I touch? Orla held out her palm near Michelle's stomach.
Course, aye.
Can I? went Aisling.
Let us? goes Maria.
Can I too? says Iona.
Michelle laughed, grabbed the hands that flew out at her, helping them in, under the Adidas top.
Whoa! You've hardly any tummy at all, Fionnula (the Cooler) smiled, peeping over.
Aye, All ma jeans still fit; what is, is all up here, see?
I can't feel.
Nah, ya have to keep your hand there.
Boy or girl?
After the scans ah've asked them no to tell, so it's a bigger surprise, more interesting and that.
Do you get lots of kicks?
Oh ... ah tell yous ... it's wild ... see when you go to Mowat the Fleshers – ah go in to get ma mum's mince and the mincer machine, it makes this Neeee, Neee noise and the wee thing starts booting away like billy-oh. Every time.

Cmon then girls, our F# sounds like that, called Fionnula and apart from Kay, the choir screed:

NEEEEEEEEEEEEEEEEEEE!

With her outstretched blazer arm, Orla suddenly broke off the touch – tooked her hand from out under Michelle's top and called, It's right enough, feel, feel!
Another couple of hands reached in.
Oh, yeah, so's it is . . .
Don't say 'it'.
A couple folk turned. It was Kay Clarke.
It's okay. That's what ah say . . . 'it', shrugged Michelle.
Manda Tassy scowled at Kay but she just turned away and pretended to look up past Wilson's Garage for the bus.
That's just *sooo* fucking gorgeous and adorable to feel it there, Orla says.
Let's feel, let's feel. Fionnula (the Cooler) shoved forwarders.
This is yous off to Finals then ya jammy lot?
It's gonna be brilliant Michelle, we're just gonna go mental ah mean it's *fuck* the singing yknow . . .
Aye, sure . . .
. . . Just go on a massive pub crawl, check out the shops, Orla's getting new boots and, eh, we're gonna try get back here for the slow dances at the Mantrap.
Oh, yous'll have a brilliant time, girls. Our Ladys loose in the city, eh?
Aye, doesn't bear thinking about.
Who's it going with yous; the Condom and who?
The Pagan. But we're getting to practise last so's we should get the longest up town, says Manda.
It's gone be filmed for telly, eh?

Aye. On late night next week.

Yous'll have such a brilliant time, girls, ah wish ah was with yous.

There was a silence.

Fionnula (the Cooler) asked, Why don't you come along with us the night to the Mantrap?

Ah, cannie Fionnula. Uhm totally skint. I was working part-time in the Superstore, fucking bass, yon Tina MacIntyre cliped on me that ah was pregnant an they fucking sacked me on the spot. Ma Dad went mental, down there screaming at Creeping Jesus but to no avail. It's complete breach of contract cause if you get hurt or lose the baby or that, lifting boxes, they could get sued, ah mean ah was stacking boxes of *cornflakes*, no way was ah going to hurt ma baby for they shower ... fair enough, ah know ah fibbed to get the job, but ah need the *money*. They fucking government saying about single mothers getting pregnant to get a council flat! *What* council flats? Get fucking real. Might be plenty council houses get built down Birmingham or some shitey place but when's a council house last built here?

Aye, right enough. Some folk nodded. Ana-Bessie and Kay didn't.

And the single Mum's allowance! What a joke. Another thing, the government going on about us girls up at pre-natal. Well it was a member of the fucking Her Majesty's fucking Navy that got me in this state in the first place!

A huge cheer of laughs went up.

Aye, do they fucking think of that!? Michelle shouted.

See the sub in the bay, eh? Manda got straight in there.

Aye. Good in the Mantrap the night, girls!

AYE!!!! a big call went out.

Well yous watch yourselves.

Do you still hear from him. The one? ... wee Maria sputtered.

He wrote a letter, aye, but ah cannie go way to the South, it was just a wee night of fun, now ma mum won't let me anywhere. I'm goan end up having the baby in ma fucking bedroom at this rate.

There was a pause, then Michelle added, I'll have to tear down ma Take That posters, or they'll scare the Baaby!!

Another big laugh went up . . .

Ah, can't believe how little you show, you just look great, Fionnula (the Cooler) was still stood with her hand in under the top, waiting for baby to kick.

Have you no *felt* it yet? Manda sort of snapped.

Aye, loads.

Feel it there? Michelle looked into Fionnula face.

Yup.

Michelle smiled, Ah really wish ah could come with yous the night. Fionnula slowly removed her hand and blazer-pocketed it.

Cmon then, Fionnula spoke, almost a whisper and *so* only-to-Michelle, you almost jumped when Kay Clarke spoke, so sudden her voice squeaked a wee bit on the 'I'.

I'll pay you in, Michelle.

Virtually all turned to stare at Kay Clarke, with her yellow Librarian badge and her green Prefect button on her blazer lapels. She had a real Tennis Club brooch too.

Michelle was quick getting off the mark, Oh, ah couldn't do that. Thanks anyways, Kay. Ah've got to get going, see yous right.

A lot, See ya's and Byeee's chorused out.

Michelle had taken two steps back and held up a half arm

50

with the fingers splayed out in a star-fishy wave. Fionnula stepped with her.

Come'n come on with us. Just the one night?

Ach, 'll see Fionnula, 'll ask the Old Dear right?

Fionnula stopped following and the pregnant young girl walked on, smiling.

Eleven at the door to Barrels, right?

Michelle laughed, no looking back. Maybee!

Fionnula turned and walked to the choir. She gave Kay a strange look but Kay was staring up at something.

LOOK! Kay Clarke pointed up, her cheek to the mournful clouds so half her face seemed blue, the other invisible and the ground level world slowed . . . stopped as, wings wide, Lord Bolivia's red head, pink-yellow and green wings, moved over the choir, like a happiness that wasn't allowed below such skies, against these curt roof angles of slate and granite.

Everyone's head turned back towards the New Chapel door which swung shut with a glint of copper.

Simultaneously Sister Fagan screamed, ran down from the main entrance to the school, followed by Sister Condron, her bucket swinging madly.

Lord Bolivia made it onto the flat roof of the amusement arcade before the first seagull dipped a wing and curved in from above Wilson's Garage, landed and ran at the parrot and stabbed it with its beak. Bolivia shrieked, took off and fell, then pulled up, powering off over the tennis court, chased by two other gulls, the rising and falling wing strokes moving into the morning.

'The sense of gigantic transition, of going Southward, downward' MALCOLM LOWRY

The bus moved along loch sides, swurled like a compass needle at their bridged-heads and travelled down opposite banks, so's you could look, cross water and see where you'd come from.

If the road was ever straight it was only to travel up Glen floors then turn the leftwards or rightness yet again into other glens or up round ridge roads.

The bus moved between mountains, along the routes and byways the Port people must use to visit cities, through the rosary of villages and outlying settlements.

Summer, like a furious rash, was upon this land. Fresh bracken, upright and astute, the stalk's growth waverings, visible close to the road as they creamed up the brae runs. The emerald of the land made the mountain gushings of froth all the more white, as they fell and shuffled from the rain days of summits into the concrete channels that narrowed their force, drove them beneath the road where cyclists would halt in bright weatherproofs, to watch the burns curl on downhills.

The Old Military roads from before the Clearances, the lifted railway, its abandoned viaducts overrun by rockfalls, birch clusters and grazing sheep; the Old Road, before the Widenings, the Cut Corners, the pulling out of Z bends, Bridge Improvements; the Old Road sometimes showing a wisp of its faded centre lines on the surviving tarmac: all these shadowed the bus's route.

Inside the girls were divided as to the differing timbres of their voices. The two nuns (Fagan still in tears) sat behind Jerry, the driver.

For some of the girls, among the swayings this way, then that, it seemed strange to be sat with Port girls on a bus journey through their village. When they had moved beyond all villages of Our Lady's Catholic catchment area, true novelty and excitement began.

Above, the sky grew clear into a conventional summer's day: overtaking cars had their sunroofs open so's you could see the thighs of the passengers. The Sopranos, sat along the back seat, had given up kneeling, looking down or across at the cars and lorries pursuing close behind them, before the overtaking.

The Sopranos had wearied with holding up the felt tip scrawled signs and pressing them against the rear window glass:

SHAG US!

and

SHAG ME!

KAY CLARKE
PHONE PULPIT HILL
797

and

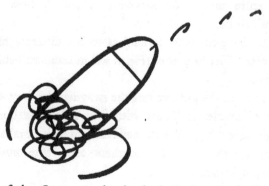

Each of the Sopranos drank alcoholic lemonade from the bottles they'd syphoned into the night before. Each flavour of alco-pop had been funnelled to an appropriate litre bottle: lemon flavoured Hooch in a plastic Natural Lemonade bottle from the Superstore. Fionnula's Garvie's American Cream Soda bottle held Shott's Vanilla Seltzer flavour. Orla had two disguised bottles of blackcurrant Hooch. She'd stood and put the empties up on the ridged luggage rack above so's at every corner or brake application, the bottles were rolling and clinking thegether or sliding forward only to roll back into vicinities and clink again further on down the road.

Kylah was closest to the bottles but she made no move to retrieve them; their sound signalled the Sopranos nascent and flagrant right to drink, signalled their dismissal of any value winning the Final might stand for.

Kylah had her own values and in music it was simply that there was the Cocteau Twins and their girl singer's voice and so much else was total shite. Though she wouldn't be able to remember the girl singer's name, Kylah had what she believed to be all of the Cocteau's CDs, (ordered from the counter at Woolies).

On the bus as it set off from the Port, there'd been the usual rows and ructions of any bus trip – like the geography one – about what musical cassettes were going to be played en route on the bus system (after Sister Condron had exposed them to the last rehearsal and announced from the aisle, 'So much work needs doing this afternoon.')

Kylah had got her way with her cassette cause the whole bus knew she would give the real impression that anything other than music she approved of made her physically ill. If tickity-tick rave music was clicking along, Kylah would put her knees up to her chin and restlessly look one way then the other, saying nothing, her complete exasperation unbearable. She'd specially taken The Cream's *Wheels of Fire* with her, cause its therapeutic length would prevent too much shite else going on and despite its baroque self indulgences, the Sisters couldn't really disapprove.

Maybe ah should get silicon implants, goes Orla.

Ah don't see what's wrong wi implants, cause, like, right, they're just bags of water, aye, like Pamela Anderson, right . . . goes Kylah, thinking *Ah was goan mention she's married to Motley Crue's drummer but ah'd best not after the way Orla was snapping when ah says that about Bon Jovi.*

Aye. So? went Fionnula, swigging on her bottle.

Well seventy-five per cent of human bodies are water, it's like a soft contact lens.

Aye? What's the other twenty-five per cent made of? says Fionnula.

Kylah paused for thought then went, Meat.

No. I meant the contact lens, not Pamela Anderson.

Everyone laughed.

I like Kate Moss's tits, but can't stand all that Calvin Klein shite that comes with her, says Orla.

The Sopranos had started playing strip poker up back the bus and Orla was refusing to join in cause of her tit size. It was the same strip poker rules they would play up the back in Cyclops's Maths class. They knew they'd stop playing, out often-feined boredom, fore it got at all interesting. Anyway, no ways would it equal the Strip Twister game Fionnula initiated at her Seventeenth, in her bedroom, when they'd all been lagered up and Fionnula had got down to just knickers.

Kylah was in a band and on Saturdays she'd take the bus out Silvermines where they practised in Scout Hall. They were called Lemonfinger and had played one high school dance, a dance at the High School Hostel for island pupils and at a youth club disco. They were good, but Kylah kept *Dab Hand* and *Low Lights* and what she thought were her best songs, to herself; still Kylah cringes to think she played the boys *Time Will Tell*. They recorded that on the new sixteen track up the amateur radio station.

Reason Kylah keeps the songs to herself is, she fair reckons she'll be needing those songs when Lemonfinger split up, or chuck her out. Reasons Kylah feels relatively secure about the band splitting up is that she'd had it off with Guitar, Bass and Drums and none of the three know she's been with the other two.

Kylah loves to be in Lemonfinger, putting her lipstick near to the microphone on each of their originals and three cover versions (*The Snake* by The Pink Fairies, *Grimly Forming*, by The Great Society and *Help Me, Mary* by Liz Phair, which makes Kylah, sound like a nubile Old Testament prophet. Drummer does some brill double beats, two fantastic vocal breaks).

Lately, Kylah has got to turning and looking at the guys when she sings *Grimly Forming*, the guitar sound climbing over everything . . .

> I looked out my window
> the cloud was grimly forming.
> Waiting for the rain I saw
> the one dark cloud forming.
> The soldiers paid no heed,
> I could hear their hollow laughter.
> Down the hills in pairs and threes
> the Red Cross girls came after.

And Kylah would move away, towards the hypothetical audience.

Kylah didn't like that song they'd wrote, *Homage to Catatonia*, its stupid lyrics went, and Kylah knew fine they were just about the three of them getting spluttering on stupid loco weed in one of their narrow wee bedrooms up each of the councils. Not that hers was bigger, she just had less records all over the shop . . . and she'd been in EACH of their bedrooms in the afternoons, checking out the differences in their penises.

There was just nowhere to sing on *Homage*, the way keeps changing; it just sounds laboured, like the fucking acoustic guitar 'prelude' they called it (which he probably got from NME or something) – that they went and tagged on *Time Will Tell*, after Kylah had a night out with the Sopranos and left them three on the sixteen track.

These chords that turn inside out were *hers*, they didn't have the right to go adding poncey, twangy bits. Kylah had sussed that a lot of cool, cool songs are just three movements of the hand, a powerful melody singing bit over, chorus, variation, chorus and that's it. Turn the chords inside out on the middle eight, discourage Spimmy from his effects pedal, talk him into changing two fingers on the chord pattern, or just bend the strings on the chord. It was simple as that 'less just naturally brilliant like Superstar, doing *Life is Elsewhere*.

One thing Kylah knows and learned from listening to Sinatra, and that Superstar guy, whose voice makes her want to hug him: the coolest singers *lead* the band . . . play AGAINST the music but never spoiling. They don't just sing *along* with the chords, sorty, 'yah yah na na guitar-and-the-singer-does-the-same'. That's just gormless, perpetual crap. You be brave enough to sing against.

Like on Kylah's CD player, a Sanyo bottom of the range that her Mum got her last Christmas – most shiny button with use is the | ◄◄ | ◄◄ 'next track' as she calls it, button.

Kylah has adolescent ears; impatient ears. Some might call this, in young people, narrow taste, or lack of experience, but it's exactly cause she tolerates so little that she still sings with her ears, no her head. You could call it brilliant taste.

The boys in the band might as well buy her roses, but cause they're trying outcool each other, they all bring her two or three CDs each, to Scout Hall every Saturday.

Kylah doesn't know the names of most of these bands that she takes home with her. She clicks them in beside the shiny | ◄◄ | ◄◄ button and listens as she puts her make-up on about to go out Saturday night. She doesn't look at the covers and often returns the discs in the wrong cases, with moisturiser or foundation thumbprints. She's over, Next-Tracking the CDs every thirty seconds, cept the odd voice she falls for, who can sing. Some famous stuff might be good but it's no use to her. Jimi Hendrix, couldn't sing – if he's so clever why didn't he write a book, stead trying to sing? Grace Slick – now she can sing, *Conspicuous Mainly By Its Absence*, better than that coughy thingy Joplin. Best of all, Jack Bruce and Frank Sinatra and that guy in the Grateful Dead – Kylah'd never seen a photo, but she couldn't listen to the guy without seeing a big Adam's apple shake when he did those vibrato stuff things – he just sounds so emotional ALL the time, and Liz Phair!

That's the way Kylah sings on the recording of *Time Will Tell*. She doesn't like writing words for songs. The way the Cocteau's girl and the Jap in the German band (who could sing!) made up their own words . . . own strange language, so it had no meaning but still felt so emotional . . . so that just goes to show! It's not *meaning*.

The boys in the band usually wrote the words and Kylah would take words home and laugh. They were hardly-disguised Love Songs to her. Kylah would find words near the sound and change them. The boys would be upset to find a line

> When I see you come out the green
> With your blue dress on

by next Saturday, changed to:

> The I see blue come out the dream
> The Long Island Iced Tea Strong

During practice, if she didn't wear tracky bottoms, the boys would gawp terrible at arse and tops of thighs and tits. Even if she turned to the cymbals of the kit, so close she could feel the air swish, when he down-smashed them, the drummer would be gloating at her pelvis.

Kylah wrote all the words for *Time Will Tell*, bout when Orla got took down to the hospital for the radiation treatment they couldn't give up in the Port, and all thought she'd die.

> Fair,
> Fair-haired girl
> Why do you still go on?
> You know the things we've done
> though the summer's just young.
> And I know seasons,
> Time passing is rough

Chorus
> Cos I've heard
> Time will tell
> Where we're all going

Kylah loves the tight camaraderie of practice. Loves the wet morning smell, the insects she dodges on the single tracker up to Scout Hall, Saturday mornings, her sleepiness evaporated on the bus – she adores the smell of the hall, its wee, cobwebby windows, the sound of rain on its tin roof, with her squatting and pissing in the toilet, the same one the boys use, its massive downward cascade as you tug the chain and approach the really loud sound of the boys jamming, which they always do while she pees. She loves Marlboro and cherryade as they relax, listening to a playback on the two-mike tape machine.

Loves the way the boys have stopped scrabbling to accompany her down the garage for cigarettes and the special cherryade you can't seem to get anywhere else, then at the end of a good day, they'll really go hysterical, swapping instruments, her on drums and one of the boys singing, *Smoke On The Water*.

It's sweet too, the way, two of them with guitar cases, walk her to the bus and wait till it comes, always wishing she would go to Silvermines Hotel for a drink but knowing she won't and if any of them have got a lift into town, saying they might see her the night and her knowing they will but she'll be in the cocoon of the Sopranos; or the night she got off with a guy just cause guitarist was hanging round in the Mantrap. She was feeling bad cause she heard the next Saturday, he'd thumbed it the nine mile home without a lift, mortal as a newt.

Kylah loved the band, the little something it gave her. So little, she secretly knew all she ever needed were the practices. She senses they were The Best Days. She felt the 'gigs' as the boys kept repeating, a strain. She got a feeling of ridiculousness. It was nerve-racking and she never knew what to wear.

There was once a fight. She'd said they needed a PA for the drums so he could play softer cause his hammering was impossible to sing above. When it got huffy, Kylah says, Mind, it was *yous* asked me to join this fucking band. It was true. The Sopranos were in the Mantrap, a Saturday night; a grunger from the proddy High walked up to Kylah and knelt at her leg to shout in her ear.

The other Sopranos were stunned, cause they were sitting at table and no guy was *ever* permitted to make a move then. The guy shouted something in Kylah's ear, she shouted something back, this was repeated, the boy rose and left.

In response to the stares, Kylah let out a burst of laugh then yelled, He asked me to join his band, says they heard me singing.

The other girls laughed.

He says yous can do backing vocals.

There were a few snorts as Fionnula and Manda turned in their seats to look through the cigarette smoke and disco light where the three grungy-looking guys sat.

If that one had tidied himself up a bit he could've been cute, Manda gravely pronounced.

Fionnula drawled, Wha'd you say?

Kylah had goes, I telt them to get off home and keep on watching their fucking Commitments video!

They all bust out laughing but during the week, Kylah's mum called her to the phone ten minutes into *Brooky*.

Hell*op*?

It's Spimmy. Asked to join our band in the Mantrap.

How'd you get my number? she says, too quickly.

Kylah's mum was stepping past the photo of the Pope in the porch to the front room; looked back suspiciously.

Kylah tutted.

You're in the phone book.

How'd you know ma name then?

Ah saw . . . ah heard you sing at the Gaelic League, your name was in the programme.

I was crappy.

When you did *Glencoe* in Gaelic . . . you've just an amazing voice.

Fionnula McConnel has an amazing voice, I don't. And *Brookside* is on.

I'll phone back.

Ya will no.

Could we meet you? Me and the other two guys in the band. We had a singer but we were just making faces behind him, he used to check his hair in the new cymbals after he leapt around.

Aye? Kylah was smiling and it showed in her voice.

Ahm sorry bout *Brooky* but it's no as good as it used to be; have you seen the old repeats with Harry Cross in?

Nah. Mum says he was a right dour so and so.

Oh! He's a legend, Harry Cross.

Listen, ah've no sung even through a microphone before but

I write songs, ah've got the brother's guitar, he's hopeless on it, no amplifier, I play unplugged.

AYE!! What are your influences?

Ma what?

What do you listen to?

Cocteau Twins . . . some of ma dad's records, Nat King Cole, Frank Sinatra, Geoff Love, James Bond themes, soundtrack to *Jaws*, and Superstar.

Cool.

I could make a cassette with me singing on it but ya mustn't play it to a single soul.

Look, have to go ma money's running out.

Oh. Right. Where yous from?

Silvermines.

Aye, ah knew it was out the villages.

Can we meet you in town on Saturday?

Suppose, for a wee minute aye.

Where do you know?

Everywhere.

Will you meet us in a pub, do ya get in?

Course ah do . . . well in Barrels.

What time?

One ah suppose.

Right. Barrels. One.

Okey–dokey.

Bring your cassette.

All right.

We're called . . . the line died.

Thunderpup, the drummer nodded, tipping his pint towards his lips.

Despite pretending to be cool, she'd washed her hair night

before though she'd all Saturday afternoon when she usually did. It was piled all up with a pink scarf in and she'd on the mini-skirt, the new Converse All Stars and was chain-smoking Marlboro Lights. They bought her a blackcurrant Hooch.

The cassettes didn't need to be listened to, those boys were going to get her in the band.

The bassist was cute but his hair was greasy and always, touch, touching it away from his cheeks; Guitar hardly spoke but he did try to impress her, saying he could play *The Man with the Golden Gun* on his 'Fender copy', that she nodded to and weeks later discovered it was a guitar.

Drummer was nice too but all that military gear shite.

I want to hear what yous sound like, Kylah said.

We brought a cassette of our last practice with our stuff on it. And there's another thing . . .

Yes? The three leaned forwarders.

This name Thunderpup will have to go.

Rest, and Be Thankful

The Sopranos had been using the undoing of singular shirt buttons as forfeits in the sadly censored strip poker. Some sat wi their blazer and ties off, since Manda Tassy sat at the side window and was losing, she'd her buttons undone down to her belly button so's you could see the little ribbon on the front clasp of her wonderbra.

Kay Clarke, arms out steadying herself, was motioning her way up the back with a box Cadbury's Roses that she was distributing, chatting with the Seconds and Thirds as she approached the enclave of Firsts.

Kay, Fionnula nodded.

Want a Roses?

No ta.

Rachel?

Na.

Manda?

Nut.

Kylah?

Aye go on then, always partial to a Rosey, specially Ian Brown . . . ah like the wee squares ones – all chocolate just, they're blue with pink roses, Kylah dangled her fingies in the box that Kay held and nicked one out, frowning with concentration.

How is the band?

Fine, aye.

No dances planned?

Nope.

I heard that your cassette was just . . . amazing.

Kylah gave a hollow, dull, Aye?

I mean I heard it was just . . . you couldn't actually believe it was you singing it, it just sounded like a *real* band . . . I mean like a band from a city . . . a dead famous big band from a city. It's going to be a record, isn't it?

Just a wee compilation CD, bands wi no records out, it's no big deal and the guitar on its start is shite. Kylah looked about, We shoulda come down here an recorded in a big, proper studio. She muttered something about money, plugged her mouth with the big cherryade bottle of hooch.

Aye, well mind us when you're famous, Manda goes, doing up her buttons.

How's your violin-playing? Fionnula smiled, out the side of mouth.

Cello, Kay nodded. Not very good, she chuckled, oddly.

Want a sip of Natural Lemonade? Chell went, tipping the bottle at her, so the alcohol fizzed inside.

No thanks.

Cmon Kay; this is the party end of the bus.

Drink up lass, Manda snorted, You'll get the toilet at Rest & Be Thankful.

Fionnula goes, Thing about Rest & Be Thankful, it's the highest up pub in the country, so ah reckon the effects of alcohol there would be exaggerated by the thin air at that altitude.

Everyone laughed.

Kay shrugged and smiled, You lot going up the town when we get there then?

Too right. Are you not?

Umm, yesss. If the Seconds get the time, we're ropey compared to you shower, she smiled at Fionnula, who shrugged. Kay went on, I was actually down with Dad last weekend anyway.

Oh oh! *Well* then, goes Manda. This must be a *real* bore for you.

How come you were down?

What? Sudden, Kay seemed a bit jumpy.

How come you were down in the capital? Fionnula goes.

Ah, just Dad was down on business so I came along for the ride, you should see River Island for clothes and Schuh for you, Orla.

Aye? Orla humphed.

What are you getting? Kay smiled.

Knee-length boots.

How much are you spending?

Suddenly, Fionnula interrupted, Hoi, hoi, hoi, what's your business how much she's got on her, what is it, you gonna give'r the money you were gonna pay Michelle in with the night? Fionnula twisted her lip.

Kay shrugged, Maybe Michelle didn't want to come out.

NO Kay, course she does. She's pregnant and grounded in her house, you ever been in Michelle's house? Fionnula snapped on without letting her answer, Staying in at night is just for folk who have nice, BIG houses that are comfortable to stay in, where ya can get a bit privacy, in a wee house yer sat looked at the four walls, or sat wi yer folks in the front room wi the telly blaring crap . . . it's a crippling feeling, magine how Michelle feels . . . staying in at nights is for . . . it's for the bloody middle classes. Fionnula had taken a brasser and she turned to look out the window.

Kay looked and swallowed, seemed to be about bursting out with the greeting. Kay spoke louder, You five are going to ruin today for everyone.

Piss off; if you want this choir to do well it's just so it's another fucking badge ya can pin on your blazer or tell your dad about; well it doesn't make a blind bit of difference to me or any of us, its just a treat to get down the city.

Why though? I mean, yous sing better than *any* of us, we all admit that, but you are just chucking it away like, like you were saying in Guidance the other day.

What? Orla turned to Kylah.

Kylah unplugged the cherryade booze, Ach. A drop squash came out the corner of her mush and she rubbed at it with arm of her blazer, and it was that cheap, nylony material the blazer was made from, so a wee dribble liquid scampered cross the cuff, not being absorbed.

Ach, ah just goes that I'm not ambitious with the band and that . . . I just want the best job in town, she smiled.

What's that?

Behind the record counter in Woolies. Only job ah've ever wanted – think about it, just sat behind there wi Top 40 at your fingertips, you can play what ya want. This lassie from the proddy High's there an am quite pally with her, mind she was hanging round with us two weekends back.

She's quite pretty, Fionnula grumbled, still looking outwards.

Aye. Well if she keeps coming out with me, it's just a matter of time before she's on maternity leave!

Everyone squawked, even Kay smiled.

. . . Then ah'll just close in there an . . . clinch the position!

Kay, Orla spoke so everyone stopped fidgeting, Kay, no everyone has to want to go to university with you.

Mind you, Kylah piped up, Ah still want to sing on a Jah Wobble's *Invaders of the Heart* CD, he gets the bestest singers; ah'm telling you!

Orla was still speaking, After what happened to me, I think we should live for today, no the morrow an . . .

Sudden-like, Kay nodded curtly and turned, began making her way, balancing very carefully, down the aisle. The Sopranos looked along the backseat at each other, mouths wide in triumphalism, showing the chewing gum's blocks.

What's up wi her? Orla popped more Wrigleys in her mush.

She's just bored, sat there next to Ana-Bessie, 'Ann, Ann, what's a man?'

Everyone laughed, making sure it was loud enough to reach front of bus.

She looked near bursting out with the greets, goes Fionnula.

Guess she just can't stand no having another fucking badge to pin to her tits.

Tits? went Chell.

Orla goes, She's got nice tits, the university boys'll love her.

Let's shut up about her and get dressed dearies, I'm fucking dying for a fag, Fionnula (the Cooler) shifted in her seat.

The Sopranos began to swing round and knot their ties.

Now the bus was moving over a pass between two colossal blocks of mountain – slabs and rations of granite burst through meagre top soils, thrusting up like broken bone through split flesh.

The whole landscape was massively ancient, under scattered screes, the exposed cliffs below the glacial glens showing time wasn't finished with the world here. A landscape from an age unslept.

At the summit, there was a huge overlook on the glen, its veering meander of the old, single track below the Main, reflecting sun on the un-usedness of its macadam, up to where the Humbers and Austins used to steam-boil their radiators outside what was once a military supply station in The Clearance Centuries: Rest & Be Thankful Hotel.

Old Jerry the driver swung in and was first off the Mud Bucket that had been specially cleaned on orders of the Mother Superior. On its normal school run, the bus windows were sometimes so filthy, the village girls couldn't be sure they'd actually pulled up outside Our Lady's.

Jerry was famous for swerving to hit pheasants on the Bultitude estates. When he copped one, he'd stop the school bus and scour verges.

Old Jerry headed off for the hotel foyer to try borrow a shaver – his own electric had burned out with a stinky frazzle that morn, so the busload choirgirls had given it tight to'm bout his 50 per cent beard – a perfect half from upper lip to the chaff point on his Adam's apple above the shirt collar.

Another two, empty, Bova tour buses were parked in the lot outside the hotel.

Don't worry, Sister Fagan, Chell says, passing her, Parrots and budgies have been knowd to survive months up home in the wild, and specially in summertime.

Oh, I hope so Rachel, The Pagan was almost snivelling again. . . . I just can*not* stop thinking of the little soul out there, lost. I almost feel like heading straight home.

Fionnula nodded, enthusiastically.

How did he get out Sister? goes Manda.

I just can't understand that Amanda, I think it perhaps may have been the janitor but I wouldn't want to lay blame on the fellow. By the time I'd trotted up to chapel on *my* old legs, there was nobody there, Father Ardlui was in the sacristy, and he'd heard nothing.

As the Sopranos bundled into Rest & Be Thankful, Chell was hissing, Parrot don't have a chance, the hoodies'll savage'm minute they see him.

Wow-wee-ow!

Yanks, Manda whispered

To get to the toilets, the Sopranos had to walk through the large lounge then turn right up the corridor with the tartan carpets.

The entire lounge was crowded with elderly American tourists, talking very loud and lifting small white bread pieces to their slow-mouths. When the mouths were empty of the pieces, they started to move very quick indeed.

As the five schoolgirls walked between tables, a good few the old people's heads followed them, the jaws work-working.

Manda lifted a sandwich off a table she passed, then grabbed another from the next empty table, there was a RESERVED sign hung on the back of the chair with this little chain attached to it and Manda nabbed that too, fixing the sign to the top button on her shirt.

The LADIES was down a corridor before the GENTS, but already a few Yank tourist women, wearing cream or fawn macs and Burberry caps, were queued, awkward-like, waiting to get in where all the cubicles had been nabbed by smokers from Seconds and Thirds, Fat Clodagh, Iona, Aisling and Assumpta most probably.

Cmon, Orla nudged, the five girls strode on, rounded the

71

right angle, Orla shoved the door, cocked her nut in and round about and they were within the magical alienness of the GENTS. It was very cold and their laughs echoed. As they brought out their cigarettes and lighters they stared at the hissing, long trough on the far wall.

Nae mirror, Chell nodded at the four screw holes above the sink and she fired up one of Manda's Camel.

Fucking men, eh? says Manda.

Ahm no sitting on *that*, Fionnula announced from the cubicle, dropping the only toilet seat, using just two fingers.

Look, Manda lifted a wee white bread piece out her blazer pocket, she peeled apart the bread and they heard the tacky ripping sound as the butter separated from the filling.

Cucumber. Manda tossed it, with a splat, into the urinal.

Yeuch, cucumber – no use to man nor beast, went Orla.

But great for a woman's cunt, Fionnula murmured from the cubicle door and they smiled or chuckled, then stopped.

The door opened and an elderly man took a half-step inward, the clothes they saw him wearing were a flat cap and very white running shoes; a blue raincoat.

By instinct, each girl jerked their cigarettes to the smalls of their backs.

Well apologies, young ladies ... apologies, the man said, backing out and scrutinising up at the door front through his glasses as it sucked closed.

The girls shrugged, blew smoke through their tittery lips.

Think he'll tell?

Na.

Will we get in the cubicle?

No ways is Condom going to come in *here*.

The Sopranos smoked, slow, luxuriously. No speaking, they were quite drunk and realising it.

Ah fancy a drink, dying for more, all ma Hooch is gone flat, Fionnula says.

Mine too.

The door opened.

Aww, I *do* beg your pardon. Another Yank old-timer, keeked in, rapidly retreated.

Suddenly they heard the rush downward: Fionnula was hovered, knickers hanging in the network of splayed tights round her thighs as she peed.

Wop, she's at it again! Kylah smiled, who was stood in front the cubicle.

Manda keeked, tutted and stepped forwards, Fionnula cooried a bit as she was, moved her eyes up to Manda's face. Fuck *sake* Fionnula, Manda tried to step in, grab the edge of the door with both fists and pull it shut. You could see she was really annoyed, but she'd have to shift Fionnula's crouched position to get the cubicle door swung shut; she sort of moaned and gave up, trying to smile it off, One of those old bastards'll have a heart attack if they see you . . .

They heard the piss stream stop. Rattle of bog roll holder as she scooped in under her.

Aye, aye, says Fionnula, thinking, *What's Manda tutting at? Mind back when we were three or four, me, her, that wee Ginty lad, aww three us thegether on the toilet seat in Manda's Mum's, peeing away, me facing front, those two on sideyways and when we got off, wee tinker Ginty had done a sneaky shite . . . a string of little curranty, purley-wurleys and . . .*

She's making me need piss too, shove over, as Fionnula stepped out to the sink Kylah shoved in, pushed the door semi-shut and went about peeing.

Fionnula turned on the cold water tap slow so's it didn't splash.

Mmm, Manda eyed Fionnula, shaking her head.

Cmon, am gonna piss in the real place, went Chell and she was stepping outwards and turning when her head moved upways, Ooo she went.

An old man Yank voice goes, Got ya!

Several other male presences made chuckly rumbles slowly.

Chell drew her fingers up to her mouth, went a brasser and stepped back in laughing.

What is it . . . ? What is . . . ? Manda was shoving her way out the pulled door and the Sopranos jostled after her.

INT/HOTEL CORRIDOR/DAY
Five teenage school girls, kilts well above their knees, chewing gum emerge from DOOR marked GENTS.
MALE AMERICAN VOICE #1
(Off screen)
Well hi there, we're real sorry to disturb you ladies but Herb here . . .

We PAN LEFT, an OLD AMERICAN CAUCASIAN breaks for it, clearly in great DISTRESS and clutching his CROTCH he pushes past the SCHOOLGIRLS and EXITS through the door marked GENTS.

TALLEST BRUNETTE SCHOOLGIRL
Sorry Mister, we were doing a bit extra swotting for our exams in there.

MALE AMERICAN VOICE #2
(Off Camera)
Heh, heh, heh, heh. You ladies from these parts? You're very fortunate young ladies, living amongst all this splendour.

MALE AMERICAN VOICE #3
Now what kinda tartan is that your kilts are made from?

SMALLER BLONDE THIN SCHOOLGIRL
That's Protestant tartan.

TALL BLONDE SCHOOLGIRL
Aye, only Protestants like us can wear it.

MALE AMERICAN VOICE #1
Now you ladies wouldn't be trying to hoodwink us in any way, would you now?

BLONDE SCHOOLGIRL WITH RESERVED SIGN
Aye we were.

The other SCHOOLGIRLS turn to stare at her.

BLONDE SCHOOLGIRL WITH RESERVED SIGN
Exams are really over.

GENERAL HILARITY among the group of girls.

SMALLER BLONDE THIN SCHOOLGIRL
They were great tho I was excused them on health grounds.

TALLEST BRUNETTE SCHOOLGIRL
Mental health grounds!

GENERAL LAUGHTER

BLONDE SCHOOLGIRL WITH RESERVED SIGN
It was brilliant right, this girl Kay that's at school with us . . .
what exam was it . . . ? Geography? SHE turns aside to the
others.

TALL BLONDE SCHOOLGIRL
It wasn't Geography, time with Kay it was English.

SHORTER BRUNETTE SCHOOLGIRL WITH THE EYES
The time with the kilt thread, that was English . . .

SMALLER BLONDE THIN SCHOOLGIRL
Protestant kilt thread . . .

GENERAL LAUGHTER

BLONDE SCHOOLGIRL WITH RESERVED SIGN
Look, we've got this girl in the class a real . . . ah don't know
what yous call it in America but she's a real swot . . .

AMERICAN VOICE #2
A damned pencil pusher . . .

BLONDE SCHOOLGIRL WITH RESERVED SIGN
We were all in early and sat down, the pencil pusher's outside,
swotting out some last poetry rubbish, so's *she* (POINTS to
TALLEST BRUNETTE SCHOOLGIRL) . . . tugs this thread
out her own kilt seam and manages to tie Kay's seat to her desk
. . . when she comes in the exam hall Kay was clattering and
banging to get the chair away . . .

SMALLER BLONDE THIN SCHOOLGIRL
Aye . . . all the teachers were shushing her . . .

BLONDE SCHOOLGIRL WITH RESERVED SIGN
Yon was a disgrace, *and* the Geography, eh? Ah mean yon actual questions!

FOCUS PULLS OUT, PAN LEFT AND CLOSE UP ON

TALLEST BRUNETTE SCHOOLGIRL
Aye. This satellite photo of some town: like a *satellite* from up in outer space and this town was meant to be in Scotland and we should know it, right!? Well all you could make out is the coastline and that was the question: 'What can you tell us about this settlement?' Eh, I mean what's that all about?

TALL BLONDE SCHOOLGIRL
So that's all what we wrote down . . . 'It's on the Coast.'

BLONDE SCHOOLGIRL WITH RESERVED SIGN
. . . 'It's in Scotland . . .'

TALLEST BRUNETTE SCHOOLGIRL
Ah guess we weren't paying much attention up the back, but a satellite photo . . . ah mean to say!

BLONDE SCHOOLGIRL WITH RESERVED SIGN
What was the other exam cracker?

TALLEST BRUNETTE SCHOOLGIRL
We all left the exam hall after the forty minute minimum was up. There's only so many ways to say, 'It's on the Scottish coast.'

BLONDE SCHOOLGIRL WITH RESERVED SIGN
What was yon Geography question, the *other* one?

TALL BLONDE SCHOOLGIRL
Seagulls.

TALLEST BRUNETTE SCHOOLGIRL
Aye. 'Nineteen-whatever was a record year for seagull hatchings on the west coast, how many seagull eggs were laid?' Ah mean what's *that* all about?

TALL BLONDE SCHOOLGIRL
Y'know. Impossible!?

SHORTER BRUNETTE SCHOOLGIRL WITH THE EYES
That was judged such an impossible exam, automatic-like, they started everyone off at D.

TALL BLONDE SCHOOLGIRL
We all got Ds.

SMALLER BLONDE THIN SCHOOLGIRL
What about you when you did Maths!

TALL BLONDE SCHOOLGIRL
Aye, Fionnula, tell him . . .

TALLEST BRUNETTE SCHOOLGIRL (FIONNULA)
Aye . . . right. (COUGHS AND FACES CAMERA) Ah had the maths formulas wrote inside the sanny bin in the girls toilets, so's a bit into the exam I asked to go to the toilet but ma piece of formulas paper was all soaked in blood cause someone had used the dispenser. Dirty Hoor.

78

SHORTER BRUNETTE SCHOOLGIRL WITH THE EYES
Ah, dinna *scum* us *out!*

AMERICAN VOICE #1
(Off Camera)
Hell, I can't play this kinda stuff to my nieces.

AMERICAN VOICE #2
Heh, heh, heh, heh.

HERB, smiling now, comes out of door marked GENTS.

TALLEST BRUNETTE SCHOOLGIRL (FIONNULA)
Hoi, aye, since we've helped you out with your holiday video
how's bout yous doing *us* a wee favour?

Where *have* you been, Sister Condron grit her teeth.
These Yank tourists got Coca-Cola for us, Sister, obviously
we didn't want to go into a public bar ourselves, Fionnula held
up the two 1.5 litre bottles, filled too near the top for perfect
realism.
Don't say 'Yank' Fionnula, they're American.
New Orleans in fact, The Pagan nodded seriously.
The Sopranos shrugged. We know, Manda says.
Jerry nodded his clean-shaven chin once and closed the door
behind them.

Post-Seventh-Hooch-Syndrome

Up back everything was moving into post-seventh-Hooch-syndrome. The two bottles, that were really a half bottle Southern Comfort lightly diluted with the Coke that hadn't gone down the toilet, were passed back and forth in an alliance of giggles and silence.

The bus was slithering and swaying into the Low Lands – instead of the impossible places, the ground now became creamy pastures; high walls, the mosses killed by city-nearness, came up close to the window – beyond the racing top-bricks, the rhododendron estates of great, mysterious wealth.

Chell McDougall was whisked onwards, manoeuvring the heavy Coke bottle of liquid to her mouth, feeling the alcohol swing inside the tank of plastic between her two palms.

Chell's auntie is also her sister!

Chell's Daddy Patrick is gone, gone and drowned: his never-found bones all broke apart on scattered places, down in Davy Jones's locker, nestled cross the rust-coloured rocks, jammed in among the slimy, thick-waving strips of weed.

Lost, lost offof the *Eilean Shona*. No funeral ever or nothing. Just gone; his shaving things still above the sink for in hopes he'd swum ashore ... His shaving things in the cabinet ... Say he was stranded on an islet or that? Then just nothing. Daddy Patrick isn't Chell's *actual* Daddy tho.

Chell and her big sister/aunt's Actual Daddy isn't round anymore. Actual Daddy was another sailor, and he was over that horizon where all the old moons and suns are cluttered up, like Buzz's scrapyard, before you could say Jack Robinson. Chell's Mum married Daddy Patrick McDougall soon after, First Mate on the *Eilean Shona* who became just bones at sea.

Chell's big sister Shirley got pregnant last summer. Guess who she got pregnant off? The youngest of dead Daddy Patrick's brothers, crazy Buzz McDougall the bee keeper, Chell's Uncle Buzz. So Chell's sister is also her auntie.

Not that Buzz is any spring chicken. Time was when both little sisters would spend a lot time out at Buzz's place near Tulloch Ferry, with his honey jars and parked old lorries and the Zebra pick-up.

Time too the sisters got took in the Zebra pick-up to get full hives off of old Cloon up near the Fort. Buzz drinking in pubs all the way up, bringing out lemonades with real lemon slices to the carparks. Driving in tears, 'Poor wee Fatherless lassies,' going on a roundabout the wrong way then mounting a grass one straight over the middle and the hives wrapped in wire driving home but Buzz still stopping at so many pubs it got night and cold in the Zebra pick-up (salvaged from the Bear Park) and as it was freezing and freezinger, the bees in the back got all silent out there in that cold, rushing night air.

They get to Buzz's place, lorries everywhere (so's when he wants one at the back out, he has to park them all the way down the single track road and tourists have been queued up for an hour). There's a telly in the garden and Buzz's old pal Snorkel is sat, watching *Panorama* with a big coat on.

The bees are silent. Buzz don't seem worried tho'. They all

just gone dozy with the cold, says Buzz to Snorkel and the wee girls.

Buzz carries the full hives into his front room and sucks all the bumble bees out with the vacuum cleaner, filling all those vacuum cleaner bags, even emptying the full one of its ousels out the back door so's some dust motes adhere to the telly screen in the garden.

Buzz sellotapes shut the rubbery openings and puts the vacuum bags full of bees by the white meter storage heaters.

In the morning when Shirley and Chell go through to watch cartoons in the gardens, the vacuum cleaner bags are buzzing angrily.

Chell takes an interest in bees there on; soon all animals. She spends all her time at Buzz's, finding the wet clay muck that glistens with fool's gold, searching out abandoned hedgehog nests filled with blind baby rats; brushing the hedgehog fleas away from their still-closed eyes; buzzards launching off telegraph pole tops and the pony trekking was at Tulloch-Ferry. Once, Shimmy the chestnut mare bucked her so high, Chell saw the unseeable-next-village for the first time. But she doesn't like spiders and only this morning, taking her shower before going down to Our Lady's, she put all the plugs in the sink and bath before stripping off her pyjamas.

One summer there were three puppies born to the bitch who died up on the farm. Chell took them, their wee eyes hardly open, kept them in one of Buzz's sheds, secret, among all the jars and the old hives, brook bodies, crown boards, smokers, hats and veils.

Chell would squeeze the wee gold tit to feed the puppies lukewarm milk from an eyedropper. She kept the puppies in a big cardboard box, lined with newspapers and an old orange jersey she'd found.

Before Buzz came up from the bees by the burn, she'd have heated a big stone from the loch, in the oven alongside the pizzas. Chell'd carry the big hot stone with the anthracite shovel, using two hands, to the shed and tie the stone up in ripped old sheets. In the morning the wee doggies would be all curled round the gone-coldness of the stone.

Chell read in one of her animal books that puppies are comforted by ticking sound: they feel its their mother's heart beating.

Chell got the alarm clock from the spare room, made double, double sure the alarm was switched off and just in case, set the alarm hands round to quarter past fiveish, just before the time it was then. Chell wrapped that clock in rag and put it in the box with the warm stone, lifted the little peeping puppies in on top.

In the morning all the puppies were dead in a mire of blood and shite. The red hotness of the stone had shattered the glass face of the clock into shards that had sliced through and cut the puppies as they fought to try and get out, shock and bleeding did the rest.

Chell cried for just that morning, buried the cut, plump bodies thegether down by the loch, wrapped in the bloody jersey.

She'd more or less forgotten about them by tea-time that night till she stepped into the kitchen in bare feet and heard the alarm clanging, way out across the yard in that shed.

Chell got less keen on animals for a while. Barbies took over for a spell with Loretta from 12 and with English Katie, all together they had six Barbies and one Ken.

They used to pierce their Barbies' ears and use common pins, the little flat tips on Barbies' lobes were earrings – the depth of the pins just fitted perfectly inside the Barbies' heads. They would play Bungee Jump Barbie with tied-together elastic bands. Sometimes it would snap from up in Loretta's top flat, especially with Ken.

When one Chell's Barbies got pregnant from English Katie's Ken, she would shove the yellow capsule from a Kinder egg up the blouse or dress. Chell'd put a wee plastic baby that you got out the Lucky bags, inside the capsule. It gave them a good fat tummy.

Primary was terrible at the end of summer holidays every year. Pick and Flick couldn't walk and she was just frightening.

Once Chell was whispering and Pick and Flick bawled out and made her go to the front. Chell stood there and Pick and Flick sat, almost face to face just shouting at her though it was only half a year since her Daddy Patrick was lost at sea.

Pick and Flick wheeled over and did that violent spin thing, both her freckly hands flat on the tyres. *Here*! Pick and Flick bawled.

Chell was given usual punishment. Kneeling. Kneeling facing the wall, staring right at its boredom. It was usual. Pick and Flick loved to get them kneeling out there, sometimes up to five of them, so's it was like they had no legs either.

That time, Chell let her head drop forward a little, forehead on the cold wall. It was a yellowy, greeny wall and it had this glaze on it, like when Chell's Mum would brush an oven minced pie with egg white: that kind of glaze. There were minute little bubbles, tiny craters you could see in the glaze.

RA-Chell!

Chell snapped her head up straight.

But you soon got bored. Chell found she could keep her

head straight but stick out her tongue and lick the wall, touch its coldness.

It didn't really have a taste as she lick-licked, it seemed to cool her down, like it does doggies with their tongues hanging out.

Kay Clarke, with her hair the way it was in primary, jammed her arm up.

Miss, Cameron, Miss Cameron, Miss, Rachel McDougall is licking the wall!

Day the school kitchens caught fire the white smoke casually rolled up the corridors past the classroom doors. Chell and the class could duck out the windows onto the hopscotch squares of the playground but Pick and Flick was sprawled in her wheelchair, whizzing round rosary beads, you could see her near greeting in the fire bells and no child wanted to help the wicked old besom escape flames but it was Chell didn't dunk out the window but horsed it back and kicked off the brake, heave-ho'd, getting lighter as yous got faster up the corridor – through the smoke that was really more like steam – Chell's spindly legs hit-hitting the seat back making her go OOF, OOF and the slap of the little girl's feet on the polished floor not stopping till the janitors caught the chair at the door to the Big End and Chell leaned, on her knees then just for a jiffy, straightening, to cross herself cause of the knowing that she'd done a holy thing by the saving of a bad person who should be all burned up in flame cause of her badnesses to childs.

Cause she was LITTLE RACHEL PUSHES WHEELCHAIR TEACHER FROM BURNING SCHOOL front pages in *The Port Star* she got Selwyn, the gay red setter puppy from Mum. Old Selwyn now, who, Saturday nights in the dark, she takes walkies up Battleship Hill slopes above the Complex, where the wood smoke from the chimney pots moves spooky through the trees. As Selwyn scrunches and snuffles round the brush, getting autumn-crisp bramble sections tangled in his long hairs, Chell hides or retrieves the tiny flags of mini-skirts, the flaps of fabric that are mid-rift-revealing tops concealed within a selection of plastic bags she has in the bushes, uphill of the boys' swing and the skitey smear of heel-scuff earth under the rope end.

Around twenty minutes later, Selwyn in his kennel down in the back green, Chell'll climb back up the slopes wearing the longer skirts and tops permitted by her mum; goosebumped in the darkness she strips and changes into skirts that would never get her front of the window, never mind out. Sometimes when it's just too icicles or she thinks there's boys up the swing, Chell'll compromise on a long top and long skirt, she'll walk down the bus stop where Manda and Fionnula'll be waiting; Chell'll whip off the skirt and she'll be wearing a tiny skirt underneath the long one.

When Chell gets home, pissed mortal, two or three in the mornings, Mum's always in bed so she sneaks in, wearing the forbade clothes, gets down to underwear in the hall, case of a Mum-prowl, she can pretend, that she was just on the way to the toilet (where she checks for hickies).

Mum leaves the back door key under the flower pots on their steep stairs up to the side door. Thing is, there are seventeen steps and sixteen flowerpots and it's pitch black there. Chell 'shites' and 'fucks' between her teeth, *Swear Mum left the key under a different pot last week to spite late late nights and ma long-lies*; so Chell's head's spinning, bent right over on the steps, scraping her varnished nails under the tipped pots, where slaters and spiders might touch her fingertips and old Selwyn the dog is out his kennel, tail slashing, paws halfway up the stair behind her, the dog's cold wet nose, sliding up Chell's thigh, sniffing her arse under the miniskirt, right up.

'Leave the Capitol
Exit this Roman Shell.'
THE FALL

At dawn, Tuesdays and Thursdays the seagulls fly uptown into the capital from the docks, cruise along the canyons and gulleys of grey air between the tenements: homes so close together, on the hour, through open windows, varieties of clocks can be heard chime the length of a street; the bleep of the electronic till in a cornershop can be heard up in top flats; the birds settle and gnash into the binliners, caw-cawing in the quiet air before the arrival of the ashbucket men.

On radios, traffic reports last longer than weather forecasts and financial reports last longest of all. A castle acts as a vague focus of a capital that apes history but seems a stage set for some idea that's been forgot, *Whatever, it's all a sham*, Manda Tassy glares out the window as the Sopranos bus crawls into the West End of the capital, the busy pavements, so many boys with the same haircuts, the girls with real different styles.

Christ, it's fucking stifling hot, I'm boiling, goes Fionnula beside, who has her sport bag up on her lap, *Like a real open country girl, anxious and over-hurried to get off, 's-if the bus'll vanish or something*, Manda thinks and says, Aye.

All the Sopranos have heard Come To The City jokes: An old woman from the Port visits for the first time, comes back to the Highlands on the late train and they ask her what the day in the big city was like; the old woman says the city is a wonderful place, so many shops and cafés and most wonderful, its all covered over with a roof of glass. (She never left the main railway station.) Or there's a shepherd from Little Australia, out past the Port, who makes it out the station and up onto the main street of the Capital one summer. The shepherd pauses, amazed outside a huge department store window, raises his staff and shatters the plate glass into pieces, What! Ice at this time of year? he shouts.

Manda Tassy slunks back, tries to be city-cool. Manda still sleeps in the cheeky, baggy T-shirts that are fallout from her fourteenth year – cartoon characters in various sexual inter-course positions. When she sat at the fold-down scullery table that morning and her daddy put her tea wi four sugars down in front, the character on the mug matched the one on her T-shirt. Manda'd hissed turned the pink character away and sipped from other side the mug, so the handle faced left and she couldn't see the character.

Now her big sis Catriona's doing well, assistant manageress at the Hairhouse, she's moved out, so Manda lives with her daddy and they eat from the plate that is largely empty. When Manda's daddy sticks his head in from the scullery a cheery voice calls, Cowboy Dinner, as Manda thumps down in the armchair and remotes the telly on, home from school – it's no cause of tomboy days when the three of them would watch westerns on telly thegether; it's cause Manda's daddy can't cook very well and they haven't paid for the Sky card this year and cause beans on toast is cheap.

On Saturday nights when Manda leaves the bathroom, towel above her tits and one wrapped round her hair, she turns into her room, pushes the door and hears the weekly sound of their poverty: the pause, never longer than a few minutes, then the bathroom door opening and reshutting as her daddy undresses and slips into his daughter's used bathwater, this poor Cleopatra, the creaminess created by two cups of powdered milk poured under the hot tap.

Saves putting the immerser on again, her daddy: look of sorrow that first winter when he had to admit the bank balance was no geared up for it and ask her to start leaving the plug in. Straight away she could understand what it had meant to him, have to ask it. Okay Dad, she had says and they've never spoke of this arrangement again for three years of milky Saturday night baths. Before she started to get weirder, when they were really close, and she told Fionnula near all, she never ever told her the shared bathwater story.

Like in primary after Manda's Holy Communion on the Saint's Day, Fionnula rustled up a silver tray for the flower petals from somewhere or other, but Manda's was the Tennents Beer one, Daddy would bash his head with on Hogmanay, wrapped in silver cooking foil, heaped with plucked hydrangea and carnation petals from Fagan's greenhouse on the Convent lawn.

Two files of little children: boys and girls marching round the lawn, the model of each Saint on a circle of tables; the procession stops at the Saint table where the children genuflect then scatter the Saint with flower petals and walk on.

Poor Daddy. Manda wasn't easy. Once her dad broke his toe gainst all the junk on her bedroom floor, he'd come barging in bawling at her to tidy the bloody place up. And there was boyfriend, Jamie Prenter that she went with for three year till Christmas past there. Prenter was a bad family, even when thirteen, Jamie's mum and dad would take him to the pub too, so's he could drive them back in their Nissan Datsun thing;

Jamie propped up on sacks behind the steerwheel, his parents, laughing and giving him ten pence for every car he overtook. He'd get his pocket money on Saturday morn, his dad've won it back off him playing cards by lunch.

Aye, Manda Tassy. Can't afford heating on winter school mornings, she'd sleep in her shirt, a panty-liner keeping her knickers okay, the digital alarm clutched to her chest – so perishing cold, she'd only to knot on her tie, pull on two jumpers, kick down the duvet, step into the ready-rolled tights and skirt and unstick last night's chewing gum from the side of the drawer.

Aye, Manda Tassy, never seen a black and white movie in her puff.

> Forth let the cattle roam,
> Tee-ra leera lira . . .

The fifth-year choir: Our Lady of Perpetual Succour School for Girls had been shepherded along corridors to a crushed up dressing room with a low window that looked over a piece of flat lead roofing to a triangle of highly overgrown grass between two spiked iron fences below. There was no view of no castle.

The rounded corridors had been stringed with long trains of schools choirs in their different uniforms; one choir was a mixed one and the boys in their plum-coloured jerseys had a fair old share bonks among them. They had prayed and now Our Ladys were singing, stood in chevron columns of the five Thirds and six Seconds and the five Sopranos, backed up gainst the white, summer light coming in the open windows. You could hear cars, lorries, city sirens in between the sings.

Fionnula and Manda were slipping in the odd yokel accent on some of the words they sang, keeping looked forwarders so's they didn't splutter out in hystericals, but hearing each other sing in the boggery accent:

FORFFF LERGHT THE CA-HILL ROAM

Then the Seconds fucked it up.

Fagan the Pagan shouted from the back, behind Condom who'd turned to her with a plaintive look.

The room seemed very quiet.

Fionnula, Fionnula Morton not Fionnula McConnel, Fionnula you and Aisling, you're steamrolling ahead, your timing is way, way out and WHY are you all following them?

Sister?

Yes Manda?

I'm famished, Sister.

Yes. We shall just run through this song then you can be on your way.

Sister, it's hard for timing without the piano. Ana-Bessie stretched her arms, showing transparent sweat blotches.

Kylah nudged Manda who nodded.

Come along now, *Forth Let the Cattle Roam*, from the start. Condom raised her two arms.

> Forth let the cattle roam,
> Tee-ra, lira lira
> Come drive them far from home
> Tee-ra lira lo
> Far across the mountains . . .

No, NO NO. Acrr-ossssss. Acrrossssss. Crisssssssp. Not 'akroash.' Acrrrrossss, acrrrossssss. Come on Again.

Far akkkkkkkkkkrrrrrrrosssss
the mountains yonder
oxen heifer now shall wander
Tee-ra lee-ra lee.

The voices divided, plunged, Sopranos skimmed atop and the Seconds made a wordless cushion beneath them all.

Now may this iron chain
Tee-ra lee-ra lee ra
bring them safely home again
Tee-ra lee-ra lo

The Sopranos held up a curtain of sound.

Grass grow green before them
Evil things abhor them.

The Sopranos and some of the others cautiously turned their heads towards Fat Clodagh.

Fat as butter
Sweet as honey

Manda reached out, as she sang and caught English Katie's bra strap through the white shirt, gave it a sharp tug and let it snap back instantly.

English Katie rose up on her toes a touch but didn't lose her note as, simultaneously, four digital watch alarms, that had been previously synchronised, started beep-beeping off on some wrists.

> May they be worth a mint of money
> When they go to market.

Oh stop, stOP STOP!! Put those watches off. Is that meant to be funny? Do you think that's funny?

The Sopranos were standing up on a raised stanchion by the window, heads leaned with boredom to one side or the other, chewing at their tongues in an attempt to provoke a mouth examination. Fionnula was staring deliberately out the window. Kay Clarke had stepped up to peer out and been trapped there when Condom started her speech.

You will carry yourselves with grace through this city today. You will wear your ties at all times. On account of this glorious weather you may remove blazers; they'll be safe left here. I know many of you have shopping money with you so look after it with great care. It is your responsibility.

The Pagan chipped in her worth, If you are not wearing blazers, have your shirts neatly rolled up above the elbows . . .

Yes, the Condom nodded. Now I want you to listen carefully. Behind the castle is a large open park around the Queen's Residence. Under *no* circumstances should any of you be in this vicinity. It is not just the danger of being lost in the park; rapes, assaults and God alone knows what has gone on in those grounds. Also. Note. At the furthest end of the main street: a shopping centre. This structure is completely out-of-bounds for you. Drug gangs operate in that shopping centre, approaching young, impressionable school-goers.

We don't want you running, The Pagan insisted.

Absolutely, Sister Fagan. No running or shouting or anything which can be considered a danger to yourselves. Anything amiss, you will find yourselves before Mother Superior in the morning. I insist nobody goes anywhere alone. Go around in groups and don't allow yourself to become separated. Men are watching all the time. Wicked, wicked men . . .

As Condom sketched the sublime hostility of a universe her church was meant to have tamed, several choir girls had been delicately shifting towards the windows. The two Sisters had ignored them cause of the warmth – even though the gathering girls had a tendency to stare outwards. Orla Johnstone seemed to be virtually falling out.

Now we're going to break for lunch. We are following a school called St Ninians on stage after eight o'clock. I want all Sopranos back here at seven. Not ten past nor ten to, did I say. Did I? Fionnula McConnell, Amanda Tassy?

No Sister.

No Sister.

No. Seven o'clock exactly. A minute later and none of you have any idea the trouble you'll be in.

Altos: the Seconds. After lunch we'll practise you first. When the singing is to Sister Fagan and I's satisfaction we'll let you go on your errands to the city centre.

Thirds. The Bass. I'll practise you after the Seconds, so let's say . . .

By now more than half the choir was up at the window, even Ana-Bessie had ambled over.

. . . After lunch then, Seconds gather here at two, the Thirds come at four then I want both Seconds and the Sopranos here for seven, together, and we shall practise, try to fit the jigsaw puzzle together. Please remember: Appearance. Let's get your appearance . . . *Correct*. You are going to be on the television set so make-up will be respectfully applied . . . Excuse me, why are you all up at the window?

The choir that had bundled around the window, turned

reluctantly to look at The Condom. Ana-Bessie, kind of moaned, There's two ... *people*, Sister.

Yes. Well get down away from the window please.

They've got no clothes on, Sister.

GET *DOWN* FROM THAT WINDOW!

Fionnula (the Cooler) and Kay Clarke had got pushed arm to arm by the window. Below them, deep in the dry, golden grass triangle between the iron rail: a girl on top was motioningly having an intercoursing fuck on a man under her; her palms fixedly back on her kidneys, elbows and arms triangles, ponytail moving every-so-softly – rolling side to side across her skinny shoulders. The two cream-coloured arse segments, divided by the dark, dark crack that rhythmically gaped open when she reached the lowest point in her cycle – showing the flat smoothness of pure skin between the buttocks there and ... and the look on her face when she turned and glanced up at them ... and the silence but for traffic and Condom's voice annoying behind them as this strange trade went on between the faces of the schoolgirls and arousal of the couple below, knowing they were stared down on them. Kay and Fionnula turned from the couple having sex just below them, looked straight at each other's faces. In surprise Fionnula blinked then, to own astonishment felt her face go a big red beamer of embarrassedness.

Outside the Concert Hall at the bottom of the steps there was a big television van with men dragging cables about. The Sopranos came tumbling down the stairs, looking around them and tugging off their ties.

Fucking hoor, fucking dirty wee hoor. *Fuck*, Manda Tassy shook her head, gave a weirdy smile, Ah mean that way she looked up at us.

Ha, ha, ha. Kylah, Orla and Chell were just laughing, faces flushed.

Hey. HEY! Manda shouted at the two baldy men hauling the cables, Yous shoulda been round the back taking pictures of what was going on there. Lucky Fagan's letting us out.

Fionnula strode glum, a wee bit ahead, saying nothing.

Ah mean did you just *see* her, the dirty wee fucking hoor, right there in the middle . . . and she knew we were there. Eh? Manda was looking at Fionnula by then.

Aye, Fionnula just shrugged.

Quickly Orla says, If the city girls are all like that, no much chance of scoring this afternoon, eh?

Look. Look! Kylah pointed.

Back, outside the window on the lead bit roof, Aisling and Iona were waving long arms side to side over their heads; they were sunbathing in their bras, skirts bunched right up.

The city was much noisier than the Port. Their senses were in kind of overload: all the colours and motion simultaneously. Their heads were moving fast, side to side to take sights in so they looked each other hardly ever in the face as they talked. In the Port they would never address each other without looking at faces. They thought the buses would say just the city's name on the fronts but they have districts no one's ever heard of up there.

At the burger place Kay Clarke (tie on) was already sat by the mirrors wi English Katie and Fionnula (Ordinary). As the Sopranos passed and nodded, Fionnula (the Cooler) pretended no to see Kay but she noticed Kay had no food in front of her, no even a milkshake for fucksake!

Oh fuck, milkshakes, milkshakes!

Look, Barbie Happy meals! Chell says.

Look, let's get those, those 99p Cool shades.

Oh, let's all get them.

Right listen. Listen, Manda Tassy was talking so loud, folk in the queue in front turned round, Ma big sister was on one of the holidays – in Spain or in Greece or Kos or one of they places and growing, right there like that, by the counter, there was this loco-weed, big bushes of the wacky-baccy, getten grown inside a burger joint by the staff. Aye!

Brilliant, a herb burger.

Puts a new light on a quarter pounder, doesn't it?

Um famished.

Barbie Happy meal for me, Chell smiled.

It's only for kiddies.

What're you getting Fionnula?

Dunno.

What are you getting?

Two cheeseburgers, large fries, chocolate shake, coffee and a hot fudge sundae.

Signs were everything and language was vanishing. No words: the gender of each toilet area, the gentle admonition to deposit used trays and containers through a flap, the yellow cone, warning of slippy floors after mopping: all had no words (the sign of a stick figure, hopelessly in motion). Language was disappearing, leaving only the tokens of pounds sterling exchanged for food, a few syllables, clicked back and forth at the counter – the lassie in baseball cap and hairnet, didn't look at any of the Sopranos (who were not looking at each other but at all the Italian tourists around them) she looked down on the touch-till system, punched in the short bursts of identifying food nouns.

*

98

Up the stair section, the Sopranos, wearing 99p Cool Shades With Each Purchase, guffawed round their table. They were penetrating milk shakes and Coca-Cola containers with unwrapped straws; french fry containers, burger wrappers and angled straws were reflected in the curved, black gloss lenses of the sunglasses.

KYLAH <	Big Burger	large fries	1 strawberry shake 1 large Coke 1 regular coffee	Apple pie Strawberry sundae
ORLA	Cheeseburger (no gherkins) 6 chicken McNuggets	large fries	1 strawberry shake 1 large Coke	Apple pie Hot fudge sundae
FIONNULA	2 Cheeseburgers	large fries	Chocolate shake	
MANDA	1 Quarterpounder	large fries	Vanilla shake Chocolate shake	
CHELL	1 Barbie Happy Meal (Cheeseburger, small fries, small Fanta orange)		Chocolate shake	Caramel sundae

Ahm sobering up, says Kylah, who sounded as if she was anything but sobering up, puff-puffing onto a scorching-looking black coffee, the white steam chittering off it, vapour matching the white rim of the paper cup, above the disturbed black liquid.

You're no sissying out, are you?

No ways, sides, ave drank tons more than you already, Manda.

Oooo.

Sambuca challenge then?

Aye. First pub, no bother.

There's meant to be a whole street of pubs, you try go from one end to the other . . .

Wonder if there's any got live music?

It's the afternoon Kylah!

But there *is* a place, there is, ah just can't mind the name; it does live music in the afternoon.

Then we'll find it, Fionnula whispered and nodded.

Ah keep forgetting, with just the one contact in, ah felt pissed even when I was sober.

Ahm really browned off singing that garbage all that terra leera lay stuff. Orla abruptly giggled and says in a high up voice, It's such total crap to be wasting our time on.

Ah know, went Manda, We were totally chronic; it's great, we'll never even make the second round.

Ana-Bessie was singing right but Kay was seeming to be no giving a fuck either.

Barely above a whisper, Fionnula leaned forward and asked, Kylah, what're you wearing?

Well, mind on Saturday night ah says ah was going to bring the silver shirt, wear it three top buttons open and my light coloured stretch pants – those shiny ones that flare out at the feet, with the little pockets here and the side zips and with the black, strappyish sandals, tan toe-nail varnish, ma hair slicked back and glossed, with a parting, and tan eyeshadow, a totty wee sliver of silver cross top of the eyelids here, lighter on the bottom then a coat of black under that, mascara and dark colour lipliner, tan lipstick to go with ma nails an toes then a glisteny lipgloss on top . . . ?

Aye, Fionnula leaned forward.

Well, now I'm no wearing that. I'm wearing ma hair down wi that Miss Selfridges denim skirt ah got fro the catalogue an the blue T-shirt, the one wi navy cuffs an collar an the white sandally high heels, red lipstick, nail varnish.

You all brought nail varnish remover?

We'll have to get every bit off for Sister Condom.

Tell yas something minging, Manda spoke round a bolus of quarterpounder, she nodded at Orla, Ma big sister was in some other hamburger restaurant . . .

What? The one where the marajoronee was growing? Fionnula gave a false smile.

Eh nah. Think it was another . . .

Fionnula went, Oh. Took off her sunglasses, squinted at the fluorescence round her and sniffed across the table.

Well, ma sister bit into something in a chicken thing, it was crunchy, and she picked it out and it was, like a *cyst* that'd been in the living chicken! Minging, eh?

Ah dinnie *scum us* OUT!

Orla held up one nugget and dropped it into her mouth.

Crunch, crunch. Fionnula smiled.

Manda goes, When ah split up wi Jamie at Christmas there, well know how ma sister shares the house up Pulpit Hill with they ice factory lassies? Well one of them was going with some farmer's son and he'd gave her a fucking turkey for a Christmas present, like a fucking *live* turkey and they had it, just running all about the carpets in the house so they got pissed Christmas Eve, chased it, caught it and didn't have guts enough to kill it so's they tried to gas it in the oven, thought it was dead and plucked it, feathers all over the place but it woke up on the chopping board and went mental. They had it running round the house over Christmas, this sorry-looking plucked thing, really horrible like, then they decided to take it back but it escaped at the bus stop and was running about the Port.

Ooo, nay chance.

If it wasny on a table by lunch-time it'd only because someone was shagging it . . .

Ah swear that's true.

Mmm, Orla put her forefinger under her left eye and tugged the lower eyelid down a couple of times.

Chell let out a huge burp.

Was that yur fanny or your arse, girl?

Whatever, an angel certainly spoke.

But what did it say?

God save the Queen and two Hail Marys.

Kylah was blinking.

What was the bet with your wee brother?

What's this?

She had a bet with her wee brother.

Ah had to swallow ma contact or he had to stuff a pepperami up his bum hole, far's it'd go.

What was the bet?

That I could be in and out the bathroom in twenty minutes.

Twenty! An ya lost!

So ya swallowed a contact, ah'd told him to fuck off.

You've got to do dares Manda, Fionnula grinned, You've got to take a few risks.

Aye, Sambuca-Sambuca challenge, Kylah growled and bared teeth.

What about when it comes out your rear end, honey?

Ah throw them away anyways. Ah get a new three-month supply from Boots on Monday.

Hi, hi, Fionnula nodded, See that guy, that Scorgie guy, the Doc Drumvargie's actual brother, tho they aye pretend they're no?

Yup, Astronaut or something, yon guy can waterski and smoke at the same time.

Argonaut, Argonaut – it's an old Greece warrior that went on seas.

Aye! Jason n the Argonauts ave seen that yon one with the sword-fighting skeletons; all shitey special effects.

Fionnula shrugged, Ah don't watch films. Anyways right, Iain Dickinson went to Amsterdam wi that Argonaut and Panatine . . .

Magine, he's just a wee baby and going wi they mental cases!

Aye, right, Fionnula leaned forward across the tumbled french fry and hamburger wrappings, So's they're coming back from Amsterdam through Paris cause they've run out of money. Iain took the most, the whole of what he got from summer in the ice factory . . .

Were you ever actually going with Iain Dickinson?

Nut. So's they get to Paris somewhere and . . .

This is them coming from where?

From Amsterdam.

Where's that?

Dutch.

Holland.

Netherlands.

You know all the bars you can take drugs in and red light districts?

What fucking dump that sounds.

Aye, ah bet there's no a decent disco in the whole place, just rave shite and guys with fucking dreadlocks and camouflaged trousers . . .

Oh don't *scum* us out!

Bet even the lassies are fucking tramps, all drug addicts with greasy hair, grungers and that, no decent make-up or clothes or that . . .

What's it called? Dutch-Holland-Nether-regions?

All of those.

What; it's got loads names, the one country?

Ah mean what's the point in going to a fucking place like yon when you could go to the sunshine, Lloret de Mar or Kos or Greece or Benidorm? Manda whipped off her 99p Cool Shades With Each Purchase, for emphasis.

So you're saying it's got three names, that's confusing?

But it's like Britain, the UK.

What about *this* place! You take the fourth bridge across the fifth or fourth to the Kingdom of Five!

What!?

It's true, the Kingdom of Five is across the fifth or fourth and ya use the fourth bridge to it!

Ah've heard folk say it.

What were you saying, Fionnula?

Ah never mind.

Nah tell us, *tell* us about The Dick.

There was a long pause and they didn't think Fionnula was going to speak. Then she muttered, Yous huv heard of Paris, aye?

The other four smiled round the table. Aye, mind, no tonight Josephine, the wee picture in the Second Year book, guy with a fishing rod and ah, goes Pecher, To *Poach* Miss! Manda laughed.

All remembered and laughed.

Chell was waggling the miniature Barbie doll she'd got with her Happy Meal, its frizzed, erect strands of blonde hair, vibrating.

They'd been on some overnight train and got into Paris real early and they'd hardly no money at all, they'd a few coins and so's they gave them to yon Argonaut and he came back wi these fish sandwiches and a bottle ouzo . . .

That's minging, like aniseedy, ma sister . . .

Aye. So's they ate the fish sandwiches and drunk the ouzo bottle and they've all day still to kill in Paris fore their train up to the ferry went that night. Just half an hour tho and Iain's feeling sick as a dog and The Panatine an The Argonaut are pretty rough too. They quiz The Argonaut an it turns out the bastard had spent all the money on ouzo after finding the fish sandwiches out back of some Arab restaurant.

Oh minging . . .

Ah *scum* us out!

So they're middle of Paris and they're getting the total skitters so they leap over into this square wi bushes in it and they coorie down wi the skitters an The Argonaut an Panatine are howling so much Iain's laughing, right, then when they pull their breeks up they find there are all these luxury apartments round the square with balconies and all these folk, wanker-folk like, sipping champagne and that, staring down at them and they realise they're having massive puddles of shite in a private garden, then they hear the police sirens. The police threaten to arrest them but in the end give them a lift to the railway station that is miles away in the middle of Paris and they're told: Get the next train out. Iain is just laughing but The Argonaut and Panatine are no looking very happy, they start walking through Paris. All the way back to that square where they climb into the gardens and there's all these little lumps in the puddles of shite of Panatines and Argonauts. It's condoms of cannabis that Panatine and Argonaut had swallowed, planning bring it back to the Port an the bastards had no even told Iain. They coulda been locked up for years if they'd got caught.

Ach, thanks a *lot* Fionnula, went Kylah, putting down the last of the strawberry sundae.

That's absolutely, totally, disgusting, Manda shook her head.

Ugch, they rolled-up condoms popped out their bum holes?

Just like having a fucking baby.

Aye shitting a melon, ma mum says it was like getting me out, Fionnula smiled.

Are you saying Dicky was selling drugs?

That was no the point of the story ah just told you, Manda.

Okay, okay! Ah was just asking.

There was a belligerent bit of silence.

Ahm, Chell went, See what you were saying Manda, bout yur sister, well ma Uncle Buzz, know the brother-in-law? You know ma family tree, it's more like a stick!

A few laughed, well Manda and Fionnula and thats what counted.

Chell went on, Well, see what yur saying, yur sister, with the turkey feathers. Ma Uncle Buzz used to fill all the cushions in his house with his *own* hair when he cut it. That's how mean he was!

Cmon let's get going. Manda coughed.

Wait, we're meant put all this crap in they bins.

To pot with that. Let's get our clothes on!

All five of them squeezed no too bad into the toilet wi the wheelchair sign on the door. There was a wee washbasin wi actual smallish mirror above. The Sopranos kneeled gently and wi both their hands would lift clothes out of their coloured Nike and Head and Adidas shoulder bags. They removed footwear wrapped in separate Superstore carrier bags so's soles wouldn't stain clothes. They took off their white shirts (cept Manda who hadn't been able to afford nothing new). They dropped their tartan school skirts on the yellow floor tiles, then put the white shirts on top that, then laid the city clothes on top of everything to keep them off the floor. They passed round two cans of deodorant, their fingers swung up near the fluorescent casing. The short hisses of the deodorant made the same noise as little zips at the back of skirts going up.

When someone entered the main door into the Ladies outside their cubicle, they stopped talking about what make-up was going to be used, so their stoops, bends, stretches and movements of dressing took on a businesslike, religious deliberation an sobriety. No girl smiled as she dressed – a ritual they each treated wi more reverence than ingestion of any transubstantial host; cause the vestiary metamorphosis was going bring about an immediate transformation that the body and blood of God's son never could.

Orla, a black sweat blossom under each oxter of her velvety body stocking – one of them she'd aye wore since her poorliness so's couldn't see her no-bra-wee-tits; Orla's thighs just dived into her pants seeming almost no thickerness from her leg above knees and her two arms were like dangly, wet ropes fappering about. As she whispered the trousers up, Orla says, Poverty goes without saying, Chastity comes despite ma best efforts and Obedience is forced onto yous, but by fuck am going for it the day. She took her retainer brace out her mouth, picked at it with the kilt pin she aye carried, then scooshed the contraption free of food fragments.

The Last of The McDonald's, Orla grimaced; replaced the braces.

Fionnula chuckled, her spread fingers, nails varnished, under the hand dryer.

Orla looked in the mirror, banged her tits a bit n sighed.

Hush honey, for a cleavage, you should get two elastic bands and tie them between the shoulder-straps across your back, it really bumphs up at the front.

If ah shout out, someone promise they'll pass me their wonderbra!

Ya can have mine.

Christ look, goes Manda, I didn't shave high enough up ma legs for this skirt.

Chell goes, Am no surprised lassie, is it a skirt or a belt?

Everyone laughed.

Aye, you'd need do yur bikini line to wear a skirt that short, goes Kylah.

Get fucked. Look at yours.

Everyone laughed again.

You wear it well honey, you look just gorgeous, Fionnula goes.

AMANDA

School shirt but last two buttons open and the sides tied thegether in a handsome bow knot, exposing her midriff and sister-pierced naval, enobled wi a cheap amethyst ring.

Top shirt buttons undone down to her big sister's wonderbra.

Electric blue, pleated mini-skirt. *Short.*

White plastic, strappy high-heeled shoes.

Big sister's G-string.

CHELL

V-neck leopard-print short-sleeved top.

Cream coloured skirt cut on the bias with brown, decorative buttons on front of waistband. *Short.*

Bare legs and just school socks under the knee-length, brown suede boots.

Leopard-print tanga and matching bra.

KYLAH

Lilac T-shirt wi navy collar and sleeves.
Miss Selfridge denim mini-skirt.
White high-heel sandals secured with silver cross-over strap.
Satin bra (black) and knickers.

FIONNULA

French Connection, viscose, long-sleeved, blue-striped shirt wi front buttoning.
Black A-line skirt. *Short.*
Black, open-toed platform shoes (from last year).
£15 white wonderbra, black cotton knickers (3 for £1).

ORLA

Crushed velvet body-top wi thin straps and black lacy shirt over it.
Black, flared hipster trousers from catalogue.
Same school shoes and socks.
No bra needed. Black G-string.

Orla; she takes Hide The Blemish an dots it on the two-days-dead spot, the side of her forehead. She squirts the big dob Perfectly Pale foundation, plasts a bit onto the spot then all over her face. She uses the sponge to blend out, bringing it down and behind her ears, making sure there's no tea-stainish tide mark round her neck.

She takes the brown eye-liner pencil and puts the tip up to the bulb of the light above the mirror to soften the end. She goes all round the eye wi the pencil. Then, wi eye-shadow, she pushes dark, chocolate brown into each eye-socket and brings it out at the corners. She gets gold Pearl eye-shadow and fingers it onto the browned eyelid to make her eyes sparkle. She puts a brown mascara on her lashes; the hairs longer and thicker.

Wi a plum liner she gives definition round the limits of her lips and fills the lip surface, taking the colour from the stick, using a brush, then she goes over the lip using the actual stick tip. With the stick from the lip gloss, she slides the clearness along then squeezes both lips thegether in a slappy pucker.

She opens the lid of the loose powder – as per-usual, some smokes out – she patters it on using the sponge being canny no to get any near her glossed lips. So much Vanderbilt perfume her collar-bones fizz then glisten.

The other girls are putting on make-up in the big mirrors, nail varnishing, using each other's bits and pieces; some Sopranos put their powder on after their foundation, some do it last thing. And they're packing up the school clothing, no worrying too much about folding the shirts. Each lassie huffed up her bag wi school uniform and shoes and make-up in.

Let's go to Jericho, says Chell, her eyebrow ring in.

Let's find some rides, Manda pulled open the door.

The Anchored Submarine

Jonah's whale, come to swallow us all, Father Ardlui abandoned trying to light his pipe for the third time and smiled at the captain beside him who'd come ashore to register. The wind gusts had regrouped then stampeded back across the pier but Ardlui noticed how the captain's hat never seemed to be in any jeopardy and McNiven, the painful Protestant, was hatless.

A morbid and curious haul had gathered on North Pier as the mirage – the low slick of the submarine with its dorsal conning tower out in the bay – threw into relief seaward views Port folk were inured to. The cove at first island (cross to, firemen versus police would sponsored-raft race each summer!) seemed much closer than as per-usual; cause of that black hull's presence, sobering, always calling the finite and true dimensions of the waters. *Usually we seem to sit on the edge of the world, as if anything that happens here really has a continuity on, across seas, but now we seem to sit on the edge less securely than before; the give of the world is tearing, an it makes our bay seem so wee which serves us right. This isn't Naples*, Ardlui thought, says, Blowy. Raising white horses!

McNiven grunted and the captain gave a forgiving smile.

White horses not a nautical term then you son of a gun? The captain didn't look the part, there again, McNiven never had either. Ardlui had says to the captain on the phone that morn: 'McNiven & Sons, undertakers, captain. They will smoothly initiate the transfer. McNiven's seen it all, captain. He's had a lad ten days missing off a trawler, balloon up below his workshop at Christiansands. Just strolled down an scooped him off the shingle. Captain.'

Ardlui glanced sideyways. The captain was hideously young, small without fisherman eye-lines from squinting the silver-sunned oceans. Ardlui looked for periscope eye. Nothing.

Orange lifeboat secured alongsides the black hull out there, with insecty movements on-deck an the lifeboat was sliding a', mashing the black bay white an green at stern then steered pierwards. Ardlui noted when the captain took off his hat. He did it when the coffin was swinging and turning in the canvas slash, then the hat was squeezed back on with three downward squeezes and a twist sideyways with that scrunchy sound on his cropped hair.

The hat came off again after the hurl in the cars, as McNiven and his glum sons wheeled the coffin into the cathedral and it stayed off as Ardlui called the Lord Have Mercy and only the organist and Sister McTavish replied.

The hat crunched on as Father Ardlui led the coffin through back sacristy, wondering if there was some way to inveigle the visitation, the black submarine with its invisible anchors, rigid on the skyline, a coffin wobbling above harbour waters, a captain with an over-casual stroll, some way to get it into his half-finished novel.

Ardlui folded stole and alb, passing them by his nose to see if the stench of the thurible was there. He took out the whisky bottle from the cupboard and blew sharply into both small glasses.

Not for me, Father.

He ignored him, filled both glasses with the Linkwood fifteen, thought, *From Brotherhood or was it. . .* ? says, Water?

Ah, no thanks.

He handed the captain a glass. The captain didn't touch it but removed a cigarette holder and was soon smoking well, with direct, confident movements, Terrific part of the country. Father, love to retire up here.

You don't find it bleak?

Well that's the attraction.

Development. That's what we need up here. I was thinking, glass-bottomed submarines would be popular in the summer!

Mmmm, the captain nodded.

I saw one in the United States, fascinating vessel.

The captain exhaled, Unusual, a town of this size to have a cathedral.

It's an honour we share with Brechin. Here's the church and here's the steeple but where the hell are all the people? A bit of a folly like our monument, the symbol of our town up on the hill there.

The coliseum structure? Very classical.

With Gothic windows! Victorian bad taste, the Greeks were never here.

The captain smiled, Well the family were relieved he could rest somewhere like this. I fully expect he'll be off your hands by late this evening or early morning. Terrible business.

Tragic, Ardlui looked out the window, clearly bored, Vision captain, that's what we need here, vision and development, you know, I sit on the Hotel Board here. I wouldn't go as far as to say as Spiritual Advisor . . .

The captain snapped his cigarette case, smiled.

Some of our patrons, for the roof-renewal project, for the Lourdes trips, are very generous. Interests to protect. Ardlui lifted the whisky to his mouth, he suddenly says, Kilimanjaro, under the snows of Kilimanjaro, captain, there are the ruins of an international airport, wild animals wandering through the terminal buildings, the drained swimming pools of luxury hotels. All built in the seventies, waiting upon a tourist rush that never came. Only wars came. Do you know what the motto of the Kilimanjaro Project was, captain?

No.

'Tourism is the flower which grows in every country.'

The sailor grinned grimly, You were in Kenya?

Eleven years, Ardlui nodded, refilled his glass and turned, It's not a mountain hanging like a dream in pink skies you need now captain, you need greater things than mountains: you need psychology, something that forces the people to come to you. We have our share of mountains. What we need are shrines. We need new miracles; all the old ones are stale or worn smooth at any rate. Sometimes the people need a new song to sing.

The captain had thanked Ardlui for his little service. It was the policeman, McPherson, the one who'd bought over that den, the Mantrap, pulled up in a Land-Rover to give the captain a lift back to the pier. Ardlui nodded to him, thought of the start of a Niall Dubh poem:

> In loveless port
> Steamers are swaying.
> The House of Stained Glass
> Above the piers,
> The sailors emerge
> Pull up their collars.
> Where my mother gave birth . . .

McPherson was planning to use the rooms above the dance hall as a brothel. He needed women from the city though.

Ardlui watched the captain trot down to the waited police car, and duck his hat without looking back, under a tremendous, vertical fall and slither of sunlight, released from a fast cloud. For an instant there was the arrowhead of a bird-shadow streaking on the earth; the priest looked up, chuckled, expecting the bright colours of a parrot.

He walked through the vestry and could see the coffin of the heart-attack sailor through the door. The captain hadn't touched the whisky. Ardlui mumbled, World full of atheists and sinners, but how they come running to us for burial in the end, he snapped the drink back in one gulp.

Citadel

Three rings of Sambuca shots were on the dark table the Sopranos surrounded, far deep into the pub. Each girl struck a match quick, on the same box.

Sure?

Aye, goes Orla.

Don't hold it the too long in your mouth, Fionnula nudged her and Fionnula's rolled-up sleeve on her blue shirt, slipped down, so's the cuffs parted and slowly cradled into her elbow.

As the Bishop says to the actress, Chell looked round and yelped.

The girls all tipped their heads back and clicked the shots into their mouths, paused, then dipped the matches down out of sight, into the dark cups of their mouths below rounded lips. In the tavern gloom, gentle blue and purple flames rose out the mouths of the five girls. There was silence as they looked from sides to sides, whites of eyes bright to each extremity, then Manda bit her lips shut, paused to make sure the flames died and swallowed that warm liquer down.

Yah.

The others followed, making faces, shaking heads, reaching for their Hooch or Bud chasers.

Hot shite.

Fucking mental.

Another! Orla stood.

Whoa babe!

Orla's goin for it.

The Pill Box! goes Kylah.

Eh?

The Pill Box, that's yon club plays music in afternoons.

Is it loads of drugs there like: the Pill box?

Nah, Pill Box is just a thing from wars, like a concrete box where'd put big guns and that, there was one on the dunes when we went caravanning up Cocklawburn, says Fionnula.

Cock what?

Thatsalottacocks, goes Kylah, in a man-American accent with her chin shoved down onto the shoulder of her blue T-shirt, to deepen her voice.

Cocklawburn. It's down The Border, she sucked on a cigarette.

The Border?

What Border?

The fucking Border.

Oh.

Right.

Kylah slid along the uncomfy bench, with a exaggerated, shielding hand, mock-whispered, Manda! maybe it's the border to the kingdom of five.

Manda laughed.

Tellingyous. It's just beautiful down there, better beaches than any Spain or Greece . . . miles to the nearest pub mind. Ah got a lift from this couple, they were twenty-one, dead nice with a static like ours. Drove me home. Mum n Dad let me out on ma life no to be drinking an I spent all ma holiday money on twelve Hooches. Ah was so wasted ah was lying on the actual back seat, ma head resting on this Kim lassies's lap . . .

Whooooaaaa!

. . . Short skirt an ma legs are actually hanging out the back door window, from ma knees, down the side of the door and it was mental . . . and her boyfriend driving right, he goes so close into the verge, on the wrong side of the road, this bush swishes by an takes off one ma shoes!

Christ.

Did ya no get him to go back?

What pair was that?

Nah, I was just in the stitches, no caring an they stopped outside our caravan then drove off, peeping the horn like mad. Ah seemed okay for a second but then ah fell over. Ah was SO pissed I'd no noticed ma legs were utterly numb with the coldness from the car wind, cause it was fucking freezing as per-usual. Ah collapsed in a heap an started crawling to the caravan but the car peeps had brought Mum to the door so's ah goes, 'Ahm no drunk Mum, ma legs got cold hanging out a car window.'

Everyone laughed.

That was me: grounded rest of the holiday.

You're a dark horse sometimes. Ya never told me that one afore, Manda stared.

Fionnula shrugged, lit another cigarette.

Orla came back with ten more Sambuca shots on a tray.

What's this?

Fionnula's dark secrets.

Och more of them! I'm no ready for that. What was it then? She couldnie stand up.

History about ta fucking repeat itself then.

What's the plan?

Get these down our gullets.

Ah want to hit the shops fore am too lagered.

Aye, shopping when yur mashed is dangerous, ye find yourself wearing weird colours.

Chell slid the box Scottish Bluebells middle of the table to formally begin proceedings.

Think we could light them with the ends of our cigarettes? Manda frowned.

It'd put the fag out, would it no?

Try it then.

Excuse me.

The girls with their backs to him turned round.

I'm sorry, it's not me, but the manageress was asking if you could maybe not do that.

Manda got herself more comfortable and says, Now what do you mean?

Well she's concerned . . . you might burn yourselves.

Pafff!

We paid for them aye . . . ah means our money's good enough, aye?

Well is it no our business how we drink then?

Look . . . well we never asked you for ID did we?

Howdye mean? Are you saying we're underage?

You're saying you'll serve us though ya think we're underage, but only if we drink certain things?

Look, it's obvious enough we're, you know, turning a blind eye to you lot, all she's asking is that you maybe go easier on the flaming Sambuca session. There was a girl up the end of the street in Dirty Dick's, scorched her throat and it swole right up, closed her oesophagus.

Kylah sniggered.

Dirty Dick closed her what?

Her throat.

Did she die? Orla smiled.

She wasn't feeling too good.

Fionnula says, Look mister. We paid for these drinks. We'll suck them up our arseholes if we want to.

Everyone looked at Fionnula then laughed.

The barman shrugged and hunched away, slapping his dishtowel.

What's he, fucking Australia or New Zealand?

'Summer Bay.'

Someone laughed.

It's Henry from Neighbours!

It's a fucking ancient old ugly grot that's what that is, Manda shouted.

Cmon, let's try wi cigarettes.

The heads went back, the tips of cigarettes were slowly lowered into the dark mouths and the flames popped up, cept Orla whose Marlboro Light faltered with an abrupt fiss then, in surprise, some of the Sambuca went wrong way down Orla's gullet.

Outside she stopped coughing but her mush was beetroot.

Sure you're okay?

Aye. Next pub? she goes, a bit unconvinced.

Fionnula went, Look, why don't we all go shopping. Meet in yon Pill Box later? Fionnula tugged the sleeve of her shirt, then crossed her arms.

Orla had straightened up. I'm going to Schuh, it's down one of those on the left.

Ah want to go to French Connection an Gap an River Island and HIV, goes Chell.

Kylah fished out a CD list the boys in the band had give her, secured by an elastic band against rolled twenty pounds notes. She looked at it glumly.

Where is it then? Manda looked at Kylah.

We'd need to ask, she says.

Everyone stood a bit aimless.

Right. Let's meet in yon Pill Box at four then.

Four then aye? For sure.

What if one us can't find it?

This place then, Manda flicked her fringe at the pub beside them.

Five Bells, Kylah squinted.

Right. Pill Box at four and here if you can't find it.

Whatever, seven at the conference centre with uniforms on, eh?

Aye.

Aye.

Aye.

Aye.

Fionnula strode along with Kylah and Chell. Fionnula turned to watch Orla and Manda move up the lane and behind, criss-crossing city folk.

It's shame we've got to hulk these silly fucking bags round with us.

Specially we get some shopping.

We could try find lockers. In railways stations or that.

The others didn't look convinced.

Are you really up for shopping?

Course.

I'd be pretty happy just to get sat and drink.

I sort of promised the boys I'd get this weird stuff you can't get at home.

CDs?

Aye.

An ah know you want a good look at stuff.

Aye, well.

How about I meet yous somewhere else in a wee while. Hour or that?

Where then?

An hour! Wi her I'll still be in the first shop, Kylah laughed, squinted.

Where are *you* going then?

Just a dander.

Aye, well please yourself.

We'll meet you in HIV in an hour then.

HIV?

HMV she means.

The record shop on the main street just there, we passed it on the bus.

Oh right, I'll find it. See yous in there then.

Aye. See you.

See you, Fionnula. Be careful, eh?

Fionnula turned and grinned, was away, among rushing people in jackets.

What's she up to?

She's been queerer and queerer lately, the crazy chick.

Kylah went. She doesn't know a *thing* about music.

Chell goes, Years ago, the day Kurt Cobain died, ah was down at the bus-stop in the morning an Fionnula got a lift in. Sandra Goretti n Patricia were there, just greeting like mad, just crying their eyes out an Fionnula comes walking up the hill and goes, 'What's wrong?' . . . I says, 'Kurt Cobain's dead.' She goes 'What happened?' an I goes, 'He shot hisself' and Fionnula frowns, up, towards the boys school and says, 'What year was he in?'

Kylah laughed, shook her hair and went, Fionnula says to me, know how Cast and that have the name of the band painted on the front of the drums an how you see that wi seventies bands.

Aye.

Well Fionnula says, when she was little she used to think there was this band, that really kept changing their image, sometimes long hair, sometimes short, sometimes crap sometimes good but aye sounding different and called Yamaha, cause that's what was on their drums!

Kylah burst out laughing as her and Chell swung left, in through the warm-day-open-doors of French Connection.

Can we see the ones ah tried on first? The black ones.

The girl turned and walked back to the counter area where she'd heaped the differing boots.

What a snotty townie, Manda whispered.

She's no thin enough for those trousers, Orla went.

She's no thin enough for the top.

The girl pranelled back towards them on her platform boots.

Ta.

I'll leave yous tae have a wee think about it.

Aye.

The girl wandered back and whispered to the girls by the till.

These are the best ones. See it's the laces ah like.

Mmm.

I like these tall ones and I like the laces all the way up an ah can get other coloured laces and wi the right skirt, covers the skinnyness of ma legs.

They're really nice, aye.

Orla leaned way, way forward – right up there – better so as to tug on the farthest reaches of the boot, gather its flappery tongue and clicking laces that she had to re-thread. She leaned so's Manda could see the lizard's tail curl of her spine at the back of her neck.

Once Orla had pulled both boots on and done the laces, you could see how out of the puff she was . . . she seemed just jiggered.

Manda?

What?

Ah find the laces and all that sexy, y'know?

Aye. They look great on you.

Orla stood up and made a funny face, Sure? No think ah look like a skinny drug addict or something?

Manda laughed, Nut, you don't. She glanced over at the girls by the counter. Orla knew too; it was her they were chatting about, cause she wasn't wearing a skirt an you could see how skinny she was under.

Look, ah can wear them now, she bended right over and pulled the trouser legs down so's the high boots just looked like neat little bootees.

The nosey townie slag came doddling back over.

I'm going to take these, Orla started hurrying to get her purse out of her schoolbag and Manda almost told her to haud her wheesht, cause you paid at the till.

Manda goes, I'll wait outside for you.

Eh?

I'm just going to look in the window; she walked out feeling like a right bitch. *Ah feel like a right cow, just cause she's so thin an gawky looking, am no wanting to be seen with her in a posh fucking city, ah mean that's just awful . . . a mean it was just a bunch of trendy-fucking-city-lassie fashion victims, if it was guys you might just understand and I'm no turning into a lezzie or anything . . . why am ah so het-up about what people think about me; who am I trying to impress?*

*

She was taking ages. Manda had put the shades from McDonald's on and turned, looking up at the castle bove the heads of all the good-looking guys, remembering the rampant feeling when they looked down on the girl's arse and knowing it was the guy's big . . . beastie, in under there, going right up in that girl.

I got you them!

Manda turned and Orla was holding out the Doc Martens box.

What! NO, Orla you can't, you just can't.

Hey ah want you to have them.

No Orla, not with your money and look, they don't even go with what I'm wearing.

I'll carry them for you.

NO Orla, no ways. Right?

But you can keep them in your bag, we've got to hulk them about and now you've finished your drink. Please. I saw how you loved them.

They were grey boots, but they sparkled, sparkled silver. Manda really did want them but she had an afraidness; awful, awful afraidness that some badness would happen if she accepted. Manda went and says, Ah mean, how ya know they'll fit me; ma shoes are aye a size too small cause it's such fucking donkeys years inbetween me getting any!

Just take them, here. Orla tipped off top of the shoe box, got in a pedestrian's way as she stepped fwd and rammed the shoe box top into an already stuffed litter bin cross the pavement. She hoisted the sparkling Doc Martens boots out, holding them aloft so's the tissue paper slithered down around her pokey, smiley face and even through Manda's sunglasses they were sure-enough sparkling. Orla put that lower box down at the side of the bin, lunged back at Manda, tissue still trailing, thrust the boots into Manda's arms till Manda laughed, kneeled, unzipped her old shoulder bag and was heaving out the almost empty squash bottle, and shoogling the boots in, flatways. Then Manda popped back up and gave Orla a huge hug, her cheek right next to wee Orla's. That cheek felt cold.

Kylah and Chell had bought Magnum ice cream lollies, were sauntering alongside the main street windows, frowning at their mouths in the sun-dark shop glass, tongues streaking out and whippling round the curved ice cream, making sure there was no chocolate on their lips. They came to a door entrance served by a single stereo speaker lashed in polythene. It was banging out *Citadel* by the Rolling Stones. A blackboard in pink chalk told of the Cocktail Happy Hour now in progress. Chell and Kylah looked at each other the once and without talking, stepped in.

Sorry ladies but you can't eat those in here.

Kylah had her head turned almost on its side, cheek on shoulder, to lick her lolly.

Three guys sat end of the bar gave the girls a steady, predatory, more-than-the-onceover. One guy says something in another language.

What IS it wi barkeepies in this town? Chell looked through her still-on-sunglasses.

I just don't know Chell, Kylah says aloud, and leaned on the metally bar top.

I'm no spoilsport, but they just won't let you bring food in. We have a menu.

Chell and Kylah looked at each other, took their sunglasses off. Kylah goes, Can we see yur cock . . . (then she lowered her voice) . . . Tail list.

Tears were in Chell's eyes and she near cracked her shite in the hysterics. Chell says, Am near cracking ma shite at you!

Leaned further over and the barman had gone a beetroot brasser, Kylah says, Have you got a liquidiser to make yur COCKtails in?

Sure.

Kylah pinched Chell's Magnum out of her fingers, passed both lollies cross the bar thegether, while going, Well mix both these in wi a bit cream, Coca-Cola, Malibu and Southern Comfort.

The two girls curled up onto the stools tapping their skirts flat on their thighs.

The barman looked at them.

Can we have an ashtray? Chell smiled.

Kylah went, And two shots of Sambuca.

Am getting real cheesed off wi her, says Manda and she took a swallow of the Hooch Orla'd bought her.

They'd gone back up onto the street where the first pub was and plumped for one called the Auld Hundred, so's Manda could try on the Doc's. There was a good juke box but no atmosphere, just some mildly bonkable city lads in Adidas tops, wolfing lager in the corner, but they were smoking Lambert and Butler! Ah mean for fucksake! When the girls come out the toilet the barwoman had put the two Hooches on the bar and the nicest of the guys called, Why do lassies always go to the toilet together? Like he was original or something an he was starting to seem more of a dippy student than anything else.

Cause we don't have a polaroid with us, went Manda.

So we check eaches make-up, Orla explained, Can't trust mirrors.

Eaches?! Eaches!! Ha, ha, ha.

Cmon, Manda rolled her eyes to the farest-away-from-the-guy area then snatched her Hooch up offof the bar and when they got over there Orla was whispering.

Steady on Manda, he was pretty cute.

It's our first pub, if we start hitting on the boys the now, they'll be a fucking queue of butchers' dogs ahind us by seven.

You know how slow ah am at coming forward, it'll take me all afternoon.

You can do much better than that.

Do you think ah should take out ma braces? She grinned and her lipstickedness slipped up over the mess of wire and silver solder lumps.

Only if you're going down on him.

I'm saving that for the bouncer at the Mantrap if he'll no let us in the night, Orla smiled.

The girls laughed, glugged back at their Hooch using two fingers neatly clicked round the bottle necks.

What's it actually like?

Ah telt you!!! I telt you at Christmas. Mind that orange medicine you'd get for upset tummies? Just like that but . . . but queerer . . . musty.

Mmm.

Ah mean there's such a fuss made bout it. But we've all of us gulped down a big grogger when we've got the cold, have we no?

Hee! If Chell was here know what she'd says?

At the same time the two girls goes loudly, AHHH, DINNAE SCUM US OUT! and they squirmed round on the seats in hysterics.

But you're meant to be such a heroic bimboic if ya do it and it's just nothing special, there's worse and besides ah've always been . . . Manda kind of leaned forwarders and dropped her voice ... Ah've kind always been in to it and, like you won't say to Fionnula nut?

No–no.

Not really in here you know? she pointed her finger into her mouth, But, more ... all over ah always liked, cause outside and that, round the back of Mantrap or down on the blaes in the dances, it's so warm when it comes out them.

Orla's was the lowest whisper, Like on your face?

Manda, nodded her head quick and patted the open school shirt down near the bra ribbon, with a flat palm, An here too, on them. Once ah saw steam come off it in the moonlight an ...

Who was that?

Ahm no telling.

Go on!

No. But ah tell you, you really need your mirror and that and you've got to hold your hair ... ah ... sorry but see ... you're perfect for it!

Orla laughed.

Got to make sure ya keep your hair the fuck out of there and no wi black on.

So it's really warm?

Hot sometimes. Ah mean ahve only done it couple times but it was something I wanted to do; see me, ah just do things ah want to, Manda lit up a cigarette. She went on, See, Catriona had these nuddy mags under her bed and I could just go into her room and look at them any time ah wanted cause she knew dad would never tell me anything, periods and that it was all left to Catriona and you know? She's just great, eh?

Aye she's great, aye. Where did she get them?

Och Ex's, same as Fionnula.

Oh right.

An there was this photo in one and it was guys, y'know, it was pretty disgusting cause it was more than one guy and they were going all over this girl's face and here, an I was really a bit freaked out y'know, it seemed heavy like, but one Christmas, Catriona got us this face cream an it was in one of those plunger dispensers, you know? So it scooshes it out on palm of your hand, when you shove it down.

Oh aye.

Well if you kind of squeezed it sudden, turned on its side, it would shoot out this white face cream.

Orla laughed, surprisingly, deep, horny chuck-chuckle.

Like then there was that issue of *More*, aye? The wanking one: 'get relaxed in bath, make sure you won't be disturbed,' all yon shite. An we were all trying it . . . well, in ma bath ah put milk powder under the hot water tap cause I like the feel, mind ah've told yous. . . ?

Aye.

So am sat there, in ma milk, going at it, in full commotion an when I happened, splash up the hand've been using, grab the face cream an go, YAH!, jet a shoot right in ma face pretending it's Rob Lowe or that coming on me so it was obviously something that was preying on ma mind.

Orla let out a real shriek of hysterics. So you pretend, it's spunk like!

Manda Tassy looked around, Well I don't do it anymore, I do it for real, but ah used to, aye.

Well you'll need try it wi all these subMARiners the night, like wee Maria McGill was saying this morn.

Aye, SubMARiners, Manda put on a big, deep voice and the two girls laughed.

Am getting really cheesed off wi Fionnula, says Manda who took a swallow of the Hooch Orla'd bought her.

*

I don't see why ya don't just buy stronger cigarettes.

It does work out that wee bit cheaper. Chell was tearing the sticky bit offof her Rizla paper and wrapping the wee holes in the filter of her Silk Cut. She says, Try. Ya can really tell the difference.

Kylah held the cigarette under her nose, squinting at it then took a draw on the modified fag.

Mmm. No just want one of ma Marlboros? She handed it back.

You shouldnie be smoking them.

Why?

Ruin your voice for the band.

What about you. You're a Soprano!

Aye, but your voice is serious. That's what happened Yolanda McCormack; fore you joined, Yolanda was a Soprano.

Never! Goes Kylah.

Honest Injuns. She smoked Silk Cut Extra Mild, great Soprano voice, then she started getting out at nights, smoking Marlboro Lights, next term she was down to the Seconds, then she starts on the straight red Marlboro and when we went on the French trip, she smuggled back two cartons those French cigarettes. Gilroy or something?

Don't know.

Anyways, they were brutal though they smelled nice. Six weeks and Condom had her singing bass alongside Fat Clodagh.

Kylah briefly held up her Marlboro. Ah fuck it, am thinking of going solo anyways and sides, ah need more fags. Want some?

Nah, I've seven here, you'd be best waiting for a newsagent, you'll only get eighteen in these machines.

Well ahm no smoking your contraptions. Got any pound coins?

Chell fished into the zipper poke of her backpack, took out a wee purse: emptied coins onto the metal bartop. The girls slid around some change, Kylah replacing everything she took with the equivalent, then going, That's forty pee ah owe ya. Kylah slid, gingerly offof the stool an crossed over the cigarette machine.

The boys end of the bar watched her, smoking her last, crossing that floor towards the machine then dropping the coins in. She punched the Marlboro icon then there was the per-usual hesitation, till the packet dunked down into the sluice. Kylah reached out a hand then suddenly paused. She bended her knees a little then twisted, turned her body as if to shield the packet from view of the foreign-speaking boys. She patter-pattered her fingers gainst side of the machine, just above her packet of Marlboros then suddenly walked back, awkward-like with a big red brasser on her mush.

What's it? Chell hissed.

Ma fucking skirt's too tight to bend down an get them out!

Chell looked down at her own.

Go give it a go.

Ma skirt's shorter an tighter than yours, Chell goes, between her teeth.

Pleeeease Chell.

Och. Chell popped down offof the stool and pranced over to the machine, pausing at one point to turn and smile at the end of bar boys who'd quite shamelessly put down their coloured cocktails, rested their cigarettes on ashtrays to stare.

Chell attempted the required kneel, crouched and gave a rapid downward tug to the riding hem of her skirt, changed position and attempted to drop further, then grimaced, abandoned the attempt and walked back to Kylah.

No way José. Not without showing that lot ma fanny or ma ass and that's no a choice am willing to make.

Excuse me. Excuse me.

The barman turned round and moved up past the fridges.

There's a problem with the cigarette machine.

Oh. Hold on there. He turned and walked to the far end of the bar where he exited the already lifted hatch. He crossed to the machine where Kylah was stood.

How much did you put in?

Oh it's no that, it's just ma skirt is so tight I couldn't lift the packet without taking it off, you couldn't lift those out for me could you? Please?

What's she cheesing you off about? goes Orla, who'd leaned forwarders and shoogled her new boot.

Och ah don't know. Like when she cracked up at Kay Clarke the day, ah mean we all know Kay's an asswipe but there was no need to give her such a slagging, the lassie was near greeting.

Aye, suppose.

And all that she was saying, what was it all? middle class and that, ah mean Fionnula would never ha says that stuff last summer when we were just all having a great time getting off with those guys. It's like now she really thinks she's got something we don't have, as if we're no all the same anymore, and she's something special.

Mmm. Maybe.

And sometimes, ach sometimes she's a bit ... tartishly bimboic. Like ah know she's got a great figure and that, but she's aye showing it off now, like there in Rest & Be Thankful, she NEVER shuts the toilet door these days, like Saturday nights in the Mantrap, LAST Saturday it was the same! Sat wi knickers and tights round her feet and lassies she hardly knows coming in and she's just so ... ach so ... like the time with Iain Dickinson, handjobbing him during the slow sets at yon dance;

133

that was the start of it. It's like everything has to be showing off now.

What do you mean?

Well look, I'll try explain something weird.

What?

See when we were aw looking down on that couple shagging at the hall there.

Aye!

Well ah was only half looking at them, ah was really looking at Fionnula, our Fionnula, an, ah can't really describe it, but ah just had this awfy feeling of jealousness, cause she was just staring at this two, fucking in broad daylight an ah think that kinda stuff's a big thing to Fionnula, ah think that's what she wants to be doing.

Aye but it is sexy for some people, they might get caught an that!

Ach aye, but it's no getting caught, it's wanting all to see, an when ah started slagging the lassie outside, calling her Dirty Hoor an that, I knew in me, inside me, ah was sorta seething at Fionnula, ah was really slagging Fionnula when ah was going on like that, bout yon lassie . . . though ah suppose yon girl is a bit of a dirty hoor doing that, it was really Fionnula ah was getting at.

Do you feel you're sort ah losing her as your best friend?

Ach, this is starting to sound like Rikki Lake.

But that must be how you feel.

It's. Manda paused. It's she needs to top everything. Like this morn when Michelle was there and you were feeling the baaby kicking. Fionnula went up last, slapped both hands on her belly and had to stand there, just for ages, gazing into her eyes, like she was the fucking father or something . . .

134

Orla laughed.

Or like Mystic fucking Meg, with these hidden powers an she goes all spacey.

Orla laughed again.

Suddenly Manda smiled again. Sometimes ah think she's on drugs. Ecstasys or that; no telling us.

Orla just smiled an shook her head. There was a bit of silentness. She leaned forward again, These boots are starting to hurt me.

Like with Catriona, she's just so cool, you can talk about anything and she tells me everything about herself, but ah feel ah know Fionnula less an less.

Thanks for that.

Quite all right.

Kylah and Chell were back at the bar and Kylah was unwrapping her Marlboros, There was this girl up there, aye, she says to the barman. Thirteen-year-old and she got pregnant from the guy who fills all the cigarette machines up our way.

The Marlboro Man! goes Chell.

Thirteen! goes the barman.

Oh aye. Back of the van in the carpark. We've got these friends right, Fionnula an Manda, an there's this population sign outside the Port, wi like, six thousand four hundred or whatever, writ on it an when that girl got pregnant they went up one night an painted 'six thousand four hundred AND ONE' at the end of it.

The barman laughed.

Chell says, She had her wee baby and ah hear, subsequently, it became a heavy smoker!

They all laughed.

Girls, the barman clapped his hands, would you like to try one of my special cocktails?

Well we're a bit short on money now.

In a lower voice, to Chell, Kylah announced, We've to meet Fionnula in HMV.

On the house, he smiled.

They shrugged, On you go then, says Chell.

Manda?

What.

I was quite, ah got really horny when ah saw them two screwing.

You couldn't see the guy hardly!

Ah know, it was a shame, but it was the idea more than anything.

Manda shrugged, lit another cigarette.

Manda, keep a secret?

What?

It's about when ah was in hospital.

What?

I tried to screw this guy who was in a coma.

What?!

Kylah and Chell tumbled from under the polythene lashed speaker, the Volkswagens of rock were giving it a more recent composition above their heads.

What way? Chell whipped on her sunglasses.

Cmon, Kylah linked arm with Chell and, one eye turned slightly towards the sun, they strode ahead.

Wow-wee-oww. Jeez-oh, Orr! Manda blew out then smiled.

Next day he was tied down to the bed wi belts, Orla sighed.

*

136

Kylah an Chell stood mong the racks of a hundred thousand CDs, Chell scanned this way then that.

What IS this shite they're playing? Kylah announced and she fished out the boys' shopping list, unrolled the twenty pound notes and looked at them.

Where the fuck is she? Chell goes, then she looked at the roll of twenties and went, How much you got with you the day?

Me maself? Thirty-three pound left.

How much they give you?

There's a hundred and twenty here.

Chell looked round, impatient once more, then goes, What was that you says bout going solo?

Do you think that's sin?

Nut. We've all been to same school but ah believe suicide is an only sin; abortion is okay, sex before marriage . . . all that, obviously anything goes, but suicide, ah can believe your soul goes to limbo. Fionnula thinks that's the only sin too. If you ask me, you were being kind to the guy, sort of.

It was the fact he was helpless, that he couldn't do anything that made me do it. That's what am really into, handcuffs and that, I'd love to try that.

Aye Orr but you should start in the shallow end. We need to get ya set up with a nice guy, you bonk the daylights out him with a flunky on then you can start trying all the bondage Barbie stuff.

Sounds okay to me.

Cmon then, let's get out here.

Right.

Fionnula (the Cooler) was moving below the high sun, the bag containing her school clothes, hung on one shoulder, her cheap sunglasses held with two fingers, the arms still extended. She was walking, pausing at street corners and looking, squinting up when it was against the sun, to read street name signs, then moving on with purpose. She had moved downhill away from main streets so the sun tended to be off behind the big, solid buildings to her left. Huge wreaths of sunlight fell out of the street ends. Buses, taxis and expensive cars moved through the bright areas.

It was very warm inside the phone box.

Hold the door open cause it's stifling in here, goes Kylah.

Chell stood ahind her, holding the door open and peeking over Kylah's shoulder.

Where's all that change ah gave you?

Holding the door with her leg, Chell bent, her hair tumbled forward and her head bammed into Kylah's ass; Kylah took a step forward, the phone in one hand, thrown outwards so's it wanged the kiosk glass.

Owww!

Sorry, Phhhh, Chell laughed and rose back up again. I'm fucking steaming, she says.

Kylah took the purse and dialled.

How come ya know his number so well?

Ah need it for Saturdays when ah cancel rehearsal an that. Here.

What?

It's just making this noise.

Let's hear.

Kylah passed the handpiece back and Chell leaned inwards so's her chin was on Kylah's shoulder.

Nope. It's no connected. Here, probably needs some kinda code or something cause we're so far away.

Code?

Other numbers on the front.

How do we find that out?

Ah don't know. We need a pub. A pub with a telephone book.

A pub?

Yup, an we're the folk for the job.

Manda. Slow down a bit, Manda.

Sorry.

Why don't we just use one of these black taxis? Look them all.

Aye but we're saving more drinks money by walking. Those boots really hurting you?

A wee bitty aye.

Put your other shoes back on then.

No ways, ah like these. We're going to be hours early at this place and what if it's shite?

Then we won't be stuck in a shite place from four till half six, we can get out quick.

They're all the same to me, Manda.

See that over there?

What?

The Highland Club Sauna.

Aye, what about it?

Know what that is?

Ah steam place, they used to have one at the Lancaster Hotel.

No no no. That's a hoorhouse.

A hoorhouse? Never.

Aye. Ma sister told me when she was going wi yon one who brought her down to the rugby. All over the city, hoorhouses called saunas.

But how can it be, just sat there like that in full view. Look, there's a fucking police station opposite! If it was a hoorhouse it'd be all hid away.

It's true!

Aye. One nil.

It's right enough. Dead gen.

They had just got round the corner when a well-gone old grey head came weaving cross the pavement at them. He was wearing a green and white striped football top from the Celtic football club team.

Lassies, lassies, ahm drunk, there's no doubt about it. Would yous know where The Buff Club is; have to meet some of the lads in the Buff Club?

Sure Mister, it's just round the corner opposite the police station, goes Manda Tassy.

Oh, thank you.

The man swayed onwards.

See. Told ya, goes Manda.

Fionnula turned the corner, looked up at the sky, held the end of her shoulder bag more loose, so's it hung right down by her shin, the plastic strap-adjusting attachments clicking on the pavement. She stopped by another shaded shop window. She gazed at herself and muttered, Fuck, fuck, fuck, fuck, young, young, young, young. She grimaced down at the bag; at a graffito dating back to second year.

Fionnula took a breath, pulled up the sleeves of her blue shirt after reaching in to test an oxter for sweat. It was dry as back of her hand.

She returned round the corner and on up the same street again. Halfway along she moved to the inner side of the pavement by the black railings. Ahead she could see the broad flagstones where the railings stopped and the frontage was. She could hear her heart beating.

Afternoon empty, that's what the bar was; that emptiness, a cupola of smokeless air in centre of the bar. Daylight too lucid and creeping into every nook and cranny. A fucking afternoon. Fucking choirs!

She stepped a little across the flagstones then saw herself in glass of the frontage, she could see the chandelier with boa feathers hung down from it then the girl behind the bar turned to look at her. Her angle wasn't too obvious so she took one long leg step and she was at the door, she reached out and turned the brassy handle then stepped in.

She had stepped in next door. It was very quiet and there were paintings on every wall, colours slapped all over them; it was like a fucking art gallery with these paintings, huge, wouldn't get in the front door of their council flat, an there were these prices beside them, £1,750, £1,690! Name of fuck. The paintings just had colours swirled all over, bit like she was feeling inside, Fionnula had to admit. £2,600.

Can I help you? A woman about her Mum's age was smiling from a desk.

Nut. Fionnula turned, stepped back to the door and pulled it open, then she turned round and says, Never ever.

She shut the door softly behind her and moved close in to the window where a framed abstract was propped up, taller than Fionnula's front room ceiling. Then out, cross the flagstones and way up the inclined broadway, schoolbag back up on her shoulder.

Got a phone book please?

Yup, the barman hoisted up a thumbed phone book, front

cover ripped away, first page ascrawl with a maze of blue pen numbers and passed it cross the bar.

Ta, Chell put it down on the bar and the few old-timers looked at the young girls as Kylah peered over Chell's shoulders. Here, oh one, six three one.

.Oh one, six three one, went Kylah.

Where's your phone please?

We don't have one.

A good few of the old-timers chuckled.

Eh?

Eh! Eh! We don't have one.

How come you've a phone book!?

.The barman pointed to a space by the window; there was a rectangle of clean paint and all round it, blue ballpoint writing on the wall, always at angles. He goes, It was there till Saturday past. Two lads were leaning against it, next thing one walked out with it under his arm. We only just replaced the handset the week before when a regular had a set to wi the wife and tore the wire out. He left wi the handset in his jacket pocket.

That's nothing, Chugg, I woke up in the armchair Saturday there, a defrosted haddock in ma jacket pocket.

Let's get out of here, Kylah goes, in Chell's ear, Chell ignored her.

But you've a phone there.

Woooo, went a coupla regulars.

That's for staff and regulars, his glasstowel squeaked on a mug he was drying.

Don't ken how it got there, the regular announced, shaking his head.

An how much do you huff to drink to become a regular? smiled Chell.

The barman laughed. Began pouring boiled water into his mug.

Are yous trying to give us all heart attacks with these skirts, an old boy in a tweedy jacket yelled.

Did that hurt? The barman nodded at Chell's eyebrow ring.

Nope, but the other one did, Chell raised both eyebrows and the barman laughed more, Jeezo, none of us'll sleep the night, eh boys?

Get them to sign the visitors' book, Chugg!

Whats that, the phone book? nodded Kylah.

The fatty barman chuckled, crossed to the phone, lifted it and pulled the extension wire out from under the shelfing. He placed the phone down in front the girls.

Thanks, Chell smiled, Do you have Sambuca?

Sam what!?

Two vodkas and fresh orange please.

That we can manage. Where are yous phoning then?

Fucking Australia! someone called.

She's leaving her band.

You're in a band, ah thought it'd be *you* in the band by the make of you.

Well we're all in a choir.

A choir! Give us a song then.

Okay, smiled Chell.

Kylah looked at her.

Cmon, Chell stuck an elbow in her, *Forth Let The Cattle Roam*.

They heard the Pill Box before they saw it. It was a low, square building without a single window. Tho a sunny afternoon, two bouncers in black bomber jackets flanked the door that was open.

Oh naw, there's bouncers.

Know what year ya were born?

Aye, goes Orla, who'd taken off her boot and was holding it in her hand, she hopped up to the bouncers and says, Hi, there's no a dress code is there?

The two bouncers laughed.

Look at ma pinkie toe, went Orla, an she bent down and took off her sock. Manda noticed Orla'd fresh nail varnish on her toenails.

Terrible, went the bouncer. We should say, we're open to the public, good DJ like, but there's two private functions on in here.

What?

There are two functions on here but you're welcome in.

Two at the same time? goes Manda.

Aye.

What are they?

He turned to the other bouncer, What is it, twenty-first and an engagement?

Ah thought it was two engagements.

Engagements? Manda gave Orla a sour look.

We're after some nice boys.

What's wrong with us?

Nothing. Yous are lovely boys, specially since yous are going to let us in for nothing.

Do yous no have your bank statements? The other bouncer went.

What d'ye mean?

Bank statements; if yous have an overdraft at the bank, we let you in here for nothing, it's well known round here, really gets the punters in.

That's mental.

We don't have any overdrafts.

We don't even have bank accounts, that's how poor we are.

Bit of smash the day though, Orla added.

Manda goes, See the chances of nice boys at a birthday party are much higher than the chances at an engagement party, when it'll be tons of the lassie's pals an, course, the million dollar question is, if it's a twenty-first, is it a boy's or a girl's?

And is he cute? chirruped Orla, speaking that quiet way, so's her braces didn't show.

And is there a band? Cause we've pals coming too; ones like bands.

Ah hear violins, goes the skinhead one, who shrugged, turned on his heels and was back in a jiffy going, One engagement: boy AND girl, one twenty-first. Boy.

Orla and Chell screamed, started getting their purses out bags.

In yous get the both of yous, went the bouncer, laughing.

Holding her boot in her left hand, Orla stepped forwarders, immediately followed by Manda.

It's not possible. Fionnula actually mouthed the words and really had side-stepped left, hard, into another doorway. There was a corner of glass window so's she was able to look up the street, beyond the buses. She was moving away, in the direction she'd first seen her. Was it her? A short skirt, real short and . . . why had she changed?

Frowning, Fionnula stepped out of the doorway and on after, but keeping one eye on her. She flicked her head to check traffic and nosily crossed to the doorway she'd come out of. Fionnula climbed up. There were all different brass business plaques. Fionnula trotted down the steps, she could still see the girl but right up where heavy tree branches were awning down quite a ways away. Fionnula started trotting up the hill.

*

145

Kylah and Chell looked at each other to know when to fade down their voices then everyone in the bar started clapping.

They sound like angels but a bet they're no boys!

You'd be right there, went Chell and she took out her Silk Cuts.

Play dommies as well as ya sing?

Aye, park those rear ends over here wi the gentlemen.

Those classy chassis.

Right ya are but've to phone first.

Aye, cmon.

Is it her boyfriend she breaking up with? The tweed jacket one looked around.

Nay, nay man, it's her band she's leaving.

A band is it?

Kylah had punched in the numbers an was staring into Chell's eyes. She picked at her lip with her teeth for a moment.

There was a traffic lights and the girl had come to stop at them with three, maybe four other people beside. Fionnula gained fast, stared, couldn't tell from the thin back of the neck, (tanned seeming), surely the hair a wee bit higher, the bare legs (too thin for tennis), the tan suede skirt, then she saw the bag. She'd been holding it to her front, clutched under tits. The unmistakable bag of a Our Lady's girl!

The green man came on and it was Kay Clarke, stepped forward cross the road. Awkward-like, Fionnula walked after her then suddenly paused, but Kay was swerving left in the centre of the road, passing the wing of a halted car then walking into the gate of a set railings, descending steps and going out of sight.

The lights had gone red. Fionnula stood, then stepped back as a bus passed, its mirror swishing by. Without knowing it,

Fionnula had lifted one of the straps on her bag, jammed the end in her mouth and was chewing.

In name of God, went Orla, holding her boot.

No one gave Orla the slightest attention. There was a boy up the karaoke; no shirt on. Chromes and glints of a drumset were behind him. Right enough there were two very distinct parties in progress – older women wi hats, grey-head husbands wi ties tugged open at the collar, circling, excited, and over-dressed young folk on one side; and all crammed in, at a long table-nook wi mirrors on the walls, lit by the disco lights, golden heaps of lager pints piled around before them, was a group of lads cheering the karaoke fellow.

The song finished and a loud jeer went up.

Davey the DJ's voice clanged through the shaky PA: Tom, the birthday boy and he's crap!! Manda started moving to the bar cause there didn't seem to be seats, Orla followed, sliding her sock on the lino when the carpet ended.

Let's see you all shaking some hair doon on that flair, but first, to add to the happy occasion, I've got an announcement to make. Shut it! Listen. They've been going out a year; they're so happy for Jim and 'Von today, Kirstin and Bobby are announcing their engagement!

A huge cheer went up. The guys next Orla and Manda at the bar cheered, threw arms round each other.

The shirtless birthday boy leapt back up on stage and bothered the DJ at his console; he leaned over to the microphone, half grabbing it, face twisted back to the club, Ah just want to say, ah just want to say, ah don't ken yous but ahm really really happy for yus!

A ringing endorsment frae Tom there. Keep working on the singing son, the DJ put on *Celebration* by Kool & the Gang (it was really *Celebramos*, the Spanish version, but no one seemed to notice: the dancefloor filled and everyone sang on top the foreign language version).

What a gormless-seeming bunch of bampots, Manda murmured into Orla's ear.

Look, there's chairs over there by the engagement lot, goes Orla.

You get the drinks ah'll try get them.

What're wanting?

Anything, Orla crossed the club floor, just as she did there was a burst of strong silver light as the bouncers opened then closed both doors; a guy rode onto the floor on an old, orange Chopper bicycle, pedalled a few circles to the cheering then got off, clicking down the stand of the bike and marching up the bar beside Orla.

Aye? the barman says to the Chopper rider but he nodded to Orla.

This girl wanting her boot filled with beer is first.

Orla smiled, Eh, two pints of your cider.

You know we're selling bottles of champagne at four ninety-nine?

Chopper guy laughed beside her.

The barman fished out one of the bottles from a dustbin, a lot of ice slithered as a bottle fell deeper into the sound of ice and water. The barman held the green bottle under Orla's face. The label on the champagne read: DUBOIS.

Orla frowned and says, Dubious!

Dubious champagne ha! went the gorgeous Chopper guy.

I'll take that too, goes Orla, getting out her purse from the schoolbag.

You want the ciders as well? the barman goes.

Aye.

The Chopper guy had been looking at her, You here wi the engagement party o with Tommy's lot?

None, ah mean no really, am here to see a band.

Aye? me too! They're mates of mine.

Aye?

Aye. Jerry Cornelius and his Taiwan Sellout.

That's great. Orla looked round. Manda was watching from a table where she was sitting, crossed legs, lighting up a cigarette; she raised her arm: a big wave, stabbed a finger at the seat she was keeping. Orla drunk a scoop of cider and slid the pint glass right down, inside the boot, rested on the bar. Some slopped out. It's a very liquidy drink. Cider, she went, then laughed goofishly. By snugging the pint-in-a-boot, in, under her oxter, Orla could carry the other pint cider in her left hand, schoolbag over her shoulder and bottle cheap bubbly, neck crowned wi two plastic cups in her right hand.

That your friend?

That's ma Mum, went Orla, smiling off, cross the floor.

Hey, big spender!

It's you he's after, Orla nodded back over her shoulder.

Chopper man? What was he saying? She says wi quickishness.

Just blowing shite. Orla bust the cap and blew the top on the Dubious, the cork leapt straight upward, breaking a purple-painted roof tile. The top of the bottle spoomered up froth and bubbles so's Orla gobbled her braces round it then unplugged the bottle. A chunk of the roof tile fell, table-centre.

Aye records, that's the thing wi the young ones these days, one of the regulars declared.

Shush.

Hello. It's Kylah, Missus Grieg. Aye. Fine aye. Is he there? Aye. Thank you. Aye fine, 'll hold on. Kylah coughed, all the old boys in the bar looking at her. There was quite a pause an Kylah whispered, Ah don't know what day he signs on. Suddenly she went. Aye. It's me. Chell gave her a light elbow and Kylah made a face back. Kylah goes, Aye, we're down now. Look there's. Aye. There's something ah need to tell you . . . yous. Yous! Aye. Am leaving the band.

There was a pause. Am leaving the band. Am really sorry but it's been. Ah know. I know. Sorry but you'll be fine without me. No. No it's nothing to do wi that solo . . . it's just, ach, it hasn't been as much fun for a while an, what do you mean? It's no, nut, nut, nut, nut, nut, nut if ah don't want to do it why should ah. Eh? It's nothing to do with dedication. Am just no enjoying it.

You tell um lass, one of the old voices called out.

What? Nut. Nut. What do you mean sack them?

What's he saying for God's sake? Chell jumped up and down.

It's Chell. Rachel MacDougall. You met her. She was at the High School when we played.

There was a long silence. Kylah stared at Chell.

Ah mean that's awful, saying you should sack them. Christ ah phoned you cause . . . nut, cause they're at school, ya arsehole. Nut. Look. Hold on. Kylah covered the mouthpiece wi her hand.

What's he saying? Chell goes.

Aye what IS he saying? goes the barkeep who was leaning by the tap, stared.

He says, do ah want to get rid of the drummer an bass player?

You think of yourself girl, a behind voice went.

Look after number one, goes another.

But that's really sneaky an he wants to know why ah done it when am down here, saying am a cowardy ben an that an. And he says that you're a dirty tinker. Kylah stared at Chell.

Oh-oh, voice behind went.

Chell grabbed the phone and screamed into the mouthpiece, You fucking little short dick man.

That's him telt! the behind voice goes.

Give it here, give it HERE.

Don't break that phone! went the barkeep.

Kylah'd the phone back an was trying to goes, Nah, YOU look here. What? That has nothing to do with anything. What? That's none of your business.

Cmere. The barkeep grabbed the phone offof Kylah.

You tell him, Chugg!

The boy's oota order.

The barkeep goes down the phone, The lassie fucking telt you, she's left yur band, now gie up the ghost quietly. Who am I? I'm her fucking new manager that's who I am.

A substantial cheer went up round the pub.

Aye, record contracts, the lot and exactly who are you, fuckin Michael Barrymore or something? What have you done for this lassie, eh? What have you done for her . . . career? She's been doon in this city, he cupped the receiver, How long you been down here?

Just the morn.

Shes doon in this city just the morn an she's got a new manager an a record contract, think about that son, an dinnae give up the day job chavvy, he shoved out the receiver with disgust, like a salute, face turned away from it. Kylah took it and, canny-like, put it to her cheek. She didn't say anything; you could hear voice, in the mouthpiece. You could see her absorbing the utterances.

Kylah's eyes narrowed, she says, Ah can tell you this. There's no point you making an issue of something like that, cause ah did it with them too.

Chell grit her teeth, beholden also, to knowledge, of Kylah's handjobbing all: guitar/vocals, bass and, yup, drums too.

Kylah looked ahead. There was silence in the plastic mouthpiece. You could hear Kylah breathing then the little fizz sound, Ask them, she nipped back. The money? Ah got it here, eh? What record company! Ach, don't be pathetic, she moved to slam the phone down, caught the barkeep's eye and wi more gentleness returned the handpiece to the cradle.

The music had been interrupted again in the Pill Box. One of the older women from the same table Manda and Orla were beached at, had struggled on stage to Davey the DJ. The younger girl and boy at the table cross from Manda, were tugging at each other excited-like.

And there's another announcement here folks, Davey was leaning over, nodding at the older woman. Aye, get up to that bar and drinks for Louise and Ali who've just decided . . . to get engaged too!

A huge cheer arose. Ali and Louise bounced up and snogged. Manda, one arm down, the hand fishing in her bag while she leaned over to yell in Orla's lug, goes, Dangerous place, come in looking for a shag but you're more likely to end up fucking married! Orla nodded, serious, as the sound system exploded with, *We're A Happy Family* by The Ramones. Manda leaned forward between the snoggers, hung something on the boy's shirt buttons. It was the little sign from Rest & Be Thankful. RESERVED.

Kylah burst out with the greeting.
 Kylah! Cmon.
 Oh. Poor lassie.
 I shouldnie ah done that.

Ach. Away. That's way it goes, lassie.

Here, here, says one in the brown jacket waving about a hankie.

Nah nah, yur okay there, warned Chell and leaned her mouth into the hair, down the side, Kylah's face, Yur fucking up your make-up baby, she whisper-whispered.

Kylah nodded, snuffled.

It's me usually does the crying Kylah, Chell had an arm round now.

Ah know. Ah know, Kylah wiped her snozzle on back her hand then goes, Crazy ah've grat an here's you, here's you wi your real daddy away lost an yur big sister married to yon looney and here's me all hetupness bout bugger all, she tried to do a big smile, teeth so white cause her face was red, but she guffed out a big sob again.

Chell drew back a fraction'n hushed, Here, yur gonna set me off, she smiled, a bit.

. . . An Orla nearly died an ahm sat here like a big, bubbly baby.

Don't worry Kylah, don't worry, we'll give them the money back.

Kylah's voice came clearer, a bit louder, Y'know fine we'll splash out the lot. She guttered a big sob again.

You could see Chell's eyes starting to go now.

Oh, ahm sorry ah mentioned your dad, it just came into ma mind.

Ach no, it's just. Is it the boys you are crying about?

Kylah almost shouted it out, Aye!

You're no at fancying one are you?

Don't really make me cry! Ah mean ah had it off wi them but, och, just to get it over wi. The way you just know fancyings are building up, an they were all over me, so's ah thought, what boys are like, suck of ma tits an they'll go back to fancying Courtney Love or that; yon Mazzy Star girl wi no voice.

Chell went, Aye well, least they were getting it from someone wi a good voice.

Aye, this is it, Kylah nodded, Ah mean ah never (she dropped to a whisper-whisper), never shagged them . . . it's just. An here you could see she was as to about resuming wi bursting out at the greets.

Whaaat?

It's just as a band.

What?

They're so fucking shite. Ahm greeting cause ah feel sorry for them cause they're so crap.

Oh.

What are we gonna do? Ah need to do ma make-up now. The two girls looked at each other.

Chell says, Bestest find some place with decentish toilets, eh?

Then what; get up this Pill place; wonder where Fionnula's got to, eh? Kylah rubbed her eyes lightly on back of her hand to check for make-up then pinched and tugged down the sleeve of her T-shirt and wi head leaned to one side, rubbed one her cheeks on it.

We go straight there?

Both girls looked each other in the face an says . . . same time: French Connection!

Think yon grot's seeing enough or what?

He's no that bad, staring right at you though, check the suit.

It's fucking boufing man, who's he think he is, fucking Bryan Ferry? Funny, ya aye see that, townies wi a fucking suit on; what a turnoff. Cannie see a lad's arse in a suit, makes them look so old, it'd be like having to screw wi Mr Eldon or something.

Even ah wouldn't have it off with Eldon, ahm no desperate as all that.

Christ he's homing in on us, get the suit, says Manda, smiling into his face as he bore down.

Hi there!

Both the girls stared.

You're no Jim Clark's wee sister are you?

Orla an Manda looked at one other and puffed big haw, haw, haws.

The guy kneeled down on his knees so the surrounding couldn't hear what he was saying but just as he'd cooried and arrived at about-to-speak-position, Manda placed her foot gainst and shoved him over so's he rolled onto his back then suddenly leapt up with a beamer. The girls' cheeks all blew out as they gigglestifled.

Fucksake dame, what fucking planet are you from? He brushed away at the arms of the weird suit even though it seemed, as you looked close, to be covered in wee ousles an dust balls, Ah just wanted to ask if you've been through the back?

Manda looked him up and down and gave a hefty sneer, Ah don't really think too much of your chat-up patter.

Guy seemed more confident now and he leaned wi two hands out flat on the table, goes, Most of the lads round here, cause yous don't seem to be from these parts, most of the boys would just say that they'd like to feel your belly-buttons from the inside. Am just being polite. He shrugged.

Manda looked over at Orla, Least that's original.

Aye. Orla barely moved her lips.

Celebrating? He nodded at the empty bottle Dubious.

We will be, when you leave us alone.

He deftly soldiered on, revolving round to survey the

afternoon pandemonium that surrounded them, Well if yous want to see me in action, I'm round at the Crash, he sniffed, pulled at his cuff, dipped his eyebrows and goes, Versace. He strolled off, up the bar.

What a curséd nuisance, Manda raised her eyebrows at Orla, took another sip of the half-gone cider.

What's the Crash?

Fuck alone knows.

Music was shut off for a moment and soon a cheer was going up, way over to the side, another engagement had been announced.

Reckon ah should make a move on chopper man fore someone gets engaged to him?

Yes. Come check out the toilet?

Aye.

What if we lose these seats?

Excuse me, will you keep these seats for us? goes Manda, picking up her sportsbag.

Eh, oh aye, the guy Manda had stuck the sign to broke off from whisper-whispering in yon lassie's lug. The RESERVED sign was sat in front him by his pint, Leave yur bags if you want.

Nah, ta but we need them.

Manda and Orla were walked round the corner, passed where the twenty-first group was, a few of the younger folk goggled Manda and Orla's gear. As Manda walked beyond the two cigarette machines toward toilets, she squinted ahead, mortal as she was. She stopped. Orla did too.

The guy in the suit, been trying chat them up was upside down, stuck to the wall ahead, about six feet up. His face looked all fatter what with the must've been rushed blood downwards, his legs a bit apart. The bottoms of his trouser legs, falled down so's could see his hairy legs. He smiled, gave dainty wee wave.

*

They entered the police station and she went first up the counter. The posters were different from outside the station in High Street of the Port, where they were all about importance of returning rockets if they got washed up astray from the firing range, or about dangers of beached phosphorus bombs, or there was one of the torn-to-bits lamb, telling townies to keep their mutts on a leash.

We need some assistance, Chell goes.

Yes.

Kylah leaned gainst the counter beside her.

We need a lift.

A lift?

Aye. We're pretty exhausted. See we're down here at St Columba Choirs final.

Yes.

An we've ... become separated from our ... from other members of the choir.

I see.

We were to meet them somewhere and we can't find the place. We've been tramping round for just ages.

I see. Well where is it you've to meet them?

It's near somewhere, Kylah blurted out.

Near somewhere?

It's near somewhere we were told not to go near so's we're hoping you could, maybe get one of your cars to take us near to, the place.

I'm not quite with you here.

Well it's a place called the Pill Box.

The Pig straightened up, I see. And you're not to meet IN there but near to there?

That's right.

Constable, Kylah blabbered out.

Mmmm. I'm a sergeant actually, he pointed to shapes on his jacket arm.

Kylah went beetroot with a big brasser of embarrassedness.

Well firstly the place you're talking about is just around the corner, take a right at the traffic lights here then a left at the next set, follow the main street there up across one, two sets traffic lights, past the Somerfield supermarket and the place you're looking for is on your left just before the BP petrol station.

That sounds a long way, Chell grimaced.

Yes, Kylah nodded, serious-like.

It's just, wi the shopping an that.

The Pig rolled forwarders a wee bitty on his shoes, so's he could make the peer down to the girls' feet where there were four French Connection carrier bags.

Mmmm, it's only about four hundred yards.

How far's that? Kylah turned to Chell, What's that in metres?

It's just, these shoes, Chell canted her leg at one knee so's the brown boot showed, They hurt sergeant, hers too, Chell added.

Aye.

The Pig leaned down on the counter, Did that hurt? he nodded at the eyebrow ring.

No as much as the other one.

What did the sign outside here say?

Police.

Aye. And how do you spell that?

P.o.l.Ice.

Mmmm. P.o.l.Ice. not T.a.axe Eee.

You mean yous are no going to give us a lift?

No. I've told you where the place is.

A mean, that's just awful. We might get attacked.

Miss. It's three thirty in the afternoon.

Aye. But look at the clothes we're wearing.

158

Miss. The clothes you are wearing are *not* the concern of the police.

Well I think that's terrible, went Chell, picking up her bags.

By the way, that bar is over twenty-ones only.

The girls kept heading for the door.

And good luck in the competition, he wasn't looking up anymore.

Outside the door swung shut.

You were amazing, you're just mental having guts to just go in there, Kylah was smiling.

What a fucking townie tight arse he was, ah used to get lifts in fro the Tulloch Ferry bobby all the time, here look, something from home; bet they'd call us a taxi from there, it'll be all decent choochters an maybe get a drink as well, ahm fucking parched for an apple Hooch or something.

With their French Connection bags hanging by their bare legs, the two girls crossed the road towards the obscuring glass of the front door to the Highland Club.

Another man in one of the over-large suits began to run as drum rolls hissed on the wee sound-system, he hit the small, square trampoline and fairly leapt into the air, twisting through it, so's he hit the wall more or less in the inverted position and stuck there his weight pulling, pulling on the suit but the velcro wall with its over-size barbs holding him pretty well, other men, including the chatter-upper, stood supping pints lager, yattering the finer points of technique.

Manda shook head a final time as her and Orla stepped into the toilet.

A Bloody Mary Theory in Tequila Heaven

Kay?

Kay turned round and it's no often you've seen her, up on bar stools, legs swingin from short skirt wi what looked like an alcoholy drink an slice lemon in front her.

Fionnula. She more moved the lip shapes of that name than actually spoke it. It was just too unreasonable that Fionnula could be stood there wearing a terribly short skirt in this sunken afternoon bar, so dark, only light source seemed rising glow from the ground level fridge, behind the bar, caps of beer bottles just visible an the barmaid sat on a stool reading the *Evening News*. Kay there, in a strange end-of-the-bar position, further into the darknesses, away from the eating area where two elderly folk were at a table wi a candle on, Kay's chosen position seeming she wanted no talk wi the barmaid.

Ah just saw you there, Fionnula was walking down the length of the bar, Kay was looked down at her skirt, You changed too!? Fionnula smiled, took her cigarette packet out the breast pocket of her shirt, the lighter was inside the half-smoked packet. She lit up, blowing smoke away from Kay, put the packet back and tugged at her fallen sleeve.

Yes, Kay nodded.

Done your rehearsal?

Where are the others; you actually on your own? Kay sorta gleered round Fionnula.

Ach, shopping an that, meeting at a pub where's live music, ah just went for a wee donner on ma own. Where's Ana-Bessie?

Jenners.

What's that?

Best shop in town.

Oh. Right. How'd rehearsal go then?

Yes? The barmaid appeared out of shadow, behind the pillar, the newspaper, centre pages folded between two of her fingers, giving her an impatient stance.

Fionnula stared at her.

Are you going to drink something? Kay was looked at her.

What's that?

Gin and tonic, a stiff one.

What flavour Hoochs you got?

We don't have Hooch.

You got Sambuca?

Yes.

I'll one of those then.

This is what Dad drinks.

Oh.

He took me here for lunch when we were down last. They do good seafood here. Fresh mussels. Ever had oysters?

Nut, eh, can ah have it in one of those wee glasses no ice thanks, Fionnula leaned over the bar, one lower leg canted up at the knee to the horizontal.

In a shot glass?

Aye, one of they. Aye. Thanks, Fionnula sorta twisted, to get at the zipper, back of her shoulder bag an took out her purse. Cannily, she had a wee wad one pound notes from the purse. Much is that? When the barmaid says, Fionnula put down a pound note then the exact in change, Look, as the barmaid put the little glass in front. Fionnula was holding out a new pound note, stretched between the forefinger an thumb of each hand, she says, JL McAdam. On back of the stiff pound note, right enough, was a profile of the great surveyor wi some sorta geometric pattern under him.

Wha's like us? If we could get away with it, the Scots would say we invented the Internet, Kay shrugged.

Fionnula smiled.

What's that?

Sambuca; have had a few already.

I've never had that.

Mmm, Fionnula held out the glass. Kay took it, seeing Fionnula's metallic blue nail varnish but wi the pinkie-nail done glossy, thick gold, loads of layers. Kay's nails were short an unvarnished.

Kay took daintiest of sips. Ummm. It's nice.

Look. Fionnula took the shot glass offof and tipped it back into her mouth, placed the glass back on the bar top without looking at it cause she held her face horizontal, so hair jutted out oddly, layered down the back of her blue shirt; cannily lowered the cigarette into her mouth then as she withdrew the cigarette, a perfect rod of blue and purple flame rose out of her rounded lips till, wi a fup-sound, Fionnula closed her mouth and swallowed.

Kay opened her eyes wider and says, How to make friends and influence people.

Uh, Fionnula raised her eyes a little as she indicated Kay's drink.

Go ahead.

And Fionnula raised that silvery glass, sweated beads wetting her palm and it actually tinkled as bubbles scooteréd surface-wards from eye of ice and lemon rind while she tipped the whole conglomeration to her lips on the rim just where you could see Kay's lipstick had been then swallowed, That's good, she viewed the globe of drink in her hand then replaced it, front of Kay.

I never used to know what Dad meant, A stiff one!

Is this us back to sailors again! Fionnula smiled.

Kay laughed, I thought it was like, shaken not stirred or something, but it just means two gin measures.

Got to watch Kay, going round asking for a stiff one.

Kay had stopped laughing and she had smiley tears in her eyes as she took big breath in. She nodded, Do you want one?

Aye, go on then, thanks. I'm pretty mashed.

Have yous all been in the pubs?

Basically. Aye. Orla went off to get boots.

What did she get?

Don't have a inkling. Ah was meant to meet Chell an Kylah in a record shop but ah didn't.

Rehearsal was pretty brutal, Kay nodded, sombre then called, Excuse me, can we have two gin and tonics. She turned and looked Fionnula, Stiff ones.

The two girls smiled.

What about that boy and girl, eh? Fionnula looked closely at Kay.

Did you see Sister Condron's face?

Aye. An ah thought Orla was goan fall out the window.

And join in! Kay says.

Fionnula let out a little yelp of surprised laugh.

Is she doing okay, Fionnula? Kay says all serious again, doing that frown thing with the skin above her nose.

Orla! Orla's fine aye, Fionnula chuckled then smiled, When

she's no worried about her hair an getting implants. Fionnula looked over at the candley lunching place. Do you know, Orla's never been for an Indian or Chinese meal in her life? She was telling me all about it.

What. Never?

Nah, why ever should she? Like how they were out in the villages till they moved to the Port. Like we've got Light of India and yon Bamboo place, folk might on occasion get carry out Saturday night but when ya grow up in the villages, well when are you goan have an Indian? Then you don't know how to order, like if you need rice and all that an in The Bamboo you've got all they awkwardness of the chopsticks conundrum. So now, if you don't grow up wi that, Orla's just too feart to set foot in those places.

The barmaid delivered the two gin and tonics. Kay paid with a twenty, swiftly looking at the picture: Brodick Castle on Isle of Arran, fore she handed over.

Thanks, went Fionnula to Kay.

Cheers, goes Kay.

Bottoms up.

Again Fionnula says, That couple, eh? an she lifted the clinking drink to her mouth while sitting downwards on a stool beside Kay.

Kay nodded an goes, If Sister Condom hadnt dragged us away we could have seen everything.

You could see everything of the girl, Fionnula says, no looking at Kay, lighting up another cigarette wi great concentration.

Kay lifted her fresh drink and swallowed some, suddenly she says, We're all to bits with the middle section on *All Around the House.*

Kay, there's no ways we're going to win the night, ahm no

164

being a contrary so and so; just to wind you up or that, it's just, ah can hear a choir when it's firing good an this year we're pretty bloody abysmal.

Suppose, yes.

No that winning should be everything.

It shouldn't be, no.

Ah think just being in the choir should be the main thing; ah mean, when we get it right an we're sounding good, it feels really brilliant to me as well, ah think it's great, but at end of the day, it's a social thing, us, the all of us, thegether enjoying ourselves, but the Sisters have to turn it into this massive big non-stop competition affair, ah mean they'd be better looking bit closer to home than trying to bum their loaf bout a Our Lady's choir; if they're trying to get the school a better image, ah mean! Fucksake you know? Twenty-seven of us pregnant this year; refuse to believe none of us give a shit about the church anymore yet they all seems a bit unchristian to me, way Condom's going mental at us to win, as if that makes any difference to the real problems in the school, or in life, an it just makes, like me and Manda, the more determined no to go along wi it. If they were more laid back I'd be that bit more enthusiastic.

Kay nodded, looked straight at her drink.

Kay, ah didn't mean any harm snapping at you bout Michelle the morn, it's just, ah think after Orla, ah've got awful, sorta all protectivey bout some folk, Michelle all pregnant and everything.

The guy could ah been nicer. That's us back to sailors again, Kay smiled at her drink.

Fionnula laughed and suddenly went, That lot, it's only getting back to the Mantrap for the slow dances they're worried about, case the place is stacked wi the sailors. Fionnula smiled, maybe to herself, maybe for Kay's benefit, You KNOW how wild Manda can be.

Oh, sure. Weirdly, Kay didn't sound that impressed, took a big swig of her gin and tonic.

Fionnula had to take a big swig to keep up.

Where are you headed now, Fionnula?

Well you got let me get you a drink back, Fionnula glanced down at Kay's thigh muscles, whished out the suede skirt. Kay musta known it was coming. Quite cleverly, Fionnula went, That's really nice, is it suede? She reached out and touched the hem of the split, the material of the skirt, so close to Kay's amazingly well-shaved, bare leg, maybe Kay could feel the just-touched-glass-coldness of Fionnula fingertips, kneading the material for that instant then quick, the hand rushing back to rehoist the gin glass.

Can we have two more of these? Fionnula kinda made a swift drunk gesture, gave a puffed out smile, the heavy bevvy starting to show.

Kay cast a look at her, from under eyebrows, had to respond, goes, If you're wondering why I'm changed, it's because I was looking at a house. A house to get a room in when I come down to Uni in September.

Oh. Ah was sort of wondering.

Meaning it's only really the Sopranos that are allowed to get done up for the city?

No. No not that. There was silence. Digs and that, eh? Was the place nice?

Well, it's an auntie to my dad; she's quite on the elderly side, very well-to-do. You wonder if I was to have a late night and everything. They have a great students' union; freshers' week.

Fionnula was frowned, counting out more money on the

bartop. Boys back and that Kay, eh? Quick, so's Kay couldnie come back on it she added, What's freshers' week?

When you go to Uni as first year, they have a whole week for parties. Kay looked a long time at Fionnula as she paid the barmaid and Kay went, You could easily get to Uni, Fionnula.

We can't afford it, and that's end of the story, coming out wi thousands of pounds of debts.

What are you going to do? What is there for you to do in the Port?

Fionnula passed latest glass over to Kay, goes, Who says am staying in Port?

It takes money to go to places.

Fionnula leaned, amazingly close, without Kay shifting the least little bit, an Fionnula went an goes, Maybe YOU'LL invite me down to stay a bit? Slainte.

Slainte. Maybe.

Seriously? Fionnula went the going aboutings of lighting up another cigarette.

Ach, ach, ach ACH! Kay shook her head on the stool and gave her body a big shiver but then a chuckle too.

What? WHAT!? Fionnula nudged her. One of those instants where it's believed someone is going say something, confirming, joyous, like the wheech of the gins up through height of Fionnula an the long suck there on the new cigarette, each intaking done wi deliberateness of real self-hatred an the last still smoking in the Smirnoff ashtray afront.

What? What do you know about me? Kay says.

Fionnula was taken aback but for a jiffy only, An what is it you know about me, up there in your house on Pulpit Hill, stared down on the Port, plugging away at yur . . . cello?

Kay backed right off but nodded to the cigarettes, Could I have one?

Fionnula stuck a blue, varnished nail toward the cigarette packet rested on the bar an slid it minutely along to Kay.

Bad habit, Kay grinned an with surprising ease, freed a cigarette from the packet, fired it up. She looked seriously, dead ahead.

See this we're drinking, smoking? That's ma holiday, Greece, Spain whatever; that's what we're drinking. All ma summer in Bella Bells Tea Rooms wi a bogging waitress skirt on. We've been talked about it two year, since before Orla got sick, but ah think we always knew, in our hearts of hearts and what-have ya-not got, we would never make it. No the five of us.

The Sopranos, Kay exhaled and grandly.

We have a good time, Kay, you don't know the half of it. A suppose it'll be backpacking round Himalayas or something wi your dad's credit card when you go abroad. Ahm no thick, ah know the score.

Nope. You're safe there. Only good thing about the Dalai Lama is Richard Gere.

With the drink in her, Fionnula smiled; no bitterness, An Australia, that's another one ave aye wondered about. If you've money to go there. Like when we went on the French trip, ah was just thinking, Christ, a whole world I don't know bout; like the cooking an way they don't have slow dances an that, an drinking wine when they're eleven; you've got all these countries no far away, centuries of history if that's what yur into, Chartres an everything; so different, an folk go all the way round the fucking world to a place, just a place where everyone speaks English. Ah mean what's there? Australia?

Kay was side-moving her head wi repeats towards the pillar, she muttered, Think the barmaid's Australian.

So what? She got out the place, her an yon Clive James, Fionnula shook her hair.

New Zealand, the barmaid called, invisible to Fionnula and Kay, behind the pillar, no looking up from her paper.

Oh. Right then! Kay called, all cheery.

The two schoolgirls looked at each other, Fionnula shrugged.

Fionnula leaned elbows on the bar, craned over far, so's ends of her hair was actual falling down the work side an it was flopping into those beer-catching basins under the tap.

Watch your hair, Kay stood and stretched an arm, cradling out the ends of the hair wi a cupped hand.

Oh, right. She called, Eh, do you have tequila?

Yes.

Can you do us two slammers? Fionnula straightened, Ever done tequila slammers?

What IS tequila?

Ah don't know but you just drink it down quick, lick salt off your hand. That's it! Lick the salt off your hand (Fionnula made the gestures) swig the drink, swallow an squeeze the lemon slice into yur mouth.

Why all the fantastical rigmarole?

Ah don't know. Tastes foul. The lemon takes the taste away, like the lassies in the fish processing, use lemon juice to wash in; that Kylah named her band after cause a girl would masturbate an it would sting.

Kay ignored, You drink it with salt and lemon? Yeuch. You don't set fire to it or anything as well?

Wait-an-ya-see. Just a couple gets ya mashed as anything. They'll need winch us out of here, she tapped Kay's arm, It'll really loosen ya up.

I am loosed up. I don't like drinking things I don't like the taste of.

Well, time to get over that approach. It'll help you sing.

The barmaid put down two small, clear glasses of liquid.

I'll get it, Kay bundled out the change she'd jammed in her matching jacket pocket. The barmaid went away.

You don't normally smoke at all, do ya?

Nope.

Ah never thought of you as a drinker either. Ah mean, drinking on your own. What's the point in that?

The barmaid slid a plate of lemon slices on the bar, and clunked two salt shakers beside. She took a tenner offof Kay.

There you go, you don't know about anyone, till you ask.

Oooo, hidden depths Kay? Dark secrets to shock? Just what Manda was greeting at me for the day.

What was she saying?

Christ ah don't know. Ah was just telling a story I'd never told her. Ah mean that's no my fault. I'm no under some obligation to tell Manda every totey wee thing that's happened to me ever.

Why what happened?

Nothing! Nothing of any interest. I was mashed right? Staying in a caravan on the border.

What border?

Jesus Christ! That's what they says too. What border do yous think? Ah don't exactly spend all ma time hanging round the Mexican border.

Fionnula, we all just say that to wind you up. We know you're a big Nat.

Aye, an by the way, we did invent the Internet.

Both girls laughed.

Cmon, do these.

You'll need to show me.

Right get . . . oh but you're left-handed, aren't ya? So salt on the hand, like this, there, aye, an you're gonna just lick it off wi your tongue, whack this down the thrapple then you gnash into

170

the lemon to get the juice out, nah, look, that's a nicer bit lemon.

I'll use this, Kay went about the fishing a more substantial an fresh-looking lemon segment fro out among the half gone ice cubes of her drink. Cubes spun round a coupla times till her fingers got hold on the fruit ration an lifted it out.

Ever hear about the time Sister Fagan bit into a lemon? Fionnula asked.

No.

The lemon went, Yeuchhhh! Fionnula all screwed up her face.

Kay burst out a hysteric an the salt grains tumbled offof her hand, Wooooops.

Right, are ya fit?

Just about, Kay re-salted the little hollow behind her thumb, the fingers gracefully curved.

Mmmm, Fionnula put out her tongue an gave the salt line on her hand a long stroke.

Uhhh, Kay licked off the salt from her hand, wetly, leaving saliva.

Ah! raised eyes looking into Kay's, Fionnula flicked the shot tequila into her mouth.

Uh, Kay frowned an slowly poured the drink into her mouth.

Ahssschh, Fionnula had swallowed an had the lemon neatly in her mouth, up to the rind-yellow.

Ah, yugs, Kay hesitated, gulped down an sped the lemon to her lips, nibbling away.

What do ya think?

An they say the Catholic church has some strange rituals! I'd need to try another to make up my mind.

Fionnula laughed, Hey, eh, sorry, can we have three more, ah mean three each, six more please!

Fionnula!

If yur goan be a bear; be a grizzly bear. Right, Kay?

It's too warm a day to be drinking.

O yeah, oh yes, she looked round in appeal, as if in the forgetting all the Sopranos were long-gone. She spluttered out laughing.

Six tequilas? The barmaid smiled.

Aye, please, Fionnula goes, a bit more serious an went about lighting another cigarette.

I'm going to be *absolutely* pissed, Kay suddenly split up laughing.

Fionnula looked at her, shrugged and tried to light her own dead cigarette again.

Kay kept laughing. You look funny, she hiccuped the once.

There you are, the barmaid had arrived, shuttling little glasses offof the tray into two wee rows of three.

Fionnula, her cigarette lit now, pointed upwards, as if she'd had a brainwave, she picked her bag from side of the stool and started taking out her purse, using both hands wi the cigarette in her mouth.

Here, Fionnula, I'll pay half.

Right-chew-are-okey-doke, plenty JL McAdam's here but what am needing is more of the old Brodick Castles, eh?

Or who's on a fifty?

Who's on a fifty pound note?

We don't accept fifty pound notes so I've never seen one, the barmaid smiled.

Not even on payday?

I don't get paid that much.

Quite right, refusing fifty pound notes, you should have a sign up, Fionnula turned a little, to illustrate the elevated position of the hypothetical sign, Nae Rich Bastards!

I don't think that why the manager refuses fifties.

NO OVER FIFTIES, Fionnula suddenly yelled, That should be a bar rule too, ah mean there's no under twenty-ones and even no under twenty-fives, she glanced at the barmaid, Which I have to put up with, so why should there no be an age limit on the other end, why should we have to put up wi these ancient old grey heid bastards gawking us?

Hush, Fionnula.

Why hush? I don't mind being barred. What's the problem being barred if yur a Townie? Fucking bar on every corner. She sat down, The problem is getting barred in a wee town like ours, Fionnula looked at the barmaid who nodded, understandingly, A wee shitey shitey shitehole town like ours. Here yous have ALL sorts of bars. Get banned fro the one, juss shuffle on to the next. What's the problem? Fionnula frowned. She'd forgot how they got onto the subject.

Kay gingerly rested her cigarette in the ashtray and began sprinkling salt on her hand.

Mmm, Fionnula goes, reached for salt herself.

Kay flicked out her tongue, fired back the shot an sooked on the previous, gnarled lemon.

Fionnula licked her salt, tipped two of the shots in her mouth an away they went. She busily picked up two lemon rations an devoured the juice out of them.

I'm looking forward to coming to the Uni. I really am . . .

Shh, Fionnula winked and pointed at the back of the barmaid.

Kay made the 'oh' shape wi her mouth, an nodded, goes, quieterish, But there's some things about the city. Just before I came here, because it was warm and I just fancied a drink, these little kids were waiting outside a chemist's. This old age pensioner came out and sold them a cough mixture bottle!

Cough mixture?

You can get high on it if you drink it.

Ah never really knew that.

Dad told me.

What is it yur dad does? A doctor but only in the hospitals?

He's a consultant.

Right.

Listen, Fionnula, Dad and Mum had a dinner party up at our house during Easter but to make it a little more fun, he asked all the guests to come in fancy dress, Kay goes, a little the quieter on third word, Theres a *gynaecologist* up at the Chest. You know, a gynaecologist?

Yes, goes Fionnula, sharp, more tequilas please, six.

Guess who he came dressed as?

Fionnula shrugged, an picked up a salt container.

Goldfinger from the James Bond film. And he'd painted his finger gold!

Fionnula stared, then just roared out in the hysterics. That's just fuckin brilliant! Ya dinnae think of doctors an that having a sense of humour.

Kay hud a kind of faraway look an was stared at her two remaining shots, Oh they really do, really wicked most times as well. Starts at medical . . .

Fionnula had held up a hand so's Kay had stopped talking. Fionnula goes, Ah was just thought about they old age pensioners, must, you know, add a wee bit on. The cough mixture price. It's state of the old age pensions that's driving the old folk to that. She laughed, says, To becoming drug dealers! Sorry sorry, what were ya saying? Goldfinger. That's brilliant!

There's this story, and I've heard it from different doctors but never from Dad! It's always, they're at medical school and one of the students, during an autopsy on a cadaver, takes the . . . a cut off man's, she dropped her voice an mainly mouthed the word, but hushed its actual sound . . . Cock.

Aye, Fionnula smiled, preparedness for the punchline.

An they go on a city bus but . . .

The BEASTIE!

Yes, Kay giggled, One medical student has it tied on a thead, all the way down an inside trouser leg, so the . . . that end bit is sticking out the trouser leg bottom.

Yesss . . .

So he sits opposite some old woman and by jiggling the thread he can make it . . . Kay laughed, He can . . . you know, make it peek in an out the bottom of the trouser leg!

Huh, Fionnula nodded, did a husky kind of giggle an lit another cigarette, she says, Just like time ah tied yur chair to the desk wi a thread from ma kilt, in yon English exam.

That was SO embarrassing. KNEW it was you, Kay grinned, reached out for another cigarette, I'll get you back Fionnula McConnel!

Fionnula just nodded, turned an smiled, hunched forward on the bar an she annoyedly tugged up sleeve of her shirt that kept falling down. Is it, is it to be a doctor you're going to do at (she dropped her voice) university then?

Law, Kay looked glumly at her tequilas, flipped one into her mouth, paused, flipped back the next one, swallowed then took the next, swallowed it down then reached out for two lemon slices she started to gnaw-gnaw at.

Make a knob peak out just like Manda, eh?

Kay's eyes were all teary, she hunched her shoulders an says, in a strainy voice, You would know.

I'll tell you this, Kay from Pulpit Hill; the walls are so thin in Manda's dad's house, that when she takes a bath, Saturday night, the old man next door knows she's right there, in her bath an

Manda can hear him wanking hisself off, sitting in his empty bath right next her there so she aye listens to her Walkman for a soak.

Oh yeauch.

Ah love Manda an everything but she's so fucking gormless at times.

She didn't do well in the exams.

Och no that Kay. She's full of all those wee town ideas. Like ah hate to say it, you want to get out of the Port, you're aw set up, you'll come down here an have a great time an get your law things but Manda, all she really, really wants, is to get pregnant, soon as possible after leaving school, to a guy wi an okay job, he'll be a mechanic, or forestry or out at the hydro or something, cause, you ever noticed how she only goes wi guys that're working? . . . Manda checks their pockets to make sure there's no giro before anything else, wi them being so poor an that, an all she wants is a bought house up the Complex, no far from her Dad, a wee boy wi a skinhead an an earring, called Shane or something, an SKY TV. That'll be her happy. Ahm no slagging that, but she's getting so big-headed on other people, like, after we saw they two shagging in the grass there . . . she was going on and on, calling that lassie a dirty wee hoor an everything. Jesus, Manda can tell most boys fro the Mantrap in the dark, by shape of their cocks down to here in her throat.

Kay burst out with laughing as Fionnula pointed to far down her neck.

Ah mean she shouldn't be so judging other people just cause, cause what they were doing . . . is different fro her . . . Fionnula sort of drifted off, hovered her hand round an round her last tequila, playfully, So law eh? Know the Prenter family, the brothers an that; Manda used to go wi Jamie Prenter?

Heard about them, yes.

You'll be hearing plenty more if you're in the law an that. Most of the stuff they're doing now, they can't try them for up home so they send them down the high courts here. Prenter family aye make a big day out of it, try to time it in wi Christmas shopping an hiring a minibus to take the family down, fucking cousins an uncles, balloons on strings out the minibus window and all to the high courts. Ah tell you, they were unreal, Manda telt me she went on a big picnic wi them one time, an they had a box of live chickens tied top of the car an a big roll of astroturf, killed and cooked aw the chickens on a bonfire, all the old aunties watching on deckchairs on the astroturf, they set fire to half the mountainside an Jamie's brother got asphyxiated by the smoke so he ends up in an ambulance . . . they had to smash down the door of a holiday cottage to get at a phone to call nine, nine, nine.

No wonder Manda sticks to boys with jobs now.

Aye, family from hell right enough but ah tell you, Manda's dottery. One time just there, she sent off for more information, something in News of the Screws she'd seen, an she was bumming the loaf, it was a holiday to London an America all for one hundred and ninety pounds. Ah telt her it was a heap of shite so she goes says she'll prove it, brings the paper in, an know what it was?

What?

It's a hundred an ninety-nine pound, two nights in London to see the musical *Chicago*!

Kay yelled out an uncontrollable laugh.

Ah mean this was in English as well! Manda cannie read, the dopeydocus.

Interpretation.

She's so funny though, she's just crazy, Fionnula smiled, all softening now.

In what way?

Och just those little ways. She's ma oldest pal, Kay. Like other Saturday night when ah dropped round, Catriona her sister had trimmed her hair. The Old Man was in the bath an she'd promised to do the dishes so's ah washed them for her. She took the hair dryer through to the kitchen to do her hair an when ah was finished, cause there wasn't really time to dry the dishes, she used the hair dryer on them, on all the plates an pans an they were done in a jiffy! She just does these really funny things that make me smile an smile, och, those sort of things make ya almost fall in love wi someone. The little things.

Do you know Catriona?

Aye. She's great, Manda's big sister? Does ma hair, an well, all us hair. Fionnula frowned, Do you know her?

No. No, hardly at all.

Oh right. But you know, Manda's aye, 'Catriona this, Ma big sister that, Ma big sister does this, Ma big sister does that,' you know?

I've noticed that, Kay says, quiet, blowing out smoke. She's just insecure.

Aye, aye you're right, she is. But it doesn't half get on yur fuckin nerves. She thinks she can make herself appear less insecure wi all the boys but it's no true an like, tween me an you Kay, she doesn't sleep wi any o them, it's all handjobs round the back then she's going, 'I've been wi him an him an him an him,' but she just means they've ruined one of her tops.

Kay laughed and moved her eyes down to the ashtray:

You know what ah mean?

I know what you mean.

Like Iain Dickinson, y'know him got Moira Grierson pregnant, or more like Moira is SAYING got her pregnant

178

cause it's aye better if folk think it was a good-looking guy. Well you know ah went out wi him for a few month?

Kay nodded, but serious, without the New Year Dance look Fionnula per-usually got.

Well Manda hud always told me she'd been wi him. Turns out in third year she took off her shirt to show him her tits an he went all red an walked away. That was it, Iain swore!

I can believe it. All talk.

Fionnula nodded but slowly, as if she realised she'd gone a bit far and to the wrong person. She coughed an repositioned herself on the stool, looked at her cigarette's dwindling progress.

Where are they all?

In some club where there's music or that for Kylah.

Where is it?

Ah don't know, Grassmarket or Haymarket, some fuckin thing.

Grass? Hay? What's the difference? Kay shrugged, an both the girls flopped into the laughings again.

Could I mooch another cigarette?

God almighty Miss Clarke, yur dad's a doctor; bad for you! There's a machine over there.

On ya go am just joking ya.

I'll pay.

It's you's the dark horse round these parts, putting away the drinks twenty to the dozen an puffing away there!

Kay counted out three pound coins an slid them to Fionnula. Fionnula got up offof the stool, walked with the coins in one hand, the other hand by her side, cigarette jutting straight out her lipstick; a wee bit on the unsteady side there as she approached the machine that sat on the ground where the dark, mirrored wall led in on the eating area. The old couple looked up an Fionnula deliberately swung round, squinted, crouching a bit to show a long side of leg, whipped her hand up the mouth an flicked her cigarette back down there, rested on the thigh, at the horizontal, a cigarette held by two blue, nail-varnished fingers. She wobbled a once, took a coin between two fingers an put it in the slot. The coin fell to the stone floor an she waddled after, dropped, rose again an circled back to the machine. Again, as she fumbled, the clumsy coin between her longest-nailed thumb and curved forefinger, it seemed to refuse to enter, jumped to the floor but this time rolled, swung out wide across the floor of the restaurant. Fionnula stumbled after as the coin doublebacked on itself then vibrated to a halt under a chair. The chair horked an squeaked as she jerked the back of it an retrieved the coin. Again Fionnula approached the machine, her hand out in hope, aimed toward the slot area. As she came close she halted, squinted at the machine, took a few canny steps, thrust out to the slot and her hand seemed to slide to the side.

Helloo there!

Miss? Poor girl must have impaired sight.

Slowly, Fionnula revolved.

The old greyhead came uprising above the table, folding his napkin and dropping it on his seat.

Oh Christ, Fionnula murmured.

Miss, that's the reflection! The actual vending machine is behind you.

Oh. Thanks. Behind Fionnula, in an alcove was the actual cigarette machine, casting its reflection onto the blackish wall. She lunged toward it, hurried the coins in an punched the icon, muttering, Fuckfuckfuckfuck. Then she was tottered back up the corridor, round the corner of the bar.

When she got back to where Kay was, there were two large, bulbous, sweating gin and tonics on the bar.

Okay?

Aye, Fionnula began unpeeling the cigarette cellophane, looking a bit daunted at the gin. Kay was sip-sipping down at her own, sorta leaning over it an sip-sipping, or more sup-supping like as you would to a soup, an onion soup. *Or broth*, Fionnula thought an says, Ah mean ah know ah've been teasing at her an am no cliping about those things but . . .

We're all insecure Fionnula, even you.

Fionnula grinned down at the gin, No sure am geared up for this.

Just as well the others aren't here. Your image an that.

Look Kay, there's no need to be mean just cause youre getting pissed. We've been drinking all the way down then at Rest & Be Thankful we got these Yank tourists to fill up a litre bottle coke wi a half bottle Southern Comfort we all went parters on. Dead funny, we were smoking in the gents toilets an these ancient old ones were bursting outside, they had a cam corder an everything, an they went, filmed us, telling stories. The others made me tell the one about you an the thread that exam day an stuff.

Mysterious an slow-spoke, Kay goes, You do not believe this is the first bar I've been in today, do you?

Fionnula could only look at her.

Kay says, I'm only joking about your image. See, you're insecure as well.

Ah never says that ah wasn't insecure.

So you are?

Aren't you?

Course, but what have you got to be insecure about?

Just. The Perpetual.

Perpetual what?

Perpetual . . . everything. Ach what's 'insecure'? Eh? A word

181

out ah *Cosmopolitan*. It's just another word for 'scared'. Ahm scared Kay, just like you probably are, scared about what I am, where am going, what job, if ah ever get one, ahm going to do, wondering if it's possible to plan anything in a life anymore. Am ah ever going to get out the Port? Who will ah get married to, if ah ever do, she smirked an looked at Kay.

Despite all the folk looking up to you? You're most popular in the school.

It isn't *Heathers* Kay, an there's nae Christian Slaters in the Port for sure. The boys are mainly groats, and stupid ones. Girls don't look up to me an even if they did, that doesn't mean I can't have doubts about masel. Ma looks or whatever.

Kay pretend-spluttered her gin, You're gorgeous Fionnula! You're really, really pretty.

Fionnula fiddled with her cigarette, nipped a nod of her head an goes, You've got better knees than me, an smiled.

Kay did this amazing thing, where she put her head right back, let out a long noise, no a laugh, a sorta cross between a sound of pleasure and a saddest sigh, Well I regret it, but I look up to you.

She's beautiful, came bulging into Fionnula's head an she says, I don't know why.

You were fairly confident ordering about Ana-Bessie and I this morning.

But that's cause everyone was wanting back for the slow dances at the Mantrap.

Kay nodded an kind of smirked, let out a big sigh an sudden, goes, Excuse me, can you make a vodka with tomato juice?

In a sorta piss-taking jump, the barmaid was at them, Vodka AND tomato juice, you mean a Bloody Mary?

The two schoolgirls looked at each other an grinned.

Anything Mary is meant to suit us.

Ever see that band Diesel Mary and Her Air Brakes? Used to play out the Barn.

No, says Kay, with the finality that circumscribed years, till recently, when she never went out at all.

You guys are drinking a LOT. It wasn't a reprimand; it was even an encouragement, Now I don't make vodka and tomato juice, I make Bloody Mary which is totally different. She began gathering in various bits an pieces, two glasses, filled with three blocks ice each, The amazing thing about Bloody Mary is, it can be drunk at any time during the day, it's neither a night drink, like . . . a Manhattan, that can only be drunk at night, nor is it a lunchtime-only drink, like (she sprinkled pepper onto the ice then doused it in a quick twist of lemon juice, a single lemon seed adhered inside one glass so she fished it off with a teaspoon), well, extra dry Martini, Martini should really only be drunk at lunch. Usually, Bloody Mary is a morning drink, a good morning drink, so you're a little late.

We'll remember though.

Fionnula leaned over the bar, You, are the barmaid from heaven.

Why, thank you, holding both glasses in one hand she lifted them to the vodka bottles an twisted her head to them, Large ones? Yes. She dispensed the vodka, swung round and quickly sloshed in the Lea & Perrins, You'll hear folk say, 'Worcester' sauce . . . even Englishmen.

Typical, Fionnula nodded, sharp.

It's Worcestershire sauce, though, and unlike Scottish Blue-bell matches, which are made in Hampshire, it still is made in Worcester, a flavouring of tamarinds and anchovies, if the truth be known, I'm working quickly, because you don't want the ice to melt. Now this is the secret ingredient, she canted backwards to grab a black bottle, A touch of Tio Pepe to smooth out and enrichen the drink. I can tell you're ten-drop-girls when it comes to the tabasco and now (she violently shook the two bottles tomato juice, threw herself into popping the tops), whatever happens, even with the largest one, you should be unable to taste the vodka, only the condiments. No! Not the condoms.

Both girls laughed.

The condiments alone. She poured in the tomato juice, stirred with her own stirrer, popped in a cocktail stick to each glass, Now I'm sorry, what's your name?

Fionnula.

And yours?

Kay.

Right Fionnula, as she spoke, she sprinkled a rust background of pepper on stirred surfaces of the drinks then using the solitary pour hole on the end of the cellar they'd had for tequilas, she inscribed a white F and a white K in salt, I'm afraid, I'm going to have to ask you to drink these up before you resume work on those gin and tonics. Here, you won't get them mixed up.

Lo and behold, Fionnula stared.

Of course, how could we not! Kay lifted the K drink to her lips, touched aside the cocktail stick for ease of access, took a sip, Ahh· yum!

Fionnula fired down a good ration the spooker, looked at the older woman an goes, It's juss . . . art. Here let me pay for once Kay, Fionnula leaned down to get her backpack.

Did you study this or something?

No, no I studied law.

Kay turned with her mouth open to Fionnula as the barmaid walked away an then both burst out laughing, not knowing if the lassie had overheard Kay talking before or not.

Just then, two woman stumbled into the bar. Yup, they had

been drinking. How much are they? one of the women went, in an American accent, but they kept walking a bit, round corner of the bar an the barmaid stepped over to them. Conceivably the statement was a leftover fro an on-going conversation; but if so, curious, how the other woman never replied. Maybe they were referring to the Bloody Marys, but when the barmaid stood afore the Americans, they ordered other drinks, rapidly an with confidence of women in their forties who know what they want to lift towards their over-powdered faces. Neither (pronounced Neether) were those drinks at the lower end of the Bar Price List and their clothes an dress were, generally, by recently dead Italian fashion designers, so money didn't seem a concern that end of the bar. Maybe they were referring to Fionnula and Kay themselves? Maybe it was some kind of remark that here was Youth an Good Looks an Vitality, perched on two stools an the woman who spoke was making some kind of comment, using irony in fact, that unlike other things she could purchase, she really knew what Fionnula and Kay had, was beyond price. Would be convenient; but working against that, you've got the fact they never even peeked in Kay or Fionnula's direction again. Curious. It'll remain a mystery what the crypticism from that American woman ever meant.

It was close six pounds for the two drinks, so's Fionnula placed the last but one of her pound notes down, an weighed them wi an empty tequila glass. She leaned close to Kay, but cause of distance of the stools apart, an so's her face could be hid ahind Kay, away fro the women's view, Fionnula was so over, that when she talked, Kay could feel the breath on her bare leg then the hair slid over the shiny blueness of Fionnula's shirt and with a cracky hiss, slumped, in gremial intimacy, into Kay's lap.

Mmmmm. You smell so good. Look them old boots. Check the make-up; know what old age is, know what it is?

What? Is old age? Kay was smiling down at the head motioning round above her lap.

Fionnula's face came up, bitty flushed, Old age is blackheads gathering in yur wrinkles, she nodded, reached out an picked up the Bloody Mary, took a fair bolt of it an says, Ah really fancy a Shott's Vanilla Seltzer.

Kay was looked cross at the two.

Any opportunity we get in life, you should just GO for it. Grab ah it. Ah don't want end up like feeling old and no, no, she took another glug, Tasted everything.

I feel like I've tasted everything in this, fucking pub.

Now there. Do you know that's the first time ah think ah've heard you swear? It's good. It's good to hear you getting your lovely mouth round a good fucking bastard swearing word like good fucking Catholic girls are no meant to do.

Oh, now don't be letting it make your day too much. I have cursed before, Kay gave her a kind of dismissive look wrinklin up the skin that way, above nose.

Cursed is it. Cursed! I like that. Aye, like no juss different drinks. Fionnula put a hand on the padded shoulder of Kay's jacket then took it straight away.

That what you do? Just GO for it? says Kay wi pretty amazing contempt.

Yes.

You, really talk a load of nonsense a lot of the time.

Even though she had one burning in the ashtray, she seemed to ah forgot an lit another cigarette straight away.

That's yours. That's yours.

Where's yours? Oh.

Kay had a cigarette in her mouth. She smoked very slowly, very carefully as if scared of making a mess wi ash.

Ah'll smoke both. She started moving both cigarettes towards and away from her mouth in a kind of rotation but ended up sat, letting a droop of ash gather on one an devouring the other.

Kay sighed. Looked straight ahead an says it. After she had says it, she turned an looked right at Fionnula.

I went to bed with Iain Dickinson too.

Much quicker than you'd ah thought, Fionnula goes, When? But then that droop ash tumbled onto one of her fingers, bumped away an touched the bar. Fionnula looked down at it, glumly an animal-like; way a dog goes, ears forward when a hanky falls to the floor.

An that's what Kay thought, *Like in the George Orwell story we did for Standard, the hanging one where the guy steps aside from the puddle although on the way to a scaffold*, an Kay says, About nine weeks ago.

Fionnula crumpled up her forehead in a way Kay'd never seen, she looked straight at her, the black eyes, slight shine on the nose-end cause she hadn't been to the toilets.

Easter, goes Kay.

Fuck, goes Fionnula, quick, so's you could see squeezing of the cigarette, the one she was actively smoking.

Ah mean that was the first time. The last time. The only time. If that's what you're thinking.

But then Fionnula was in open confusion. Without reason she turned head fro side to side, ashtrayed the active cigarette an started on the longer, saw across to laughing American women who drank fro glasses wi a tall green bottle front them. She gave away all the weakness by saying, But, ah mean, how?

Pardon?

Well ah mean, why? Ah mean, ah never thought ya even knew him.

Ah don't, Kay was onto the gin that was left, her Bloody Mary was done.

Like where'd you meet him?

The Mantrap isn't the only pub in town. Just cause you and the Sopranos are always there. We met at the Barn.

The Barn? Right. Fionnula nod-nodded as if to convince herself. How did ya get out there, taxi?

No. I got a lift out, Kay looked bored.

Right.

Fionnula tried to appear more cool. He's a nice guy Iain, eh?

Laugh. Kay just laughed. He's just a guy.

Didn't work out then?

She laughed again, Not really no.

What happened?

Just a one-night thing. I didn't want to go out with him or anything.

Wow, look ah won't go tell. Manda an that.

It was a doubtful look Kay give.

Ah won't!

She shrugged an blew smoke right onto the ashtray so some the ash, a butt rolled a little. She reached out, took a long series of sips from the gin. Fionnula watched her.

Where'd it happen? Fionnula goes, in a voice, grave with morbidity already.

Ah! She gave this side smile out of her mouth.

Fionnula volunteered, Wi me: back of his brother's car out a party at Christiansands.

Kay wasn't interested.

An at his parents one aftrnoon, Fionnula droned on.

Funny you mention Manda. It was at her sister's flat.

What, Catriona's! She wrinkled up her nose, gave a wee shake of head in lostness.

What's it matter? Kay goes.

Ah just don't . . . ya met at the Barn an went back to Manda's big sister's? What about your folks?

They were away, they're always away. They're away till next Monday just now.

You spent the whole night!

Yeah, she reached back behind her neck and let out her hair, she moved her head fro side to side to side, brown hair; it going down and sliding cross back of pale jacket then she was bending to the backpack, putting her big hairclip deep down way in it.

Where was Catriona?

It is *her* flat, Kay's voice had went, down by Fionnula's feet.

An yous two, rolling offof the sofa. It was really question rather than visualisation.

Kay sat up straight on the stool, Wasn't really like that either, she grinned. We were drinking this vodka Catriona had in the house, mixed with tomato juice, we thought they were Bloody Marys but it was so yuggsy we had to gobble down pickled onions in between each gulp, an we were puffing out at one another, having this halitosis contest!

What?

Bad breath.

Oh right. Grant's voddy?

That's right. That was IT! I've been trying to remember but that was it. Grant's!

It's fatal an the cheapest. So just started snogging him drinking this stuff?

Yesssss. Catriona mmmm, too.

Catriona snogged him too!!! Both you snogged Iain in the same room?

189

Kay went about mooching, lining up and lighting another cigarette, says in first breath, In the same bed.

Eh? Fionnula goes.

We were all three in bed the whole night.

You were in bed with Manda's big sister and Iain?

Kay Clarke nodded an inhaled nicotine.

Fionnula looked at her, straight at her.

Right there, Kay says, You think am totally disgusting, don't you? You looked down on me for being quiet, now you look down on me as being tart, like Manda would.

Fionnula took a big breath, her hand went out to stay, shook a bit, Nut, nut, Kay, that's no it ahm juss, ahm just takin it in and. You don't know what am thinkin at all.

You don't think am totally disgusting? She bolted the rest of her gin.

Fionnula took a huge pause, a big breath, Manda would. Manda would but ah don't. Ah mean Jesus, this is amazing!

No it's not. You an your Sopranos will make it amazing but.

There was another long pause. Fionnula blew out air. You don't know what's raving through ma mind Kay. I promise ya now if you want I won't breathe a word.

What do you think of me?

Am all mixed up but, but it's a mix of . . .

Disgust . . .

Would you let me speak? It's no at all disgust it's a mix of amazement an. Christ. That's what am feeling. Ah first ah thought it was . . . at first ah thought it was. It's jealousness.

Jealous?

Fionnula nodded slow, looking at Kay. She suddenly goes, They didn't, kind of, they didn't cajole ya into it?

Kay smiled; not going to cry at all now, More like I coaxed them.

Fionnula swallowed, her heart was bammerin in her chest. Am burstin, comin wi me, we could, talk more in there?

No, I'll watch the bags.

Right, right, okay. You will stay there, aye?

Kay gave her the frowny look an kind of laughed, Yes.

Fionnula stepped quick to the toilets, swayed a good bit an biffed the door, she checked the mirror an saw the nose shine but she'd left make-up in her bag so's lifted a sleeve to it an her lips were jibberin, jibberin, Jesussussusus. Her hands were shaking as she hovered in the cubicle, then sudden, she paused, banged the door shut an slid the lock. When she'd finished she was somehow stood looked at herself in the mirror, adjusting her skirt tho she didn't remember leaving the cubicle. She touched her face a few times but was shakin her head, shakin it side to side. She put her hand between her breasts on the blue shirt to feel her heart goin then she breathed out an tried a half-hearted smile. The sleeve fell down on one arm but she walked back through, no even bother pull it up.

She saw Kay kinda hunched on the stool, you could see the lovely suedey roundness of her arse an the tight calves going straight down to dear-looking leather shoes.

Aye, Fionnula nodded, daft-like, as if they'd just met in a pub back in the Port. A bit drunkly awkward she got back on her stool.

Kay. Am no going tell anyone but, with ... with three of you there, was, sort ah, girl on girl stuff happenin too?

Course there was. Kay was smoking another.

Fionnula nodded, kept nodding way beyond reasonableness. Later she would realise it was so Kay wouldn't see her shivering on her stool as downwards Fionnula's stomach dived and simultaneous a jellyfish sting, right in her fanny, and up, in an awful wonder came its warm spreadingness. She noticed the ashtray had been emptied. *That was a good barmaid*, What's it like? she heard her voice go.

It's really good, Kay says in a way that sounded to Fionnula like she might be talking about a bowl of soup or a drink.

Fionnula says, almost angry, Ah've always wanted to try it.

Kay goes, Well Catriona is really ... she's got her belly button pierced ...

Fionnula spoke over her, Ah've really wanted *bad* to try it but, in the Port y'know, like if you got found, like even snogging, a girl. Fionnula had to stop but in case Kay started again, she went on, An that's why one of the things a feel is jealousness here cause, cause you're no aye getting folk hanging round ya, like Manda an that, you have a bit of space an got away wi that scot-free but someone would be sure an clipe on me. Even, mind that time when Kylah had to pretend she'd got off wi a guy so she wanted a hickie?

Kay made a puzzled face.

No remember? She fiddled wi another cigarette, It was so as to go an put off this groaty guy that was asking her out, she was goan say a big Hiya to him wi this huge hickie on her neck; so in the book cupboard of Cyclops's room ah volunteered an ah really gave her a big love bite, ah felt, ah was really turned on (she lowered her voice), wet an that, but Kylah juss laughed. It was a good love bite too! Ah mean ah was in Love wi Kylah for months after. It's been really lonely at times for me.

Wow. An me thinking you were the least lonely girl in the world.

It's just. Fionnula shook her head, Ah think ah like girls as much as boys. She paused a long time, Maybe more.

Try it then.

I'd like to.

But, I mean have you been feeling like that a while?

I've been feeling it for years now but it's so, so confusing. I got off wi this guy once in France just cause he looked like a girl. And now, to find you've tried it am, we all, I was thinking you were such a quiet wee soul, but it's like they say, quietest rivers run deep. Look, Kay, we didn't really get on and that before, but you've told me something important to you and I'm blathered, am completely mashed, we both are so look, before I saw you up on the street there I was down the bottom. There's a bar there, a place called Tarantula. Heard of it?

No.

It's, lesbian an gay place. And it was Catriona mentioned it to me an now ah see why.

Catriona isn't lesbian! Just that bit bi. Manda doesn't have a clue, Catriona won't tell her cause she knows Manda would freak out an she also knows what a bunch of gossips you all are. How was your bar then?

I was too scared to go in, ah was just shakin, feelin like a wee small town girl an it's weird, ah come up here an meet you an . . . like it was getting bad. Look. Don't start telling them, but sometimes ah would look at Kylah or Chell or Manda an I'd really want to start snogging them an there was this awful time, juss day before Orla was going to Lourdes an we were kissing each other bye just two of us and I really wanted to ram ma tongue down her throat an I couldn't believe ah wanted that, ah mean she was ma friend and she was so awful awful poorly, but sex was still on ma mind an it made me feel so sick at maself. You can't go on having sexual attraction for all your friends, it drives you mad an that's why, ah've always known, soon as I'm out of Our Lady's am away fro the Port an down here in a jiffy.

I'm not sure. I was really drunk that night and it just happened.

Would you do it again wi a girl?

Sure. Safer than boys. I would but I don't think I'm lesbian, I like boys too. Cocks. The way they always say, in stories that it'll be throbbing, but it isn't at all. From the stories you think it'll be like a wild hosepipe!

Fionnula laughed, Was that your first time? Iain?

No. Second, first was this great guy down in England, he was really good about it all an careful ... Iain an Catriona, were kind of mad.

Can we have more gin and tonic? Kay smiled at the passing barmaid, Do you want one?

I've no more money.

Two gin and tonics.

You've had an awful lot to drink.

Fionnula and Kay smiled at the barmaid.

It's a bit late now, went the barmaid, she began chopping a lemon, I guess you've both moved into Lunar Caustic.

Fionnula an Kay looked't other, gave a weirdness nose wrinkle each.

Cheers.

Thank you very much indeed.

Kay there dished out another Brodick Castle purple sheet though the change musta been fair mounting up in her matching jacket pocket too.

The barmaid put down more change and gin, she only served wi bottled tonic, never asking.

Kay turned an smiled strange at Fionnula.

Fionnula went, Kay, ah, oh.

Kay's fingers had sorta sprung out an Fionnula thought, *They could do some beige varnish,* but the glass went over, bounced an the g & t liquids fished out cross the bar surface, an the iceblocks slid on further cross the black wood while the glass bulb bounced without breaking an rolled in a semi-circle fore coming to a stop against the ashtray.

Fionnula hád been so staring at the glass, didn't see Kay's head kinda go down, an one leg start to slide offof the stool then, all-a-sudden she canted sideyways an Fionnula was goin, Whoa!, an she was up, throwing arms round Kay so the palm of one hand came directly against the breast but Kay slid on past her, even a slim seventeen-year-old is heavy on the way down to tequila heaven, so Kay sorta kneeled as she fell an swung away round so her back banged gainst the bar, loose coins crashing out of pockets an she was sat facing the door. Fionnula was kneeled with her, panic and nervous laughter in her voice as she goes, Are ya okay, ya alright? An the flood of spilled gin had come back, an inundation of it was spattering down fro the bar edging, going all dark on Kay's jacket, an Fionnula was doing little slaps on Kay's sort of tanned-seeming face but her black eyes were gone beneath closed lids.

Kay KAY!! Cmon, wake up!

The barmaid appeared an kneeled down by them.

Um, hi. Ah think she's kiddin on.

She's not kidding. Not after my Bloody Mary. Ambulance.

Oh no you cannie, ah mean we need to be up at the conference centre at seven.

She's not going anywhere, goes the barmaid, she was walked round the back, dialling up.

What's happened? went an American accent.

They had eighteen tequilas, a lot of gin and a lot of Bloody Mary.

Yeah? Hey invite us when you go out next time!

Then Fionnula was gathering both their bags with one hand, the other stroking Kay's forehead as she lay there, completely unconscious, a small smile on her lips.

It's a Marsupial Thing

In the Pill Box, Kylah was up the karaoke doin *Somebody To Love*. It was obvious she was going to tank it.

It's obvious she's goan to tank it, says Chell so all attention turned back to Chell again, Manda an Orla were on either side of her, but they'd gathered a weird retinue. A guy in an anorak called Danny, who had a plastic bag wi books in it; Kylah an Chell had brought him from the foyer of the Highland Club an he'd insisted on showing the girls where the Pill Box was. Then joining them.

The guy in the velcro suit, who'd been stuck upside down against the wall over by the trampoline most of the afternoon, had finally interpreted his previous snubs as excuse enough to sit down at the table with a pint. Then there was The Divorcee, who'd recently moved into Velcro Suit's flat. They were all paying attention, an would pay even closer attention when Chell put up a nail-varnished finger to touch the ring on her pierced eyebrow. Chell touched the ring on her pierced eyebrow an says, Here's another. This is another true story about the Port. We had these male strippers comin to the Mantrap which is just a brilliant nightclub. We go there every Saturday night that they'll let us in. But this was a really poxy bunch of strippers, like they were the third cousins of the Chippendales, a swear some of them were disabled an there

196

were only a couple of bonkable ones, so they're down to their G-strings and we're all going mental, all the women, y'know? An when the nicest whipped off his G-string, an threw it into the crowd, it came right over an hit my pal Fionnula, who was beside me; it hit her right in the eye, then she got knocked over, cause all these right old boots were fighting over it, aye? Like that game up in Orkneys or somewhere: all the men fight for that leather ball, pretending it's an Englishman's head, ha ha! Well all the old boots were fighting for the guy's G-string an one went off wi it. Couple ah days later Fionnula's eye is all swole, runny an weepy so she thinks its been damaged by the fuckin flying G-string. She goes to the doctor an it turns out on that eye, all her eyelashes an eyebrow is infested wi pubic lice.

Aww, yugser!

Doesn't that just, scum ya out!

Look that girl over there, look at her dancin, that's the weirdest dance ave seen for yonks.

Where?

Her over there by that pillar, Manda goes.

There was a girl by a pillar, she was standing straight but as *Somebody To Love*, wi Kylah on vocals, overwhelmed the sound system, the dancin girl was moving her left leg three times to the right, really close to the floor then she did this silly little turn an moved her other foot, the right one, cross the floor, turned an repeated, left foot, right foot.

Aww, it's like *Top of the Pops Two*, when you see them folk dancin in the nineteen seventies!

Look at her go!

Are yous blind or something? Look! went the Velcro Suit.

What?! She's a crap dancer.

She's not fucking dancin?

What's she doin?

Use yur eyes Christsake girl, she's dropped a glass. She's clearing up the broken glass with her feet.

As you looked closer you saw it was right enough, that's what she was doin, she wasn't dancin at all, just using her feet to clear the glass shards off the fringes of the dancefloor.

So this, this, this this, this-this-this-this.

Yes, Danny?

This, sch, sch, sch, sch, schooool, you-you go to. Is it an all gi-gi-gi-girls school?

Aye. It's a convent school Danny, wi nuns an all that.

Know what they call it, in the town? The Virgin Megastore?

And is it? goes The Divorcee.

We've had twenty-seven pregnant since last September.

How many pupils. Thirty? Velcro Suit goes.

There was one lassie pregnant before her confirmation!

Look, ah don't understand all yur pape Roman foolery, am a good Protestant who hasni been to church for twenty years, what age are you for confirmation?

She was thirteen.

Jesus.

It was the man fills all the pub cigarette machines right up the west coast that did it.

Dirty bastard.

Subsequently, the baby became a heavy smoker.

You aye say that, 'subsequently'.

What is a confirmation?

Ach, it's complicated. It's like, a religious MOT.

Christ, ah bet you lot just run riot in the school.

Oh dozens of stuff!

Mainly in Cyclops's eh? She's got a class of thirty or something, but only ten of them were in the class, eh? Swots like Kay Clarke an that eh, at their desk, an there were twenty

198

of us hiding in the big book cupboard all quiet an we were there the whole of the class, some others talked the stupid cow into believing we were all off sick.

That's nothing, what about time wi the fireworks?

Aye we'd all been separated, so we started setting off these bangers in class, smoke an everything, but she's such a deaf, ditsy cow, we told her it was the tops of the pens popping off she was hearing, an she believed us! You know the nuns, the sisters, they're all so dottery, it's like they're aw in the last century or somethin, an you can just run rings round them, wheedle them into anything an that just makes a us disrespect them all the more, like at least Mr Eldon's a bit sussed.

Mind bloody knickers.

Oh don't scum us out.

It was Cyclops's time of the month, an these floral dresses she wears! You could see right up.

Aye, all this blood showing on her knickers between her legs.

It's a notorious school. We have a Debs night, for when you're leavin eh, an the last one got a drug raid fro the police, lots of boys from St Columba's got done.

The karaoke was over and Davey the DJ was playing more fight-friendly sounds. A boy was walking towards them from somewhere on the far away side of the dancefloor, it was Orla he was headed towards but he was squinted at her weirdly, he bent over and goes, Would you like to dance? My . . .

Right, Orla interrupted him and was up straight away. They moved into the dancers.

Boy's dipping into our honey list, The Divorcee grinned.

Hoi, we're no one's honeys. How long ya been divorced then?

Come back to the flat wi us and I'll show ya! The two men laughed.

Kylah appeared.

Where's the prize then?

That was only the second round.

You've plenty admirers now.

Do you need somebody to love?

It was The Divorcee again. Kylah ignored him. She'd already talked to him and he listened to all the wrong bands.

Check out Orla. A guy asked her up, says Manda.

Kylah kneeled to talk in Manda's ear, How are you getting on wi them?

Christ Kylah, The Divorcee on the left thinks he's fucking Billy Connolly. What's the point paying fifty quid to sit in choochter hall wi the draught up yur skirt when you can hear all the Big Yin's routines from this wanker for nothing!!

What bout Velcro Suit?

He's so full of bullshit it's oozing out his shirt collar. They've asked us back to Theirs, want to come? Chell goes.

Think ah might just stay here an have it off wi the cigarette machine. The talent's fucking shite, eh? Sure those two're safe?

What, you mean AIDS an that? went Manda.

Naw naw, I just mean SAFE! You should maybe bring Danny too, he's sound, they wouldn't axe murder yous wi him about.

Aye, he's sweet, harmless, it's a shame. Tell you AIDS is the least of your worries wi those two dicks, more like Mad Cows Disease.

Somewhere near dancefloor centre, Orla leaned close to the side of the lad's face. I got something to confess, he says, I wear glasses.

You mean you don't know what ah look like?

I like your atmosphere. An your perfume.

200

Orla gave him a smile (all the Sopranos were wearing the same perfume from the same bottle). She goes, I can confess something too, I wear braces, on ma teeth, retainer braces. I'm meant to keep them in another six months.

I'll put on ma glasses then an you put in your braces.

It's a deal. They stopped dancing. Each removed the relevant containers, Orla fitted her braces as he put his glasses on. They started snogging.

Yur wee pal's goin for it, says The Divorcee.

They all looked over an Orla was in face-up snogs wi the guy who by then seemed have glasses on. They held the clinch for ages, even when they started moving back towards the table, even when they were right beside, an Orla put out a hand in a little flapping move, then even when she pointed up urgently at her mouth.

They're fucking stuck! goes Manda.

Chell started goin into the hysterics.

You shush, it's her braces, went Kylah. Is it your braces?

Orla and the guy with his mouth stuck to her thegether tried nod but that seemed a bit painful. Kylah stuck a finger in an the guy's tongue came free.

Wow! went Orla.

Its ma stud, went the speccy guy, he put his tongue out and there was a silver stud in the middle towards the tip.

Got stuck to ma braces.

Velcro Suit an The Divorcee were laughing, Kylah scowled an turned to Orla an the guy, Have you two been properly introduced.

Ah don't know if that's really necessary now.

Well ah don't know your name but this is Orla.

Hiya. I'm Stephen.

This is my best pals, Kylah . . . she's in a band.

Hiya. You are a great singer.

No really it's just a great song.

That's Chell an that's Manda. Our pal Fionnula's no here yet. If she's comin.

The guy says to Kylah, Have you heard of Holger Czukay?

Is he related to Keyser Soze? says Kylah.

I'm up on all the pop trivia, says the guy with the stud in his tongue.

Are you?

Yes. Do you know who the lead singer of Echo and the Bunnymen is?

Let me guess, is he called Echo?

Good guess but no, anyway when they played Glastonbury it was so muddy he had two roadies to hold up a binliner on each of his legs so they wouldn't get covered in mud.

That's what being rich and famous is all about, having someone else hold up your binliners on each leg when you're wandering across a sea of shite.

Do you know what Sammy Davis Junior said being black and famous in America meant?

No.

He said being black and famous in America meant he could be refused entry to exclusive clubs and restaurants that other people could only ever dream of going to. Do you know Michael Stipe likes to send his remote control toy cars onto the stage while his support band are playing to freak them out?

Who's Michael Stipe?

You're not really a pop trivia person, are you, Kylah?

No I'm not, Stephen.

Excuse me, I have to make a phone call. He removed a mobile phone from inside his jacket pocket and quickly dialled a number. He listened for a period of time, blocking his other ear to keep the noise of Davey's Disco out. It was, *Somebody's Gonna get Their Head Kicked In Tonight* by the Rezillos that was on. Davey had introduced the song describing it as, That old favourite.

Everything okay there, he smiled, switched off the phone then returned it inside his jacket.

Orla and Kylah looked at him.

The speccy guy, Stephen, says, I'm looking after the flat for, The Man. The Man, he likes his budgie, you know, budgerigar, the little bird, he's very very keen on it ah mean let me stress VERY very keen on it, very attached to his budgie. You know you can get these baby listening devices, kind of a microphone, to hear what's going on in the next room, well you can actually phone it up on the mobile and listen in, make sure everything's okay.

Does it speak, the budgie?

No, no it doesn't speak, but you can understand when it's distressed, you can hear it banging about in its cage, and you don't want it to get distressed, not The Man's budgie. I mean they're lovely things, the wee budgies, but they have their practical uses too. Take for instance, when you're skinning up, skinning up with someone's business card, I find those Scotland Against Drugs business cards excellent roach material, so say you're skinning up, something great just comin on the telly, like an Open University programme on geomorphology, or a programme for the deaf, or the headlines in the Gaelic language, so me and The Man are skinning up, and you drop the last wee chunk of blow, drop it on that fucking brown carpet. Funny isn't it, how it's always a browny carpet . . . that's you, you would think, crawling round on the carpet, nose to the pile, only finding old toe-nail clippings, no more dope! Up the river in a canoe wi no paddle, rapidly approaching a waterfall, but oh no! All The Man does, is, he sets down his wee yellow budgie on the floor, it does scavenging across the carpet and in seconds, the little bird's found the wee lump of dope. Obviously the common budgerigar has no taste for cannabis resin, so he always spits it out, and bob's your uncle, if you'll forgive the pun if you noticed it, your cannabis is retrieved by the budgie. That's not all! When The Man's lady comes over, it's a touching sight to see The Man place the little budgie on his Lady's shoulder where, with real delicacy, the budgie undoes the back of her earrings allowing her to remove them. Always delights The Man that!

Has the budgie never swallowed any dope?

Eh, the one before this one did.

What happened?

Eh, The Man, got a pair of nail scissors, cut the budgie open an performed an autopsy on it. Was surprisingly easy to locate the digestive tract and the dope was recovered. We were assisted by an Open University programme on taxidermy we's seen the night before.

So do you share the flat wi The Man?

Oh no no no no, I just look after the flat when he's away. He's away on business a lot. Do you want to come up the flat? he smiled at Orla, It's just round the corner, and I really think I should change the budgie's cuttlefish.

Orla kind of turned to Kylah, whispers, Come back wi us, wi that pierced tongue oh his he must be into all kinky stuff.

Orla, he's a bit weird.

Cmon, Chell n Manda'll never let me go on ma own, a mean look at the time, it's no as if it can take long.

Okay then, but listen, don't mention the scissors an the budgie thing to Chell.

Right then.

Kylah leaned over, Ahm popping back up wi Orla to his flat, juss keep an eye on him? Where are we goan meet to get changed back?

Well look at the time, doesn't look as if Fionnula's comin.

Why no go back to McDonald's, ah could go another burger an the mirror's good there, cause we'll need to tone down the make-up a bit?

An get nail varnish off too.

Aye. We're going back to their place for coupla quick drinks. If yous want to leave your uniforms give them us, their place is just above here. Danny'll you help us carry their uniforms? We've got them all in bags here an are going to change later cause we've got this shopping as well.

I'll help you carry them, Danny smiled.

Aw right then, Hi Orla, you can leave your uniform wi Manda, they'll look after them.

Orla nodded an kneeled, took out her purse, also took out her rosary beads an transferred them into the purse.

Well, see you later, alligators.

Aye, see yous, come on, drink up an off to our house of fun, goes The Divorcee.

For some reason, Manda, completely mashed, was leaned across to Chell, going, If you're going on holiday what ya should do is buy a *Cosmopolitan*, that's what ma sister does, cause you get all these free shampoos an moisturisers an perfumes all in one go for nothing that you'll need on holiday.

Then everyone was standing up, an draining last drinks and moving towards the door where the light was at a filtered angle by then, wi edgings of gold and it slashed eastly across the Capital. They began walking up the pavement, all of them dazed by sudden brightnesses and movement of traffic.

Chell goes, Am a bit famished again, ah really fancy a crisp sandwich, smokey bacon in a morning roll.

Everything you need in our palace, goes The Divorcee who was walking up the pavement ahead of them, his keys anxiously out already.

Well, ya got smokey bacon crisps an a morning roll?

Nut.

All right there, Danny? Chell called back.

Gr gr gr rg rg rg . . .

Good, good.

Are those car keys?

Aye.

Oh, hey Manda, he can give us a lift to the exhibition centre. He's goat ah car. That went to you after the divorce did it?

Here, don't get him started, shouted Velcro Suit.

Do you want to see a picture of ma wife?

Your ex-wife? Aye.

The Divorcee started rummaging in his wallet.

Did some folk get killed there in a car crash, goes Manda.

Eh? went Velcro Suit.

Against that monument thing, did some folk get killed in a car crash cause there's all flowers round it?

They're wreaths! That's the fucking war memorial, ya dummy!

Here you go, The Divorcee handed Chell a photo.

Aww, is that you on your wedding day?

Aye.

That's you in your kilt eh, y'know ah used to think a sporran was just for holding down men's erections. Your wife was gorgeous.

Aye. She was that.

What was her name?

206

Ailish.

Look Manda, his ex-wife was really really pretty. How come yous split?

It was a sort of incompatibility of personalities.

Velcro Suit went, Aye, she hated your fuckin guts and you hated hers, cmon man, get wi the programme here.

This is the gaff, The Divorcee put the key in the street door an they walked up to the first floor, their feet echoing high in the stairwell, Danny's plastic bags rustlin away behind them.

Where'd ya meet that guy? Velcro Suit nodded back.

Some place down the road.

Strikes me as bit weird.

You strike me as a bit weird.

Chell was going, So when did you marry, how long were you together?

Five years, went The Divorcee, shoving the key into the lock.

There was a door mat outside the door on the landing wi PISS OFF written on it.

The five of them trooped into the hall an The Divorcee led them through to a front room where there was a big telly an a long couch. The walls were painted different pastel colours.

Sit yourselves down. Chell, what would you like to drink?

Do you have Peach Snaps?

No, I don't think so.

What do you have?

McEwan's lager.

Oh.

Aye. Two crates in the fridge. Tell you what. I'll bring one crate through, all right, Danny son?

Aye, aye great thanks.

Velcro Suit went banging through to the kitchen.

Chell and Manda slumped down on the couch, Danny was on an armchair. Manda remote-controlled on the telly an it was an American chat show.

The Divorcee says, The telly an the couch are mine, came out the house after the divorce. He's selling up this place y'know, he nodded to the windows, so I'll be looking for to buy a place. Take the furniture with me an get a wee place, yknow, this one, he had nae furniture till I moved in, only a mattress. He nodded, solemnly then stepped out, I'll gie him a hand.

Christ, these two are as much fun as a day in the morgue, Chell whispered.

What one do you want? goes Manda.

Ah don't really care, says Chell, The Divorcee's the nicest guy but you get the impression Velcro Suit might be the better snog, he's got a good body for such an ancient bastard. They both looked over to Danny. Looked at each other an burst out laughing.

Danny we think you might be our man yet! Manda screamed out laughing.

Danny smiled an shrugged, he hadn't taken off his anorak.

Velcro Suit, rammed in the door wi a crate of beer cans an plonked it down on the table.

Danny reached out, eased a can free fro the tight pack, cracked the top an began sucking on it.

Make yourselves at home, like Danny's doin, am just going to, Velcro Suit put on a fake low voice, Change into something more comfortable. He walked out an turned left down the corridor.

The Divorcee balanced on the edge of a armchair close to Chell. Chell sighed an goes, Ya can sit beside me here if ya want to.

Montell Williams on the American chat show slipped a microphone under a guest's nose and says, So you're in a street gang an you wanna get out of it?

Chell and Manda sighed simultaneously.

Hey! I've a video from ma wedding here, want to see it? It's hilarious, well Danny there might no like it, The Divorcee lunged forward and took out a video fro under the big telly. As he freed it fro the case, you noticed it had SPEECH IMPEDIMENTS, wrote on the side of the identifying label, which is kinda unusual when you think about it.

The Divorcee manually changed the channel an inserted the video. It began with the best man's speech, though sometimes the video image would swing round to show The Divorcee in Highland Dress wi his ex-wife in her white wedding dress. The Divorcee started laughing, sat wi his legs crossed, rocking back an forth on the floor.

Chell and Manda went goggle-eyed at each other.

You soon heard that the best man had a speech impediment, and it was this The Divorcee was rollicking in the hysterics at in front the telly, suddenly, The Divorcee burst into tears, put his hand across his eye, made a dash for the door, hit the wall so the light went out, then raced up the corridor where they heard a door slam. Chell an Manda looked at each other, tried no to laugh, jamp up an walked after him.

He was locked in the toilet an the girls could hear him sobbing.

Are you okay? Chell called. Only weeps an greets came in reply.

What is it? Velcro Suit's voice called from the other end of the long corridor. His bedroom door was ever-so-slightly open.

So The Divorcee wouldn't hear, Chell clopped down the length of the corridor, stopped outside the bedroom door an says, He's crying an he's locked himself in the toilet. Manda had followed.

Didn't think that would take long, came the voice on the other side of the door. There was a silence and they could hear laughter an the best man's voice coming from the living room.

Come on in here girls, called Velcro Suit, but his voice sounded different.

Chell pushed open the door into what musta been the largest of the rooms wi a huge double bed with a metal bed head. Close to middle of the floor, near a stereo system, was Velcro Suit, doing a perfect handstand. He was completely naked, his cock was erect and he seemed to have shaved under his oxters an painted them blue, some sorta ink was running up the vibrating muscles of his arms. His eyes looked all white in his flushed face an his mouth goes, Forget him girls, he'll be in there for hours, have a bit of fun, six bare legs in a bed, the perfect cure for the common cold.

Ah don't have a cold, goes Manda.

Must admit, that's some joint yuv goat on ya, what's that stuff? smiled Chell.

It's the ink from squids, sepia, rub it in to a man's shaved oxters an he keep his hard-on for hours. Cmoan, yon cunt'll be in there hours. Thinks am selling the house! Am only putting it up for sale till the miserable bastard moves out, whoaaaa!

Velcro Suit started to fall. There was a mountain bike leaned gainst the wall next him an, though he started to curl his legs, his right foot didn't clear the bike an hit near the chain. The pedal swirled round an round, an came to a stop. Velcro Suit stood up an gazed down at his foot as a slow-swelling circle of blood appeared on the black floorboards.

Aaagh, went Velcro Suit an lifted his foot a little, no drops, but a steady little stem of blood was speeding fro the end of his big toe. Chell stepped nearer an you could see the flap on front the big toe was just hanging off.

Oh Jesus, you okay?

Towel. Get us, och that crazy bastard's in the bog, chuck us a fucking shirt or something!

Manda, who juss had her hands up at her mouth turned an began to pick some shirts up from the floor an pass them to Chell. Velcro Suit was sat on the end of the bed by then. Chell passed a white shirt an he wrapped it round his foot. Both Chell an Manda noticed his cock hud gone soft so yon squid shite wasn't all it was cut out to be.

You'd better get up the hospital.

Aye, aye.

We'll phone an ambulance.

Nah nah fuck that juss phone us a taxi . . . ach ah'll do it.

The girls followed as he walked up the corridor, one foot shrouded in blood-stained shirt that he swung forward only walking on the heel of it. As they passed, Danny was still in the front room wi all the shopping an schoolbags round him, drinking beers an watching the wedding video where members seemed to be dancing by then. Velcro Suit seemed to pass and Danny stared at his nudeness but without any expression. Velcro Suit stopped, the girls reversed as he took a few steps back, scowled at Danny an slammed the door to the living-room tight.

When he picked up the phone there was blood on his fingers. As he phoned a taxi, Chell knocked on the toilet door, You okay in there?

There was a pause. The flush went.

Yur pal's had an accident, he's cut off most of his toe.

I want Ailish.

Oh dear.

She's beautiful.

Get out here an shag these lassies, *they're* BEAUTIFUL wi pierced eyebrows an belly buttons an Christ knows what else an they're here in our house now! Ya daft cunt, an am stood here wi the blood pishing out one end of me.

Just you worry about yur self an watch yur mouth, hop-a-long.

Aye, away an get yur trousers on.

Chell turned back to the bathroom door and goes, Look, you're goan have to get over this, ah don't mean now, but sometime real soon an yur mate really has cut hisself bad.

Wi me an Ailish, it's a marsupial thing, y'know?

Eh?

He called from behind the door, Like animals that've pouches. Ah really need the security. I need to be in her pouch.

In her what? Manda scrunched up her forehead.

Chell whispered, Ah think he says pouch.

Weirdo.

Shush.

Come on out. We'll all go back down the pub an have another drink.

The door buzzer went.

Get the door! Velcro Suit called.

Manda picked up the intercom phone, Aye? Eh, aye we phoned a taxi, don't know his name but you'll recognise him, his toe's got cut off an he's bleedin to death. Eh? Aye he's making a bit of a mess. Aye ah'll tell him. Manda hung up the intercom an yelled down the corridor, He says to take some old sheets an towels or that so's you don't mess in his taxi.

Fuckin dosser, Velcro Suit appeared at the far end of the corridor, his right foot sockless in a white Reebok wi blood oozing out of its leaky joints, I'll do a shite on his fucking taxi

212

floor. He limped along the corridor toward them, Which one of yous is coming up the hospital with me?

Eh, nah, we've got to meet friends.

What! You're letting me go up to the hospital alone?

We'll wait here for you.

Oh come on, ahm bleedin!

We'll wait here for you.

That'll be right, Velcro Suit opened the door an swung his leg out, slammed the door ahind him. Chell noticed there were blood footprints right up the corridor.

Are you okay in there?

I'll never forgive maself.

It could be worse. Does he have kids?

I don't know.

Manda coughed.

Do you have kids?

There was no reply.

Don't think he's killed hissef do ya?

What? Drowned hissef down the lavvy pan? went Chell, an Manda smiled, cause it was good to hear her talk frivolous about drowning what with her Actual Daddy gone over that horizon where all the old moons are cluttered up like Buzz's scrapyard, an her Daddy Patrick gone too, gone and drowned: his never-found bones all broke apart an scattered places down in Davy Jones's locker, nestled cross the rust-coloured rocks, jammed in among the slimy, thick-waving strips of fucus.

Manda wandered through the kitchen door that was next them and opened the fridge; it was empty part fro another crate of the McEwan's beer, an a mayonnaise jar so old the contents were yellow.

Chell laughed, That was just classic, starkers wi his beastie sticking out an his couping over.

Silly arsehole, Manda let out a harsh laugh. Look the state of this place, she yanked the tap closed cause a small drip was going into the sink that was stacked wi dirty dishes.

Tell ya, goes Chell, 'Ll be glad to get back the Port away fro these townie nutters. Least you can get a decent snog, or something more anytime, offof someone ya reasonably know so he's no gonna knife ya or anything. Wonder if there'll be sailors off the submarine in the 'Trap the night?

Manda whispered, Let's get shot of this place, over McDonald's an change, wait for Orla an Kylah turn up.

Aye, okay ah wish he'd get out of there though, am burstin to piss.

Hi, Chell's needing in to go to toilet.

I'm not coming out till Ailish comes home.

Christ.

Tell you am goan pee ma pants.

Do a Fionnula an go in the sink!

Chell whispered, All the dishes!

Well we're no goan do them are we? Minks anyway, the dishes should be done.

Any kitchen towel?

In this place! I'll get one of his shirts.

Nah, nah ways, might have octopus blood on it or something, ah've wee bit tissue here, shut the door, an lean gainst it. Chell undid and stepped out her skirt all the way, moving the buttoned waistband through the knee-length boots an putting the skirt neatly over back of a chair then she pulled down her knickers, she looked up at Manda an says, Sure you've got yur weight on that, ah don't want yon Danny burstin in?

On ya go, says Manda, looking.

Chell put both hands flat behind her on edge of the draining

214

board an shoved herself up on the sink, bent forward an pissed, she looked in, under the hair of her, an goes, Splashing but it's going in a soup bowl on the top there, hee. She kicked her legs a wee bit so the heel of her knee-length boots banged on the under-the-sink-cupboard door. Then she'd finished an she hopped down, dapping wi the tissue an dropped it onto the top dishes.

You weren't wearing that wi your uniform too, were you? Manda nodded at the leopard-print tanga Chell was pulling up.

Nah, the bra's matching too. She tugged up her leopard-skin top to show the matching bra, It would show through a school shirt like yours.

That'd be quite sexy though.

Ah guess, Chell shrugged, pulled on an up her skirt. The front door banged an Chell jumped, hurriedly pulled the skirt rest of the way. Manda leaned forward from the staring at Chell an pulled the kitchen door open. No one was there. Manda knocked on the bathroom door.

What? went The Divorcee's voice.

Manda an Chell wandered down to the living-room an pushed open the door. Danny was gone. Their bags holding the uniforms were in a jumbled order.

Fucking bastard's robbed your purses, ah've mine here, she tapped the pocket in her shirt an leaped forward lifting up on a bag, then she saw the note on the table and flew over to the window which, wi the warm day, was a few inches open, Fuck, he didn't take ma Docs!

What?

Manda banged the window up an the old weights rattled, she stuck her head out and there, up the side street walked Danny. Chell stuck her head out too, Fuck FAAACK!! You bastard!

Hey, hey stop that guy, he's a thief!

A few folk looked up an walked on.

Danny, who had Chell's other knickers on his head, tugged them off an looked back before trotting onwards, a school tie, bearing the colours of Our Lady Of Perpetual Succour School for Girls, trailing out of his plastic bag.

We'll never catch him.

Chell kneeled and scrabbled about in her bag . . . He's left shoes and socks, an ma fuckin blazer but he's taken all our uniforms!

What the fuck're we goan to do?

Chell was leafing through her purse, He's no taken any money, just clothes the fucking perve, she looked up at Manda as if she was goan greet.

Manda looked down at the note:

HOW ABOUT SOME LESBO STACK ACTION
THEN WEE PIERCED WHORES? I DIDN'T KNOW
CHILDISH TITTERS WERE INCLUDED IN YOUR
SERVICES I'LL TAKE YOUR LITTLE SCOOL UNI-
FORMS AND THINK OF ME WANK INTO THEM
EVRY NIGHT

Chell started crying, Orla n Kylah are goan kill us.

Hey now, Chelly Chelly, she kneeled an gave Chell a big squeeze, Cmon, let's get out of here.

You Are Now Entering a
Drug Friendly Zone

The nurse came out, looked both ways an nodded at Fionnula who jamp up, Is she okay?

You can come through now.

Is she all right?

Doctor's seeing her now.

I thought you might have to pump her out.

No, she's been sick.

Ah thought she was gonna die.

The Accident & Emergency was just up the corridor, the nurse walked past a series of booth-things wi pulled curtains; a man was moaning ahind one. The nurse moved aside a curtain an Kay was lay out on a thin bed wi wheels, her arms encircling a grey basin that had a lot of yellow sickness in; her shoes were off an you could see her small toes that Fionnula couldn't ever remember seeing in PE or swimming an all. There was a real youngish doctor standing above her an Kay mumbled, Can't I persuade you then?

The doctor turned an looked at Fionnula, he laughed and he says, I'm already married, Kay.

Kay moved an flung out a spurt of sick in the basin that glugged, showing how deep it was. At the same time she spewed, a fart came from her arse. Kay looked up at Fionnula, there were tears in her eyes an the little mascara she'd on had run, she says, He won't marry me, ah can see why not at the moment but everyone deserves a second chance!

Fionnula was about to smile at the Doctor when Kay shouted, You're a fucking prick like all the rest! A slaver of spit came dangling.

Kay! goes Fionnula an she stepped forward.

The doctor took a step towards Fionnula an smiled, She just needs to go home and sleep it off.

Right. Am sorry.

Fucking ball-less, hi HI what university did you go to? Did you have a dead man's dangling cock hanging out your trouser leg on the bus, you dirty man, you dirty DIRTY doctor, I'll tell your wife on you! Kay yelled.

Well she should sleep, he scribbled something on a form. How much did she have to drink?

Ah don't know, she says she was drinking earlier, twelve tequilas four . . . six gins . . . Four Bloody Marys. Fionnula looked at the doctor and says, There were no drugs or anything like that, ahm sure of that. Ah told the nurses when we come in on the ambulance.

The doctor looked at his watch, You're too young for that sort of kind of drinking, are you not?

Is it okay if she leaves now? We kinda huff to be somewhere.

I don't think you've any choice. The sister wants you to be out of here in ten minutes, obviously there's a bit cleaning up needed.

Kay yelled, Sister who! Sister Fagan I'd bet. She laughed, some private thing, muttered something they couldn't hear. Do you have any? On no! She shouted an put her face in her hands as if she suddenly remembered something.

Mmmm, went the doctor and he moved out, beyond the curtain. The man in the next cubicle moaned and Fionnula heard the swish of the nurse's uniform.

Kay looked at Fionnula.

You okay?

There was sick all down one of the lapels on Kay's jacket, Fionnula stepped to the little sink an says, They asked for your name an address, so look, ah gave our address, ma dad an mum's cause like, ah thought you might be out all night or something but also, ah thought, they might try and phone your folks and you'd be dead offof them.

Smart thinking Watson, Kay nodded and she burped.

The basin swayed an swilled a bit so Fionnula took it off her, squeezing up her cheeks at the smell an look of it, she bent an slid it in under the bed.

I told you they were away, Kay nodded.

I didn't think you'd remember a thing about what either of us says, went Fionnula. She tried to roll up her shirt sleeves, facing the wall an dookin a wad some folded bluey paper towel from the dispenser under the sort of pipe tap. There was a hoiking sound, a sharp crack ahind her an something touched the back of her left calf as she turned, Kay had hoiked up the most amazing amount of spew down off the bed onto the floor, AWWW KAY, Fucksake! She backed into the corner. Kay moaned, spat an tried to lay back but more came up. Fionnula shoved over an sat where the pillow shoulda been an put an arm round Kay to try hold the hair away from her mouth. You no got an elastic band to put your hair back? Kay didn't reply, just gasped breath. Some of the ends of her hair were wetted darker than the brown wi vomit. Fionnula reached round Kay's shoulders, grabbed the ends an pulled the hair back, bunching it thegether in a single fist at the back of her jacket collar.

The curtain whipped aside an an older nurse was there, Can you be quiet and move out here now please. There are seriously ill people in this ward.

Fionnula looked up, This lassie's no feeling too hot either.

This girl is drunk. There is a man having a heart attack over there.

Fionnula scowled dangerously, She was brought here in an ambulance unconscious an we're juss going. Her dad's a dead famous doctor ya know.

She's been sick, she had too much to drink. This is a hospital, not a bar.

Well can you call us a taxi? We're no from this place, ah mean I don't have a clue whereabouts I am.

There's a phone in reception though I doubt a taxi will be wanting to take anyone in that condition.

Look here you fuckin old boot, you're a nurse, no a fuckin policewoman, fucking right this hole is a hospital an this lassie's ill, an we're leaving in a minute so quit terrorising her ya fucking ugly fat bastard, go on, get out our fucking sight ya, look that fuckin crucifix round yur neck, a fucking *Jesuit*, Kay eh, shoulda known, goan, fuck off FUCK OFF. Fionnula threw the wet towel at her but cause of her hunchedness over Kay, there was no aim an the paper touched the nurse's shoulder an fell to the floor.

I'll get security.

Get the fuckin queen see if ah care, ya fuckin bitch.

Kay spat on the floor an went, Fuck off a minute will you, an let me get on to feet.

The nurse was gone, Kay laughed an says, They really are overworked, we shouldn't be shouting at them.

Ah fuck them, it's no fucking BUPA, ma old man pays his taxes every month.

Where's ma shoes? What's the time?

It's fucking twenty past six.

Oh Christ, I can't sing like this.

Yes ya can, we can make it, ah don't have a clue where the fuck we are, the ambulance went for fuckin miles, we're on the fuckin outskirts, but you seemed to have enough money, we'll phone a taxi. Ahm meant be in rehearsal at seven so ah've gotta go change, take off ma nail varnish, we can tidy you up a bit, here, Fionnula kneeled near the spewed-on lino an started putting Kay's leather shoes on for her. Kay sat on the edge of the bed wi her face in her hands. Sometimes she chuckled then went sudden quiet.

Fionnula took her hand and helped her onto the floor.

Okay?

So so.

Take your time. I'll just get the bags, Fionnula cooried, reached out an took the fallen wad of damp towels, used it to scrape the spew offof the back of her leg an the raised heel on her old platform shoes. She dropped the tissue on the floor an picked up both schoolbags, shouldered them on her left an linked wi Kay using her right arm.

Like she's a hundred year old, thought Fionnula as they walked up the ward's length, an says, Ah'll phone a taxi. A younger nurse turned round and looked at them, she looked a second too long an Fionnula goes, Are you seeing enough?

Pardon?

Ah says are you SEEing enough? Then they had to turn to the left, Poor Orla, eh?

What?

Having to had been in these places, she pushed open the door an they were back in the waiting area where Fionnula'd been for ages. Just as they moved through, a guy was getting trundled past in a wheelchair, there was something up wi his foot, all blood guntering over the top of his white trainer on one foot.

Ooops, wonder what happened to him? Fionnula whispered.

I think I'm going to sick up again.

There's the toilets, I need to phone. Here, you best get in uniform, she handed over the bag.

You got change?

Aye.

By the phone, Fionnula put her bag down between her feet while she waited for a woman to get off. Three orderlies were over at the door, one goes to Fionnula, Were your two frae that party over Burdiehoose.

Eh? goes Fionnula.

You an yur pal, were yous at that party?

Nut, goes Fionnula.

Yon classic wi the toe off was he from the party as well?

Nah, goes the wee one.

What's this? goes the fat one.

There's a party down there, we've had a steady stream ah casualties aww day; boys caught in their zips, lassies hurt fightin, suspected overdoses; the lassies were saying they kept cawing the ambulances fae a box cross the road that they'd had Telecom come in an fix special, for convenience of folk cawing taxis an that, but in between . . . incidents, they'd gone out to caw again an the fuckin phone'd been vandalised. It sounds a fuckin riot down there, the orderly took out a wee sheaf paper, Look, ah made sure ah goat the address, um goan get some of the ward nurses an go straight down after the shift!

Can ah ask you something?

You can ask me anything.

Fionnula smiled, Where are we? Ah need call ah taxi.

Little France General Hospital, they'll no take ya tho,

222

specially after the toe job there, you'd be better goan down the bus-stop.

What do you mean?

Aww the taxi drivers are the fuckin sisters' old men, it's the sisters organise aww the taxis out here.

Aye, noone here gets out alive, he laughed.

Fionnula didn't know what they were joked about an she dialled the big yellow taxi number above the phone.

Yes.

I'd like a taxi please at Little France General.

Yes. What department are you in?

Accident and Emergency.

Oh. Name?

McConnel.

Ah have McConnel down here as drunk and disorderly, two females.

What the fuckdye mean?

Hitherewhydoantyawatchyerlanguage.

Eh? Yous are a public service, how come you've lists of details like that, are you the secret service or something?

So you are drunk an disorderly?

No we're not, an we need to be at the exhibition centre at seven. Ma friend had a violent reaction to food.

So what yur saying is, yur friend could be sick at anytime, an in a taxi it can take us an hour an a half to clean it out an get it back on the road again. A taxi can make a hunner pound in an hour.

Ah bet that's the fare into town too! Ah mean this is bang outta order, this is unreal, are you saying yous as ah taxi company choose yur customers!

Aye. We've just taken a fare over to Casualty at Little France, toe cut off, pishing hooring blood all over an if that's no bad enough, the dirty cunt gets down an does a shite on the taxi floor; an you're telling me ah cannie choose ma customers.

Well fuck you! Fionnula slammed the phone down an muttered, Townie cunt. Hey, she called over to the orderlies, Can ah've a wee shot a pen?

Fancy goan a party later? the guy wi the address in his pocket flicked up a pen.

Eh, ah cannie no, sorry.

She phoned directory enquiries, wrote down two other taxi company numbers an phoned the first one, Hi ah need a taxi urgent down to exhibition centre.

All right, where are you?

Little France General, Accident an Emergency.

It's no you that did the shite in the taxi is it?

Oh Christalmighty! Fionnula put the phone down an walked away.

Hoi can I have ma pen back?

Kay was both hands on a sink, throwing up into it. Spew clods had blocked the plug so's each fresh a-boaking fell an splashed liquids onto her blousey thing an jacket.

What an image of Love, thought Fionnula, an says, Okay, we'll have to take the bus.

I'd do anything for a toothbrush.

That might be a bit premature. Cmon, you've got to get changed. Condom'll kill us if we're caught in this. Your stuff in there? Go get changed; don't lock the door. Ah don't want you crashing out in there, no battering doors down.

Fionnula stepped into the cubicle next Kay; she didn't shut door proper an it kept swinging inwards an she bopped it closeer. She changed into her school shoes last so's no huffing to endure cold feet on unclean-feeling tiles through her tights.

Ya fit. Kay? she knocked the door an pushed it in a wee bit. Kay was stood, no tights, school shirt open, Fionnula looked at the longness from below Kay's belly button up to the white, front-fastening bra (so no choir un-doings from behind) an above, on, the longness and flatness went, between the pointy breasts, complete up to the neck where it at last started to curve out over her throat that moved as she spoke. Fionnula thought, *Iain an Catriona had that*, an goes, Eh?

Am I white as driven snow? She was halfway up doing the buttons, face chuffa'd down at them wi no trace of double chin.

No. A bit lipstick would be an idea, yur a wee bit washed-out-looking. Fionnula stared as Kay packed stained clothes into her bag. She passed her blazer, as Fionnula took, metal donked gainst edge of the door: the Prefect badges, suddenly odd, like they come from a long time ago.

Kay crossed to the mirror, Look at the sick in my hair, oh God.

Best to leave till it's total dry and crunchy then just brush it out.

Voice of experience? Kay managed a smile.

I haven't had experiences you have, she handed her the blazer.

Kay looked wi brown eyes, This is one I'm trying to forget, she goes quietly, an she was putting on her lipstick. Fionnula had out a bottle nail-varnish remover an was scrubbing at her nails wi a grab of bog paper. Kay moved away an Fionnula suddenly felt hurt.

Smell of that, Kay smiled.

Oh sorry.

Kay was ducked into her bag an had out a little bottle of perfume. It was so small an probably expensive, Fionnula couldn't make out a name on it.

Want?

Fionnula held out her arm, back of her hand up, Kay put the bottle in, underneath the arm on the wrist, where veins show, the fat glass neck pushed in on the pulse an together, in time, as Kay continued to press, looked in each other's eyes, Fionnula twisted her arm, Kay keeping the bottle pressed on the wrist, above that clenched fist then lifting it smooth so one, two, three blobs hit the blue veins.

Don't waste it on me . . . Kay righted the bottle an Fionnula massaged the perfume in an lifted her wrist to her nose, Oh lovely.

It's Mum's. I pinch it, syphon a bit into this.

What is it?

Don't know, Dad got it for her in Italy.

How are you feeling?

I don't think I can get on a bus.

No. Leave your tie till we get out of here. Ready?

The door of the Ladies opened and the orderlies saw what were now two schoolgirls, walk out the exit and down the driveway with its saddened shrubs. At the bottom of the driveway they turned right an were gone.

The bus-stop was on a long straight section of road. All the glass had been cunted out an little diamond piles shivered in among the hedging roots where it mustn't of ah been no sweeped up.

Look at the time, goes Kay. It's okay for me but your rehearsal starts at seven.

Ah know. An where the fuck's all the buses then?

Are you sure it's this side of the road? How do you know it's not the other?

Fionnula looked down the road, Maybe we should walk a bit,

if we got to a busier place there might be taxis about, then am saved.

Let's walk down a little then, see what's round that corner.

And begin to walk is just what they did, Fionnula keepin looking back over her shoulder, for as to a bus. Round the corner there was another long straight wi the appearance of files council housing off to the left.

If we could find a phone box, an the street name we could phone taxis fro somewhere in the estate here or maybe find out where we are.

Are you sure about it here?

Come on Kay, they speak English. Fionnula started down a street. A few of the houses seemed boarded up. Kay an Fionnula walked quiet, past a couple ah flat blocks an there were pint milk cartons out on the window sills.

Why are there pints of milk out on the window sills? goes Kay.

Manda's dad used huff do that.

Why?

Keep it fresh. No fridge, Kay.

As they approached the end of the hill of tenements, Kay goes, Look, we'll get a street name here. At the end, the street nameplate was missing, just a rusty stain showed where it had been. Sprayed on the pebbledash were the words, HIBS END OF THE STREET!

What does that mean?

Don't know, went Kay.

They walked onwards, the sun was falling all over the way, so birds flying in the opposite direction of the two girls, above the telephone wires, seemed jet black gainst the clear sky. It was cooler in the shadows.

They passed a block spray-painted on the end in big pink

letters were the words YOU ARE NOW ENTERING A DRUG FRIENDLY ZONE.

I think we should turn back. Fionnula? This place looks, rather dodgy.

Anything downmarket from a Barratt house an you're calling it dodgy, Fionnula smiled at her so no to make it seem too nastyish.

Just then a helicopter went over, dead low, Don't worry Kay, there's the Barratt helicopter now, Fionnula laughed. Though clearly marked on the bottom of the chopper were the letters P O L I C E.

Up ahead there was a variation on what ya might call the dominant architectural style of the area. A block-like red brick place wi gold letters: The Broadsword on the side wall. There was someone outside: a restless-looking young man in a white T-shirt.

Fucksake lassies, nice, but ya might ah left the uniforms at home, ya know, like, it does ma image no good if am seen sellin to school kids . . . if someone got a photo or that, ah cannie even take yous in the foyer wi those togs, ach tae fuck. He looked both ways, Cmon just nip in a minute. He nodded to the door of the pub an vanished inside.

Don't, Fionnula!

I just wanted to ask . . . Fionnula and Kay stepped after him into the carpeted foyer.

Fionnula goes, Ah just wanted to ask ya where we are an if we can call a taxi fro here? Kay was kinda looking at his arm tattoos.

Like ma tattoos? he smiled an tugged up one arm so's you could see them, This one is Basi, one ah ma favourite designers, an this one . . . that's the Armani logo . . . but get this, he tugged up the left sleeve an there was a rectangle logo wi a sorta compass in the middle wi the words Stone Island round an round it. He says, Stone Island, exact same as one of the labels, you know, ah was finding it expensive keeping up wi all the new stuff that was coming in, aw the labels ah like to wear, so's a thought it'd be cheaper to just get the labels tattooed on. Permanent like! Now what'reya wantin? Es?

We're no into drugs. Sorry. We're . . .

There was a sound, Kay rushed her schoolbag up to her mouth, it was all unzipped and she spewed up into the bag, spat then zipped it closed.

Oi. Fuck! went the guy.

I didn't want to ruin the carpet, Kay smiled weakly, wiped her mouth wi her blazer sleeve.

Ruin the carpet! Fuckin look at it lassie, see that over there, that's a blood stain frae the night Gurrly Dobson goat fuckin stabbed. Pour it oot your bag! We piss on this carpet when we're too wasted tae get to the bogs.

Yur fuckin clothes'll be ruined Kay, that's a beautiful skirt.

Mmm, doesn't matter, look, I've to go outside.

Are yous two up on something? You must be, whatdye mean, ya don't like drugs? Two fine young things like you, let me introduce you to some good ones.

Kay walked out an the door swung shut.

Look mister ah swear, we've got to be getting somewhere quick, all we need is a taxi, or some directions into town.

Into town? Straight up this way, take a right at the shop, left when you come to the big road, that'll take you down The Toll, there's buses and all sorts. Excuse me, but I think I'm passionately in Love with you, or your friend, or both of yous, ah don't really have ma emotions about yous sorted out yet. Is there a chance I could ask you out tonight either, or both of yous?

No. I'm away the night.

Didn't think I recognised the uniform. I'll give you every drug on me for your phone number, he produced a pen. Fionnula smiled an right there, in the foyer of the Broadsword, she wrote down the name of the Port an the phone number of her parents on his arm.

He reached into his pocket. That is the most beautiful thing on ma arm an that's a lovely part of the country, ah mind once . . .

Bye! goes Fionnula an she stepped out.

Well what a bargain, the guy says, on his own, in the foyer, That's what ah like about the younger generation: a certain dignified restraint.

Kay was sat on a wall cross the road, her grim bag swung between her legs.

Yaokay?

Uhhuh.

Cmon, this way.

They hud gone straight up the way, taken a left at shops where a big group girls hanging outside, started to follow them. The girls looked bout fifteen an ventually one out-stepped Fionnula an stood afront her. Fionnula an Kay an all the girls stopped.

What fucking school are yous from?

Fionnula let out a big sigh.

Are you oan drugs, look the state of her, fuckin junkie.

She's just out the hospital, twelve tequilas an a load of gin an vodkas. Look. Ah'll square wi yous, sorry for being in yur patch but we've got to get into town, all our teachers are there an we got spewin drunk, she passes out an we ends up in Little France, Accident and Emergency; am mates with . . . your man at the

230

Broadswords there, know what a mean? So we swung round to see him, now we're just trying to get back cause your man's, on business you know . . . ah just popped round to give him ma phone number, we're no wanting trouble here, just be on our way after sayin hello. Cmon back an ask him if you want?

They're mates wi The Man, one lassie muttered.

Shut up, goes the one wi the gold rings.

We're gonna get killed if we don't get down the road on the bus.

Ah don't give a fuck, yous might get killed here, yous should be doggin it anyway, like us, stead of posin round here. You musta have plenty money for yon drinking.

Ah think that's quite cool, leave um alone, Mary.

Shut it. Let's see yur purses?

I don't believe this, Kay moaned.

Show them yur bag Kay.

Aww fucksake! The girl wi the rings stood back, as Kay opened her bag an held it out.

Aww, mockit!

Told ya.

All my money's in there, in the pockets, says Kay, Help yourself.

What about you?

Fionnula took out her purse an showed to the leader girl. The girl took out the single pound note an handed the purse back to her.

Let's see in your bag.

Fionnula opened it an the girl ruffled, Mmm, you're no ma size anyway. She coughed an handed the bag back. Got any fags?

Fionnula took out her packet, slipped free a cigarette an gave it to the girl then quickly lit it. She didn't offer anyone else.

Keep em, goes Fionnula. The girl slipped the pack into her plasticky kagool.

Yous best be goin, the girl says.

Fionnula went to walk on an the girl stopped her. She held out the single pound note, and she looked round her gang to make sure the point struck home, Am givin yous this back, no cause am shittin it off The Man, but you'll need it for bus fares.

Right, Fionnula nodded, hard as fuck an did a singular chew at an imaginary bit gum.

Say hello tae The Man frae Mary McNiven, right?

Aye.

The girl moved aside an Fionnula stepped on, the single pound note still held in her fingers. Kay zipped in behind her an followed. They walked on without turning back, Kay goes, God, I almost died of fright. You were quick with your wits there.

Fionnula growled quietly then muttered, Um goan come back here an bite her fuckin nipples off. No one fuckin tries rob me.

Kay went quiet.

They would have killed me if you hadn't been there. Did you see their faces at my bag of spew! They both laughed.

Ach, they don't kill anyone. Just wee lassies. Just didn't have time to fight.

Fionnula? Did you give your number to that drug guy? He was frightening.

He was honest, Fionnula smiled.

You did?

Why? Kay turned to her. I didn't ask the doctor to marry me! Jealous? She smiled.

Kay looked back, very pale.

I wish you were, Fionnula suddenly says. She grit her teeth, faced front an kept walking.

Kay says nothing, then goes, Where are we? We're not going to make it for you at seven, we'll be lucky to make it for eight. I mean where in hell are we?

Ah don't know, I think we missed it. They came to a bigger road but it led off to the left, not the right. Private cars sped round it. Then in the distance, they could see the castle, last of the sun tamling its heights and huge marmalade screes of cloud way over behind it, startin to fill a sky wi colour. Fionnula says, There's the castle, this is a big road, it'll lead us straight in, but as what way to go then ahm none the wiser, we need a map or something. We've got to keep going; that's life.

So they did keep going, on up the road replete wi private cars cushing by but nothing in the way of public transport.

Christ Kay, goes Fionnula, to keep her spirits up, If we do get a taxi, it's goan cause a rumpus when the driver finds we've only money at the bottom of a bag a spew. Awful touchy about taxi cleanness in this city, she chuckled.

And on and on, till they came to a roundabout, the grass at its sides muddied, the high arc lamps already on, despite the generosity of the evening light, an the cars jostlin round, beepin and fightin all in a hurry to get to where an why, an it was possibly one of the ugliest places in the land, for these girls who came from a town, hunched round a harbour like a classical amphitheatre, where the ocean grew still in a trapped bay an the mountains of the islands seemed to hang in the skies of summer nights and in November the sea turned black while salt gathered in the window corners of even the furthest-back houses. An even though Fionnula's family was hidden up the back, in the dip of land where history put council housing, away fro the Victorian resort villas, even there, was saving grace of the skies where clouds would always move faster than anywhere these girls would ever travel to and where the dying light of day would falter in the slow-moving coal-fire smoke above where owls an foxes moved in the grey-black woods of the shelterin hills, hundreds of feet above the bus-stops.

There was an absurd council seat, that presented the southerly view across the roundabout, Kay dropped the bag of spew an flopped down.

I'm sorry Fionnula, I'm sorry, just a breather. We're lost, aren't we? It's my fault you're going to miss the rehearsal. Drinking like that. I'm an asshole.

Kay. It was fun. It was a laugh. Think how we'll look back on it. We'll get there for eight. I'll be in the deepest shit you can imagine but we'll get there for eight. Fionnula sat by her.

It's my fault though. I'm crazy.

You're not crazy.

Kay says, Fionnula, I've got the fat belly.

What?

I'm pregnant.

The traffic circled the roundabout. They were really saying these words wi a good bit loudness.

She looked at Fionnula. It was dusking out now and you could see the whites of their eyes but the brownness was black, same as some of the lurking bushes of the landscaping ahind her.

Fionnula opened her eyes and mouth wide, says, By Iain. By Iain you are pregnant cause of the night wi him and Catriona. The way she had says it: obviously not questions. She was speaking out these things to try and bring them clear into the world, the way a baby would come or an aborted foetus would hit air. But. Jesus, have you told your folks?

No.

Have you told . . . ?

234

I've only told you. Ana-Bessie wouldn't be able to handle it, I thought about going to Catriona but . . .

Jesus, Kay . . . fuck . . . how long?

About nine weeks. I was at a place today, a clinic place for abortions. That was a lie about looking at rooms. I'm . . . I was going to apply for halls of residence. It's just, my parents are such bloody Catholics, they're dead against abortion. Even with Dad a consultant, but he's in some pro-life pressure group in the profession, yet . . . all these tears came into her black eyes and they caught the arc lamps as soon as they pushed out, an they were, in their way, quite beautiful. Her voice was steady tho, This would break their hearts, an I'm so expected to go to university . . . she shook her head and looked, hopelessly, at a yellow cement mixer circling the roundabout. And peeling off in the city centre direction.

Look Kay. Now, you want to get rid of the baby. Or you feel you have to get rid of it for university?

I don't know anymore. I mean, I don't want a baby, what can I do with a baby? It's a total disaster, my whole life is a total disaster just in two months it's gone crazy. And drinking an smoking like this with a wee baby in me, she burst out a sob.

Shush, goes Fionnula.

I was drinking and smoking like that today, to make myself have to have an abortion, acting as if I've already decided to get rid of it but . . . I know I haven't made up my mind, I'm denying it. I've done an awful bad thing and I should pay for it.

KAY that's just more Catholic bullshit, like your mum and dad. You've done nothing wrong . . . it's just baddest fuckin luck . . . Fionnula reached out and that was it . . . she took the hand; was it the left or the right? Fionnula will never ever remember, and Kay's head just went right down on Fionnula's blazered shoulder and the crying came and came as Fionnula, numbed, put the arm around her, realised she was hers for the taking but shivered, stared out cross the ridiculous roundabout. God had delivered the girl to Fionnula. *Look at the cost, ahm going to fuck her, just a matter of time*, but what Fionnula felt was anger, not anger at Iain or Catriona, not anger at Kay's folk, not even anger at their absurd religion, but anger at the sky and the roundabout and the whole charade that puts a young, lovely girl, lost in a city; unknown as to what she really wants an too lonely to imagine. Fionnula was seething that the big jigsaw was meant to fall at random into any old picture but why The Perpetual was just pain, pain, pain, Orla witherin away or drowned fathers an a so-called family tree more like a straight stick of Chell.

Kay, cmon it'll be okay.

For all my parents being posh and Pulpit Hill, you tease, but now I'm just like Michelle or any others this year.

I know honey, we've no right. Kay, know it doesn't help but I admire you, you've really gone for it, and no one can take that away from you an keepin this to yourself; that takes nerves of steel. You're braver than ah ever could be. Come on. We need to get goin. And it's then, it's then she feels it in her left hand cause her right one has gone over, other side of Kay, an is rubbing up an down Kay's arm, squeezing the odd time when a bad sob comes an she can feel the crown of her head, pushed in at her neck, hair all compressed an Fionnula has even girned her eyes tight shut just for a jiffy, suddenly not sure if this touching will make it easier to take Kay's face in her hands and kiss her and understand she is transgressin what is fair; much more than Catriona, an Iain, on that night that Fionnula'll always be trying to better. There's something in her hand and wi her arm still round the pregnant girl, she's kneading it an remembers it's the pound note, an she rubs its greasyness wi her thumb. Fionnula breathes in an swings the arm off Kay who straightens an rightaways rubs up at her eyes. It feels horrible to peel away from the realness of Kay, an Fionnula is unfolding the pound note in her two hands now an she sees what it is an she says, Kay! in a bright voice and there, in the evening light it's JL McAdam hisself . . . inventor of the tarmacadamed road an there is his face on the pound note beside the grid of streets, the layout of the main streets of the capital city!

It's a map!

And so, with the pound note folded out in her palm, then clutched safe in her fist, arm in arm bumping thegether wi Kay's tired movements, the two girls traverse through the thoroughfares and boulevards, the map on the money leading them back to the place of their appointment.

That Taken Glow

Manda an Chell walked into the police station, two shoulder bags an Chell an Kylah's French Connection each. The Pig looked up fro the *Evening News*, Hello. Again.

We'd like to report a theft, went Chell.

I'm sure you would, is it something you have stolen or have you actually been the victims of . . . theft?

I BEG your pardon, goes Chell.

Is it something you are confessing to stealing or have yourself had something stolen?

Manda turned to Chell an goes, I thought you says he'd help us!

Shush. I don't like your attitude sergeant, we're here to report a theft.

Not from the pick n mix section of Woolworth? Or not knives and towels from British Home Stores?

What are you talking about?

Would I be correct in supposing you're from the school called Our Lady of Perpetual . . . he looked down at a sheet of paper . . . Succour?

In a hushed way, Chell goes, How do you know?

Just a hunch, nodded The Sniff.

Quieter now, Chell goes, We've had, some clothing stolen,

and we thought we should report it but, eh, maybe we won't bother.

Oh really. Did you want a signed receipt for insurance purposes? Versace was it, a few Gucci handbags and a Leica camera? Why don't I just give you a receipt and you can fill it out yourselves, consult some of the shop windows on Princes Street!

A para polisman! Manda giggled, looked at him an says, You're like John Cleese.

Chell goes, A man stole our school uniforms.

The Plod stared at them.

We weren't wearing them at the time, Manda suggested wi a real innocent helpfulness.

Hush, snapped Chell. She doesn't mean anything was going on at the time, Chell added.

Who was this man? asked the Flatfoot.

His name was Danny, where did you meet him? Manda turned to Chell.

We met him in the Highland Club, announced Chell.

What! goes Manda.

Oh! goes The Filth.

You never told us you met him there! Manda shouted.

What's the matter? Yous never asked.

What the fuck were you doing there! Manda yelled.

We went to phone a taxi, when YOU, she pointed at The Scum, Wouldn't help us book a taxi.

It's only for men in there, Chell.

There were loads of lassies in there!

No wonder. It's a brothel, Chell!

Eh?

It's a brothel, ya silly cow.

Don't call me a silly cow!

Hoi HOI! shouted the copper, This is too much! Now a whole bunch of lassies from your school have been trooped in an out here all afternoon. Did your best to clean out the pick n mix counter at Woolies then it was down to BHS where yous took whatever you could, kitchen knives, towels whatever. All of it on the security cameras. Now the ladies . . . the nuns from your school have been absolutely frantic, so I suggest you forget about all this and get up to the exhibition centre now, before you get into any more trouble.

Shoplifting, brilliant! goes Chell, That's just fantastic, it's no just us that're in the shite then.

Aye but we've still had our uniforms nicked, goes Manda, Ah've lost a kilt an tie to an extreme an dangerous pervert who's loose in your city.

Come on, we'll just have to face the music.

Ah hope we do get expelled. No ways I can ask Dad for money, how am ah goan tell him ah lost my kilt?

Least you've got your shirt.

Nae use without a tie, snapped Manda.

Ladies, ladies, the fashion discussion outside unless you want me to take down details of the theft.

He's no exactly likely to hand it in, is he? Walk in with all these stained clothes at a polis station, ah mean he had ma knickers on his head!

Le Couchon automatically glanced down at Chell's legs an she caught his glance.

Chell goes, Ah yur okay, ah've got ma leopardy tanga on.

Manda burst out in the hysterics.

The Snoop went a brasser of redness.

Kylah sat listening to Orla in McDonald's, casionally squinting

over the top floor tables. Orla (braces in) says, He's coming up
on the mail train, am goan meet him at the station when it gets
in at four.

Really think he'll come?

Aye.

What there's guys fro the submarine in the Mantrap?

Well that's supposin any of us get in, an supposin the sailors
are there an supposin any are cute and supposin any of them
would go for me.

But you'd consider pulling twice in the day?

Normally anytime but the night? No. No ways. Ah've asked
him to come up an it wouldn't be good to copoff wi another.
An ah know for a fact he might be into stuff I am.

Kylah made a slurp noise in her drained Coke, Like what?
She leaned elbows on the table.

Juss stuffff, Orla raised her eyebrows. Stuff I want to try.
Getting tied up an that.

Kylah leaned back an laughed, Getting tied up at four in the
morn, that's mental? What else are ya gone do?

Ah know I can stay at Fionnula's or Chell's or yours an that's
great, though, ah dont like being round your brother's cause ah
get so embarrassed, but if yous go home ah might stay up wi
him all night, walk to the castle at Christiansands, watch the
sunrise . . . if it's no pishing wi rain. An don't forget, station
buffet's open at six these days so we could go sit there. He says
he'll have to get the early train back out and down here for his
. . . work.

That's so romantic. You've got That Taken Glow bout you
already.

That what?

That Taken Glow a girl gets when shes into a guy. It makes
girls more attractive to other guys too.

Nah.

Ah swear it. Like yur no going wi anyone, no one asking you out, then one guy asks ya out an he's nice an yur sorta thinkin about him an then five or six guys are all asking ya out cause you've got That Taken Glow. Quite amazing really, an ya wish they could just all ah asked ya out, nice an steady, one after the other. Maybe wi gaps between. Life is never ordered like that, Kylah squinted at her watch. They'd already took their nail varnish off but Chell an Manda seemed to be cutting it a bit fine wi the uniforms an they had Kylah's bag of French Connection clothes too.

What happened wi you an the band then, Chell says something?

Oh Orr, we were totally mashed an ah decided leave them. Ah phoned them up from this pub full of old men; ahm no too sure bout it now, it was sorta, cause we were getting out of money an the boys had gave me all this cash for CDs and ah went and never bought any, an me an Chell took all THEIR money an spent it on drink an those clothes fro French Connection. Now am sobering up the old guilties are starting, ah! Kylah screwed up her eyes, Is this the dirty tarts? Aye, YA SHAG THEM THEN? Kylah yelled. A couple fathers fro family groups turned an stared over but Kylah couldn't see them.

No smiling at all. Schoolbags hanging fro their each shoulders an those French Connection bags danglin near the ground, Manda an Chell moved through the fluorescent tables towards them.

Hurried-wise, Manda skimmered into the slidy seat, gaspin, slidin the bags way under the table an goes, Yur fuckin uniforms've been nicked!

Oh, nice one, Kylah put her finger up to the contact lens-less eye an tug-tugged down at the skin, We really believe ya.

It's right enough Kylah, am sorry, goes Chell.

All four girls stared at each other.

Dead gen? goes Orla.

What about ma French Connection stuff? went Kylah.

It's all here, it was strictly school uniforms he was into. In a hushed drama-y voice, Manda looked at Orla an goes, We're no fucking joking, these two met him when they were hanging about in a fucking BROTHEL, yon one ah pointed out to ya, they fuckin thought it was a pub!

A few more of the fathers were glaring over.

Oh come on! Don't blame it on us, Manda! Fucksake, goes Chell.

This pervy Danny . . .

Him, goes Kylah, he was okay?

She's right enough Kylah, goes Chell.

Okay! This seem okay to you? Manda flicked the note down on the table, Kylah shut one eye, turned it the right way up, Orla leaned in to read it too.

Jesus! Ah thought he was okay. Kylah opened her other eye. He didn't . . . try anything back at that flat did he? Are yous okay? Jesus. Pervert bastard, Oh fuck, eh? Just the thought of it.

It really scums ya out, doesn't it.

Aye, even if ya got the clothes back you couldn't wear them, Orla shrugged.

Manda pensive for a tick, lightin a cigarette goes, Suppose if you soaked them in Lux for a couple of days . . . Aye. Manda slumped, back seemed to relax. We've got yur blazers right, but yur blouses an kilts have gone an whatever underwear ya had in there is a sure goner too.

The fucking mink run off down the street wi ma school knickers on his head!

Yous are jokin.

Pffff, are we fuck!

What about shoes? Kylah was rummaging in her school bag.

He left shoes an socks.

Fuckin cunt. Fuckin bass, goes Orla, A fuckin pervert!

Kylah goes, Wha da ya mean it was a brothel? The Highland Club!

It's a brothel.

Ah mean we were only in a few minutes, the women were a wee bit weird wi us but once they found out we just wanted to call a taxi they were perfectly polite, an so was that Danny, says he could show us where it was.

Ah bet he fuckin did, goes Orla.

Ah mean ah asked if they had a bar an ah thought it was a bit weirdy they didn't but part from that it just seemed like . . . some city place.

What're we gonna, do? Can't turn up in skirts as short as these. We'll be fuckin crucified.

What can we do?

What did you buy in French Connection?

Kylah goes, We bought juss skimpy wee tops an skirts.

So short they'd be up our ass cracks . . . shorter than this! goes Chell, gestured down at her skirt.

Fuck.

That's no all. The mood isnae gonna be good. Seems like loads of the Seconds and Thirds were done for fuckin shopliftin, aye! Ah went back that police station we went to, try and get some help an all he went on about was Our Lady's pupils that'd been in an out aw day on shoplifting charges!

Who?

244

Everyone part fro Kay Clarke an Ana-Bessie I'd magine.

But, fuck, this is for TELLY. Condom an the Pagan are gonna go ballistic.

We'll look more like fuckin En Vogue than a convent choir.

Any brainwaves?

There was no talkin.

Chell goes, See they Hari Kishnas jivin round in the orange robes we saw, nick their fuckin gear, wrap it round us, turn up an tell Condom we've converted.

It's no funny, Chell.

Chell shrugged.

She'll freak out juss as much as we turn up in this state.

Look at the fuckin time, all we can do is get some of the make-up offof us an get up there.

They took final sucks on half-gone cigarettes an nibbed them. They started gathering their stuff thegether.

The window in the rehearsal room where the girls had watched the couple fuck below them, earlier in the day, was still open, allowing in a cool night air, some starlings were still flittering wi the last streaks of eastern light.

Through walls you could hear other practising songs an successful applause in the auditorium as Catholic school choirs from all over the small nation competed for the title and £15,000 cash prize to the music department. Since the music department of Our Lady of Perpetual Succour WAS Sister Condron . . . the purity of her spiritual quest for victory in the competition might be understood.

Sisters Condron and Fagan were standing before a subdued collection of Seconds and Thirds who were shuffling uncomfortable, even before the door opened an Manda Tassy, a French Connection bag held over her pelvic area, was propelled into the room by the bulked pressure of Kylah, Rachel (eyebrow stud removed) an Orla shuffling behind her.

Sister, we're sorry but our uniforms have been stolen.

The silence was so perfect, the scream of a passing starling sounded awful loud.

We weren't wearing them at the time, Manda added again. She lowered the shopping bag so the true length of her skirt was visible.

We were trying these clothes in a shop Sister, Orla hurriedly lied but it was too late. Sister Condron had fainted.

It was a male teacher wi a quite nice body from a next door school an a fatty janitor type who helped Sister Condron into a chair an assisted her come round. Chell was in tears by this time and Fionnula McConnel an, bizarrely, Kay Clarke had been found to be missing.

Sister Fagan had already promised the Sopranos full range of possible retributions so they stood, huddled in a cluster, Manda wi an arm round Chell, sometimes whisperin thegether but shunned by the frank, but at least correctly uniformed, thieves of Seconds an Thirds.

Manda whispered, Where's Fionnula? to Kylah.

Kylah shrugged an goes, The only good thing about our situation is, they canni expel all of us ... it's just gonna be couple a scapegoats.

Aye, us, goes Manda.

Sister Condron's recovery was miraculously swift. She glared at the provocatively dressed girls of the highest voices wi a clear loathing and she suddenly asked in a furtive voice, almost an uttered thought, What clothes do you have in the bags?

Manda cleared her voice an announced, in a loud, confident

voice, They belong to Kylah and Chell . . . Rachel, Sister but they are not suitable.

NOT SUITABLE! Listen to you Miss Tassy, standing there in those clothes telling me what is and is not suitable! I didn't ask what was suitable, girl. I asked you to describe what the garments are.

I have two tops an a skirt, Sister, says Chell.

I have a top and a skirt, Sister, Kylah nodded. Then the door opened and Fionnula McConnel an Kay Clarke, both wearing uniform an tie, walked in. For some reason, Fionnula was clutching a single pound note. Fionnula was about to speak up into the silence when her eyes locked on the other Sopranos, still in casual dress, but she hardly hesitated, announced, I'm sorry I'm late Sisters; Kay and I got lost and Kay is no feeling well, Kay smiled and nodded, strangely quiet, then she turned and vomited onto the carpet.

Sister Condron hardly looked at her then goes, Kylah take off your clothes.

Apart from Kay Clarke spitting onto the pat of her vomit, and the hardly perceptible carpet-shuffle closer to the window, all was silence.

Sister Fagan gave Sister Condron a startled look.

Somebody help get Kay's clothes off. Kylah, you have the strongest voice, I want you to put on Kay's uniform, Kay can wear whatever monstrosities are in those shopping bags. Kay, Rachel, Amanda and Orla shall not be singing tonight, nor I imagine any other night. Ever. Fionnula and Kylah in Kay's uniform will form a skeleton, emergency Sopranos. Sing more pronounced, stronger, sing for your lives, ladies. If you will go to the toilets or the bus and change now, we will have time, perhaps, to rehearse both songs. I will never forgive any of you for this. Never.

Night Comes On

Under the hole in the ceiling, up at St Orans, above Port, Ardlui had forsaken the novelistic stance before the manuscript pages for a fat, amber tumbler of whisky aclink with ice. He was rolling a Spanish cigar back and forth thoughtfully in his lips. Behind him, up the wall, he could sense the novels he'd transported from town to town in his father's pigskin suitcase then as years went by, in crates of the Holy & Apostolic from one part of the world to the other. Books he hadn't read for twenty-five years but which travelled with him for the day he would read again, hoping they would punch his heart as they had: Bernanos, Mauriac, early Percy. Through the window, darkness was driving back the island mountains, leaving only the blue sheen of the bay, the rip of the submarine's length. Random headlights turned the big sycamore across the road silver, as shadows of its own branches writhed round its wide trunk then the vehicle passed, leaving night once more.

Ardlui sighed, shook his head, he took one of the Sensor Technology pens and moved it to a clean tablet of paper where he wrote:

> Meet again with: Kirkham Constructions
> John Brotherhood
> Fax Diocese, hint at a miracle/vision. (The Dio'

consults the commission for official verification. e.g. CONVINCE THE BISHOP and you're made)

Re-read unofficial histories: Lourdes, Santiago but especially Knock and Medjugorje in Bosnia. That is our blueprint. Probably all destroyed but try to research construction contracts for airport at Knock, runway length, landing systems. Possibility of runway extension at Tulloch Ferry? Remember Kilimanjaro!

THE VISION: Girls. They must be girls. Get pupil lists for Our Lady's.

Ardlui chuckled and leaned back, *Most are probably on drugs anyway. That policeman, McPherson is seeking his girls and I am seeking mine.* He went to refill his whisky glass. When he sat down again at the table, he reached out, wrote in larger letters across the top:

MIRACLES ARE THE FLOWERS WHICH FLOUR-
ISH IN EVERY COUNTRY.

Ardlui sat back, tossed the pen on the desk and grinned. The telephone rang through the house and he drunkly waited for Mrs Mac to answer till he remembered she was long away home. He did not cross to the bookshelves and push the footer of a button that makes the phone there leap into life with a rash jangle. He sat, wishing he had the courage to put the light out and let the darknesses gather about him and fill out all the problematic dimensions of the front room but there were no curtains and he was afraid he would be seen, sat at table long into night-drinking, though it was this he desired most of all; listening to Messiaen's *Quatour pour la fin du temps* as in the old days. He glanced up at the torn plaster where the scandalous chandelier had been smote down by the prayers of the most pious old age pensioners. Leaving the page of notes before him, Ardlui gathered up his novel manuscript. By collecting it in his hand he could throw it together at the table lamp on the corner. Like a tall person falling, the lamp tipped over then tumbled off the edge as pages scattered or slid along the floor into the far corner and settled under the radiator. A chaos of shadows redefined the room as the lamp fell but its shade protected the bulb and it bounced, hysterically then lay still, the open top of the shade flooding light in, around Ardlui's legs. By stretching out a substantial brogue and sliding the alabaster base of the lamp towards him, the vulnerable shade cradling the bulb came beneath his heel and Ardlui put down the whole weight of one side, crumpling the shade, twisting the metal frame aside and finally, with a crack, the bulb went and but for the blue water down in the bay below the room was black and silent.

New Face on the Mental Scene

The bus moved through cushions of darknesses, sneaking to lands that are high; sodium orange of cities' sky behind as they climbed back into the far places, sealed in together in the warm cabin, lighting dropped low and girls silent.

All Sopranos slept, cept Orla in a seat to herself. Sometimes she put a cheek gainst cold glass of the window; when she restlessly took her face away, a crescent of condensation stayed then shrunk on its own dimensions, leaving only the black night and its frightening lands. The red glow of tail lights illuminated only high verging and the barks of outer, roadside conifer trunks. When brakes went on, the red glow might reach deeper between the forest trees, showing the mangle of winter-fall before just the owl-black, pine marten world began.

Kay Clarke curled up, slept opposite Orla, her long brown hair fallen over the seat edge, ends curled on the floor. She was wearing the shortest of skirts, one Kylah had bought at French Connection. The headlights, when Orla looked up the aisle, past the restless Seconds an Thirds, were boring leftwards or rightwards as the bus went the other way, always skimming over the elegant, long centrelines as they languidly swung westly or east.

There was a high bit of the moon somewhere above, when it cleared the black tree tops, it was leaking its distinct light onto

Kay's lovely bare legs. Then as the chain of villages began, even Kay's body shifted, as if some old, hoary memory stirred, even in the youngest hearts that Time hadn't had occasion to polish properly yet.

Orla thought of the name Stephen. No the guy, just her mouth moving the shape of the word an then wondered if he really would board a train in the capital and make a four-hour journey through the darkness where she'd laid a path of thoughts about him. *All the Love Songs in the world, like that strange one Kylah sings,* Nature Boy, *but they don't actually teach us anything about love, we're none the wiser, no rules laid down in love, no history like there is, in say, medicine, this big mystery at the centre of the world, silent an huge like a god,* then Orla lifted her hand to her mouth an she took out her retainer braces. They were wet wi silver strings of saliva an slowly the moon came across them and it was too beautiful, an as Orla was startin to cry quietly to herself, she crushed those braces into a sore complex of wires, digging her palm an held them as the bus passed inwards through the nightsmoke, that you could sometimes smell, as it neckerchiefed by, in Five Mile House, and round the Concession Lands of the flooded New Loch, through the pass to Back Settlement an under the lit bridge at Tulloch Ferry.

A few of the Thirds and Seconds quietly alighted through the villages, each girl spoken to by Sister Condron. But the Sopranos were no waking. Orla dropped the mangled brace onto the bus floor as they passed the welcome sign, up back of the Complex, that Manda an Fionnula had once vandalised, an the bus seemed to spin like a crane in the air as it took the hairpin an slipped down into the marine basin of the Port, the crouching hunk of the submarine still out in the bay.

The bus stood, engine switched off outside the school on

McAdam Square. Sister Condron was at the bottom of the aisle, an arm out to each side, a hand holding on to the top of the seats. Sister Condron announced, Ana-Bessie, you can leave, you should just go to classes after eleven tomorrow.

The Sopranos and Kay yawned or stretched up the back, uncurling, squinting out windows.

Sister Condron goes, I want the rest of you in early enough to hear eleven o'clock prayers and intercom messages. Each one of you will be going up to see the Mother Superior. So many of you, we will have to call you up in groups of two or three. Perhaps we should give out tickets.

No one laughed.

Be in prompt before eleven. You can rest assured I will be seeing the Mother Superior in the morning with the gravest of individual reports about what has happened today and your parents will be contacted. You are free to go. Could Kay Clarke and members of the Sopranos stay on the bus a moment.

The Thirds and Seconds shuffled off. Cars, wi their exhausts producing smoke, were parked round the square and various girls began to disperse towards them, ducking in, to sit by unseen parents. Each parental car sat a little too long then began to move into the night, courteously giving way to one other, dismembered-seeming hands waving through streetlight-reflecting windscreens.

Sister Condron says, I believe the six of you have been abusing alcohol and not wearing your school uniform. If they were stolen from some of you I don't think that is to any loss, for after the pandemonium of today I don't think ANY of you will need uniforms of Our Lady's again. I am going to talk to the Mother Superior now about your immediate suspension and eventual expulsion from the school. How surprised and disappointed I am to find you, Kay, suddenly part of this . . .

lunatic fringe we've always had to endure. Announcements will be made on the intercom tomorrow regarding each of you seeing the Mother Superior individually. Sister Condron collected her bucket of books then slowly got down off the bus an began waddling up towards the New Chapel.

The Sopranos an Kay started to amble towards the front.

We're dead, goes Manda.

See the submarine's in girls! goes Orla.

Ah don mind getting expelled, goes Kylah, Ah'll just go on the waiting list for Woolies, but ma folks'll go spare.

Mine too.

Kylah goes to Jerry the bus driver, Ah have ma Cream cassette there?

Could you hear what they were saying behind ya Jerry? goes Manda.

Enough to know yous aren't their favourites the night. You shouldn't be in pubs at your age, could yous not've screwed the heid the day? Yous know how much the music means to her.

Jerry, music is the LAST thing on her mind.

It's right enough.

Night now, goes Chell.

Aye, have a good day the morrow, sounds like fun.

They stepped off the bus one by one, an the door hissed shut. The old Mud Bucket dieseled it off cross square an past the garage, making for the buspark. The Sopranos an Kay stepped over to the length-of-legs school wall; they sat in a libertarian dark, any-old order but Kay upwall, beside Fionnula.

Ana-Bessie had waited special an she crossed over from her Old Man's car.

Quite a skirt! Ana-Bessie goes to Kay.

Wha's wrong wi it, Kylah snapped.

We must be about the exact same size, Kay goes to Kylah, up the line.

Aye ah guess, Kylah nodded.

Maybe you should sell it her, Kylah? Manda sneered, quietish.

Suddenly Fionnula goes, You look dead bonny in it Kay, you should keep it on, hit the Mantrap an ravish a few salty dugs wi us, coming, Ana? Fionnula gave Ana-Bessie the full stare.

No, eh no I can't, that's my dad's car over there I just . . . I just wondered. She tried to cut Fionnula out and talk to her friend direct, I was wondering what she said to you, Sister Condron. Do you have to report to her tomorrow? went the little nosey voice.

I'll tell you about it later, Kay smiled.

Oh. All right. See you tomorrow then, Ana-Bessie coughed and walked off, giving a little wave backwards then hurrying the last few metres to the car to give her father the gossip.

As the car drove off, all busied themselves lighting cigarettes an Manda side-glanced as Fionnula offered Kay a cigarette without askin, Kay gave a weird look an smile to Fionnula, let her light it for her.

There was long silence an then Fionnula says it, Girls, am tellin ye we're all gonna get expelled. If it hud just been the clothes an the lateness an that, an ah think like them nickin out the shops, ah reckon they'll just get suspensions but us, cause there's alcohol involved we're for the chop.

There was other silence.

Manda nodded an the others scraped their feet a bit. Manda looked at Kay an says, You'll get away wi it, wi yur dad an yur university an that.

Kay looked Manda an says, I'm not getting away with a thing. I'm out, I can assure you, for lots of reasons.

Fionnula jumped in, Look, Kay's in it as well, she's going have do her exams up the Proddy next year or something, ah tell you, they've been wanting to get shot of us for ages and now we've really put ourselves in it.

How come ya went an got so pished? Orla leaned forward an looked straight at Kay.

Good company, Kay goes.

Like ah says, goes Kylah, Ahm just headed for Woolies record counter but for Kay, it's a shame, an ah tell yous honey ah think you *should* KEEP those clothes they look so good on ya!

Fionnula laughed an Kay smiled up and says, Kylah, you're so talented, how can you just say that you're headed for Woolies . . . ?

Manda muttered, Here we go . . . it's fucking young business-woman of the year.

Are you saying she's not talented?

Of course she's talented! But what good it is being talented in this dump? Who's interested in talent here? You don't see Richard Branson out the Barn dishing out the fucking record contracts do ya EH? Manda moved her cigarette.

Know what we should all do? Fionnula says it quiet. We should all just get out of here, live in the city.

What about you Chell? Orla leaned forward an blew out smoke.

Pfff, know me. Ah juss wanta work wi animals an that, ah only stayed on the year cause yous all did; don't give a fuck if ah get booted.

Orla?

Orla shrugged an sort smiled but frowned simultaneous. Ah don't think yous should worry too much cause ah tell yous, they won't throw me out an they can't let me stay and expel yous.

What makes ya think that they won't expel you?

They won't. I'm their wee miracle, their mascot. They wouldn't have the guts throw me out.

Jesus, Orr, it's been a pretty bad day for them. Condom is fuckin BEELIN at us majorly.

Know what we's should do girls? goes Fionnula.

This time they decided to listen.

If they're goan give us all the fling, if we're getting expelled themorrow, am fucked if am going home an getting tidied up like ah was goin to Holy Communion, an what's the point, cause none of yous have bloody uniforms! Know what we should do? We should make it an all-nighter.

Aye! whispered Orla, I am.

Just each of us phone the folks an say we're stayed at eaches else an be out the whole night, juss go for it an stumble in the morn wi our fuckin heads high.

Go where all night? When we get fired out the 'Trap, there's nothing, says Manda.

Till six an the buffet opens at the station, says Orla.

We may meet sailors, we might be out getting hurls round the bay on the submarine by then girls! Chell shouted.

More than fuckin hurls!

Are you saying go into the school dressed in our clothes? Manda asked.

That's the half of why we're getting the boot, a mean admit it, it's all sex and clothes that freaks those frigid old cows up at this fuckin tip, we'd be better off shot of it, Fionnula flicked her head violently backwards, just missing the iron railings, hair jumped up at the mossy statue of Our Lady's silhouette, lurking high in the glooms.

Manda goes, Being smart is getting away wi fun an no getting caught; we got caught. We're in shite an now yous are saying we should just rub their noses in it the more?

What, are you planning a university career too? Fionnula kinda spoke out, no looking at Manda, just staring at the ground.

Fuck you, Fionnula, Manda kinda twist-snarled her mouth an bit at her cigarette.

There was silence.

Am tellin yous, it won't be a problem, goes Orla.

Look, goes Kay, My mum and dad are away till Tuesday, you're all welcome to use it as an alibi, you can say you stayed over at my place. You can even go there if you want, like this guy of yours who's coming up Orla, take him up to mine, it's not a problem.

Wayhey! Party-times, goes Kylah.

Get the sailors up, spunkin on the Axminsters.

There yous go! Fionnula smiled.

There's showers, Kay shrugged.

An needle n thread so Orla can make a handbag out of this lad's balls eh?

Should a heard the two of them in the bedroom this afternoon! goes Kylah.

Everyone laughed.

Away, ah was just snoggin him!

Where were you? Manda goes to Kylah.

In the budgie room using his mobile phone to phone Mum, see if the submarine was still in the bay!

What about the singing the night, eh?

Fionnula laughed, We fuckin extra stunk! She indicated Kylah, Me an her were juss lookin each other goan, 'Ooooo.'

Cheese Feast wi extra cheese stunk, went Kylah, smilin an shakin her head. Then Kylah goes, Look, Kay, ah mean yur bag smells weird.

Mmmm, Kay nodded quickly.

She fucking threw up in it, Fionnula laughed, She did us proud this one the day. Took on Mexico wi the tequilas. Tequila Sheila's got a fuckin rival here!

Away! Right enough? Kylah was smilin at Kay. Manda was frownin.

Fionnula says, We ended up in hospital, ambulance there, nee naw nee naw nee naw right through town.

Chell goes, Me and her were in a brothel by mistake.

It's true. I was out for the count, Kay smiled, looking sleepy an it made her eyes different.

Crashed out in this bar we were in, we just ran into each other by chance.

What a day, girls. If we're chucked out the school it'll been worth it, Orla says, an looked up dreamily.

An Orla's in Love.

In lust.

Manda nodded Fionnula, Let's get over North Pier bogs for make-up an so's you an Kylah can change, make whatever phone calls an get us in the Mantrap.

Let's educate a few sailors!

Tell you, what we need is a wee drappy drink, eh Kay? smiled Fionnula.

YES! The girls called out.

Time to go down below!! Ha!

Aye, fuck the morrow an fuck Our Lady's an its crapness.

Forth let the cattle roam! Fionnula called.

TEERA LEERA LAY!! The girls roared in response an burst out laughing.

They began walking, a delicate formation takin place, Manda an Orla at lead, Kylah an Chell behind an Fionnula wi Kay way back, all talkin away, twenty to the dozen. About the day's goins on!

What's this, is Fionnula in love wi Miss Spewer all of a sudden or somethin? goes Manda in Orla's ear.

Orla shrugged her shoulders an goes, Don't get annoyed at her, no the night Manda, ah just feel like everyone getting on thegether. If Kay has loosened up enough to get spewin drunk she might be a laugh, an wi her no being a face, maybe she can do the talkin to the bouncer?

The six walked along the esplanade in the cool night, pointing out into the darknesses of the bay an shouting, 'Ooo arr Jim lad', 'Portland Bill, I'm Portland Bill', 'I'm Captain Birds Eye', 'Pieces of eight', an the one that got loudest laugh o all, 'Aye aye fill her up with a fish finger Seaman Stains', an weirdly it was Kay who shouted it fro the back in the best of bad, Cornishy Dorsety accents.

The six of them stood outside Barrels. Kay was still in Kylah's new French Connection gear an Kylah an Fionnula were dressed up again. Nail varnish had been re-applied an Chell's eyebrow stud returned to its rightful place but there was no sign of Michelle McLaughlin outside.

Kay and Fionnula gave each other the most daring of furtive looks.

She's nooo turning up goes Chell.

Guess no, nodded Fionnula, she tugged up the sleeves of her shirt though it seemed a bit on the side of chilly an she lit another cigarette.

That's just the way it is, eh? She's broke an grounded an her glory days are over, Christ knows she shone in her time, goes Manda.

Fionnula openly scowled at her.

Here she is! Orla called, Michelle! Don't believe it.

Michelle McLaughlin looked a bit odd in Kay's direction,

then smiling at all, make-up, wearing black lace shirt an short, pleated skirt, no bump the-tall showin, stridin towards on legs in black tights, tall an boney, an high boots on her feet. No different than year an a half back.

Hey sexy ass! Chell shouted as Michelle crossed the road, looked both ways tho a one-way street.

Hi YA, how'd it go?

Aww a classic.

We came second last.

Or twenty-second as Condom calls it!

FuckSAKE ya bimbos, goes Michelle, eyes lighted again on Kay, flickering only for the jiffiest of jiffys at Kay's legs, skirt, etc. etc. Michelle goes, Hi YA Kay!

Hi Michelle, off the hook?

Aye aye, listen girls, ah says to Old Dear ah was staying over at yours, Chell. Ah mean am no invitin masel over, it's just, know how it is, if ya say you're NO staying over, ya huff to be back at some stupid fuckin time, two or three an it's crampin yur style like fuck, snoggin in double quick time an your knickers are still wet by the time ya get into bed!

MICHELLE they all called.

Dinnae scum us out, Chell was heard to call, deep in the mix.

See the sub's still in!

Aye, the 'Trap'll be thick wi them.

Listen, will yous wait here while ah go the hole in the wall, get some cash, goes Orla.

Once Orla'd crossed the road, Manda goes, She's been spendin like billy-o all day.

Ah couple of them watched her round the corner.

We've loads a gossip for ya!

Okay, let's get round an in there.

Kay, am no meaning anything by it, but wi you not bein such a kent face there, why no you an say Michelle do the talkin to the bouncer right, an let's all get our ages right? goes Manda.

Fionnula goes, Right, mind we have to be born in nineteen seventy-eight, am goan do the talkin if there's any trouble I'll go for it an claim am nineteen, yous all claim yous were born in nineteen seventy-eight, but mind, it must be BEFORE the day's date so's get yur dates right an stick to them an we'll bluff'm down. Ah think that's a good idea, Kay an Michelle go in first, like we're all a group thegether an no knowing their faces so well they should just wave us through.

What if they search my bag? goes Kay.

Aye, there's a problem.

All ma money's in it as well. I haven't plucked up courage to look.

What happened?

Spewed up in it. These are Kylah's clothes I'm wearing. Long story.

Michelle roared in the hysterics an held her fingers near her mouth, then she goes, Let's see, an crossed to Kay.

Don't open it, it's really smelly, goes Kay.

Michelle knelt an unzipped the bag, Mmm, where's yur money?

In the pockets of the jacket.

If we could get the money out I'd just chuck it away.

Oww hush lassie, we can leave it behind the bar in here, eh? Angie would let us, long as we don't tell him what's in it, you can pick it up themorrow, goes Chell.

Right, watch this girls, Michelle took something out the breast pocket of her black shirt an started attacking it wi her nails.

Whoa, everyone went.

Michelle unpeeled a condom an held it up, Surgical glove, she goes an all laughed. Who's got the shortest nails?

Me, an it's my sick, goes Kay, took the flunky then began forcing it onto her hand.

Everyone laughed. Take note now Kay, went Manda.

Well girls, it's obvious I'm no expert, went Michelle an tapped her stomach.

All laughed. Kay had her hand quite deep in the condom an some of them could smell the familiar, sharp, rubbery an lubricant tang. She was easy able to snap it over her wrist.

Ever seen one that big? goes Kylah.

We saw a cock the day. Oh it was a cracker. A cracking laugh, ah mean, his cock was nothing special . . .

Where did you see a cock?

On a nude man doin a handstand. We'll tell you.

Kay put her hand in and hooked under the neck of the jacket, Keep back, keep back, she says.

Don't worry.

A couple walked out Barrels main door. That guy works in the Hydro showroom an what's-her-name used to be in Our Lady's. They looked queerly at the gathering, as they walked hand in hand the couple twisted their heads to look at Kay.

Aye, went Fionnula.

Aye, went Manda.

Hi-up, went the man one of the couple, What ah yous doin?

She was sick in her bag an all her money's in the jacket. That's a condom she's using.

Right. The couple walked on.

Nosey parker, Manda muttered.

Kay had removed the jacket an wi her unsheathed hand got

out a jumbled mix of notes; tens, fives an ones in there. She left the weight of coins an shoved the jacket back in.

What's goin on? Orla was back.

Major operations.

Kay shoved the jacket down in an peeled off the condom.

Whos is the flunky? goes Orla.

Mine.

Kay dropped the peeled condom into the bag, Evidence of a good night there, she nodded down at the bag.

Fionnula laughed really loud.

Why d'ya still carry flunkies?

Michelle says, Orla, juss cause I'm pregnant doesn't mean a can't have sex. It's no the end of the world.

Oh aye. Sorry.

C'mere. I'll take it. Chell, who'd snogged Angie in the past, nipped into Barrels.

Fionnula goes, Orla, mind say you were born in nineteen seventy-eight. You're Aquarius anyway, eh?

Aye.

Just stick to yur birthday then, eh.

Michelle an Kay approached the jaw-fringed door of the Mantrap. The bouncer of the island was alone at the portal.

The five Sopranos followed wi a perfectly feigned casualness, as if they were about to cross their own bedrooms.

Hi.

Aye, he looked at Kay's eyes an dared a once-over of the legs.

Still moving towards, he bein too embarrassed to really challenge female strangers, bein complete an comfortable wi the male Saturday combats but bewildered by midweek girls, Kay and Michelle started to sweep by.

Sailors in here? goes Michelle.

Aye. Loads, but there was a little hesitative gap between Kay an Fionnula to avoid appearing to barge in, suddenly, the bouncer had gone an stepped into it.

Any ID ladies? hands folded in front of groin as habit demanded for certain male ́enquiries.

Sorry, VD did ya say?

EYE DEEEE.

O we're all over eighteen, smiled Fionnula trying to step round him.

Hey now, steady. Any proof of that?

Cmon, we were in here two week ago.

Ah don't recognise you.

That's cause you're new.

I recognise you. Have you got a sister though?

Nut. You must be thinking of me.

Kay had come back up behind the bouncer, but Michelle seemed to've gone on in. Kay says, Is there a problem?

Could you move on, inside please.

They're with us . . . me.

As the bouncer had his back to the Sopranos, Chell put two fingers up above his head, curlin them up like pretend rabbit ears, or little Devil's horns.

Can you just go back on inside please?

Well they're with us. We're . . . I'm not going in if they're not. They're all . . . old enough.

The bouncer turned back to the Sopranos, Chell whipped her hand down, Aye well, let's see. The bouncer put one hand up to one wrist an tugged up his sleeve, then he pulled up the other shirt and dinner jacket sleeve of the arm: writ in thick pen from wrist to elbow, inverted so they came against his face the correct way up. The left arm read

YES 18
born
20 May 1978
Or before
Aprel 78
March 78
Feb 78
Jan 78
1977
1976
1975
or longer ago.

The right arm read

NO no 18
Born 21nd May
1978
or after
June 1978
July 1978
August 1978
Sept
Oct
Nov/Dec
also
1979
1980
1981
1982
to today.

Right you. When were you born? The bouncer looked at Kylah between his held-up hands.

Nineteen seventy-eight, goes Kylah.

The bouncer squinted at the abacus on his arms, concentrated, What date?

I'm Capricorn.

Eh?

Am Capricorn, do you no have that information there? What date? DATE!?

Look, this is daft, am eighteen an ah was in here two weeks ago.

You don't look eighteen to me.

Oh I'm eighteen, okay.

The bouncer looked at her.

January the ninth.

Fionnula goes, Look they're all eighteen, this is daft, look at me, am nineteen years old and we go in here an spend good money an you're puttin up this scene, ah mean it's middle of the week, you've let all kinds of psychos in there but you're making it difficult for a bunch of girls in a group.

If you're no eighteen you don't get in, it's the LAW. Am just doin ma job. You look eighteen so you're in, but yous and you can forget it, he pointed to Chell an Orla.

Oh fuckin come on! The lassies are same age as us.

As for you Capricorn, ah don't much believe you so's you can try another night.

Fuck you, goes Kylah an walked away. She shouted Fionnula n Kay, Yous go on in, have a laugh an come round Barrels fore two okay? Cmon Orla.

Manda was still stood afore him.

You can get in. Cheer up. You're in the best place in town.

Manda gave the look of relief. It was major social humiliation to no get past the bouncer but once in, gave him look of deaths an walked on.

Fuckin wanker, goes Manda as they walked down the fairylight-lit corridor to the cloaky. They could hear the beat so slow sets hadny started.

He was such a fucking . . . arse, goes Kay, standing beside Fionnula.

Fionnula and Manda gave in their bags an took the tickets.

Cause Kay was using swear words, Manda looked at her an gave Kay an open sneer.

They walked on an Manda blethers, Right then, where are these fortunate sailors, eh, fortunate to meet you an me Fionnula, eh?

They went through that door wi the fire-glass, into the pink then blue flashes an novas of the bar an dance floor but juss through it, there was a noticeboard, one of they wi the horizontal grooves you stick little white letters into:

CLUB OF THE PORT WORKERS: SOCIAL NIGHT UPSTAIRS IN SAINT COLUMBA ROOM

Ah fuck, went Manda an she rushed fwd, hopped up the deadly two steps at end of the bar, from where you survey the still-winter dancefloor and its rich pickings.

Three things happened simultaneously: Manda's big sister, Catriona, across the silver of the reflecting floorboards, lifted a hand to wave from amongst The Hairdressers. Over the furthest corner of the Mantrap, where two young men were sitting at different tables wi half-gone lager pints an out-folded *Daily Records* afront them, a kick-fight broke out. Behind Manda, three marshals fro the car ferry pier, tore open the front of their reflective jackets. The velcro fixers made rips loud enough to hear above DJ's Twenty's fodder. The DJ so-called, account of his guarantee never to play any record that hadn't been in the top twenty. He was padlocked, a bit above the dancefloor in a cage of barbed wire, to protect him from being carried out and thrown off the pier on Saturday nights as happened on his first engagement. A small key to the padlock, painted red, hung round his neck, in case of a fire.

The marshals lowered their jackets onto stools an gently sat before their newly blistering lager pints. They never bothered to turn, look the boys who had sat back down after throwing a few wild punches an were now just shouting at each other.

There were four people on the dancefloor. About fifteen local men along the bar.

Name of fuck, Manda held out her arms, let them slap back gainst her in despair. Look at it!

Michelle came trottin down the stair.

Fionnula was staring over at Catriona. Fionnula looked at Kay, lifted her forehead an elongated her cheeks in a forced smile.

It's fucking shite, so much for sailors, he meant aa those old moaners of the fishing boats. Michelle shrugged. Where's the others?

Never got in.

Past that twat-fuck. You fucked off quick enough, goes Manda.

Noways was ah getting knocked back. Next time am out I'll be trying to sneak in a pram past him.

What do you want to drink? goes Kay.

Save yur money on me thanks Kay, all ah can have's a glass water, goes Michelle.

Lemon Hooch, goes Manda.

Ah'll help, goes Fionnula an stepped over with her. Manda watched them go.

Before Kay even got to the bar a boy walked along the railings an leaned to her ear, Kay shook her head an the boy walked away, to the toilets, try and pretend he'd been going that way anyways.

See that! MacKay boy just asked Kay to dance.

Bastard never asked one us.

Awful pale the day but she looks great tho eh?

Who?

Kay Clarke. Ah never knew she was hanging round wi yous.

She's no.

You don't like her, eh? See yur sister over there.

Aye.

There was a long bit of not talkingness. *You Sexy Thing* was started playing.

Michelle coughed an went, Where the others?

Barrels. Might as well juss go round, this is crap. Manda, who'd been leaned on the railings, turned an looked down the bar. Another boy had come up, leaned between Fionnula an Kay, touched Kay's shoulder an says something: Kay smiled so's her teeth shows, an says something back. The guy talked a little more an went down the bar where he was sat with another guy. Manda says, Fucking hell, they're sniffin Kay.

Aye, goes Michelle, Know how it is in here. Nothing like a new face on the mental scene to raise the sleepy cocks.

Who's that again? goes Manda.

What, Scobie MacIntosh?

Nah, no him, that guy far end on his own. Cute. See him about.

He's spoken for. Bit of a quiet case, he lives wi yon Morvern from the Superstore, used to live up the Scheme.

270

Oh right he's the guy; that's a bonny bonny lassie.

Kay an Fionnula came back over from the bar.

You're doin okay. Ta, goes Manda, taking the Hooch.

Kay smiled an shrugged, sipped from a clear half pint.

No into Scobie Doo? It'll be slow sets soon. Ya gotta have someone snog for slow sets, Michelle looked round then at Kay's drink, You on the water too, Kay?

Mmmm.

What're *you* drinkin? Manda nodded, aggressive at the glass.

Malibu an coke, Fionnula whispered, almost inaudible.

Manda slipped her Hooch bottle in the wee round holes along the wood top of the railings, If ah ask Scobie Doo to dance, will you ask his mate?

Aye, sure, goes Michelle, But he won't slow dance an snog me when the sets come on; he knows fine ahm pregnant.

Depends how many pints he's had. See yas.

Manda and Michelle walked along the bar then went down on the dancefloor wi Scobie Doo an mate in tow.

I'm really fed up wi all this, goes Fionnula. You no going over, talk to Catriona?

Kay just laughed, took a swig of the water.

What? Fionnula took out a cigarette an offered one.

No thanks.

On the water an no cigarettes. Haven't made any big decisions, have you?

No.

What are you thinking?

Looking at those two, I'm wondering who's worse off, Michelle pregnant or Manda not pregnant?

Manda's got other problems too, you can't be too hard on her though she can be a pain.

You'll just say I'm just snob but, this is so small town, isn't it?

Aye.

Like Catriona just isn't even going to come over and say hello. And do you know why?

Why? goes Fionnula.

Cause she's scared. It's not that she doesn't like me. I know she likes me a lot and she's really not shy about things we've done to each other. She's scared of this damned little town. If we were in the city she could come over and hug and no one would be gossiping. And it wouldn't be such a big deal about what's happening to me. And it wouldn't be a big deal for you. You know. What you were saying today.

Ah know what you mean. Fionnula nodded. Sometimes it makes ya want to do something to fuck it all up. All the fuckin wee lies an hypocritical folk.

Some of those lies are not so wee.

Kay an Fionnula looked at each other. If I have an abortion I'll have to leave. I'd be thrown out. Either way I can't lie about what's happened, Kay shrugged.

You won't tell them everything?

Suppose some things are irrelevant.

Don't fuck up your university, Kay. You're brainy. I've always been jealous of you, just too much a big boots to admit it. You've got enough problems. You need the support of your parents, no matter what happens. I've got nothing. I can take ma clothes and leave this town.

And end up what? homeless on those streets today, sucking cocks for the price of a Big Mac.

There's homeless folk here, says Fionnula.

I know.

It's just, cause there's still dregs of a sorta community feel, homeless are sleepin on folk's floors, hid away or in leaky caravans. Like ma cousin Tommy; he's a goodlooking boy. He's got this caravan down the Borders, works the roads an stuff then he comes up here an does the surplus at the Alginate and sleeps in the front room wi his dog. Its 1996 an this country can't give its people a roof over their heads. It's funny, isn't it! How in smaller towns, folk won't allow other folk to lie on the streets but it's okay in a city. So there is good stuff about bein stuck in a glory hole like this. But cause folk are kinder, all gets swept under the carpet and politician folk can ignore it cause no one'll fight it. They say there's goan be changes in this country. Well I think the only thing changes you in this life is the people ya talk with, the people you sleep with, people you work with. Every other bastard is either lying through his teeth or trying to sell ya something. It's only other people that change your life.

Just then the lights sunk an a deep blue stained the smoked air round them as the slow sets began. Below on the dancefloor the pale faces of the tall boys fell on the upturned lips of Michelle and Manda.

There's no fuckin fish boxes or nothing, goes Kylah, slowly moving her lit lighter from left to right an back again, then a gust battered it out.

Kylah, Chell and Orla were nowhere near Barrels. They were round back of the Mantrap, below the Ladies Toilet where the wee open window was. The rear of the Mantrap had an extention wi no ground floor windows. The corner of it was right angles to the Lynn, the subterranean river that flowed under most of the town, from where it went under, front the Superstore, to where it emerged in the little swan-marauded estuary, to rear of the night club. It was test of high school boys guts, at night, to splash up the tunnel fro the sea-end at low tide an no poofy torches, emerge soaked an slime-wrapped, climb out into the Superstore carpark an go for celebration pints in the Politician. The only bar that would have them.

In winter gales, even though the small waterbreak onto the shore wasny angled on incoming seas, breakers severed on the wall then their tops smashed gainst back of the Mantrap extension. Burst waves would chuck black seaweed bunches as high as where they hung from the rone pipes. Once a wooden fish box went through the first floor window and Sgt MacPherson, who owned the Mantrap, posted it to Grimsby wi a bill and invoice. In the hurricane an orange, calor gas cylinder was found up on the roof.

Kylah an Chell looked at each other.

Orla goes, Less we draw lots, odd one has to give the bunks up to the other two but she cannie get in.

Ach, must be a way, goes Chell. She strolled down, close the shore where a bit of a breeze was getting up an the tiny stars were faintly going. Then she saw it, Hoi!

Orla n Kylah walked over.

Yer jokin ah hope.

Please yourselves. Snogging sailors or not. That's the choice. Slow sets'll be started soon enough.

We need gloves or something, more of Michelle's condoms!

No ways, it'll be all dry wi this weather.

Chell jumped down an stepped over, crunchin shingle. A huge mountain of seaweed the county digger had dumped there after clearing the shore. Chell shoved both hands in an tugged out a double handful clutch, Cmon, some posh folk eat this.

Aye, that's fuckin posh folk.

I'll make a heap here, yous two gather in an pile it up under the window.

The seaweed was dry, powdering dusty stuff bashing offof it as Chell tore out huge, puffy chunks that smelled real bad. It was raising such dust, Chell would take a few backwards steps, throw the weed up onto raised level of ground an move round to escape the clouds. In twenty minutes or so they had stripped all crusted, outer lining an the weed was getting more damp an rubbery deeper inwards. Little trickles of water were coming off the hangin ends, drapplin cold drips cross her bare legs an when she lifted a hand to move hair away from her face, Chell's fingers came too near her lips an she tasted the sea water sealed within those weeds; so there she was, dwarfed by this, in the dark, hoikin lumps out it an she got to thinkin about the creepy crawlies might be in that pile rotted weed, not just spiders but others, those leaping, trilobitey things when you coup a stone on a salt seashore, or little baby crabs, so young their top shell's still transparent an you can see all inside things. All manner of sea beasts might be trapped in the seaweed-skimmed shore debris, an now the stars were almost gone above Chell, an the chopped moon was letting light fall out less often, an she could hear the water clucking down behind her an as she pulled a slab of wetter seaweed, in dead light of the hole, sure for the splittest of instants it's the grey gaping face of Daddy Patrick! fixed in there as she screamed an fled backwards, fell on her arse but was up, an leaping off the shore onto the pounded earth at back of the night club.

What? Orla giggled. Crabs is it?

What is it? goes Kylah.

Chell was hunkered low as if pissing, face held down an she would've put her hands up to her eyes but for their minkinness wi the briny salt weed.

Kylah stepped over, kneeled likewise an put an arm round her shoulder, Whatsit?

Ah thought ah saw ma dad.

What's up? Orla was stood, a long wrapper of seaweed in both arms.

She thought she saw her dad, Kylah goes quietly.

What one? Orla went an goes.

Hush Orla!

But Chell just sniggered an shook her head, she stood up an let a big breath, says, Do've ah big wet arse, ah fell? she swivelled round her arse an stuck it out in the almost non-light. There was some sand an just scabs of seaweed, the dried bubbly ones. Kylah brushed at Chell's ass, rubbing the sand off and smacking her softly as she finished.

Yur fit. Okay?

Aye. Am sorry. Yous'll think am mental.

No honey. It's okay for us.

Ah swear. Ah saw him right there, buried in it, staring out at me, she pointed back to the heap. Wi the lights fro the railway pier behind, the heap seaweed was outlined, but appeared just as a black mass.

It must be all the sea stuff, goes Kylah.

Aye, went Orla.

There was no talking, just waves hit-hitting on the concrete lip.

Look at the state of ma fucking hands, goes Chell, in the morelight of that wasteland, she says, Someone else take a shot on the mound eh, am fuckin knackered.

Kylah an Orla looked toward the dark shore. Kylah licked her lips. Orla coughed.

Ah think we've got enough to climb in, says Orla, an followed over to the pile she'd been building.

Kylah looked back at the shore then hurried after them.

They stood round the pile below the window an Chell jumped

up on it. It shrunk down a bit an she trampled round, like as if it were grapes, to solidify it more. The sill of the window was near tit-level an with a heave she was up an through it.

The window was too small to turn in an sit so's she had to grab top of the cistern an pull herself in, Fuck, you could break yer neck, she says, an pulled on through, one leg, bent over, straddled the sill an swung the other leg. Chell put both palms on the wood an lowered herself. Her arms started shaking, she turned her neck far she could, dropped eyes to gauge the drop an let go. Her left knee-length boot skite-ed away an hit the sanny bin as she went over, slammed the cubicle door appallingly loud so's the whole frame vibrated, the actual heel cunted off, went gibbering cross the tiles, hit the skirtin and rebounded, shooting away off under the toilet door, Ooo-yah, goes Chell an she stood up, one hand jabbed out as her busted-boot-foot-sunk back, heel-wise.

You okay?

Am fuckin in so ah am, but a bust ma boot. Yur gonna huff watch yerself.

Kylah's hair in its tied-upness appeared, an her ringed fingers, curled up on the window frame, wi a pull she was in over her tits but she just pitched on screamin an Chell lunged fwd.

Whoaa!

Kylah swung a moment on her pelvicky area that let Chell get under as she slid in, an her upsidedown face, all red an fattened up, like the stupid cunt on the velcro wall, came onto Chell's shoulder, an her laughter-breath was whacking into Chell's ear.

Fucksake Kylah, ya loon!

Chell took weight of Kylah on her shoulder an lowered herself, bringing in the demin skirt that fell right down an Kylah was screamin, both hands flayin wild up there to try cover her arse an fanny. Chell concentrated, holding Kylah an movin backwards so Kylah's feet just slid down the wall an sideways then she suddenly slapped them on the ground as Chell came up against the toilet roll on the cubicle wall. Kylah was still laughin an leaned her weight on Chell.

Get up, Kylah.

Kylah stood up an stopped laughin, says abrupt but quieter, Ah don't think Orla'll make it.

Chell leaned down an took off her boots. Fuckin ruined, she goes.

Orla pulled up an her face came into the window.

Chell slammed down the toilet lid an stood up on it. It was made of some shitey cheapo stuff so it buckled in but she leaned out, Orla, cmon.

Wi seeming no fear, Orla bounced up, got elbows over the sill an shoved herself inwards so she was hung half in, half out, she put her arms out an Chell got them.

Got her? Kylah grabbed Chell's legs more, as to steady her an Chell put arms round Orla an by twisting on her axis, wound the wee girl in, Orla laughed but Chell put out an arm to steady them an the entire prefab toilet walls came free, wi little puffs of powder from each ceiling screw, the cubicle walls shuddered in a westerly direction, Orla's feet shot in an her sudden weight sent Chell crashing onto the wall that bent all out of shape.

Chell an Orla were lying on the ground. Chell noticed the cubicle booths had been stuck to the tiles on the floor by these small sucker things, Only a fuckin policeman would fit heap of shite stuff like this, she says.

DJ Twenty spurted a blast of dry ice cross the loneliness of the empty dancefloor. More a cosmetic to hide its spaces than anything. Michelle and Manda were mashing an tonsil-tickling

Scobie an his mate, turning in the ultraviolet light, the white smoke.

Fionnula, teeth blue in the low light, had drained her Malibu an Coke an Kay had nodded to the empty glass. They'd walked up the bar an another boy had come over an asked Kay to dance. They'd ordered more drinks.

Can I have a red wine with two spoons of sugar in it? Kay goes.

Eh? The barman goes.

Don't say 'Eh', goes Fionnula.

The barman looked at them.

Listen, put two spoonfuls of sugar in the red wine, went Kay, I'm pregnant and it's good for me. I shouldn't be drinking and a Malibu and Coke.

Fionnula laughed and goes, Hush, honey, look!

Chell came walking down fro the stairs. All the guys looked at her strangely, amazed they were so pissed they'd missed her before; she seemed smaller, then Fionnula saw she was carrying her long boots.

Hiyas!

How'd you get in?

Climbed in the fuckin window out the back, where the fuck're all the sailors?

Tucked up in their spunky sub.

What do you want to drink?

Get us a pint of cider please, Kay. Ta. Fuck it, no sailors and all that effort.

There's none here, just the Port workers up the stair.

Michelle and Manda are in there!

Yup. What happened to your boots?

Bust them on the way in, but Orla was saying she bought Docs for Manda an they're in her bag.

What's all this?

Chell looked down, an all over her dark, leopard-print top were millions of little islets of ultraviolet blue, all the little dust-motes off the seaweed, Oh fuck, ah look like I've got the worst dandruff ever, she bashed down at the fabric above her breasts, Who's goan want dance wi me? She looked round, Mind who would ah really want to dance with? Ta, she took the pint cider an guzzled a big dollop offof the top.

Orla an Kylah came down the stairs an went spinnin cross the dancefloor thegether in a mock waltz then put their arms up an started twirlin their hands round.

There's an idea, goes Kay.

What? goes Chell, no even looking at her. She shook her head an goes, Ah telt them to try blend in to the background a bit, she says an took a swig more cider.

Kylah had fallen over on the dancefloor an Manda had broke free of her snogger, she helped pull Kylah up an hugged her, then she saw all the ultraviolet motes on her and was swishing her palms around Kylah's lilac T-shirt. Chell watched her an minded Manda gogglin at her fanny when she pissed in the sink at those guys' place. The boy Manda had broken away fro, stood stock still, kinda bemused, awkward an watchin.

Time After Time came on.

Orla came boundin up the stairs laughin and goes, We jumped in the back window on a pile of seaweed. We're stinkin of seaweed.

Beats spew, went Kay, an they all laughed.

Chell laughed and goes, What are we like the lot of us?

Manda had gone back to snoggin the man, turnin slowly on the spot, next to Michelle who had stopped makin any attempt to dance an was just massively snoggin the other guy on the spot.

Kylah came up the stair offof the dancefloor an laughed, Hiya!

I'm buying everyone drinks, goes Kay and I'm drinkin wine with sugar in it.

Hey, let's taste, goes Kylah, Mmm, can I have one then?

Kay an Fionnula looked at each other an burst out laughin.

What? goes Kylah.

Oh, nothin, we're no laughin at you honey. It's somethin else.

When Kay went up the bar, Kylah goes, Hi, do you know what Kay's like on cello?

Ah've never heard her since second year, but she'd been getting tuition ah think. How?

I'd really like try sing along to it, like solo voice an a cello, be weird.

Mmm, sometime, sure you can. What were you saying bout you left the band?

Ah was feeling bad earlier but am glad ah did now. There's always a time when it's best to go solo. Grace Slick or that. Ah was thinking, maybe come up the night, wee fuckin jam session wi posh Kay.

Wouldn't mind a wee jam session with her maself, Fionnula thought an says, Aye, maybe.

An since we're same sizes, wouldn't mind checking out her wardrobe, Kylah nodded to Kay, up the bar, the old Port marshals harmlessly flirting wi her, in Kylah's new clothes.

Fionnula stared, laughing.

Whaaaaaat? Goes Kylah in a kinda cutey-pie way.

Fionnula just shook head an says, Kylah, you're a star, you're a star already an you should mind that.

Chell goes, Ah wish Manda would get shot of that grot, ahm

sure you can catch something offof this carpet, she nodded down at her feet.

Aye, athlete's foot, worse than the pool.

Athlete's foot! More foot and mouth.

Thats what Michelle's doin wi yon guy.

They laughed.

Ma little toe's been sore all day wi these boots, goes Orla.

Aye, they're nice tho.

Kay arrived wi sugared wines.

Ta, that's fucking great, goes Kylah.

So you bought Manda a pair Docs, Orla?

Cmon. We all know she's no money.

They all nodded.

An ah've got a pair. Or rather, I don't, she goes an tapped her tits.

All laughed.

Ah feel like a slow dance but no wi anything in here. Am bored out ma skull, goes Kylah an she stamped off, somewhere up towards the toilets.

Last one the night, the DJ barked an the last orders bell whanged behind the bar.

Stockard Channing's voice filled the blue light, the opening moments of *There Are Worse Things I Could Do*, offof the Grease soundtrack. All the Sopranos put down their drinks simultaneously.

I'll take the hassle if you will, goes Fionnula, an she could feel herself shaking.

Let's go for it, says Kay.

Chell had grabbed that boy who'd first made move on Kay, Don't you stand on ma fucking toes, she says, draggin him away fro the bar.

At first, The Night Fionnula McConnel Slow Danced Wi

282

Kay Clarke, they weren't star attraction, cause Kay and Fionnula were already conjoined mong the ultraviolet, thick in dry ice, when Kylah spun onto the dance floor doing a pretty good waltz, her arms wrapped passionately round the sanny bin. This raised a good chunk of unheard laughs an smiles till, cautiously, men began to cross over from the bar to the railings by the floor.

Fionnula felt she had to keep whisperin as Kay leaned against her, hair all over her face, she was so nervous she wasn't enjoyin it, stuff ravin through her mind, Fionnula says, Ah don't know why you're worried about getting expelled cause, if you, if you had baby, being expelled's perfect cover for being away fro school. You get expelled but you don't get all the stuff ah having to leave cause you're pregnant.

Manda had stopped snoggin her man an stepped aside of him when he moved in front her, so she could watch, stood by the rails. When he saw what she was looked at, he fair lost interest in Manda. Even Michelle had broke off to watch; Catriona an The Hairdressers up in one of the booths all stood up when Kay an Fionnula's slow dance took them close to the stairs and out of sight of the furthest booths.

The song had finished an the full lights come up, an it was in the clear and vivid light, Fionnula had goes, Kiss me.

Ice and the Pearl

Outside in colder, breezier air, the dark round back of the Mantrap, Kay was leaned gainst Fionnula's arm, then there was a bit distance to where Michelle stood. Manda was over by the pile of seaweed, helpin Orla first, make the jump down from the wee toilet window, an promisin catch her. Chell tossed down the backpacks an made an easy jump wearing Manda's new Docs. The sanny bin came flying out first, missed Manda and made a real din, then Kylah jamp, crashing into the pile of weed an collapsin it, laughing an standin.

Halooo! Kylah called.

Hi, Fionnula went, quietly.

They began to move round the front, Fionnula an Kay walkin a little apart, Manda in front. There was a crash back in the darkness where Kylah seemed to ah disposed of the sanny bin.

Kylah came running, running out glooms an started walking longside Kay, It would be brilliant to one day, do a bit singing with you, if you want, on your cello, Kay, eh?

That'd be brilliant.

Just like me, wailing away, you, maybe me on guitar, like that's kind of stuff am into doin rather than bands, me out front wi a circle boys round gawping. The music should be first, see ya, she ran on, so she was hopping aside Manda.

What the fucka ya doin? Manda goes.

Eh? went Kylah.

Don't fucking talk to them.

What're you on about? goes Kylah, but they were beside the door of the Trap, so Manda juss did a big huff out.

Ladies. The island bouncer nodded.

Kylah visibly sped up an turned her head aside, but suddenlike Manda stepped over to him, What're ya doin after?

Why, where are you goin?

Barrels.

Kylah was stopped at the corner when Orla and Chell an Michelle an Fionnula and Kay caught up.

Can ya believe that? goes Kylah. Fuckin Manda Tassy's been there!

That's musta been why he juss let her in. She looks youngest of us all, goes Michelle.

Fuckin acts it as well, Fionnula grumbled, but the others says nothin, just flickered nervousy looks at Kay.

No lookin at Fionnula or Kay, but in her own ways of eloquence, Kylah goes, A mean, when yur wasted enough, you'll snog, that's way it goes, I've near snogged ma brother out of boredom when ah've been pissed enough, eh? But wi him!

Aye, Chell an Orla quickly agreed an that was it. If Fionnula an Kay had been willin to leave it at that, they might of had the whole thing forgot, an put down to another wild night.

She kept slaggin him to fuck, goes Michelle.

You could see Kylah really tryin defuse the whole vibe that was buildin, tryin go along wi it so far hersel, but then Manda was catchin up so they all walked on an into Barrels an it was Orla up the bar, turning to Fionnula, an Fionnula goin, Whisky, triple whisky.

You don't drink whisky.

First time for everythin.

An course every cunt was lookin, an fuckin Catriona an The Hairdressers over in the corner by the juke box starin, an half the useless bastards that was just in the Mantrap, specially the men, cause it's such a poxoid affair of a town, that the night club's actually a good place to catch a quiet pint! Fore you have to face yur grim local for final orders. An the marshals, were lookin cause it's all the Catholic girls who're hot on each other, most of them are ex-merchant navy an just'll laugh it off an forget by their stocious bedtime, but you can't separate who was who, as in, who just starin cause of Kay's legs an being a new face on the scene, an who is staring cause in this town, rumours are down the street fore the wind is.

Manda was straight up, openly lookin back then talkin quick to The Hairdressers and Catriona, who had a dead expression on her face an Kay ordered a tequila through Orla an smiled at Fionnula, I just want to see how quick I'm sick.

Fionnula shook her head an leaned on the bar, like a man would, but alas, Michelle and Chell had found the booth by the door so Kylah was over there yakkin nervous about anythin so Kay an Fionnula looked at each other.

That'll be £10.66 please, says the barman.

Battle of Hastings.

Battle of Hastings, says Kay an Fionnula, simultaneous, quick, then both burst out in hysterics.

Stay here, goes Fionnula. Let's fuckin' stay here. If you're gonna burn your bridges burn them, an she takes a swallow of the whisky and curdles her face right up.

Ah think men put water in it.

Fuckin salt water.

Look at Catriona, look.

Fionnula turned an Kay held out her arm an gave this real quayside wave.

Fionnula laughed openly as Catriona juss had to stand, rigid, wi her wee sister in front her, layin off so furiously the ponytail back of her head was shakin. Fionnula laughed more, this wasn't just laughin at the situation, it was a laugh AT Catriona.

Under breath as she waved more, Kay muttered, Wave back. Wave back, remember me? I licked your fanny.

Fionnula was really laughing by then, Ah don't think you did it well enough, Kay.

Oh I did. I can assure you, I did, the way she was reacting at the time.

Ah see! laughed Fionnula, a deep laugh. Obviously that kind of thing happens every night to · Catriona Tassy, an she's strugglin to remember yur face, or maybe somethin else!

They both laughed.

Cmon, let's sit, an they crossed to the booth where Chell, Kylah, Orla, an Michelle were.

The girls all stopped talkin when Kay an Fionnula arrived. Kylah did her best goin, We were just saying, mind when Anne Curran got suspended and she was so bored she started comin into school every day.

First time she'd come in on time in her life!

It was right enough! goes Chell, Her attendance was perfect after she was suspended, it was brilliant!

Then they stopped her comin in.

Ah don't think they'll have that problem wi us.

Manda had begun traversin the bar floor towards them, slowly getting closer. Kylah got visibly jittery, Did yous hear the sub had someone died in it? That's why it was ashore. A guy had a heart attack an his coffin got took ashore this afternoon.

Died of too much wankin! Chell gave out a laugh as Manda

stepped over Kay's leg an slumped into her seat, sucked huffy on her Hooch. There was an all-round silence. Everyone smoked. Everyone drunk.

Ah think you're really selfish, goes Manda.

Is that what your sister says, so you're sayin it? went Fionnula, no lookin at Manda an then Kay looked a bit the uncomfy cause Manda's bullshit was not worth comin out wi what her sister had done an Kay gave Fionnula a warnin look.

Ah mean I have to come out to the Mantrap as well every Saturday an now we're the laughin stock of the town cause yous are so pissed.

Ahm no that pissed.

Fionnula, ya can't go around doin that, people'll think you were lezzie.

Fionnula leaned right forwarders, Don't tell me what I can an can't do, the school an the church are at enough of that without ma friends startin.

Friends! Some best friend that does that. Everyone knows we go round thegether Fionnula, Manda looked an there was pain in her face right enough.

Manda, it doesn't matter, it's nothing, can't you see how it doesn't matter? It's you makin it out somethin . . .

But she was on a roll, You've really been getting on ma nerves lately, ah doan know why, am just ma usual self but you've been weird, an now this. Manda looked near to greet.

Manda, ah don't want talk about it, ah just want to get pished, we're fuckin young, you're actin like a forty-year-old already.

Am ah fuck, it's just you're immature, don't value yur friends an you'll regret it, ah mean, where'd the fuck YOU come from? she turned on Kay.

Fore Kay could get involved, in a direct line of energy that cut everyone else out, Fionnula glared, shoutin, She was sick, ill, ah found her.

That doesnt make sense, how'd you just meet her in that huge city an why she have a change of clothes?

Cause she was lookin at a flat for university . . .

That's not true, Kay snapped.

Yes it is, went Fionnula.

Chell and Orla looked from girl to girl an sipped their drinks an nibbled at their crisps.

Kay Clarke goes, I was at a clinic that I'd telephoned from a call box round the corner from here a week or so back. It's basically an abortion clinic. That's where ah was today, just talkin to a doctor and a counsellor woman.

Fionnula put her face in her hands, Nooo.

Kay Clarke looked at Michelle an says, Michelle, I'm nine weeks pregnant.

Probably never had the Sopranos been so quiet an so still for so long. Fionnula coughed.

You okay? Michelle, smiled. You seem okay, better than I was but . . . its goan be different for you, eh?

Manda mumbled, Wasn't to know an ah don't think tonight helps matters, but she was just starin at Kay Clarke, eating this all up wi her eyes.

Chell goes, God, Kay, why didn't ya say?

Why, what difference should it make?

What're you gonna do? says Orla.

I haven't been able to decide. It's obvious I'm not fit to be a mother but my parents are against abortion.

Well I'm gainst it, but ah mean for me, ah don't believe in it, ah do think it's murder, a sin, but that's for me, ah wouldn't judge another girl, that's for you to make up yur own mind, Michelle shrugged.

289

It's a shame but it's no a sin. Abortion, Orla insisted, lookin round.

Jesus, Mother of fucking Hell, went Chell, slowly shakin her head, lookin down at Manda's Docs bought by Orla an on her feet.

Cause if that's a mortal sin, all the stuff they say is, is, juss by having sexy thoughts it's mortal sin, like we were saying the day. Whereas all am hopin is to be doin some mortal sins after four, Orla smiled.

Well, wear a condom, we say, goes Kay.

Aye here, goes Michelle, takin another out her pocket.

Its okay ah've got.

Look, ah think ah'll get home, goes Kay.

Everyone looked at them. Fionnula sat still, her face long, an looked ahead.

Kay stood an shrugged.

Who was it then? goes Manda in a bored-pretended voice.

I wouldn't of thought it would be you to ask that, says Kay.

Manda gave her a bad look.

Ask your sister, Manda. Your sister knows who I got pregnant with.

What the fuck's ma sister to do wi it?

She'll tell you somethin.

Fionnula coughed an goes, Am goin to walk her up the road, where are yous goin?

They all just looked at her.

When this place shuts am goin wait for the mail train to get in, then maybe be in the station buffet, ah'll be round there sevenish cause if the guy turns up, he's only here a few hours.

Look, just come up the house, don't be floating around, I just need a shower an a sleep, Kay shrugged.

Ah'll get your clothes in the wash, Kylah; tune the cello.

Aye, aye, look, if yur okay I'll come up themorrow or somethin.

The island bouncer came in, smiled at Manda an went over the bar.

Fionnula picked her bag an walked wi· Kay to the door.

Kay and Fionnula walked side by side, the narrow lanes that wound round tiered cliffs an steep slopes of Pulpit Hill, threaded the corners, streetlight bulbs fitted in old gas standards, so they seemed to be of the Port in another time, halos hung under the graceful cast-iron curves, sheltered wi a saucer shade.

See in winter, this lane always freezes, I have to walk to school down it cause Dad leaves for work so early. It was so slippy that winter I got the perm, remember it?

Mmm, Fionnula smiled.

Well I'd to go so slow down the ice here, with my feet sideways, it was taking me three quarters of an hour to get to the bottom. Know how when you have a perm, you never brush it, so in the mornings I'd put mousse and lots of water on, to control it. By the time I got to the bottom there, it would be all ice in my hair and I'd be crunching it out, like the sickness today!

Fionnula laughed an they both walked forwards, looking down on the ground, sort of swinging their feet forward an a bit side to side. The hill was so steep, so they kind of wove their way up the road.

Kay goes, That was the Christmas my ear started to hurt, sorer and sorer so Dad took me to see Dr Drumvargie on Christmas Eve an he looked right in an he realised there was something there an he took out this tiny but beautiful little pearl from right in my ear.

Never! How was it there?

It must've been there from when I was little; four or five cause I had no memory of it. My mum never had pearls though so it's a mystery where it came from.

That's beautiful. Pearls in your ears an ice in your hair.

They looked straight at each other an they laughed.

Kay's house was very big-seemin an dead quiet. There was burglar alarm that Kay had to shut down when they got inside. She had to rush to this box on the wall an ya could see she could do it in the dark. She says, Sometimes I wonder if this is to keep burglars out or me in. In summer, they'll go to bed early an turn it on an I'll be up late, just open my window cause it's a little stuffy and all the alarms will go off . . . what a commotion.

All walls seemed have stuff hung on them in frames, no just paintings but documents an photos and in the hall an up walls of the stairway, no just in rooms where you lived.

They went straight up to her bedroom an Fionnula soon saw that was cause all was there. Telly an video an even a kettle an a desk wi computer; the duvet was all frumpled down an Fionnula saw the cello by the big curtains, varnished like a piece of furniture. There were no posters on walls, like paper posters, they were real paintings wi frames on them like the ones Fionnula had seen earlier in the city place wi just colours on them. Most of all; Kay had a all-to-herself bathroom an shower next her bedroom.

You've got a gorgeous bedroom. Is it okay to smoke?

Ah, eh, Kay started to laugh. I was going to say no, but why? Mum's got some nose, she can smell one cigarette two days later when I've forgotten someone had one. She can even smell when I open a bottle wine. She doesn't seem to be able to smell pregnancy tho.

They both laughed.

Here's me pregnant. My wee world in tatters and I'm worried about smoking! On you go. There's no ashtray just use a saucer by the kettle there, Kay lifted her pyjamas off the pillows, I'm just dying for a shower. There's red wine in there and gin but I think the tonic is flat an there's nice liqueur things. She went into the bathroom, Put on the telly if you want.

But don't try to escape out the window?

Don't you dare try to escape out the window Fionnula McConnel, she smiled.

She shut the door. Didn't lock. If there is a lock on your own bathroom, in your own room. How would we know?

The sound of a shower vashing on a plastic curtain came.

Fionnula sat on end of the bed. She held out her hand an it was shakin, crossed to the wee closet an took out all four of the wee liqueurs. She sat on end of the bed, using her whole fist to twist an crack the wee screw tops, liking the scratchy openin sound they made, an sittin on that end of that king-size bed, just staring at things wi her black eyes, she drained each of the bottles in quick little sips, her feelings somewhere between waitin in a dentist's waitin room an a doctor's.

The island bouncer pushed in the door, felt an a light came on. It was a small wee first floor flat wi a bay window clogged by loads house plants, he stepped in an Manda stumbled after, waved the half bottle Orla'd bought her, Beautiful, she shouted. Michelle, Chell, Kylah an Orla followed an the door was shut behind.

The bouncer says, Make yourselves at home. Girls. No need to undress straight away, an he let out a laugh. Only Manda smiled an she shoved open another door that was a wee room, seeming only to have a wee beddy mattress on the floor.

Mon, Manda went, an pulled at him.

Hold on, let me get the home brew out. The island bouncer went into one other toty wee room where they could see a tiny sink, an a miniature fridge that sat on the floor. They saw a dirty shower curtain. The bouncer kneeled an lifted up this white, plastic barrel, so full of brown liquid you saw it strain wi the weight an the girls had to move aside as he swung it low, into the centre of the carpet.

Kylah was over by the window looked out cross main square where no cars were goin round.

Birmingham Lager, he says. Ah tell yous, a put a clutch of magic mushies in it.

Hurrah! went Manda.

He moved over an put on the portable cassette player. It was set to the radio an musta been the new, crappy local FM station cause it was Jimmy Shand givin it waaldy. He left the radio goin but in one step Kylah was on it, switched off the radio an started clatterin among the few cassettes.

The bouncer was back in the little shower room, frantically fingering clean a couple of mugs an pint glasses.

Michelle an Chell had plonked themselves on the barely-room sofa.

Bouncer came in an kneeled on the floor. He turned the wee tap an started filling the pints. Cause it sat on the floor he could only half fill, then he passed them over, still looked down.

Manda leaned in the bedroom doorway, slugged her pint an goes, So, ma–oh–so–fantastic sister is a pervy lesbian an Iain Dickinson's a pervy double dad. He'll get a fuckin citation fro the Vatican at this rate.

Chell took the pint glass offof the guy, kneeled on the floor, she rose her eyes heavenwards cause her back was to Manda off to her left an she took a snifter of the liquid in the glass, made the motion of putting her finger to back of her throat an the mime of vomiting into the glass.

Michelle nodded gravely.

Friends, friends friends, goes Manda an shook her head.

Shooglenifty started on the tape machine doin *Waiting For Conrad*.

An the cream on the cake, goes Bouncer. He opened a drawer an brought out two toothpick grass joints. He lit one up, exhaled the rich, oily bouff an passed to Kylah who sat on the floor.

No thanks.

Cheers but nah, goes Chell.

Am pregnant.

Have a blast, the kid'll do well at school.

No thanks.

How's your sex drive these days then?

Sorry, ah only fuck human beings.

Kylah an Chell laughed.

Help yourself to my body doll, he passed the joint to Manda who took an smoked on it.

Chell goes, See all that stuff on your arms, ah know it's hard to remember all those dates, so ya ever considered getting it tattooed on? A pal of ours was down in the city wi us the day, an she was tellin me she met this guy who'd all those designer fuckin labels that guys love pose round wi, actually tattooed on, to save the bother of buying them all.

Ah have thought about it, he nodded in seriousness. But there's somethin ya have to keep in mind. He smiled secretly.

Oh, what's that?

Have you ever thought they might change the legal age for night clubs? he took a sip home brew.

Pretty unlikely. Suppose the fat fed who owns the place might snuff it an then they'd start lettin anyone in anyways.

Orla let out a funny laugh.

MacPherson's a good man.

MacPherson's a good man. Listen to you. Does he know you're on the whacky baccy?

I'm sure my secret's safe wi yous.

Oh yeah. Got a phone?

Kylah laughed.

Well I'm almost sure I'm going to let you in on Saturday night but ah might just need one more wee encouragement. Good beer?

Aye, it's okay.

I'm really curious if you have piercings anywhere else?

Wonder on.

He walked over an touched Manda's pierced belly button, Last time I examined you it was just the one. No more?

No ways am letting ma lezzie sister near me again.

Time just to check, he walked into the bedroom.

Comin, Chell? goes Manda

Eh?

Are you comin? Cmon.

In there wi him! Are you mad?

What's the matter?

Get lost.

Manda kneeled down by her, Cmon Chell, please, just watch then.

Fuck*offff*.

What's the matter? Manda put her hand on Chell's leg. You just need to watch, ah just want you to be watching. She changed tone of her voice. Ah don't trust him.

Don't do it then.

We're right next door here, goes Kylah, to take the pressure off Chell.

How about it, Kylah?

You're pissed Manda, let's go.

No NO! NO NO! no. It's good here.

It's shite. We'll go wait in the station for Orla's man. You come too.

Cmon, sex out! It's no just Kay an Catriona, it's never too late to juss . . . freak out.

Once they hear your sexy moans from in here there'll be no question, goes Bouncer's voice, an one of his Hush Puppies flew out the bedroom door, hit some pint glasses in the shower room an one seemed to smash.

Manda shrugged an on all fours crawled towards the bedroom door, halted, circled, collected the half bottle an crawled in. Chell stood, grabbed the door handle an whammed the door shut.

Kylah turned the music up.

Fuckin state she's in, eh? We'd a been safer off wi Kay an Fionnula.

Michelle leaned over an poured the beer into the big plant pot aside her.

Wha's this? Chell's foot had come against something, she reached down an pulled, it was a shinty stick.

That's what he'll be using on Saturday night.

What else is down here? Chell shoved her ass right up in the air an peered under the sofa, Wow-wee-aaow, she slid it out. It was an extra-large, deluxe blue box of Astra fireworks. Michelle an Kylah squeezed round as they lifted the top off, smelled the sweet smell of the gunpowder, saw the spilled diamond-like black granules in the bottom, touched the rough, skelfy wood of the big rocket's stem.

Sparklers, brilliant, Chell grabbed one out an Kylah put her lighter to it. It hissed, phuttered and rasped into life, wrigglin towards the wrist as it shot out gold an white flakes of light. Michelle an Kylah had their own an were circling the room. Chell switched the light out an night-time was in the room, an the white smoke rose up to the ceiling, retinal streaks cruised behind eyes, jamped on back of their eyelids.

Cmon, let's light a Roman Candle.

Does that one no blow something up at the end?

That's a banger.

He's a fuckin banger.

Shush, he'll hear.

Above the music all they could hear was the heavy shaggin of Manda next door.

Fuckin arse, cmon. Chell took out a Roman Candle an looked round, she crossed to a tall plant by the window an shoved the firework into the soil of the large tub, lit the end.

Simultaneous, laughing, all three girls ran for shelter of the wee shower door.

The room turned the most spectacular green an a thick crawling smoke began to fill that only refracted the light more. Everything turned pink, then purple and then a cactus of golden tears flew into the air an there was an energetic fizz as the red bottom of the candle shot up among the leaves of the scorched plant, where it came to a stop and flamed for a few moments.

Jesus, get the window open Chell.

Chell stumbled cross the floor, kicking the loose cassettes. She knocked a smaller plant offof the windowsill an it came free of its pot, a slab of soil tumbled out on the carpet. Chell forced the window up an the smoke tumbled out; a huge parachute of white vapour that instantly shot up, rolling over an folding on itself, tumbling above the highest lamp posts of Main Square an rushing off, towards the cattle mart buildings.

Cmon, let's do a wee firework display!

The girls fell on the firework box; out came the biggest cone, its bottom packed heavy an made out of green wax. It was called Mount Saint Helens. They placed it on the windowsill, for good measure three or four tall thin Roman Candles were jammed into the soil of the other plants. The girls were lighting the blue touch papers indiscriminately, so's the fireworks started blastin off at different times, lighting the room all over; a whizzing section leaped to the ceiling, hit it an dived out the window. Mount Saint Helens burst through the adjacent plants then exploded, sending out strips of flame all across the darkened room.

Next door Manda moaned an called, Oooo, the fuckin colours!

Chell stepped to the firework box an lifted every other firework out. Let's try a rocket, she goes.

Here, watch your face! goes Kylah.

Ach, it's easy, look. Michelle grabbed a bottle offof the telly. It was some kinda posh wine bottle or somethin an there was a fake rose in it that she tipped to the ground. She put the smallest rocket's stem in the bottle, pulled down her black shirt, so the cuff covered her hand like a glove then she held the bottle by its base, pointed out the window. She turned her face well away from the contraption, Light it, she goes.

Kylah put her lighter to the fuse.

The rocket hissed violently a moment then shot out, horizontally across the square, dipped for a second then bent upward, an wi a scream, trailin orange light, it curved over the buildings on the far side of the square an vanished.

The girls roared in laughter.

Moan, let's set off the big one!

All them!!

Chell put all the remaining fireworks deeply into the soil of the scorched earth policy of blackened houseplants.

That rocket's too big to set from a bottle.

What about that, if we took the cap off, Michelle pointed to the home brew barrel, We could angle it out the window an fire the rocket out the hole in the top.

Aye, if we tipped some out.

Ah cannie lift that.

Fuck that, Michelle bent an just opened the wee tap so's the beer started to glug out onto the carpet. It flooded the floor.

What about down the stair? Orla giggled.

It's the Sally Army office down the stair! laughed Kylah.

Oh, that's okay then.

The beer poured down through the drenched carpet an Chell tipped the barrel, like a telescope, so it was angled out over the roof opposite an into starless night sky above Portworld.

Orla goes, Will I light them, cmon, I'll light them, fireworks are beautiful cause when they explode in the sky they belong to everybody, an wi that pronouncement, Orla began lightin a single Roman Candle.

No Orr!! Wait!!

Juss set if off, juss set it off!

The first Roman Candle started to sputter so Kylah lit the big rocket. Chell ducked down almost behind the barrel, there was a huge roar an the room filled wi silver smoke. The barrel rocked back upright an they all rushed the window.

Missed it!

Shit it's gone.

Kylah kept leaned out the window to get a breath of air.

Light the rest an let's scram.

Kylah could hear something odd. A steady sound an she wondered if it were Orla's train come in, dead early, maybe cause of speedy gonzalez Simon driving, bringin in Orla's speccy weirdo. Then she frowned. It was a bell ringing. An far cross Main Square, opposite The Royal Hotel she saw the side window of the first floor on the bank was broken. There were bars on that window. There was hissing an blasting all round Kylah, dazzling lights, acrid smoke, a heat near her arm and she saw a single, long thread of white smoke feed out of the broken bank window an get jerked away by the wind way cross that square.

Fuck, goes Kylah, an it was then MacPherson, some constable in the police car wi the blue light flashing, came swinging into the square through the one way system an stopping outside the bank.

Shut the fuckin window, shut the fuckin window! whispered Kylah and with all her weight, she got her nails on the frame an crashed it down closed. She yelled, Put them out, put the fireworks out, its fuckin police; the rocket went through the window of the fuckin bank!

The room was filling wi smoke, Kylah stood an the smoke hit her in both eyes sheer agony. She fell to the ground again an found a still half-full pint glass. She poured it on one firework an the flamecolour died as the beer spilled off the hard compost an down the sides of the pot all over a low wee table.

Whats happenin? goes Michelle

The Pigs is outside the bank! Put out the fireworks! Kylah grabbed at a burnin Roman Candle but it was hot an she yelled an tossed it on the sofa, which went on fire.

Michelle just picked up the pot three of the fireworks were spurtin off on an chucked the whole potted plant cross the room. Orla dived for cover.

Get on the ground; the smoke's less on the ground, goes Chell, Are they outside?

Kylah was on her knees, Ah burnt ma fuckin hand. They're outside the bank, fuckin rocket went through a window on the first floor. Orla, ORLA, get a towel out the shower, wet it, an block the bottom of the door, there's smoke detectors out there right down the corridor, if they go off the brigade an the police'll be right over here. It all no smokin here, she chucked beer on the smouldering sofa.

No smoking! goes Michelle, Yer fuckin jokin look this place. All was virtually dark an it was crawlin through the thickest fog the girls were doin.

Orla had the shower running an she was coughing. She threw out a wet towel that splatted down next Chell an she jammed it in where the light was, under the door.

Put the music off.

Kylah kicked out and hit the cassette player that snapped off.

Get in the bedroom, get in the bedroom, or we'll suffocate.

Chell shoved open the door into the bedroom.

Uhhhhhh, Uhhhhhhh, Uhhhhhhh!! Eh?

Orgy! The bouncer screamed then a wall of smoke an the four teenagers crashed in an slammed the door.

The bouncer sat up, screamed, Fire!

Shut the fuck up, the police are outside, Kylah scrambled to the window, knockin over things on the way.

What's the fuckin smoke?

Fireworks, ya daft cunt, shut up.

Ma fireworks! Have you dangerous wee bastards been muckin wi fireworks?

Kylah moved the curtain aside an orange streetlight leaked in, showing Manda lying on her back wi her tits leaned off one side. What the fuck's goin on? she mumbled, Get in here wi us the now.

Shut it, went Chell.

Smoke was seepin in fro the other room an the blocks of streetlight comin in the panes of glass lit up the vapour in rectangular sections.

We open the windows an they'll see the smoke, says Kylah. What're they doin?

Just lookin up at the bank window. Lookin round. They must think it's a stone someone flung. Ah saw smoke comin out but there's none now. Manda, get your clothes on for fucksake, we need get outta here.

Jesus. Yous've sent a rocket across the square, the bouncer coughed, We'll get busted man, the lot of yous, Christ ah can't breathe.

Busted for what?

All those plants next door, they're cannabis plants, fifteen of the beauties, ma pride an joy. Ah'll have to pretend I've got motor neuron disease or something!

Ah wouldn't worry too much about that, there's no much evidence left.

What're they doin now?

They're getting back in the car. They're goin, they're fuckin goin! The car's round the square, aye they're off.

Open the window, goes Orla.

Kylah pulled the curtains full open an rattled the window. A tumble of smoke pushed out an she says, We'd best lie low a bit, they'll be coming back. Just get this smoke out. Kylah stood an laughed, opened the door into the livin space.

Christ! goes the bouncer at the smoke pummellin in.

Kylah crashed up the main windows an the smoke clouded out. Kylah leaned herself into the air an breathed deep as two guys came dashing over the square fro the direction of the Superstore.

DONT JUMP! DONT JUMP! they were screaming. When they got under the window they shouted, It's okay we've called the fire brigade, on ma mobile.

Ya fucking bastards! Kylah screamed down at them an she ducked into the room.

In the distance sounds of fire engine sirens could be heard.

Kay came out the bathroom in her pyjamas wi hair wet, lengthened out down her back an says, Do you want a shower?

I'll go without. If you don't mind, Fionnula went.

Kay gave her a look an sat beside her.

Well maybe, goes Fionnula an she stood an went into the bathroom then turned round an came back out again, Nah, am okay. She came back in an sat by Kay.

Kay stood an went over to the telly. Here were candles, an she lit one, an those stick things that make a good smell. Kay held up the packet the stick things came from an says, Aphrodisiac scent!

Mmm, Fionnula goes, suddenly thinkin, *I've got to get out of here!* an saying, That means it turns ya on, aye? Her hands were shakin so much she thought they could suddenly shoot out, violently to the left or the right.

Know what I do every night now? I play, cause I think, if the baby in me got bigger an I decided to have it, as it got older, the vibrations would be good for it. So I play. I sit here, an I wrap my legs right round, it like when you're ... fucking with someone, a boy or a girl, Iain, Catriona, whoever. Cello vibrations go right up the legs an, it's like they're goin in here. An arty washing-machine really.

Fionnula laughed.

You're not meant to play like that and it makes it difficult so I do easy stuff.

Mmm.

I play with no clothes on.

Mmm. Fionnula whapped her tongue round her mouth to make sure it was wet an says, On ya go then.

So Kay Clarke took off her pyjamas very slowly in the candlelight in the big house up Pulpit Hill an while Fionnula watched, Kay played that cello, her legs (that Fionnula suspected she'd shaved again) round the curves of that instrument so's her feet, an those long toes, were actually placed thegether on the wood of the instrument. An Fionnula watched, feeling physical stuff but realising she was at mercy of Kay, no the other way round and Fionnula was liking that an she was thinking how Kay was an amazing person in many ways an how, just in a day, all your beliefs can be turned round, everything can change at the mercy of a girl who had pearl in ear an ice in hair an sudden Fionnula felt very happy, very excited at what life was going to lay before her. Isn't it amazing how some things turn around?

The mail train came drumming into uncovered platforms at the station: engine, one coach of mail, one of seats. Orla was stood further up the platform. Rest of the Sopranos an Michelle were hidden back in the station building trying to hold up Manda an they had been dodging round Port draggin Manda this way for half an hour, through back lanes an long-ways-round, over folly and round lighthouse pier, wearing their blazers now in chilliness.

The guy stepped out the coach door an smiles, goes to Orla who had a too long walk towards him: Good morning. Good morning morning morning MORNING! An he looked at his watch. I feel like Spencer Tracey in *Bad Day at Black Rock* already, he says an he whipped his arm behind is back.

Orla didn't have a clue as per-usual; stood on tiptoe an they kissed, quite briefly on the lips.

Thanks for coming. No glasses?

No braces?

We've chose our masques, Orla smiled.

Stephen goes, Sometimes vanity can be a compliment. Just a mo, he ducked back in dark coach an emerged wi the budgie cage, draped under a big tartan blanket he'd razored a wee slash in, so's the handle you hold the cage with, came through.

Couldn't leave him down there on his own. Not The Man's budgie.

Where're you goan put it?

I'll just carry him round.

Christsake. I was hopin we could walk out to this old fallen-down castle.

We can do that.

Fuck, it must be the budgie, he's got the budgie wi him! Kylah whispered.

Aye.

Hi Kylah, he goes. Do you know Phil Spector invented Thousand Island Dressing?

What's Thousand Island Dressing? goes Kylah.

You get it in Pizza Hut, says Chell, It says it on the handle of the spoon.

Who's Phil Spector then? goes Kylah.

This is our pal Michelle.

This is Stephen.

Hi.

Aye.

306

This is the budgie, he kneeled an lifted up the blanket so's they could see it. He's called The Onan Two.

You mean The Omen Two?

Nah nah. It's a common name for a budgie, he had one before called Onan, but that one had to be dissected, so this is Onan Two. You know, from the bible, Onan? He spilled his seed on the ground. He was the first wanker.

You cannie be far behind, Manda slurred.

Welcome to our little town, smiled the guy. So I hear you broke into a bank and are gettin chased by a mad bouncer?

I shagged him, Manda muttered.

Orla goes, We'd kind of destroyed his flat and burned all his heesh plants to death wi a wee firework display.

What are yous gonna do? went Orla.

See when they've unloaded the mail. They don't lock the coach cause ah shagged Peter Macauley in the passenger coach, goes Chell. She needs to crash out, she flicked her head at Manda. We could sit it out there till the buffet's open up in here.

Right we're way along to Christiansands, he's to get the seven forty so we'll see you the buffet thefore.

Right.

As they walked along the seawall, Orla says, Ah don't mind, but you fancy Kylah, eh?

Stephen, holding the budgie out, awkward-like from his leg goes, She's very attractive. ·

Orla nodded, I'm what you want though, an you know why? Cause you'll have an interestin time with me. When we were settin off the fireworks ah was thinking, I'm on a short fuse myself.

Your temper. You don't strike me as having a temper at all.

I don't. Only for important things. I don't mean my temper.
Oh?

I mean my life.

They were walking along the esplanade, across from closed shops. Look, Orla says, pointing out to the defineless hulk across the bay, A submarine. A man died on it so they anchored to send him ashore. The girls thought there would be sailors in town the night.

And up there your famous folly?

Aye. This mega-rich guy had them start building it in far-away-days and olden times to try give work to the stone masons, cause they were all on the dole, if they hud dole in them days, but know what? The mega-rich guy went bust!

Ha! The moral of the monument that crowns your town. Charity is Dangerous!

Aye. But ahm no from here. Ahm from a wee village out of town. You passed it on the train. In the dark.

An they were getting into dark that helped cover multitudes of crimes, where the streetlights were deemed no longer a justifiable public expense, an the old, ancient, medieval night crowded round them.

They had walked way down, past the cathedral where just around thirty minutes before there had been a military police truck outside an they had loaded a coffin in the back an drove off followed by family members in another car.

Orla an the boy wi the shrouded budgie cage passed the tall, broken glass-topped walls of the estates.

See that, can you see it? Orla goes. There was a needle of rock stood alone in a field wi vertical cliffs of trees behind, They say that's where Fingal used to tie up his dog.

Who's Fingal?

He was a giant. An the castle we're goin up to is haunted, haunted by the Green Lady an by the Black Hand.

Black Hand?

It's a big black hand that chases ya. Don't ya believe in ghosts?

No.

You're with one now. I'm a ghost, says Orla. Just the night, Chell saw her dead father in a pile of seaweed. Ghosts are everywhere. That's why I'm good for you.

Cause you're a ghost?

Yup. You can do anything you want with me an that's what men wish for. Its a once in a lifetime experience for you.

These chicks are the damaged goods, was what Stephen was thinkin an he says, I'm sure it's lovely scenery but I can't see a bloody thing.

They walked on. What musta been mirrors an bells an whatever amusements were hung in the cage for the budgie were the main sound, tinklin an touchin an gradual, the loomed bulk of the fallen-down-castle was above them. The front was sheer but round the corner was a steep, windy path they climbed up through, he holding out the cage an, when he fell, an swore, all the time, holdin out the cage to protect. As they climbed, Orla goes, I've been here alone an lonesome so much it's good to be wi you, wi a boy! They were moving among walls with rustlin ivy on them then there was an interior building, a dank, soil smell an the sound of water drippin. He had a real sense of elevation an you could see lights of Port way, way back there in horseshoe curve, arc lights where the big, outer island ferries were tied up sending bars out, into the bay where there was just the conception of further islands ranging out to oceans.

There were small saplings wi breezin leaves an they sat under them, the budgie cage to Stephen's side.

Like it here?

Atmospheric. Wish we had music.

Orla proclaimed, I think you should screw me. Screw me silly. I want you to tie me up, my wrists an my ankles, but you've to tie me to a tree as well – facing the trunk, an while you're doin it to me, from behind, I want you to have these, the right way round mind, in me, an just as I'm climaxin, you've to draw them out, fast, but not too fast, sort of da, da, da, da, da, da . . . that sorta speed, Orla dropped the clicking clutch of rosary beads into his groin, an no fussin wi condoms, ah've never screwed thefore so there's no problem wi me.

There was a silence.

The guy went, Ah . . . mmm . . . gotcha! Whatdo ah tie ya up with?

Laces. Shoe laces, I've tons, these ones on ma boots, these ones, she produced the rainbowy laces she'd been forced to remove that morn, An these ones, she took out the new laces she'd used in the school shoes. Don't worry, am all prepared.

Well, I thought we might smoke a wee joint, sounds like I'll need the relaxation.

Whatever, but don't you get too out of it, Orla goes. Can we have that fuckin blanket to sit on?

Oh, but The Man's budgie'll get a chill, they get chills easy.

Ach, I'm getting jealous of your affection for that budgie already.

Then there was a huge hissing sound, way below them, an something moving, moving out in the water, seeming as big as a house, the conning tower of the submarine was driving through the narrow inlet, its huge, sucking presence swinging around as it moved awaywards.

Fionnula'd been disappointed then as they got ruder, way

beyond the just snogging it got mentally good; you knew where it felt bestest till Kay had whispered, I'm aghosted and it's nice to do things in the morning too, and they'd laid near, fingers holding, all sodden with sweat from one atop the other, and close, sometimes murmuring things and halting a sleepy sentence with kisses till Kay slept. Fionnula lay beside, smoking for hours, stroking the girl aside her, the ash so deep in the saucer she'd emptied pot pourri out of, its gentle powders, as she placed a knuckle in to stub, reminded her of softest snow. She lay, waiting for dawn, knowing it was a bad idea that she wasn't going to fight, it was a bad idea to fall in love . . .

A dead, Brazilian light had slowly pressed itself down on everything round Orla, Stephen and the bright colours of the forlorn budgie in the cage. They lay wrapped in the tartan rug that had covered the budgie, under a birch with thick enough trunk to have tethered Orla through the wages of her contentment and past the darknesses into the sliding, gunmetal colours, till the grey air revealed burst clouds, trailing down onto the shards of ragged islets beyond a still and dark bay.

Within the wrap of blanket, Stephen paused to lift and light the fourteenth, out of his trainer shoe which was operating as an ashtray.

Above them the midget-voice proceeded:

> Hail Mary Full of Grace.
> Grace Yak. The Lord is with Thee.
> Blessed are thou Blessed are thou
> Amongst women
> Wipe your bloody feet
> Blessed fruit of thy womb

Squinted, Stephen reached for his glasses and says, For fucksake!

Lord Bolivia, in red and emerald splendour, like a burst firework, knifed down and landed on the budgie cage. The huge parrot twisted his beak down, giving one eye to the little budgie within and in an effortless movement, clamped his claws onto the cage corner then took off. There wasn't even hesitation; with the cage dangled beneath him, Lord Bolivia powered out, over the cliff heights and slightly descended with the cage hung under, budgie smirling wings, flying, across the bay towards the secret forest where all the escaped exotic birds. dwell.

The Sopranos

The station buffet was empty after the train went. Orla walked back in very slowly, yawned and crossed to the counter. The guy serving was pouring a pint of lager, Aye, he goes.

Morning, went Orla.

The guy stopped pouring the pint then raised it to his lips and took a good swallow. He put the pint down, What can I get you?

A Coke and a coffee.

A Coke and a coffee.

She crossed over to the window seat where she put down her bag then walked back. The guy behind the counter fell over. He stood up again, brushed at his trousers and poured out from a Cona coffee flask, says, Milk and sugar's there. Is that guy your boyfriend?

Suppose; aye.

The English guy serving nodded, slid the coffee over to her then turned to the dispenser and poured a Coke, Your pals about, the two tall ones an that, the one in that band?

Kylah? She might be in, we've been on an all-nighter. Don't know where she's got to; she left the band though.

All-nighter, you wanting one of my Full Breakfasts? I'm just sitting down to my second. He nodded sideyways and there was a large breakfast sat on the counter by the till, a knife and fork next. He used local words in his accent.

Nah, no thanks. That your second pint since six?

No way, he laughed, handing the Coke to her, It's my fifth.

She laughed, says, How much?

The railways pay for that one.

Aye? That's really kind.

No bother, I'm quitting here anyways. Theres free plays on the juke box if you fancy, some good stuff on there. I was getting so driven mental here by all that shitey fodder I've fitted mainly my own CDs in there. You should see their faces sometimes! I've changed all the heavy metal albums to reggae ones; that aye gets the best reaction from the motorcycle boys. I just sing dumb and say it must be a technical fault!

Orla laughed and walked to her table. The guy behind the counter sat down on a stool behind the drinks dispenser and began eating his Full Breakfast and sipping from the pint. That guy was obviously a bit of a hero. He'd been cautioned by that police, MacPherson, owns the Mantrap. The buffet guy got arrested in John Menzies. He was writing all these sort of anarchist slogans on wee scraps of paper and going into the bookshop sections, slipping them into all the novels and touristy Rabbie Burns stuff.

Orla sat looking out the window where some cars for driving lessons were already heading out, across the station forecourt. The bay looked different without submarine an the wind was no longer raising dapples of white horses for the sky was clear an looked heatwavish for to be like that so early. Fionnula was crossing the forecourt towards the station. Orla put her palm against the glass, a smile on her face.

Oh Jesus, goes Fionnula, walking toward the table, eyes

314

closed a wee moment, splayed hand spread out over forehead and face a moment, in mock-shame.

Hi there.

Do it? went Fionnula, eyes wide now.

Aye! goes Orla and both girls screamed, jamp up throwing arms round. Orla sat, leaned forwarders, goes, It was, it was great and everything but there was nothing to it really, Orla looked over an dropped her voice, Wasn't sore or anything, not in the fanny, it's just, it's a wee bit kinda like you think everything'll be different and, I just feel the same, a randy wee besom.

Fionnula shrugged, He's a nice guy.

Bit weird.

Aye. Ah must get a drink, pretty hung over.

Orla pushed the Coke across.

What, are you sure?

Just take it, listen, am no even going to ask about Kay and all with what she must be going through.

Fionnula smiled, She's sleeping. Pregnant and sleeping.

Orla raised her forehead, I've thought of it myself, trying with a girl.

Aye? Fionnula didn't know what to say.

I've enough trouble not getting the boys without starting not getting the girls! Listen, Manda shagged the grot island bouncer from the Mantrap, no condom or nothing, bad time of the month and she's all para now.

Fionnula laughed, Twenty-eight, twenty-nine, it's gone be a record year up at Our Lady's! Jesus! You were careful, weren't you?

No ways was we bothering with condoms, look at me, I'm a jaffa, nae pips at all.

Famous last words, Orla. Wi a city guy you've got to be careful of the HIV and whatever.

Aye. Wouldn't worry about that wi me. Orla looked bit shy and goes, What was it sorta like with you?

Fionnula leaned forward, Sorta like you'd think. The other knows where to touch and how and all that, no like a boy.

Fuck, goes Orla, a little too husky.

Manda was just going so mental in Barrels maybe it egged us on a bit.

And Kay with Manda's big sister and Dickinson at the same time, eh?! Fucking big threesome and Manda suddenly stopped going, 'Ma sister this ma sister that,' last night and it was all 'lezzie whoor; what if Dad finds out,' you could see she was furious, then what? When she got into bed wi that sheep shagger she grabbed Chell, trying to get her to come too!

Manda?

Aye! She's just jealous of you, telling you, she would go for it with you now.

Don't give me ideas! Fionnula looked out the window and gave a guffaw, shook her head.

Yous haven't been getting on eh, but I think she's just a bit mixed up herself, sex-wise you never know what's going on in folks' brains.

Aye, but the whole Port'll know now about me and Kay an the lot; just as well we get the chuck from school.

Yous won't get the chuck; they can't chuck me out and they won't to yous.

I don't know Orr, Fionnula footered the last cigarette out a pack.

My sickness has come back, Fionnula.

The cigarette stopped still in her fingers.

There's no need to go for tests and stuff I can just tell, all these coldnesses going through me and weird turns and I'm no having that radiation again.

Orla.

It's not me yous should worry about, it's Mum. Poor Mum cause she lost a wee baby way before I was born and now she's going to not have me.

Don't say that, Orla.

It's true, just believe me. That's why they'll no throw me out Our Lady's, imagine the scandal if they expelled me an I'll be gone in six month.

Oh Orla, don't say these things, it's scary.

Suddenly at the window there was the formidable sight of Chell, Kylah an Manda, waving and smiling, but sort of staggering all over the pavement. They didn't seem to know the side door was open so they pushed and pulled and clung to each other along, beyond the window, through the main station doors.

Orla grabbed her hand so Fionnula actually jumped with fright, the little hand gripping the longer one on the formica table, Don't go an say to the others the now, Chell'll be all in bits an that . . .

I'm in bits Orr . . .

Aye, but you're like me, you'll cope.

I just feel all hopeless, me an Kay fussing about her being pregnant, as if that's near as important and here's you with . . . this. You really must see, Fionnula dropped her voice as the other Sopranos came in the far door, See the doctors.

Orla just smiled, nodded, looked at the three girls as they strode up to the table.

Won't fucking BELIEVE what happened to us! goes Manda, actually smiling at Fionnula, face all alive with gossip.

Listen, listen, listen! went Kylah, turned over to the guy behind counter an went, Hi.

And suddenly Orla felt a huge surge of hurtness that the Sopranos weren't immediately turning attention to her and her news an Orla thought, *We really are alone. Amazing, I'm fucking dying but I still have a big head. I'm still demanding attention as if I was alive, like the way sailor in the hospital deserved it though he was a goner like me. Cruel life: it sets up all these goals early on like, then by the time we've achieved those goals, they've got to be totally meaningless to us. Ah sort of wonder if I should sometimes write down the twenty or thirty things that I'm sure I've sussed out in seventeen year. Maybe I'll write them down in the fucking hospice . . . the hoss-piss.*

Where have yous been? Fionnula was saying, Kylah shoved in next her and Chell moshed in at Orla's side, Manda parked herself sideways on the seat of the table across.

There was a silence that gave Manda the field to own up and she says, Orla tell you?

Nut, goes Orla.

I seriously copped off wi the bouncer, shagged him and I really regret it, as you would, but I was totally out of it and these lot near . . . Manda giggled, Burned his room all up wi fireworks, but tell them where we've been.

Kylah goes, Well we went over to the Superstore bakery, warm and hide out a bit with the bakery girls, mooch some morning rolls an have a crack an that, an we got to thinking, really shitting it about getting expelled, right?

Fionnula looked at Orla and Orla met her look.

Chell says, We were thinking, if we saw the Father, if we goes and saw Father Ardlui, just sat down an explained a wee bit what happened . . .

No every single wee detail . . .

Just that our clothes were taken by a pervert.

That we hadn't been drinking, sort of.

Manda goes, I thought he might at least admire us for coming over to his Mass at seven in the morn.

Fionnula looked at them, her face all scrunched up, Yous went to see Father Ardlui?

It was so embarrassing dressed like this, we's had to take communion.

Yous have been to MASS!? goes Fionnula.

Manda goes, Swear as I went up, I was mortified, I thought felt his stuff running down my thigh, I thought it was goan drip out on the stone right in front the Father, like that day Ana-Bessie's sanitary towel fell out on the way up the aisle!

Ah don't scum us out, Chell goes.

All laughed with the remembering.

But Father Ardlui was mental.

He went mental? goes Fionnula.

Nah, nah, goes Kylah. He IS mental, he started talking all this stuff and you won't believe . . .

What? goes Orla.

Right, listen, says Kylah, He takes us in the back after all the morning crowd staring at us and we sit down and start explaining what's happened and he suddenly says he already knows all about it so the Mother Superior musta been on the phone to him about the choir even earlier or last night and as you're talking to him you get the impression he's no really listening. He's miles away.

Sudden like, went Chell, He starts talking all this fucking weird stuff about this place in where you were saying yesterday, Eva Herzigova.

Bosnia Hercegovina, Fionnula shook her head an lit cigarette.

Kylah went, The gist of what he was raving on about was some shrine thing they had there and this wee unknown town

319

had become, like massive, cause folk, Catholic folk, were making pilgrimage to this place in their thousands and thousands and how lassies like us had had to milk cows and shovel shite an stuff once but now there's jobs galore.

Manda goes, I thought he'd forgot where he was again an was launching into one of his sermons!

But he sorta kept hinting at things, then Orla, he was going on about your trip to Lourdes and it was a miracle how you were well again and he was going on about this place . . . what's it called?

Knock knock who's there?

Knock in Ireland? goes Orla.

Aye, he got these bits of paper and starts reading out shite, like how many tons of concrete they used to build this airport there and how many men were employed . . .

Manda goes, It was getting like one of Mr Eldon's fucking geography lessons!

Orla goes, Aye it's right enough; place in Ireland right out the bogs and there was kids or something had vision of the Virgin Mary there, so they got an airport built an everything. We were goan there if we couldn't afford Lourdes.

Kylah goes, By this time he was asking us if we ever had dreams, like religious dreams and he goes if we could tell the difference between our dreams and our thoughts when we prayed. He says our characters weren't formed at our age.

Manda laughed and goes, Christ we were sort looking at each other; here's us, and it's lucky the cathedral doesn't fall down when we enter it, an we're all hung over as fuck and hanny slept and I've just rolled out of bed with a man, an it's eight in the morning and he's going on as if we're applying for jobs as nuns!

It was sheer mental to start, goes Kylah. Then of a sudden he starts saying he could be a big influence on the Mother Superior even though the future of the choir is in doubt an we've done a big awful thing an that and he does it just there, right in front of us he goes and asks us straight out. Us! Of all the girls.

Asks you what? goes Fionnula.

Chell crouched down, almost to the table's surface and hissed, To lie!

Manda an Kylah nodded thegether, quickly.

Lie? About what happened the yesterday!? goes Fionnula.

He says if we lie he'd get us off it wi Condom an Mother Superior.

What d'yous mean? goes Orla, You didn't need go near him. We're no going to get chucked out anyways.

What did he ask yous to lie about? Fionnula wasn't smiling.

We were to ask yous as well, the more the better he says, it might be good cause we're a Catholic choir; even that we can sing!

Lie about what? Fionnula says slow.

Father Ardlui wants us to says we all thegether saw some kind of apparition of the Virgin Mary, so's he can take it to the church an if they approve it, they can build a shrine, get more folk coming here all year round, hotels, airports an all that like in Knock.

He says it's the nicest job creation scheme ever.

Fucking hell, went Fionnula, He asked yous to pretend we'd seen a miracle happen? What did yous say?

Chell goes, I asked him if it would mean a McDonald's in town.

They all laughed.

Aye, I'd do anything for that too!

What do you think we told him? goes Kylah, Told him in the nicest way to fuck off, we werenie lying for anybody, he'd come to the wrong folk.

Chell goes, The all of us are no angels and we do sins and that but I'm no lying over something like that just to stay in that, all-out-poxy-fucking-dump-hole Our Lady's.

Christ, Fionnula shook her head, We should try sell the story to News of the Screws.

Fucking classic, eh? goes Kylah.

So that's it then isn't it? Manda smiled, held out empty hands. We're out.

I just can't believe that, he's so total nuts, Orla mumbled.

Kylah called out, Hoi, if I put stuff on the juke box will you turn it up?

Yup. There's free plays on it.

Brilliant, Kylah meandered over to the juke box.

Like reggae?

Good when you feel like this, Kylah smiled.

Hit the hard rock CDs, I've fitted reggae in there. Rough night? How about a Full Breakfast on the house for all yous.

What's this?

Nothing. Smash the system, no one comes in here till closer nine anyways.

Aye serve them up, cheers, loads of fatty bacon but no eggs on one.

Want some wee beers, I can put them in Coke cups?

We'll take anything that's coming our way.

That's the spirit, the guy behind the counter smiled. Hear you quit your band?

Aye, who says?

Your wee pal over there.

Aye, maybe headed for a city, get a band thegether there, work in a Woolies.

Oh aye?

Aye. Kylah crossed back to the Sopranos. Fucking hell he's

322

making us five breakfasts for nothing and beers in Coke glasses, he's mental.

The Oppressed Song by Bunny Wailer bounded out the speakers.

Chell goes, I was saying, it's goan be a cracker day an we should go out Tulloch Ferry to my sister's place, paddle in the river and that.

Fionnula goes, What about at eleven?

Well, we're bound to get suspended with these clothes on and we could catch the twelve twenty-five out to Tulloch Ferry, it's only a wee walk up the bridle path an backroad on a day like this.

Aye?

Aye let's go for it.

I'm out of fucking fags and totally skint, goes Manda.

I'll borrow you, goes Orla and she reached for her bag.

Orla, went Fionnula.

Orla looked her back in the face as she took her purse out. You could see all the twenties she'd got out the machine night before, meant for Greece or Spain or wherever holiday thegether. You're out of fags too, Fionnula, Orla smiled and she took a crumply fiver and held it out. Fionnula didn't take so Orla put it down on the table in front her. I've only a twenty Manda, Orla went.

Well I'll give you all the change after I've got the ticket, cause I couldn't pay back a twenty for months, goes Manda. Ta.

Don't worry about paying back too quick, Orla warned.

Fionnula was looking at Orla across the fiver.

Take it, I know you're dying for a fag.

Fionnula accepted what Orla had told her by reaching out, taking the fiver in her hand and gripping it tight, she accepted everything that was going to happen until the end.

Mmm, those breakfasts smell yummy, Orla smiled and goes, Think I'll get a few bottles Hooch and that when we go out on the train.

Aww steady lassie!

If we drink like yesterday we'll really be seeing the Virgin Mary.

Here we go again!

Forth Let the Cattle Roam.

Teera leera LAYY! they all bawled, laughing, looked at each other and none appearing much worse for wear as the day's sun came silvering over the bay and the tips of the back country hills, already in full summer flush in this time of their lives.

Acknowledgements

'**L**ong Orphanage of Railway Stations', a line from an Apollinaire poem, I see as the source of several sentences here. 'In The Loveless Port the Steamers are Swaying', is a beautiful line from an André Salmon poem. The image of the free bird spiriting the caged bird to paradise is from G. V. Desani's *All About H. Hatterr*.

Hospitality and Guidance when in Los Angeles: straight to Mark Richard and Jennifer Allen. In New York do as Tina and Jean Margaret do x x x. Irvine Welsh for proffered kindness not forgotten. Robin Robertson for Olympian patience. Thanks to David Godwin. Holger Czukay, of CAN, thank you for the Scottish aubergines that keep me going; we'll dance with Nessie again soon! Joe McAlinden and SUPERSTAR: the strength to carry on that lies deep inside and their amazing album, *Palm Tree*. Hollie and all St Tequila's convent girls!